Players

Karen Swan lives in Sussex with her husband, three children, two dogs and her car called Meltchet.

Visit Karen's website at www.karenswan.com
or you can find Karen Swan's author page on Facebook
or follow her on Twitter @KarenSwan1

By Karen Swan

Players
Prima Donna
Christmas at Tiffany's
The Perfect Present
Christmas at Claridge's

KAREN
SWAN
Players

PAN BOOKS

First published 2010 by Pan Books

This edition published 2013 by Pan Books
an imprint of Pan Macmillan, a division of Macmillan Publishers Limited
Pan Macmillan, 20 New Wharf Road, London N1 9RR
Basingstoke and Oxford
Associated companies throughout the world
www.panmacmillan.com

ISBN 978- 1-4472-6516-0

A CIP catalogue record for this book is available from the British Library.

Typeset by Ellipsis Digital Limited, Glasgow
Printed and bound by CPI Group (UK) Ltd, Croydon, CR0 4YY

Visit **www.panmacmillan.com** to read more about all our books
and to buy them. You will also find features, author interviews and
news of any author events, and you can sign up for e-newsletters
so that you're always first to hear about our new releases.

This book is dedicated to my mum (even though she isn't allowed to read it because of the rude bits), whose tireless devotion to her grandchildren and steadfast faith in me enabled the book to be written.

Acknowledgements

Enormous thanks must go to:

My husband Anders for his unwavering enthusiasm for holding lengthy discussions with me about non-existent people – the characters are every bit as real to him as to me and I adore him for that. And anyway, he's very handsome.

My delicious children – because they're my reason for everything.

Dad, Aason, Andrew and Eilidh for it never once crossing their minds that this book wouldn't one day be published; Vic and Lynne for all the cups of tea (sadly this page is as far as they're allowed to read of this book); Rod for having such a great job, Tash for jollying me along; Wallcoot for stifling her yawns; Molly Stirling for her excellent taste in books; Jenny Geras for her incisive and sensitive editing; Emma Kirby for giving me the confidence to set out on this path in the first place; Lizzie Buchan for her kindness and great advice.

Chapter One

Hugh Summershill knew better than to try to discern or understand the subtle rivalries that women engage in, but he did know that Julia McIntyre was the type of woman his wife, Tor, sniffed at. She'd think Julia had 'let herself go' (even though she was only a size fourteen – he'd checked in her labels one languorous afternoon, wanting to go back to La Perla and get that lacy all-in-one thing he'd seen in the window). Her hair wasn't poker straight, but bouncy with a soft curl which she just left to dry naturally, and she had milky skin with rosebud-pink nipples that had clearly never seen the sun. She wasn't polished, sophisticated, thin or fashionable. In fact, she wasn't any of the things that Tor prized – she wouldn't even have seen her as a competitor – and he'd often wondered whether, subconsciously, this was why he'd gone with her: a random act of spite to his wife, whose perfectionism was alienating and aloof.

He lay back, enjoying the feeling of her breath on his stomach, the spring breeze whispering over him and making him shiver as they lay naked and entwined on the daybed on her veranda. The background rumble of buses and steady drone of rush hour traffic kept his senses rudely aware that this was Battersea, not Bermuda.

'Hmmm, you like that?' she smiled, blowing air rings on his hips. She shifted position, placing herself between his legs, inching downwards, her hair fanning silkily across him as she traced wide meandering S-shapes over his torso with her breath.

She felt him stir and looked up at him, pulling herself forwards, grazing her curves against him, giving him some of what he wanted, but not enough. Nowhere near enough. He grabbed her, ready again, and she giggled at his lusty appetite. Poor Hugh, he'd clearly been starved for years.

'You know,' she said provocatively as she straddled him, not remotely done with him yet, 'this could be how we spend every afternoon. Can't you just imagine it, darling? You and me and this?'

Her hands fluttered behind her, cupping his balls, and she began grinding with intent.

'What . . . do you . . . mean?' he groaned.

The late afternoon sunlight caught her hair, drenching her in apricot light. He didn't know whether to fuck her or eat her.

'I mean I don't want to share you any more, lover,' she purred, leaning over him and biting his lip. 'Let's make this real, once and for all. I want you to move in.'

At the exact moment her husband was ravishing his mistress, Tor Summershill was also reclining in splendour. The sun was low in the sky, ready to drop like a fat peach from the tree, and Tor was stretched out on a teak steamer, eyeing the honeyed glow on the children's naked bodies that made them appear even more luscious than usual. Their busy baby chatter as they tucked into their lawn picnic was nothing more than a tranquil buzz, and Tor made a mental note to get some more of those diddy organic cocktail sausages – so much easier for little fingers and milk teeth.

Mmmm, bliss, she sighed. Still, having a garden bigger than a bikini helped. There weren't many places in south-west London where you could stick the kids out of earshot in an orchard. One hundred and thirty feet of London lawn came with too many zeros for most people.

God, Cress was lucky. She sighed deeply, breathing in the first delicate scent of the night-flowering honeysuckle, and stretched out further. Where the hell was she anyway? She'd been gone ages.

A distant crash and flurry of expletives answered her question and she shaded her eyes to search for her friend, just as the french windows burst open and Cress's slight, angry silhouette stomped down the lawn to the summerhouse. Oh God, what? What? WHAT? Tor frantically scanned over the list of possible disaster scenarios that might explain Cress's crossness – a leaky nappy on the Aubusson? Some broken antique blue and white porcelain? Felt tips on the Frette bedspreads?

Cress set down the tray of freshly-made lemonade with a clatter, and abruptly presented Tor with a glossy red sword.

'Uh, thank you,' Tor faltered. 'What's it for – besides battle, I mean?'

'Can you believe it?' Cress muttered. 'Rumbled already. And it's only bloody May. Bloody kids.'

'What's rumbled?'

'Christmas!' sighed Cress. 'That sword was part of my Santa stash. One of the kids has found it. God knows which one. It was lying on the stairs.' She stood there, hands on hips. 'If I put it in their stockings now, the game is up. They'll know Father Christmas is a myth, I'll be exposed as a liar –

because it will of course be *my* fault that he doesn't exist –
and that'll be it, end of their childhood; next stop, smoking
and snogging behind the scooters . . .'

'Jago's at a boys' school,' Tor interrupted.

'Precisely!' Cress exclaimed triumphantly.

Tor grinned and took a sip of lemonade. 'Did you make
this?'

'Yes. Why, is it disgusting?'

Tor laughed. Cress was many things – mother of four,
business dynamo, social butterfly and intoxicating to her
husband – but domestic goddess? Not a chance. Every dinner
party was spooned from a caterer's Le Creuset, and when
she stopped breastfeeding after three weeks, she joked it was
because her milk was off.

'No, it's great,' she lied. She took another slug of lemonade
to prove her point, and tried not to shiver.

'Well, that's it. Big Yellow Storage for me,' Cress continued,
settling herself noisily on her steamer. 'The kids get into
everything now and there just isn't the storage space in these
houses.'

Tor looked up at the detached seven-bedroom pile and
weighed in sarcastically. 'Yes, you're right. Five thousand
square feet and not a cupboard in sight. It's pitiful. I don't
know how you've put up with it for so long.'

Cress idled a hand in the grass, brushing it casually. 'Hey,
why don't you get one too? Our spaces could be neighbours.'

'Thanks, Cress, but I really don't need to pay for any more
square footage. Our mortgage payments are crippling
enough. And anyway you know I'll just want to decorate it.
Think about it – no natural light, low ceilings, no original
features. My basic nightmare.'

Cress laughed, and they both tried not to drink the lemonade.

Tor squinted over at the toddlers now running amok around the crab-apple and plum trees. Marney and Millie were four and three respectively, but they still shared the padded thighs, bare pudgy bottoms and high, rounded tummies of their eighteen-month-old brother, and she felt brimful of love as they staggered shrieking through the sprinklers. She felt tempted to jump up and join them.

But only momentarily. Lying back doing nothing, for once, felt so good too. And anyway, Cress's stunning Swedish nanny, Greta, had emerged from an hour-long phone call to her boyfriend back home and was herding the children into fluffy towels.

Tor noticed that Cress kept squinting at her mobile on the table and checking the signal.

'So, what's happening at work?' she asked. 'You've been travelling a lot recently.'

'Tchyuh, don't I know it. The air hostesses miss me more between flights than the kids.'

'Mmmm.' Tor squinted at her in the sunlight. Cress's emotional isolation from her children – which she buffered with a stream of nannies – was scarcely acknowledged and certainly never discussed. Cress was all about achievement, control and perfection, and Tor understood her friend well enough to know she needed to keep this 'blemish' below radar until she figured out how to nix it.

To look at her, nothing – apart from the red sword – was out of place in Cress's world. Not her career, not her house, not her marriage, not even her hair. Cress's bob – tinted a shade too blonde – was so sharply styled it looked like it had been cut with lasers. The style was perfect for framing her small heart-shaped face and offset her steely blue eyes, but Tor was always on at her to let it grow out a bit more, get it to look 'a little more relaxed, more natural'.

But then nothing about Cress was relaxed or natural – why should her hair be any different? She was a mini dynamo, a five-foot-two vortex of energy – running between deadlines and flight schedules and spinning classes and bedtime stories. That hair had to toe the line.

Cress raised her face to the sky and shielded her eyes. 'But yuh. I guess you could say work's going . . . well.'

Something in her voice caught Tor's attention. Tor looked back at her friend. Wearing giant shades and a tiny green towelling beach dress that showed off a figure few thirty-three-year-old mothers of four could boast without drastic plastic surgery, Cress was brushing the grass casually in a bucolic manner. She looked uncharacteristically relaxed.

Tor was instantly suspicious. 'Cress, what is it?'

'Hmm?'

'You're trying to tell me something.'

'No, I'm not.'

'Yes, you are.' Tor looked at her, suspiciously.

There was a long pause. 'You want me to beat it out of you.'

Cress giggled. 'I do not.' She began humming lightly. Tor's flecked hazel eyes narrowed further. The women's friendship spanned fifteen years – formed over a mutual ex who had two-timed them at Bristol University – and there was precious little they didn't know about each other. She sank back into her chair, then suddenly gasped and clapped her hand over her mouth.

'Oh my God – you're having an affair!'

'Sssssht! Tell the neighbours, why don't you!' Cress looked

annoyed. 'Actually, no. I'm not having an affair – and I'm shocked that you think I would.'

'Then good God, woman – what is it?'

'I'm *considering* having an affair.'

'No!'

'Yes.'

'No! Who with?'

'With whom,' Cress corrected. 'With Harry Hunter.'

'Nooo!'

'Yes.'

'Nooo!'

'No, you're right. I'm not really.'

'Oh, for God's sake.' Tor, deflated, sank back into the chair and absent-mindedly took another sip of the rancid lemonade. Dammit.

'But he is completely delicious, isn't he?' Cress asked rhetorically. 'And who could blame me, now that I'll be working so closely with him. I mean, I do think Mark would actually understa—'

'What?' Tor shrieked. 'What do you mean, working so closely?'

'Well, he's signing with me on Monday – that's what all the travelling's been about.' She smiled impishly and threw her arms around herself in a hug. 'Oh yes. That man is mine, all mine. I'm pinning him down to a five-book deal. Plus backlist.'

Tor couldn't take it in. Harry Hunter? She couldn't believe she was only one degree removed from him. Oh please, please, let her meet him. Harry Hunter's face was more familiar to her these days than her own husband's. But then, Hugh was never anywhere to be seen and Harry Hunter was everywhere you looked – bearing down from bus billboards, beaming out from the society pages, falling out of nightclubs in the gossip columns, and flirting up a storm on the telly chat-show circuit.

You'd have had to be living in Neverland not to know who Harry Hunter was. He was the publishing world's latest sensation, his books selling by the millions, topping best-seller lists simultaneously all round the world. He'd been translated into thirty-eight different languages and now Hollywood was adapting the books into blockbusters.

His breakthrough book, *Scion*, had been a sleeper hit which had swept the nation, and then the rest of the world, only five years ago. He'd quickly followed it up with *The Snow Leopard* and *The Ruby Route*, which were critically mauled but still sold in their millions because of his name. But it wasn't so much his sales as his torrid, tempestuous nine-month marriage to Lila Briggs – the chart-topping, multi-platinum-selling, stadium-filling singer – which was played out through the tabloids, that ensured that the former housemaster's name had stayed in the headlines ever since. Six foot three, with a curly mop of buttery blond hair, flashing green eyes and rugby-muscled shoulders, he was now a rampant lady-killer, rarely seen without his signature cashmere tweed jacket on his back and some society darling on his arm.

'God, I'd leave Hugh in an instant if Harry Hunter even so much as looked my way.' She stretched dreamily at the thought and Cress enviously noted her muscle tone. Tor had danced her way through her teens and twenties, and although at fifteen and five foot eight she had recognized that she was too tall and not quite good enough to make the corps in a professional dance company, her recompense was an easily toned, low-maintenance figure that made Cress – who fasted for one day every week – want to weep.

In fact, much about Tor's effortless elegance made Cress well up with envy. Her unbleached, rich caramel hair – blonde around her face – that fell in sheets to her shoulder blades; her distinctive almond-shaped hazel eyes that didn't need mascara; and those faint freckles – which opened up in the sun like daisies – covering her cheeks and nose, which kept her forever looking no older than twelve.

'Well, I'm glad you feel that way because, to celebrate, I'm throwing a welcome party for him next week, and you're invited – naturally.'

Tor's jaw dropped.

'No!' She was struck by panic and took all her wishes back. 'There's no way I can party with Harry Hunter. I mean, you know I'll get drunk after half a glass and start to stutter and suffer stress incontinence . . .' Her voice trailed off as she clocked Cress's bemusement. 'Well, what's the dress code? You know I've got nothing to wear.'

'Cocktail,' Cress said, crunching hard on a clutch of ice. 'And I know precisely the opposite.' Pre-babies, Tor had slowly but surely scaled the heights of fashion retail. It hadn't been a meteoric rise, owing to a sensational lack of ambition, but the design houses' sales teams admired her easy chic and instinctive eye. She could put together a rail that even they hadn't considered, and more often than not she left them with more tips for the forthcoming season than the other way round. She was always invited to the first round of buying appointments, sat in the front row at the shows, and by the time she fell pregnant with Marney she was chief buyer at Browns in South Molton Street. It was a nomadic life, though, regularly flying to Milan, Paris, New York and Los Angeles, and not one she'd wanted to continue once the children were born. She wanted to be a hands-on, stay-at-home mother, and although she increasingly found herself drawn to interior design these days, she still had a wardrobe of eveningwear that Cress lusted after like a little sister.

'Well, I'll still need something new. This is no time for hand-me-downs,' Tor muttered, trying to work out how much weight she could shed in a week and whether she'd be able to get Fabien for a blow-dry at such short notice. Did Hugh have anything in his diary?

Talking of which, how had they left it for Kate and Monty's tonight? Was he going straight from the office? She tried his mobile but it was switched off.

Tor checked her watch and started gathering the children's beakers, swim nappies and discarded clothes.

'Millie, Marney, Oscar,' she called to her waddling, toddling brood. 'Over here, please. Let's get you dressed.'

The sun had plopped from the sky now and her legs goose-bumped in the dusk. She shivered and shrugged on her pale grey cashmere jumper (M&S, machine washable, but with the label cut out, who knew?). There were only two hours till dinner at Kate's, and with three kids under five and still bath and bedtime to get through, it was a tight schedule. Time to get a shift on.

Cress waved and smiled cheerily as Tor reversed out of the drive. She closed the front door slowly and leant against it, deliberating whether to make the phone call, or go and bath the children. She could hear their shrieks and splashes three floors away – God only knew the amount of water there must be on the floor.

She checked her watch. He hadn't rung – but then she'd known he wouldn't. The New York flight was due to leave in twenty minutes. She pressed her fists against her eyes as she faced up to the fact she was out of choices. If she was going to stop him getting on that plane, she was going to have to play her hand.

Navigating her way past the abandoned toys and strewn clothes – Greta could pick them up – she marched past the children's bathroom, just as Felicity, her youngest and barely three, clambered over the side of the bath.

'Mummy!' she yelled. Darting past the towel Greta was holding wide like a windbreaker and throwing her arms around Cress's legs – her long, wet hair slapping Cress's thighs – she rugby-tackled her to a halt. Cress wobbled and fell forwards on to her hands in a rather ungainly downward dog position.

'Oh Flick, get off!' Cress said crossly, trying to push Felicity off her legs. 'You're getting me soaked.'

'But you're already wearing a towel, Mummy.'

'No. It's Juicy Couture and it's dry clean only,' she said huffily.

'Now you know that's not true,' said an amused voice.

Cress tried to look back over her shoulder, but being still a dog that was downwards and not suitably warmed up, she couldn't. She peered through her legs instead.

'What are you doing home so early?' she cried.

Mark was standing at the top of the stairs, pulling off his tie. 'Meeting ended early,' he grinned, faint laughter lines tucking in around his clear blue eyes. He oozed mischief and looked considerably younger than his thirty-nine years. Even the sprinkling of salt in his pepper-black hair seemed to twinkle. 'And clearly you were thinking what I was thinking.' He walked up to her and planted a kiss on her butt cheek. Even after nine years of marriage, the chemistry between them was as strong as it had been the night they first met, when she had been embroiled in an affair with his married boss and he'd had to smuggle her out of the bank's summer party after his boss's wife made a surprise entrance.

Felicity extricated herself from her mother's heap and – along with Orlando, four, Jago, six, and Lucy, seven – threw herself at her father instead. Mark disappeared under a wriggling mass of pink limbs and downy hair.

'Come on, you lot. Bedtime story,' he said, giving Flick a piggyback up to the nursery rooms on the top floor. 'I'll be back for you in a few minutes,' he winked to Cress.

Cress winked back, and blew goodnight kisses to the children, who didn't notice. She blanched at their unintentional slights but decided to put that one down to the excitement of the moment.

Anyway, she had other things on her mind. She didn't notice Greta standing in the bathroom, holding the damp towel across her chest and listening to every intimate word between husband and wife.

Cress stalked across the landing to the master bedroom, her perfectly pedicured feet sinking into the plush cream carpet, and shut the door behind her. Picking up the red leather Smythson diary she'd left on the bedside table, she flicked through the pages until she found the number she was looking for.

She stared at it. Her destiny lay in those digits. Everything she had ever worked for, striven for – hell, neglected her family for – came down to this. It was do or die.

Her company, Sapphire Books, had risen to spectacular heights in eight short years, presciently foreseeing the blogging phenomenon as a kissing cousin to the publishing industry. While the naysayers decried these web books as the

Napsters of the publishing industry, she saw beyond the initial drift. Though the most successful blogs boasted millions-strong readerships, they appealed mainly to the computer-nerds. Cress knew most people preferred to read from a physical page. They liked the feel of a book in their hands when they were in bed, on the bus or at the poolside. And she knew that her precision editing and slick polish could package the same material to an even broader audience.

Her first six blog-books had gone straight into the top ten of the *Times* best-seller lists, but sales on titles since had cooled and she needed to look beyond diarists and virtual lives. She couldn't afford to stay so niche. The blogging trend was peaking and Sapphire Books needed to break into the mainstream.

As usual, luck had been on her side. Her first foray into fiction had been picked by Richard and Judy's all-powerful book club and sales were now nudging a million copies. But she had nothing with which to follow it up.

So when that innocuous brown envelope had landed on her desk, handing the biggest name in publishing to her on a plate, it had seemed too good to be true. Clearly, it wasn't something she could show to her legal team. She had to do this alone. It was dodgy ground. Oh, who was she kidding? It was criminal, face it.

She'd tried doing it straight, meeting him socially at various parties in London, New York and Boston, letting the acquaintance bud until she felt she could table a meeting with him.

They'd met up at the Portobello Hotel – small, intimate and off the corporate track, like Sapphire – and she'd delivered a sensational pitch, boasting of Sapphire's impressive profitability and its reputation as the fastest-growing, most dynamic publishing company around. They were the mavericks, just like him. The chemistry between Harry Hunter and Sapphire – between him and her – was sizzling, and Harry had been surprisingly impressed.

He'd only agreed to the meeting, intending to get to the pink and black lace balconette bra she was wearing beneath her grey georgette blouse. But her impressive engagement ring had winked at him like a jealous child on a single mother's first date – no woman kept her ring freshly polished after nine years of marriage unless she was still in love with her husband – and when he'd suggested finishing the meeting 'somewhere more private', they had stalled.

He liked a challenge, but he didn't have the time he'd usually devote to breaking and bedding her. Manhattan was waiting, and she wasn't even in the same ball-park when it came down to money. Reluctantly, he'd had to let her go for the time being but, not wanting to burn his bridges – knowing they'd bump into each other again on the publishing circuit – he'd left it that he'd 'consider' her proposal.

The minutes had ticked by all week and she'd barely slept. She'd fingered the brown envelope constantly, like a worry bead. Did she dare cross the line?

Now, she couldn't put it off any longer. Time, tide and air traffic controllers wait for no man. She had to do it.

The phone rang five times before he picked up.

'Cressida,' he smiled, though there was a faint note of impatience in his voice, now that she was no longer an imminent prospect. 'I'm sorry. I meant to get back to you. It's been a crazy week.'

Cress had seen the pictures of him in the *Mirror*, tumbling out of Whisky Mist with a blonde on each arm.

'I know. I won't keep you,' she said levelly. 'I just wanted to check you weren't getting on the plane.'

'What?' he said, alarmed. 'Has something happened? Is there a security alert?'

Cress could hear a rumble of commotion around him.

'No. No security alert. Nothing like that.' Cress heard him break off to reassure the passengers around him. 'Sorry. Didn't mean to panic you,' he was saying, with what she could well imagine was a boyish grin. There was another pause. 'Yeah, sure. Who should I make it out to?'

He came back on the line.

'Sorry. Autographs,' he said, clearly cradling the phone on his shoulder. Cress visualized him scribbling on various people's magazines, cheque-book stubs, arms – breasts, no doubt.

She waited.

His voice was distracted. 'So are you ringing to tell me there's something new you can do for me?'

'In a way, yes.'

She paused, letting his frustration mount.

'Which is?'

'Well . . .' She took a deep breath. 'I can agree not to tell the world about Brendan Hillier.'

Chapter Two

Dinner was supposed to be at nine sharp, but it was already half an hour past that and Kate was still waiting on one couple. Monty had gone back out with the last-but-one bottle of fizz, but they hadn't catered for the pre-dinner drinks lasting two hours and he'd soon have to start on the Pouilly Fumé. Bloody hell. He hated the food and booze being out of synch.

Kate stirred the sauce in silent fury. They'd been tense with each other all week and she knew he was deliberately avoiding ringing her at work. If she confronted him, he'd hold out his palms and blame back-to-back meetings, but they both knew they were in retreat from each other, from the red stain they'd woken to on the bedsheets, and what it meant. Again.

She didn't ask why any more. There were no answers, no more tests, no more doctors. Everyone said they should just hang in there – count themselves lucky that there wasn't an actual reason for failing to conceive. It meant it could still happen. They just had to have Hope.

What those people didn't realize was that Hope was the worst part. Counting the year, not in weeks or months, but in private twenty-eight-day cycles, thinking maybe this month would be the month – constantly on the watch for water retention, talking herself into nausea, deluding herself she had a heightened sense of smell, praying that her tightening waistband signified the beginnings of a new life, not a new diet – only to have it dashed month after month after month.

No, Hope was not her friend. And when those oh-so-well-meaning people squeezed her hand comfortingly, support and sympathy written all over their faces, her smile was frigid with resentment.

Kate took another sip from her glass and looked at the clock. At this rate they wouldn't get to bed before 1 a.m. Not that it mattered so much – after all, the one upside of not having children meant late nights could easily be supported by lazy mornings. But as a top libel lawyer in London's most prestigious and profitable reputation management firm, Saturdays were often her busiest days. She had to have a clear head for threatening the editors who were getting ready to bump up their Sunday circulations with juicy scandals featuring her celebrity clients. She was on first-name terms with all the newspaper editors, London agents and LA publicists, and she had the home and mobile numbers of most of the football premiership and several Russian billionaires.

Tor walked in with an empty glass, looking stunning in a cream silk backless Temperley dress. 'I've come to join you,' she said, going straight to the vast American fridge and pulling out the last remaining bottle of Moët. 'I'm fed up with being ignored by my husband.'

Hugh had come to Kate and Monty's straight from the office, and Tor was sulking that he hadn't bothered to come home first to get changed – his suit was rumpled and he needed a shave. She hated arriving at parties on her own – even when they were being hosted by their best friends.

Apart from briefly asking her if the children had finished their supper and whether she had money for the babysitter, Hugh had gone on to spend most of the evening engrossed in conversation with a rather voluptuous – well, plump actually, Tor thought – freckly woman with a fabulous mane of treacle-coloured hair that she kept tossing about like an excited pony. Hugh liked women with some meat on their bones. He probably thought she looked as though she would be good in bed.

'Any reason why you're starving us all?' Tor asked.

'Well, clearly because you've just let yourself go and really need to lose the baby weight,' Kate drawled.

Tor smoothed her dress over her tummy and smiled back, self-consciously.

'Joke!' Kate cried, tossing her auburn hair off her shoulders. Her friend's insecurity was maddening. A neat size ten, Tor had never really shrugged off the body fascism that came from an adolescence spent staring at herself in a mirror all day, practising kicks and pliés next to five-foot featherweights who could tuck their ankles behind their ears. But quite what she had to be insecure about was beyond Kate. Keeping herself to a size twelve was a constant battle. She knew that inside her gym-honed curves was a size fourteen waiting to burst free. Not that being curvy was all bad. She was tall enough to carry it off – five foot nine in stockings – and Monty said her magnificent cleavage was his pride and joy, his own set of twins to play with.

'Good tan too,' she reassured.

'Thanks – this one didn't leave me smelling like roast beef. Here, sniff.' Tor held out her arm and Kate sniffed appreciatively.

'Well, hello, ladies,' said a smooth voice. 'Do you need

any help with that?' They looked up. Guy Latham, an old uni friend of Monty's, had sauntered in. He did something 'technical' in the City. Looking taller than his six foot in an exquisitely cut bespoke grey suit, lime silk lining flashing, he was clearly doing well.

His wife, Laetitia, confirmed his successes with some ambitious networking of her own and was completely terrifying. She was one of those slick charity hostesses you always saw in the society pages at the back of *Tatler* and *Country Life*, and was best friends with Daphne Guinness and Tamara Mellon. Brought up in Martha's Vineyard on America's East Coast, she had been bred to the power charity circuit, and her life revolved around lunches, shopping events and 'intimate soirées' with the great, the good and the generous. Tor, Cress and Kate thought she was a social climber with ropes on her back, but Tor couldn't deny her presence here tonight added a frisson of exclusivity to the gathering.

Guy took the bottle from Tor, who was going faintly purple.

'Allow me,' he said, taking the bottle from her. Without taking his gaze off the two women, he expertly opened the champagne. It popped elegantly and he poured them two fresh glasses.

'Now. As you were,' he said with a wicked smile.

'Huh?' Tor was lost.

'Sniffing each other. It looked surprisingly erotic.'

They both frowned at him, Tor in confusion, Kate with thinly veiled disgust, her green eyes flashing.

'Oh well, it was worth a shot,' he smiled. He picked up the magnum and headed out of the kitchen. "Don't do anything I wouldn't do, ladies,' he called over his shoulder.

'God, he's patronizing,' Kate muttered under her breath.

'I eat his clients for breakfast and he treats me like the little woman.'

Tor took a sip and enjoyed the feel of the bubbles fizzing on her tongue. 'Forget him. He's a prat.' She walked over to the door. 'Tell me this: who's the fat bird who's been chatting up Hugh all night?' Tor watched them, feeling suspiciously like she was spying on them. They seemed so – intimate.

Kate tutted disapprovingly. 'You cannot, in this day and age, call someone "a fat bird", Tor Summershill. That's the kind of slur that brings me lots of money.'

'I guess,' Tor conceded. 'But she is chatting up my husband.'

'Yes, I noticed that.' They stood at the doorway together, glasses in hand and eyes narrowed. 'Her name's Julia McIntyre. Guy suggested we invited her. I can't stand her but she's just destroyed her husband in the divorce court, so Monty's angling to invest some of her millions.'

'Aaah.' She turned back, bored by her husband's flirting. 'Anyway, back to my original question. When are we eating? I'm going to pass out with hunger in a minute.'

'I'm just waiting for one more couple.'

'I take it there's a life or death situation which is making them so bloody late?'

Kate chuckled. 'There is, actually. He's an obstetrician, stuck at a birth.'

Tor rolled her eyes and pulled a goofy face.

'Oh, hang on. You know him, don't you? James White – wasn't he yours?'

'Oooh,' Tor smiled, bending at the knees. He'd delivered all her and Cress's babies, and they both had a long-standing crush on him. 'God, is he really coming for dinner? How fantastic. Who've you put him next to?'

'You, of course.'

Tor's stomach rumbled loudly and she clapped a hand over it. 'Well, look, I really don't think you can hold up dinner any longer, even for the deeply charismatic Mr White . . .'

'Uh, Lord White,' Kate corrected, smiling.

'Is he a Lord?' Tor whispered, intimidated.

'Well, when you deliver the royal babies, you're going to be top of the list, let's face it.'

'Wow,' Tor muttered. Did Cress know a Lord had de-livered her babies, she wondered? Surely not. Else she'd never have heard the end of it.

Her tummy rumbled again.

'Well, *Lord* White could be hours, yet. And if you don't get some food down everyone's throats, I swear they're going to be so lashed they'll start playing spin the bottle. And I, for one, do not want to have to kiss my husband.'

Kate chuckled.

'I'll send Monty through, shall I?'

With the zeal of the half starved and completely pissed, Tor manoeuvred everyone towards the round pedestal table while Kate started ladling out the portions of monkfish, which by now were looking tougher than a Thai kickboxer.

Kate had laid the table beautifully. Her parties were always themed. Tonight's was Oriental Pearl. The black linen table-cloth was set off by a trail of white orchids that fragrantly wove around dainty tealights, and tiny ecru blind-embossed place-names perched on antique ivory chopsticks – a night-mare to read but they looked great.

Tor stood behind her chair – she saw she had Guy Latham to her left and James White to her right. Hugh was opposite her but might as well have been in another room for all the attention he was paying her. She tried joining Guy's conversation with Monty, but it was something about the pensions crisis and she stood awkwardly mute as she ransacked her brain for a single opinion to offer up on the topic.

Thankfully, she was saved by Kate triumphantly setting down the meal, and all conversation ceased as everyone inhaled the aroma.

'Apologies, all,' smiled Kate. 'We shall have to start without the last guests. Please tuck in.'

Nobody needed to be told twice, and over the clatter of forks, Guy and Monty picked up their conversation where they'd left it. For a few moments, Tor didn't care. She was just grateful to be able to eat at last – she'd skipped lunch so that her tummy was flat for this evening and felt exceptionally light-headed. If she could get some food into her system, she might sober up a little.

Kate had calmed down from her inward histrionics in the kitchen and was sitting regally, feeling satisfied that her evening – if not her life – had finally come together.

The doorbell rang. Typical!

She sprang up and came back into the room moments later, crying, 'A little boy. Hurrah!' Everyone cheered, even though none of them knew who'd just had the little boy, and raised their glasses in a display of drunken conviviality.

Then just as quickly as the table had roared approval, it fell silent. Following Kate through the door came a ravishing brunette, petite, with porcelain-fine bone structure and an elfin crop. With a casual hand on her shoulder was a tall, dark-haired man with strong cheekbones and deep-set chocolate-brown eyes. He was carrying a bottle of Pétrus, which cheered up the men, who were depressed that the Parisian – for what else could she be? – was accounted for.

'Everyone, this is James White and Coralie Pedeaux.'

The men perked up again upon hearing that Coralie was not yet married, conveniently overlooking the fact that they all were. Monty – desperate not to let his long-awaited supper go cold – briskly did the introductions while Kate served up the last two portions.

The latecomers took their seats, James kissing Tor on both cheeks before tucking his chair in and shaking out his napkin. 'How lovely to see you again. May I call you Victoria, seeing as we're off-duty?'

'Oh, please, call me Tor.'

'Tor, then. Are you well? You certainly look it. Hospital gowns clearly didn't do anything for you.'

'Thank you.' She smiled brightly at the compliment and nodded towards Coralie, who was positioning herself daintily between Monty and Guy – both of whom were holding out her chair. She was wearing a navy knitted dress, with a deep scooped neckline and a tantalizing scarlet ribbon that threaded over a small but perfectly formed décolleté which had clearly never breastfed three children. A shapely back wasn't the only reason Tor preferred backless styles these days.

'Your girlfriend is far too beautiful to be sitting at a dinner party in the inner city suburbs,' Tor asserted in mock outrage. 'Shouldn't she be at a grand prix or on a gin palace in the Med?'

James laughed. 'I know. Half the time I take her out, she gets taken to the VIP area and I get barred at the door. It's so embarrassing. I have to keep pretending I've been paged.' He shrugged self-deprecatingly, and she laughed.

'Have you been together long?'

'Mmm, about a year? Just under, I think. Or is it more?

Hang on a second.' He frowned, mentally scanning for a reference point.

'Oh, you're such a boy.' Tor scolded gently. 'So rubbish with dates. Tsk.'

'Yes, I know. It's pathetic.' He hung his head in mock shame, and Tor giggled.

He was surprisingly relaxed off-duty. She leant in conspiratorially. The champagne in the kitchen had hit her and she felt playful.

'Of course, are we allowed to speak?'

He looked at her, puzzled.

'Socially, I mean.'

'Ah.' He leant in. 'Are you a spy too, then?' He looked furtively round the room. She giggled again.

'No. But you know jolly well what I mean. You are – were – my doctor. Doesn't our meeting here contravene the doctor-patient relationship, ethics, thingy?'

'Oh, I see, yes, the ethics-thingy.' He nodded sagely. 'Well, are you pregnant?'

'No, I'm not.'

'Are you planning to get pregnant again?'

She snorted before she could stop herself. 'Chance would be a fine thing.'

He cocked an eyebrow.

'No, no.' She coughed and fidgeted. 'Definitely no more.'

'So you're not planning to see me again?'

'No.'

'Charming!' He grinned, and she thought how boyish he looked. He'd always seemed so – patrician, in his white coat. He picked up his knife and fork again and leant in to her. 'Then it's OK. We can meet here, no jeopardy – or thingies.'

They smiled at their japes, and she was surprised at how

completely at ease she felt in his company. She knew, of course, that sitting next to James White at a dinner would be considered by most of south-west London as a huge coup. Cress would just die. She might have Harry Hunter, but Tor had James White. He was the best obstetrician in London, and Cress used to joke that it was worth getting pregnant just to see him. Nearly all his patients were madly in love with him – he was their knight with shining stethoscope – and would gladly make up excuses to increase their ante-natal visits and delay being discharged after the birth. Oh, the cruel irony of having to be pregnant by another man just to see him!

Being a James White patient was like being in a very exclusive club – one for which the husbands paid dearly, at over ten grand for a C-section – as he only took four patients a month. Those in the know took their pregnancy tests at four weeks and often booked him before their husbands even knew they were pregnant. Cress, typically, had cunningly forged a close telephone relationship with his secretary – the gatekeeper – just to get first dibs.

'So how do you know Kate and Monty?' Tor asked, just as he put a forkful of food in his mouth.

'Mmm,' he paused, trying to chew quickly. 'Old family friends. And then Monty went out with my baby sister for a while. Not long. Couple of months? Broke her heart of course, the scoundrel.' He tried to scowl. Tor laughed. 'Naturally, I threatened to beat him up with my very heavy medical textbooks, but he wriggled out of it with a David Bowie album and the secret of his bacon sarnies.'

'Yes, they are legendary, aren't they?' Tor smiled. Monty's renowned breakfasts had been the bedrock of the three couples' friendship as the toll of Cress and Mark's, and Tor and Hugh's consecutive babies and broken nights rendered them all unfit for night-time socializing for a good few years. 'Gosh. So that must have been ages ago.' Tor paused, trying to work out dates. 'Because Monty and Kate have been together since – what – they were sixteen?'

'Um . . .' He refilled his glass. 'Yes. But they broke up for a bit at the beginning of university. As I understand it. That's when he had a dalliance with my sister.'

'Ah. This was all before my time.' She uncrossed and recrossed her legs.

'How do you know them?' James, tucking into his dinner, didn't look up. He was clearly famished. Close up, his eyes looked tired. She wondered how long he'd just worked for? He'd been up all night for her with both Marney and Millie, although Oscar had been a planned C-section, mid-morning.

'Well, it was the boys who were friends first. My husband was at Wellington with Monty so they've known each other since they were only just out of short trousers. I met them when Hugh and I got together after university, and Kate and I just clicked immediately. It was like I'd known her my entire life.'

'Is your husband here tonight?' he inquired politely.

'Yes, he's over there.' Tor nodded briefly in Hugh's direction but she was eager not to bring him into the conversation. She was beginning to find his ceaseless admiration of his buxom dinner companion embarrassing. She hurried along. 'Actually, I always thought you were married.' Tor was sure she recalled seeing a photo of him at the Gold Cup polo a few years back, with a stunning brunette.

'I was. Until three years ago.'

'Oh, I'm so sorry. I had no idea.' Tor felt embarrassed.

James shrugged. 'It was a long time coming. Casualty of

my job, unfortunately.' He sighed. 'The hours are long, unsociable, demanding. You can probably imagine. She grew tired of going to dinners and parties on her own . . .' Tor resisted the urge to empathize with his ex. Her situation was quite different. Definitely.

'. . . of me getting out of bed in the middle of the night to go into the hospital. Can't blame her really. In the end, she . . . well, she's remarried now, to a colleague of mine, a plastic surgeon. Much better hours.' He smiled wryly.

'Still or sparkling, Tor?' Guy interrupted.

'Oh, still, please. I've had enough bubbles for one night,' she smiled.

Guy filled her water glass and emptied the bottle. 'James?'

'Yes, same, please.'

Tor scanned the table and saw another bottle further down. It was too far from Guy. 'I'll get it,' she said and stood up to reach over to it, the side of her dress falling forward and inadvertently casting James a superb flash of her breasts.

Guy joined their conversation, trying to engage James in the pensions discussion, but he heroically resisted, keeping the topics to Cornwall versus Norfolk and the differences between baby boys and girls. Tor fell a little bit more in love with him for being so sweet to keep her in the conversation, and the rest of the evening flew by. In fact she felt quite disappointed when the doorbell started ringing solidly at quarter past midnight, as everyone's pre-booked minicabs arrived so that they could dash home to relieve the babysitters.

Monty was holding Tor's coat open for her when James came to say goodbye.

'It's been such a pleasure seeing you again this evening,' James smiled down at her. 'But remember . . .' He looked furtively left and right. 'You haven't seen me.'

She giggled and he kissed her on both cheeks. Coralie was standing at the door, shivering. Without a word, he placed his jacket over her bird-like shoulders, and guided her out. A moment later, Hugh sauntered up, hands in pockets. Where had he been?

'Wasn't that our baby doctor chap?'

Whatever his insouciance, Hugh must have been jealous of Tor's spirited conversation with James, for he was all over her in the taxi. She had intended to be cross with him for ignoring her all evening, but as he slid his hands around her back and under her dress, she was too pleased by his ardour to care.

They gave the taxi driver quite a peepshow, writhing on the back seat like teenagers, and when they got home, Hugh kept the taxi running outside and vastly overpaid the babysitter, practically pushing her out of the door. Tor was plumping the cushions on the sofa in the drawing room when he came up behind her and deftly untied the velvet ribbons holding up the top of her dress so that it fell to her waist. She gasped in surprise that he couldn't even wait to get upstairs. The skirt of the dress was too tight to pull down, so he hitched it up, revealing the tiny white lace G-string she'd worn on their wedding day. It rolled down easily beneath his fingers, and he left it suspended around one ankle as he bent her over the sofa. They were both frantic with hurry. Five weeks – the last time they'd had sex – had been long enough.

Chapter Three

Summer had come early this year, and even though it was only May, Tor's days were spent on the commons, teaching Millie to cycle without stabilizers, making daisy chains, blowing dandelion clocks, and playing hide and seek behind the massive conker trees.

There were two commons to choose between – Clapham and Wandsworth – and each of these grassy London plains sat atop hills on either side of a square mile valley, which estate agents called Between the Commons, but which was better known to the locals as Nappy Valley, due to its extraordinary claim of having the highest birth rate in Europe. Tor didn't know whether this had actually been substantiated or not, although it was hard to refute if you wandered down the chic Northcote Road, which snaked along the valley floor, on a Saturday morning. Two out of three people were either boasting a bump or pushing a pram.

With such a high density of young children in a confined area, competition to get into the nursery and pre-prep schools was arguably fiercer than in any other part of the country – hell, in Europe, surely – and the desire to be part of this club meant house prices had skyrocketed. Like the garden squares of Notting Hill and Chelsea, the Nappy Valley grid had become one of the most exclusive enclaves in London, and the commons flanking it sat like extravagant green entrance gates to a plush country club.

Each common boasted a playground, where everyone congregated when the sun shone, recreating urban scenes of the traditional seaside pastiche. Children scampered around the park-keeper's hut and played with the plastic dumper trucks, which – in an unspoken display of middle-class manners – no one ever took home; towering sandcastles were built, collapsed and jumped upon; ice lollies were bought and fought over; dogs slept in the shade; bicycles were pedalled furiously and then abandoned.

Tor enjoyed being a main player in the sorority that had formed there. Compared to Cress and Kate, with their high-flying, demanding careers, Tor knew her days read like an exercise in off-duty indolence, but to the initiated there was a competitive element as fierce as anything in the workplace, and as the HQ of the Nappy Valley 'professional mummies', it was a veritable hotbed of tribal rivalries, gossip and innuendo.

After a solid hour's-worth of playing Poddy 1-2-3, Tor was relieved to finally sit down and she dug her toes deeper into the sandpit (partly to hide her unpedicured springtime toes) as she waited and watched for Millie to come back from weeing behind the oak tree.

'Tor Summershill! I was talking about you only earlier.'

Tor looked up. She was disappointed to see Jinty Adams – the world authority on motherhood – plop down next to her, looking nautical and somewhat oversized in blue and white striped cropped trousers and a gauzy white blouse. Giant shades sat on the top of her head and she had pulled her hair back into a ponytail that was supposed to look effortlessly chic, but just made her look like the captain of the netball team.

'How are you, Jinty? It's been ages,' Tor said politely.

'Hasn't it though?'

'Have you been away? You look annoyingly healthy.'

'Oman. Just got back. Have you been?'

'No, not yet.'

'Oh, you must. The kids just love it. It's the new Dubai, you know.'

'Mmm, so I hear. Where are yours?' Tor scanned the play-ground.

'Oh, the twins have got tennis club and I left Rosie with Fräulein. Felt Eddy and I needed some quality time together.' She squeezed her four-year-old, who was looking particularly petulant at this idea.

Jinty had three boys and a girl, and belonged to a growing breed of mothers having four or more children. Once upon a time, one child had been a 'starter', two had been 'neat and tidy', and three was a 'proper family'. Now the goal-posts had been moved and the most competitive mums were having four, five or more. Tor wasn't sure her body – or her marriage – could take it.

It was academic anyhow. She and Hugh hadn't discussed having a fourth – probably because that would involve having sex, which would mean he'd have to come home occasionally, so that was a spanner in the works. As a self-employed architect, he was always either working late at the office, on site or pitching for new business at drinks parties. Wherever he was, it wasn't at home. Was this normal? Were all marriages like this – or just hers?

'Are you thinking about any more?' Jinty asked, reading her mind.

'No, I don't think so.' She shook her head and looked down at Oscar, who was sucking sand off his fingers. 'How about you?'

'Heavens, no. God, the cost is prohibitive,' Jinty said in a confiding tone. Tor quickly calculated that she must already be paying nearly £48,000 per annum on school fees – net! Was that not considered prohibitive then?

Jinty carried on, without pause. 'But that's not a problem for you, is it? I mean, your husband appears to be doing awfully well. I see his company car parked outside the McIntyre place all the time.'

Jinty looked straight at Tor, who was brushing the sand off Oscar's hands with baby wipes.

McIntyre. McIntyre. Tor felt she knew the name but couldn't quite place it. Jinty saw the frown of confusion on Tor's face.

'Opposite me, you know,' Jinty added helpfully. Tor remembered that Jinty lived in Spencer Park, over the other side of Wandsworth Common, an exclusive enclave which backed on to eight acres of private parkland.

'Oh, you mean the Spencer Park job,' she bluffed. 'Yes, that's certainly a . . . lucrative contract.'

'Yes. She's a very rich bunny, is Julia. Got plenty of money to burn. And time.'

Tor looked at her. Julia? Julia McIntyre. She definitely knew the name.

'Of course my Gordon knows her ex terribly well. They sat the bar together.'

'Her ex? You mean she's divorced?'

'Yes, didn't you know?'

Tor's head whipped up. That was it! The rich divorcee at Kate and Monty's dinner. Tor's brow furrowed. She felt strangely bothered by this connection, remembering how she had cornered Hugh all evening. I mean, it was fine for him to talk non-stop to a divorcee at a dinner party, but she hadn't known that he *already* knew her. Why hadn't he introduced her?

She tuned back in to Jinty.

'. . . Yuh, she caught him at it with a trainee. Such a cliché.' Jinty rolled her eyes. 'But it all worked out terribly well for her in the end. Got, what, three million, was it? Plus the house. And now she's got your husband.'

'I beg your pardon?'

Jinty laughed, though her eyes didn't. 'I mean in a professional capacity – of course.' She put a reassuring hand on Tor's arm. 'Oh, must go. There's a swing free. So lovely to see you again. Think about Oman, OK?'

'What kind of name is Jinty anyway?' Kate bitched loyally, expertly chopping and dicing carrots in preparation for her next culinary masterpiece. The children loved eating here, and always wolfed down their vegetables – even sprouts – with no problem. Consequently Kate thought Tor's children were the world's best eaters – further confirming her opinion of Tor as supermummy – and had no idea as to the amount of tomato ketchup (which smothered anything green) they got through at home.

Tor was sitting at the oak block table, an untouched mug of tea steaming in front of her, her hands running absent-mindedly along the undulations of the wood, which had been rubbed to a marble smoothness over the years. It was just a typical Saturday morning – the girls cooking up breakfast, brunch or lunch (depending on meetings, delayed flights and dinners the night before) while the children jumped on sofas in the sitting room and the men played football on the common.

Except that today didn't feel like usual. It was as though her world had changed, shifted slightly off its axis. It was two days after her conversation with Jinty and she was still rattled. She'd picked up on the subtext – who could have missed it, frankly? – and couldn't quite dismiss it out of hand.

Tor watched Kate sauté the onions. She liked the way Kate had combed her thick auburn hair into a loose French plait, with wispy tendrils falling forwards, framing her face in a soft-focus haze. Her striped blue and white linen smock fanned out gently over her teeny pot belly (the nearest she was going to get to a baby bump, she would joke, self-consciously) and in her boy-cut jeans and battered plimsolls she looked like a young Charlotte Rampling.

'Oh, Kate. I'm probably just overreacting. You know what she's like. Not happy till she's ruined someone else's day.'

'Well, imagine how bitter you'd be if you had to live with those thighs. Ooh, the chafing.' The women chuckled. 'Honestly though, I can't bear the cow. Who does she think she is, spreading malicious rumours like that? Doesn't she know who she's messing with? *Tu problema, mi problema, amiga.* Just give me the word and I'll put together a case against her for crimes against fashion. You could easily have her for emotional distress – I mean really, horizontal stripes on *her* bum? There's not a jury in the world would find against you.' Pause. 'Except maybe in Fiji.'

Tor laughed.

'Seriously, Tor. You've got nothing to worry about. Hugh's crazy about you. Everyone can see it. So he works crazy hours? He's got his own business. It's part of the job, unfortunately. Just wait till they get bought out by Fosters. Then you'll be laughing.'

Tor nodded appreciatively. She understood why Kate thought everything was rosy. She and Hugh never argued, he helped with the kids . . . But privately? When it was just the two of them? What would Kate think if she knew they'd only had sex three times so far this year?

Her head hurt just thinking about it. 'Have you spoken to Cress?' she asked, changing the subject. Tor had been avoiding Cress's calls all week, knowing her best friend's antennae would pick up her anxieties immediately. 'Has she signed him yet?'

'Oh my God, yes! I can*not* believe she's got Harry Hunter on her books. God only knows what she must have done to get him.'

'Knowing Cress, sold her granny – or one of the children. Where's the party going to be, do you know?'

'Eight o'clock at Kensington Roof Gardens next Saturday. Paparazzi central. She wants to get maximum exposure of her new purchase,' she said.

Kate leaned back against the worktop and dropped her head back, closing her eyes.

'What are you doing?' Tor asked suspiciously.

'Imagining him – exposed.'

Tor guffawed. 'You're trying to get pregnant with your husband! You're supposed to be having filthy thoughts about him, not strange men.'

Tor straightened up and grabbed her tea. 'Having said that, it goes without saying we need to encourage him to have filthy thoughts about us. I definitely need to get a new dress. Do you think Hugh would leave me if I added another zero to the Visa bill?'

'Yes,' Kate chastised. And then reconsidered. 'Although if it means you get to pull Harry Hunter, I personally think it would be worth it.'

And they burst out laughing, just as the children came charging into the kitchen, thinking that this looked as good a time as any to ask for ice cream cornets.

Chapter Four

The post landed on the mat with a thwack, startling Cress so that she jogged black coffee over her milk-coloured cashmere dressing-gown. Tch. Not a good start.

Mark picked up the bundle of mail from the hall and, kissing her affectionately on the forehead, dropped it on the worktop.

'Looking forward to today?' he smiled, pouring a cup of strong builder's.

She rolled her eyes. 'It's a glorious day and my four beautiful children are mine, all mine. What's not to like?'

'Mummy, I hate butter on my croissant,' Lucy whined. 'You know I hate butter. Greta never gives me butter.'

Cress rolled her eyes. She couldn't keep up with her children's dietary preferences, which – thanks to Greta's indulgence on the matter – appeared to change on a weekly basis.

'You'll have a great time,' he grinned, seeing her nervousness and annoyance merge into a fidgety irritation. He ran a hand through her hair, and let it fall through his fingers. He kissed the tip of her nose. She had smudges of mascara around her eyes – last night's lovemaking had left her exhausted and for once not giving a damn about going to sleep with a full face of make-up. And he loved her for it. The less she cared about perfection, the sexier he found her.

Since signing Harry Hunter to Sapphire Books – all of twelve days ago – she had actually relaxed. Just let go. After eight long years of what felt like almost total absence as she got Sapphire off the ground – reappearing only for the conceptions, births and birthdays of the children – he'd finally got his wife back.

Of course, the children were used to their mother's limited presence in their lives – they didn't know any different – and Cress had always 'made it up to them' (as she saw it) by insisting on paying above the odds to get the very best nannies on the market. But even with Norland trainings and Montessori certificates, they never seemed to last very long. Cress was a demanding taskmaster, and in seven years they'd had eleven nannies. One was sacked for taking the children to McDonalds; another for letting Jago whiz around the block on his bicycle without a helmet; another for buying Lucy the acrylic, and not the wool, school jumper.

After that one, Mark had determinedly made a stand about not sacking the latest nanny on some flim-flam excuse. He didn't want a constant stream of strangers filing through their home and populating their children's lives, he'd said. If a nanny was to be sacked, it had to be for a properly sackable offence, and not from a fit of pique.

And so far, Mark had his fingers crossed that things appeared to be going well with Greta. She'd lasted nine months already, which was far longer than most, and she seemed very settled. If Cress was sniping, it was running straight off Greta's back – one of the advantages of a language barrier – and the children adored her. He just hoped not too much. Privately, Mark had observed that the sackings usually came when the children bonded with the new nanny and called for her over their mother.

So when Greta had asked, at the last minute, for the Wednesday off, to see her boyfriend who was coming over from Sweden, Mark had been delighted. He knew Cress was frantic with Harry Hunter's big welcome party in a few days' time, but this was a plum opportunity for them all to spend some quality time together. At Mark's prompt, Cress was taking them up to the Science Museum and then to Kensington Gardens for a picnic, and he hoped he might be able to get away from the office early and join them as a surprise.

He patted his suit jacket, feeling for his BlackBerry, before remembering it was in the bedroom. He bounded up the stairs two at a time, eager to make the 7.48 a.m. He had a big meeting with the head of Equities at nine, and he had to do some emails on the train.

He was two strides across the landing when the bathroom door opened in front of him and, from a mist of hot steam, Greta's tanned and lissom legs emerged. In spite of his rush to get to work, his eyes dragged his feet to a stop and travelled lingeringly up from her ankles, past her taut knees, stopping at the pale blue sea-island cotton shirt that fluttered at the tops of her smooth thighs. The shirt swamped Greta's frame. Only two buttons had been done up, and as she jumped back in surprise, the shirt billowed open to flash a pair of daisy-print knickers.

Mark swallowed but couldn't wipe the surprise from his face.

'That's my shirt,' he managed finally. Cress had bought it for him for Christmas a few years ago. It had been one of his favourites.

Greta blushed a becoming pink and nodded, staring at the floor. 'I'm sorry,' she whispered.

He stared at her, incredulous.

'Why are you wearing my shirt?' he whispered, hurriedly, casting a glance down the stairs. If Cress came up and found Greta standing in his shirt, there'd be blood.

Greta shrugged, flashing her pants again. Mark's eyes darted down, before he could catch himself.

'Mrs Pelling, she threw it in the bin,' she whispered, looking at him beseechingly. 'She says you not want it any more. She says the collar all frayed. Look,' she said, going to reach up to show him.

'No! No! It's fine, Greta, I believe you,' he whispered again, trying to minimize her movements. She was wearing his shirt, but only just. The sweep of her neck down to her shoulders was exposed, and her skin looked so silky he half thought it might just slip off her altogether. 'But I don't understand – why did you take it *out* of the bin? Why are you wearing it?'

Greta blushed harder but she kept his gaze. 'I don't know,' she said, with a look that said she did. She shrugged again, the shirt shifting.

Mark looked away quickly. He wished she'd stop doing that.

'I just always liked it,' she continued, feeling braver. 'It always looked so nice on you. It matched your eyes.'

Mark looked back at her and was astonished to find her staring at him, a small fire in her eyes. Holy crap – was she giving him the come-on? No! What would she see in him? At thirty-nine, he was nearly twenty years older than her. And anyway, he loved his wife. After years of playing second fiddle to Cress's career, he had her back again. Things were the best they'd been in years. He'd be a fool to risk it all for . . . for . . . for a stunning . . . He'd be a fool. Besides, it was such a bloody cliché, fancying the nanny. He had more about him than that.

He coughed, nervous his voice was preparing to flee, along with his principles. 'Well, I don't think it's, uh, appropriate, Greta, for you to, uh, wear my garments.' Garments? He'd never used that word in his life! 'If Cress put it in the bin, I think it had better go back in the bin. And stay there.'

Greta bit her lip and looked at the floor. 'Of course, Mr Pelling. I am sorry.'

Mark nodded. 'Right. Well, I'd better go,' he said brusquely, turning and striding back down the stairs more casually than he felt. It wasn't until he got to the office forty minutes later that he remembered his BlackBerry was still in the bedroom. Nor did he remember a word of what was said in the meeting. Nor did he remember to surprise Cress and the children in the park. All he could remember was Greta standing in front of him, in his own, favourite, shirt.

Chapter Five

Tor bustled about the kitchen, wiping ketchup off the walls and nearly breaking her neck slipping on a rogue grape underfoot, as she tried to restore it to its usual gleaming perfection before Hugh came downstairs. He'd come home early tonight – for once – and she peered into the fridge, wondering what to cook. Not expecting him home, she'd had some of the children's pasta, but that was several hours ago now, and it wasn't really enough to qualify as a meal. She settled on fillet steaks, mushrooms and a salad, and having put the oil on a high heat, began chopping spring onions and tomatoes. The oil began to smoke and spit, and she was swearing under her breath when Hugh sauntered in.

'It's your own fault for standing within spitting distance,' he smiled, taking her reddened wrist and gently sucking on it. He'd changed into his running kit – ancient faded blue jersey shorts which practically stood up on their own and a university rugby shirt. He dropped her wrist and walked over to the dresser for a water glass. 'I'm off for a run.'

She took the oil off the heat. She clearly wouldn't need that for another forty minutes then. 'So how was your day?' she asked, pouring herself a glass of white instead. She hadn't had a chance to speak to him alone yet. He'd come in and gone straight up to put the children to bed, but she'd seen instantly that there was a charge about him this evening. Something had happened.

'Bloody fantastic actually.' He turned to face her, beaming. 'We've been invited to tender for the new council offices contract – two-year job, thirteen million pounds!' He couldn't have grinned any harder.

'No!' Tor gasped and put down her drink. She squealed with delight and ran across the room, throwing her arms around his neck and covering his face in tiny kisses. So it had all paid off then. The lonely evenings spent on the sofa had been worth it.

She pulled back and looked at him. 'Why didn't you mention anything about this before? I didn't even know it was a possibility.'

'I didn't want to get your hopes up. You know what it's like. It can get depressing.' He squeezed her around the waist. 'I wanted to come home with some good news for a change.'

'It's nice enough that you're just home for a change,' Tor teased, then instantly regretted it.

Hugh had set up his architect's firm, Planed Spaces, with Peter Golding, a friend from McCarthy Willis, where they'd both done their apprenticeship. They'd been going now for six years and it had been a long, hard slog. The corporate and commercial contracts were elusive and they'd had to concentrate on a density of smaller-scale domestic projects. Sure, there was no shortage of redevelopment projects in Wandsworth – everyone puts their money in their property and their children – but it was a piecemeal existence. Even the most extravagant home was small change to a commercial project, and although on paper the Summershills were far from paupers, the day-to-day reality was they often lived hand-to-mouth: their car was second-hand, with over 80,000 miles on the clock, most of Tor's new 'school run' clothes came from Topshop, and she'd started buying her branded products at Morrisons.

This council contract could change everything and herald the next chapter for Planed Spaces. She felt a surge of excitement. Perhaps this would be a new chapter for them too.

'So do you think . . .' She hesitated. 'How about you and I go away for a weekend somewhere?' She winked.

'Hey, hold your horses,' he chuckled. 'We haven't won the contract yet. We're merely invited to tender. We're up against three others. We're submitting plans end of this month, so we'll hear after that.' He kissed her on the forehead and wriggled out of her hug.

'Well then, let's celebrate the invitation,' she persevered. 'Don't go for a run. Stay here with me. I'll find something with bubbles for us to drink . . . a scrap of chiffon for me to wear . . .' She giggled.

Hugh began jogging on the spot. 'It's tempting,' he smiled. 'But I've got to start thinking about the brief. And you know I always come up with my best ideas when I run.'

Oh! She felt exasperated. Even on a good day like today, he seemed out of reach.

He threw his leg up on the kitchen table and pushed his head down on to his knee, doing some hamstring stretches.

'Right,' she said flatly, as she watched him. Tor cradled her glass, feeling the chill in her palm. 'How's the McIntyre job coming along?'

'Oh. Um, OK, I think.' His voice sounded strange, Tor thought, although he was upside down. He switched legs and his face was obscured. 'I'm not really involved with that job.'

'Really? Jinty Adams told me she sees your car parked outside all the time.'

Hugh stood up and frowned at her, as he began jogging on the spot again.

'She lives opposite,' she explained.

'Right. Well, anyway.' He turned to go, eager to drop the conversation.

'It's funny. I hadn't realized she was that Julia who monopolized you at Kate and Monty's the other week.' She raised an eyebrow.

'She – she did not monopolize me,' Hugh blustered. 'I spoke to plenty of people that evening. Anyway, I was networking. What does it matter?'

'Oh, it doesn't. I just would have thought you'd have introduced me to one of your clients, that's all.'

'I just told you. I'm not really involved on that job.'

'So why's your car parked outside the whole time then?'

'It's a company car, Tor. Anyone in the team can use it. Look, what's going on?' His eyes narrowed and he shifted his weight. 'I hope you're not trying to suggest anything – it's beneath you.'

'Well, so long as she's not beneath you,' Tor shot back.

Hugh froze.

'I can't believe you just said that! . . . For God's sake, Tor. What's wrong with you? Do you really think I'd . . .' His voice trailed away.

Tor stared at him, trying to find the truth. She knew that Julia was a threat. There had been an easiness between them at the dinner party, an intimacy, which didn't seem appropriate for a business relationship. And she hadn't been able to shake the feeling that the flames of Hugh's passion that night had been fanned by his dinner companion's magnificent décolletage, and not by Tor's admirably you'd-never-guess-she-had-three-children flat tummy.

But she couldn't deny that Hugh looked sick. His pallor was grey and he sagged forward, like she'd shot him with an anaesthetic dart. He turned away from her and leant on the worktop.

Tor relented. 'Oh God, I'm sorry, darling. I didn't mean anything by it, really I didn't. I don't know why on earth I said it. Just forget it. I let paranoia get the better of me. I'm an idiot.'

She came up behind him and wrapped her arms around his waist, resting her cheek against his back.

'Come,' she said softly, trying to turn him round to face her. 'Please don't go for that run. You can go in the morning. Stay with me.'

Hugh shrugged her off.

'Do you really think I feel like having a cosy night in with you after you accuse me of fucking another woman?'

And before she could reply, he'd stalked down the hall and slammed the front door. Tor winced and stared after him, chewing her lip.

Carrying the bottle of wine into the sitting room, she steadily emptied it, watching the telly without seeing anything, before finally going up to bed wondering where he'd gone (he never ran with money in his pockets) and when he'd be back.

He eventually returned after 1 a.m., by which time the oil was as cold as the salad, and the steak had long been returned to the fridge. Tor hadn't bothered to eat hers. That pasta could count as supper after all.

Chapter Six

The next morning, feeling hungover to hell, she left Hugh sleeping, and got up with the children. While their bottles of milk warmed, she went for a wee, took off her watch and rings and stepped on to the scales. She just couldn't understand the people who weighed themselves in the chemist's, wearing jeans, coats and shoes. Most of the time she had to resist the urge to trim her nails first too.

She exhaled and looked down. She'd lost two pounds! She felt elated. She tried to give a punch of glee, but her hangover intruded.

Cress's party for Harry Hunter was being held tonight. It was guaranteed to be the social highlight of her year – everyone they knew was married now, so there were no weddings to go to any more – and because no one in Nappy Valley ever seemed to get divorced (clearly all the baby-making kept them blissfully happy), there weren't even any second marriages to look forward to. The fortieths were still a good few years away, so it was all just christenings and children's birthday parties now and they weren't any fun because you couldn't get tipsy and flirt with the dads.

Millie and Oscar began bellowing for their milk and Tor moved back to the kitchen. As she handed it over to her sucky calves, the phone rang and she ran into the study to pick it up before it woke Hugh – penance of sorts, she figured.

It was Cress.

'Cress, only you could ring at seven thirty a.m.'

'Well, let's face it, hon, I knew you'd be up.'

'All ready for tonight?'

'Fuck no. The caterers are threatening to bail out because they've double-booked with a Saudi wedding and say we didn't confirm in time. Mark missed his flight from New York so he's still over there, Orlando's got chickenpox, and I still don't know what to wear.' She drew breath.

Tor laughed. She knew what was coming.

'Anything I can do to help?'

'Well, since you ask – can I come over and raid your wardrobe? I've been too busy dealing with Harry's contracts to go shopping,' she chortled. 'And you've always got such gorgeous stuff and I never see you in half of it. I'd be doing you a service actually.'

She was over within the hour. Tor had jumped into the shower and climbed into her favourite pair of battered Sevens, which were as soft as her winceyette pyjamas.

'You look gopping,' Cress said, glancing over at Tor – who was pale and black-eyed from last night's bottle of wine – as she rifled through her confection of rainbow-coloured chiffons and slinky slipper satins. Tor had put on a DVD of *Angelina Ballerina* for the children and collapsed on to the bed. (Hugh had got up and gone for the run he didn't go on last night – which begged the question, what exactly did he do then?)

'God, Cress, I'm having a shocker. I just cannot handle my drink any more.' Or my marriage, she wanted to add, but didn't.

'Hmm,' Cress said, eyeing Tor closely. 'We may have to slip you in through a side door.'

Tor snorted in derision.

Cress pulled out a sumptuous Dolce & Gabbana satin shift sprinkled with deep red poppies. 'Ooh, très kitsch.'

'That one's fabulous. You've got to have no hips at all, but, see the bra inside? Makes your boobs looks wonderful.'

'Hon, nothing could make my boobs look wonderful. Mark says I have tribeswoman tits.'

Tor burst out laughing. 'I'm sorry, what the hell are tribeswoman tits?'

'Oh you know – empty, longer than elephant ears.'

Tor tried to stop laughing. 'Cress, you cannot say that.'

But Cress continued: 'You want to know what's so awful? He won't let me have an itty bitty bit of Botox for my brow cleavage' – she pointed to a microscopic wrinkle between her brows – 'but when I jokingly said I needed a boob lift, he said "OK!"' She stood there, hands on hips, in mock outrage.

'. . . So I can't have a small painless injection which will make me happier every time I look in the mirror, but I can undergo major cosmetic surgery just to return his happy sacks to him,' Cress grumbled. Though she whined and whinged and made Mark out to be just awful, the reality was the Pellings enjoyed a blissful marriage. Tor was sure Cress made up the stories just to make everyone feel better. It was accident, rather than design, that they had four children. They just couldn't keep their hands off each other – tribeswoman tits or not.

'What are you wearing?'

Tor sighed. Even the prospect of socializing with Harry Hunter hadn't galvanized her into shopping action. Try as she might, Jinty's words remained resolutely rattling around in her head. 'No idea.'

Cress spun round, her eyes narrowed. 'Not like you. Whassup?'

Tor shrugged lightly. 'Nothing. Just been ... busy, you know.'

'Hmm.' Cress turned back to the wardrobe, unconvinced. 'What about that cream dress you wore to Kate's the other week? She said you looked bloody sensational. Said all the men were dribbling over you. And one in particular.' Cress cocked an eyebrow. 'James White?'

Tor looked up in shock. 'He was not! You know how polite he is. Kate's just being a minx. I assume they're still going tonight, by the way?'

'Yup. I get the feeling she could really do with letting her hair down, actually. She's just finished that case, so she's barely seen daylight for weeks.' Cress paused. 'And you know the latest round of IVF didn't take?'

Tor shook her head. 'Oh no. That's their second, isn't it? How many more are they allowed?'

'Just one I think, next month. But who can tell? That might be it for a while.' She lowered her voice to a ridiculous stage whisper that the children could have heard from the play-room, had they wanted to. 'Just between us, I think the strain's beginning to tell.'

Tor shook her head. 'Honestly, it's just so unfair. I mean, they're childhood sweethearts. Who else is going to blaze the trail for living happily ever after?'

'Tch, you are such an innocent, Victoria Summershill.'

Suddenly, Cress shrieked. 'Oooh, oooh, what's this?'

She pulled out a scarlet strapless dress with a mini bow at the waist and a pleated chiffon skirt.

'Oh, that's Chanel. A corset that'll kill you but you'll die looking gorgeous,' Tor said.

'Can I try it on? Pleeease?'

Tor shrugged. 'Sure.'

Cress whipped off her pale blue cashmere tracksuit, revealing a soft tan and hard muscles, and wriggled into the Chanel. 'Do me up.'

Tor gave a little tug of the zip and in an instant Cress's wiry athletic size eight shape was transformed into a modern-day Jessica Rabbit – all curves and dips and undulations. The two women stood staring into the mirror, agog. Tor was first to speak.

'God, who knew a dress could do that?' She shook her head in amazement. 'You look better than you did on your wedding day.'

'I do, don't I?' Cress admired herself in the mirror. 'Whatever you paid, worth every penny. I'd have paid double.'

'That's because you can,' Tor sighed. 'Well, that's you sorted. Now if someone could just arrange for me to be abducted by aliens and replaced by my better-looking self, we might just have a party on our hands.'

Cress smiled. 'Only if your replacement can dance better as well!'

Chapter Seven

When he came back from his run, Hugh took the children swimming and out for lunch, leaving Tor time to get her hair and nails done, and legs waxed. He was maintaining a hurt silence and spoke only to communicate his whereabouts with the kids. Her tentative caresses, attempts at apology and inquiring looks were shrugged away with disgust.

Tor sat in the kitchen, nursing a strong coffee and wondering what to do with herself. She wasn't used to having free time. It was only 1.30 p.m., and with all her appointments out of the way, the afternoon yawned ahead of her. She still couldn't think of a single thing in her wardrobe that she wanted to wear tonight. And she knew the only thing for it was to hurt the credit card. She grabbed her pea jacket, bag and keys, and jumped into the car.

Traffic was the usual boggy nightmare trying to get over Albert Bridge, but as soon as she swung off Embankment, on to Royal Hospital Road, it was surprisingly light and she was in Walton Street fifteen minutes after leaving home. She rarely came here – the boutiques were seriously high-end, proffering bespoke scents, Italian shoes, bedlinens with thread counts in the high hundreds, and vintners which sold Cristal in the quantities most offies shifted lightly oaked Chardonnay.

She sauntered along slowly, eyeing up the expensively

clad – mainly European – women who sauntered out of the formerly ubiquitous Daphne's, hell-bent on spending several hundred on lingerie before making it up to their men with a couple of hours of – what did the French call it? – *'cinq à sept'*? The men seemed happy with the drill. They were all lean, tanned and wearing calfskin moccasins with blazers that were impeccably cut in pastel linens.

Tor slipped on her oversized eBay-bought Chloë frames and looked back to the windows. She felt pale and plain again, and very much like a housewife on a day trip. She hoped no one would notice her. She walked more quickly, eager to get to the boutique.

It was at the end of the road on the right, just before the parade of Georgian townhouses. It looked forbiddingly smart, but she hadn't come all this way just to end up in Hobbs. She took a deep breath and pushed open the door.

She was instantly greeted by a manicured French voice. 'Good afternoon, madam.'

'Hello.' It was so quiet in here, so polished – even her breathing sounded clumsy. Tor smiled and scanned the shop, looking for a colour or print that would tempt her and take her away from the overt attentions of the assistant.

She spotted a rack of floaty dresses, and made her way over to it. Most of them were shorter than her nighties – the ones she never wore except to seduce Hugh in – and she flicked through them idly, but there were some hopefuls. She picked up a shell pink number with a pretty plunging back, a heavy cream satin babydoll with square neckline, and one which particularly caught her eye – a sensational viridian chiffon, overlaid on sea-green silk, with a scooped front and criss-cross back. The skirt was bias cut, clinging the hips and just kicking out at the knee.

She smiled in anticipation – she always knew what would work on her – and looking for the changing room, tiptoed over the marble floor. The changing room reminded her of the one at her wedding dress fittings, sumptuously wide to allow for all those hoop skirts, heavy curtains spilling dramatically into pools on the floor.

She quickly undressed and put on the pink. Yeuch, no. Too pale. She looked like a prawn. She got it off quickly before anyone saw her. She had a horror of being made to walk out into the shop, modelling the creation for all the other customers.

She took off the hanger the cream babydoll, which now looked alarmingly short, as the bell above the door jingled and a couple of Europeans walked in. They were speaking in French, and Tor noticed that the assistant's voice had lost its froideur. Tor heard the man speak – in beautiful English – to the assistant. Could he possibly have a cup of tea? Tor suppressed a laugh. He obviously did this kind of thing a lot. Hugh would have to be sedated to come into a shop like this, not least because of the price tags.

Tor checked out the price of the babydoll – £489 – Holy Cow! It had better make her look sixteen again. She slipped it over her head and began doing up the exquisite little buttons up the side. The fabric felt gorgeous and the mini puff sleeves sat at the perfect point, showing off the dip at the top of her arm, just below her shoulder. It made her feel delicate and waif-like, like a 1960s redux of a Jane Austen heroine. She wasn't sure she could still do quite so short – it stopped a good three inches above the knee – but perhaps with the right shoes? She absent-mindedly twisted her hair up, revealing her slender neck. Certainly one to consider.

She began unbuttoning again, just as some Morcheeba

started up and the tinkle of tea cups sounded on the glass table. She heard the brass rings of the curtain next to her being pulled along the rail. She couldn't wait to try on the viridian dress. Quickly she stepped into it and pulled it up, juggling her breasts into position in the little scoop and smoothing it over the hips. Looking down, it seemed a little tight. She frowned and checked the size. Size ten. She felt instantly depressed. So much for those lost pounds.

'Do you require any 'elp, madam?' The manicured voice enquired loudly – and frostily – again.

'Oh no, no, I think I'm OK, thank y—' But before she'd finished, the curtain was pulled back with a flourish and she found herself in the middle of the shop.

'Mmm. Would you like to try the next size up?'

Tor froze. It was like one of those nightmares when you dream you're naked in the middle of Bluewater. There she was, still in her black ankle socks, primrose yellow bra straps on show, standing in a dress that was one size too small. And sitting on the white leather Barcelona chair right in front of her, almost as though he was waiting for her, was James White.

He looked as shocked as she felt, though he recovered first. Probably because he's not the one dressed like the tooth fairy, Tor thought bitterly.

'Tor! How marvellous to see you,' he said, jumping up to greet her.

'James! What on earth are you doing here?'

She needn't have asked. The curtain next to her whisked back and there, an image of perfection in size eight viridian chiffon, stood Coralie Pedeaux.

'Darling, you remember Tor, don't you? Tor and her husband were at the Marfleets' dinner.'

'Mais bien sur. 'Ow are you?' Coralie nodded her head graciously, though Tor could see she didn't remember her.

'Very well, thank you. Gosh, it's just lovely to see you both again.' She wanted to get the hell out of this dress as quickly as possible. Coralie looked sensational – the colour made her eyes flash. She looks like a mermaid, Tor thought.

'So that's how it should look,' she tried to laugh, and indicated Coralie's outfit. 'I knew I was doing it wrong.'

'Nonsense,' James argued. 'You look super. It's a great colour for you.'

'Ah, well, you're very kind, James. And quite the most polite man I've ever met.' He smiled, Coralie didn't. 'Well, I'm just going to slip into something more flattering,' she said and she stepped back behind the curtain, pulling it tightly round and leaning against the mirror. She closed her eyes, smarting against the humiliation.

She pulled on her jeans and jacket, and quickly applied some blusher and lip balm. 'I'll take this one, please,' she smiled to the shop assistant, holding up the cream babydoll. Sod the cost, she just wanted to get out of there.

'Wearing it anywhere special?' James came and stood next to her. Oh, thank God, she'd grabbed the joint credit card. It really would have been too awful to have her card refused in front of him.

'Oh well, yes, actually. A friend's having a party tonight. Rather glamorous – by my domestic standards anyway. She's a publisher and . . . Oh you know her, of course. Cressida Pelling? Well, she's just signed Harry Hunter, so it's like an inaugural welcome tonight. I expect we'll all embarrass ourselves and gawp like teenagers. How about you – I mean for Coralie's dress? Must require something suitably fabulous. Cannes, perhaps?'

He chuckled. 'Um, well, not really. I mean – work's gone crazy and I've been working all hours, again – so I said I'd treat her.'

'Wow, lucky girl,' Tor smiled. 'Hugh will leave me when this bill comes through next month.' She paused. 'That's if he doesn't go before.'

Her hand flew to her mouth. 'Oh God, I can't believe I just said that! Why did I say that?' She made a twirl in the air with her finger and waggled her head like a crazy woman.

James was looking at her. He put a hand on her arm. 'Is everything OK, Tor?'

She looked up at him. It would be just so lovely to tell someone, to tell him. But the curtain was pulled back again and Coralie, dressed in red linen micro shorts with matching safari jacket, sauntered over, brandishing her dress with intent. 'I think this one, don't you?' she said, snaking her arm around James's hips and pushing her curves against him, like a pocket Venus.

'Of course, darling. It looked very nice.' He looked at Tor, who had fixed a benign smile on her face. The assistant handed her the bag.

'Well,' Tor shrugged. 'So lovely to see you both. I really must get back to the wastelands of SW11. My parole officer will be looking for me.' Coralie looked at her, perplexed. The irony was clearly lost in translation.

'Joke? I meant my husband.' Tor felt awkward and kept her gaze away from James. She was backing towards the door. 'See you both again soon, hopefully.'

She had no idea.

Chapter Eight

Two consecutive courses of Pilates and tennis lessons had paid off and her legs looked lithe, lean and tan. Worn with some flat thong sandals embellished with coral embroidery, she looked more ingénue than Baby Jane. Good going for thirty-two. She admired her reflection in the antique mirror propped against the wall. Goodness, the difference twelve hours and a £500 dress could make.

Hugh came in and sat down on the bed, towelling his hair. He'd just had his shower and smelled of limes, his signature scent. He was naked bar the towel around his waist and Tor admired his physique – buff and athletic, not too muscly or macho; the kind that came from twenty years of daily runs, rather than pumping iron. His hair was still conker brown, and if there was any grey, it was hiding.

Feeling her eyes on him, he looked up. She felt locked by his pale grey eyes as he took in her appearance. The shimmering highlights, bare legs, new dress. (Actually he didn't appear to notice that the dress was new – which was a good thing given the size of their overdraft.) He sat up and put his hands on his knees. He still hadn't talked to her. Well, not unless you counted Neanderthal grunts.

Tor took his appraisal as positive and, sensing an opportunity to make up, crossed the room and sat on his lap. The dress became indecently short when she sat down – she'd need to watch that.

'Darling, look,' she began. 'I'm sorry. Truly. I know I was a witch. I don't know what came over me. I know you'd never have an affair. You know I know that.'

She didn't know anything of the sort but they couldn't go on like this. He didn't say anything, just placed his hand on her thigh and looked her up and down. Then, slowly, he began kissing her exposed neck, inched a hand up and cupped her breasts. She hoped his hands weren't greasy – this fabric would show up everything – and to distract him, put her hand on his crotch. He was already hard. With one hand, he undid the towel so that it fell open on the bed and leaned back on his forearms, regarding her lasciviously.

She paused, taken aback by his cavalier attitude. His eyes were glazed with lust and cool anger. He was testing her, daring her to make it up to him. It was clear there would be nothing for her from this. He wanted cold, selfish, one-sided sex. This was his revenge.

She slid to her knees and wet her lips, trying to look more in the mood than she felt. Although she still wasn't sure he was a faithful husband, she instinctively knew that right now she had to play the good wife. She bent her head and took him in her mouth, teasing him as she flicked her tongue lightly. She heard him moan, felt his body stiffen, his fingers roughly entwined in her hair, and as he pushed her head further and further down, she had to resist the urge to gag as he came. She hated the taste, but she hid it with a smile, kissing him lightly on the lips.

'I love you, darling,' she said, stroking his cheek.

'I know,' Hugh said, but his eyes remained closed.

Tor stared at him for a few moments, then got up and

walked into the bathroom. She shut the door behind her and as quietly as she could, began to discreetly brush her teeth.

They walked in hand-in-hand and Tor felt like Cinderella with her prince. Cress came running over, a delight in scarlet. 'God, I hope they let you in the main entrance after all,' she beamed impishly. 'You look amazing.' She kissed them both and grabbed them each a bellini from a passing waitress, who didn't slow down.

'Hmm, watch the staff,' Cress murmured. 'They're pissed off they're not at the Arab wedding. Better tips, you know.'

Tor giggled and scanned the room. It was full of strangers and familiar famous faces, though she could see Kate and Monty standing in a far corner, propping up a knackered-looking Mark.

'He made it then,' Tor said, nodding at Mark.

'Yes, bless.' Cress smiled. 'Got in an hour ago. Literally showered and got dressed again. You boys are going to have to get him tanked up if he's going to last the evening.' Cress put a hand of mock pity on Hugh's shoulder.

'You can count on us, Cress,' he smiled. 'Come on, let's do our duty.' And he led Tor across the room. Tor lagged behind, letting her arm stretch out, liking being led like a little girl.

'Spotted him yet?' Tor interrupted. Kate looked quizzical. 'You know, the rarely-sighted, blond-tufted, tweed-bedecked bird magnet, known to migrate to the sunnier climes of Cap Ferrat in high season, preys on Botox blondes?'

Kate giggled. 'No, he's not here yet. Waiting to make his entrance. Probably standing in the alley around the corner, having a crafty smoke.'

Tor took in the bling hanging off Kate's ears. Kate always

treated herself to a piece of fine jewellery when she won a case, and she now had a bounty that warranted a security guard and a Swiss bank vault. The only piece she would never buy was a particular ring for her left hand – the token eternity ring that Monty would give her when she'd given birth to their first child.

'I see you won again.'

'Yes,' she sighed happily. 'Fell like a house of cards on the third day. Not quite a knockout, but near enough.' She fingered the diamond peardrops hanging from her earlobes. 'And these were winking at me from Graff. It would have been rude not to, really. Cheers.' The girls clinked glasses in celebration. Tor hoped nobody would notice her studs were cubic zirconia.

The little group fell into easy banter, enjoying the frivolity and merriment of such a grand occasion, eyeing up the other women, spotting fashion disasters, who'd had cosmetic surgery and trying to guess who was cheating on whom. The gardens looked beautiful, theatrically lit with low-level lanterns tucked away behind shrubs and flaming torches perched atop the walls. Purple and orange banners were swagged like Bedouin tents and vast daybeds were scattered all about, with glamorous couples lounging around like Talitha and Paul Getty in Morocco.

The views over London were spectacular. Tor zoned out of the conversation and looked around, identifying far-away neighbourhoods and people-watching the little streets. She had just located Westbourne Grove when she heard a commotion. She turned around to see Cress, standing with a microphone and with one arm linked through the arm of quite the most beautiful man Tor had ever seen.

She gasped. The international paparazzi had not done

Harry Hunter justice. They'd need to try harder. He was taller than she'd imagined and there was a twinkle in his eyes that was just downright filthy. He was wearing a midnight blue velvet smoking jacket – not her kind of thing at all, far too dandy – but, good God, he wore it well.

She went and stood with the group. Kate was speechless too. 'I think I'm wearing too many clothes,' Kate murmured.

Monty's mouth dropped open.

'I'd watch your wife with him, mate,' Monty said to Mark teasingly. 'If this is how they react from the pits, imagine what it'll be like working at close quarters.' Mark looked more awake than he had all evening, and regarded Harry Hunter with fresh eyes.

Cress had finished gushing about how pleased she was Harry had chosen to come to Sapphire Books, blah blah, and they were crossing the room together like newlyweds, graciously accepting thanks and best wishes. Tor felt like she was in a receiving line, and she suddenly fervently hoped Cress wouldn't come over with him. She didn't have a clue what to say to him. He was far too gorgeous. He should consort only with nymphs and demi-gods, surely.

She grabbed a couple of bellinis from another speeding waitress, and she and Kate took several swigs.

'Now look, Harry,' Cress began earnestly, indicating to the little group. 'You don't need to be nice to these people. They're not in the industry and can't do a thing for your career.' Everyone chuckled nervously. 'But they are my dear friends and so, I guess, I would so love it if you could just try to pretend to like them.' She crinkled her nose and he laughed.

It was clear from the razzle-dazzle in Harry's eyes as he took in the impeccable women that he had no intention of snubbing them. He adored adoring his adoring public.

'This is my best friend and interior designer, Victoria Summershill.' Tor nodded politely, discreetly sucking in her tummy and flashing a toned thigh. 'And her husband Hugh, here, is an architect.' Harry quickly sized up Hugh, who had come and put a protective arm around Tor's waist.

'Monty is a rather good stockbroker and I think he earns almost as much as you do, Harry.' Both men's eyebrows shot up. 'Ha ha, not really! But I'm sure you can do some bonding over Sunseekers or the new Vantage – or something. He's also jolly lucky to be married to Kate.'

Kate nodded soberly. Cress caught sight of her new diamonds twinkling like glitterballs and leaned in.

'God, I love those earrings, hon – they make Tor's look like cubic zirconia.' Tor privately died.

Cress leaned in to Harry and muttered in a mock whisper, 'Watch yourself. She's a libel lawyer and a complete ball-breaker. Those rocks are her trophies.' She paused. 'Rather like your girlfriends.'

Everyone laughed. Cress was always great at breaking the ice.

'And of course, last but not remotely least, this is Mark, my poor beleaguered husband, who has to put up with me.'

Everyone felt relieved the summations were over, not least Harry, who was terrible with names and couldn't remember a single one, although he had clocked which husband was guarding which wife.

'It's a pleasure to meet you all. You look terribly normal, though I suspect you can't be, seeing as you're such great friends with Cressida.'

'Ah, she broke us long ago,' Monty smiled.

Cress rolled her eyes, and caught sight of a paparazzo lurking in the corner.

'I just have to see to something. I'll catch up with you all in a bit,' she said, and she raced across the gardens like a Jack Russell out ratting.

'Well, she's done you proud tonight, Harry,' Kate said. 'This is a super party. The guest list reads like Debrett's.' She narrowed her green eyes as she scanned the room. 'Actually, I'm sure I've sued half the people here.'

Harry looked at her, intrigued. 'Who do you work for?'

'Moreton Parker. We're not the biggest, but we are the best.' Kate went straight into the spiel. She was proud of her career, and highly ambitious. She was up for partner this year. Bringing in a name like Harry Hunter could be her meal ticket. Heaven knows, there were flies on him. 'I've been keeping up with the tabloid coverage on you. They're really fond of you, aren't they?' She jutted out a shapely hip and held his gaze. 'Barely a day goes by without them finding some opportunity of putting your picture on the page. Do you ever feel they're lining you up as the new David Beckham?'

'All the time. Who does he use?'

Bingo. 'Us.' Kate smiled and reached into her tiny beaded clutch. 'Here's my card. Call me if you like.'

Harry slipped it inside his dinner jacket, without looking at it. 'I shall be sure to,' he said with a smile. Monty frowned again.

'So, uh, I bet everyone asks you this all the time, but have you started work on a new book yet?' Tor asked hesitantly, worried about sounding boring, or stupid, or both.

'Yes, Cressida's already cracking the whip. She's just signed me to a five-book deal and I have to deliver my first manuscript by Christmas. She keeps telling me how I mustn't keep my public waiting.' He rolled his eyes.

'And is it true your earlier books are going to be made into films too?' she asked earnestly, like a student newspaper reporter.

'Yes. Miramax bought the rights for *Scion* – which has already been made – as well as for *The Snow Leopard* and *The Ruby Route*. I'm writing the screenplays for both those films as well, so it's going to be a busy year.'

'However will you find the time to stay in the papers?' Kate asked archly.

Harry looked at her, his interest piqued by the amusement dancing in her eyes. 'It's a constant battle,' he smiled back devilishly.

They stared at each other for a moment, and Kate nodded in recognition, already imagining telling the partners she'd landed Harry Hunter.

There was a long silence. Tor took another gulp from her drink and wished the boys would be a bit more hospitable. Just because Harry was world-famous, internationally renowned and gorgeous didn't mean they had to be rude.

Hugh clearly couldn't be bothered to get involved in the conversation at all and engaged Mark in a lairy argument about who should captain the next Lions tour. Monty was just weighing up which splinter group to go with – the husbands (very tempting), or Harry and the wives – when he spotted a familiar figure moving through the crowds towards them, and did a double-take.

'I say, fancy seeing you here.' He thrust forward a friendly handshake.

James White responded in kind. 'Hello, squire,' he smiled.

Harry started suddenly upon hearing his voice and spun round. Stiffening, he looked at James, who had put his hand back in his pocket and clearly had no intention of offering it.

'Lord White,' Harry said with a hint of sarcasm.

'Hallo Hunter,' James said levelly. 'How did you manage to crash this party? Slip a fiver at the door?'

Harry chuckled, but there was no smile in his eyes.

Tor looked on, shocked. What on earth was he doing here?

Kate dropped her cool demeanour and, shrieking with delight, kissed James on the cheeks. Cress dashed back over, having unceremoniously ejected the gatecrashers.

'How on earth do you two know each other?' Cress asked, trying to think how she could have missed James's name on the guest list.

'Ah, surely you can guess: *"Bright with names that men remember; loud with names that men forget"*,' James replied enigmatically, staring at her.

'Huh?' Cress replied, perplexed.

Harry sighed dramatically. 'Eton. We were in the same house. He's quoting Swinburne, trying to show you how clever he is.'

'Oh,' Cress said, embarrassed to have missed the literary marker – it was supposed to be her specialism, after all.

An awkward pause ensued, as both men failed to fill the gap with a merry anecdote or embellishment from their schooldays together.

'Right,' Kate said slowly, sensing the tension between the two men.

James looked away first, to greet Tor. He liked her hair worn up like that, and she looked a vision in the short creamy dress.

'Definitely the right choice,' he smiled, flicking his eyes down at her dress. She smiled shyly, and as he kissed her hello, his hands felt firm on her back. Tor saw Kate's eyebrows shoot up.

'We ran into each other on Walton Street this afternoon,' Tor explained quickly. 'I made the mistake of trying on the same dress as Coralie. Big mistake, huge,' she said smiling, paraphrasing the *Pretty Woman* scene. 'Where is she, by the way?'

'Oh, over there somewhere,' James said. 'Ran into some acquaintances on the way.' He looked at Harry. 'She'll be over in a moment, I expect.'

Tor craned her neck and could just make out Coralie's petite form. She was wearing the viridian dress and looked every inch the magnificent peacock. Almost as though her ears were burning, Coralie glanced up and, seeing James standing with the guest of honour, left her companion mid-sentence and wiggled over.

Tor didn't like her, though she couldn't really specify why. There was a coldness about her. She wondered why – besides her obvious beauty and stupendous figure – James was with her. She didn't seem his type. Not that Tor had the slightest clue what his type might be. But somehow she hadn't reckoned him as a trophy hunter.

'Aren't you going to introduce me, James?' Coralie simpered.

'Yes, of course, darling. Coralie, this is Harry Hunter, struggling author.' Everyone chuckled. 'Hunter, this is Coralie Pedeaux.'

Coralie proffered a delicate hand – as limp as a dying swan, Tor thought – and instead of a polite handshake, Harry kissed it. This time, Kate and Tor rolled their eyes at each other. Yet again, they'd been eclipsed by La Parisienne.

A speeding waitress zoomed past with a tray of mini fish

and chips, and Kate's eyes lit up. 'God, I'm starving,' she said. 'I haven't eaten all day.'

Tor looked at her friend's plum silk jersey Ungaro dress. You could tell. There wasn't a lump or – more to the point, a bump – to be seen. She looked more like a fashion editor than a lawyer in her outfit, accessorizing with some jumbo turquoise bangles pushed up on to her upper arms and turquoise-feathered Pocahontas-style Manolos.

'Quick, catch that waitress,' Kate said to Monty, grabbing his sleeve, and before you could stop them they were weaving through the crowds, trying to rugby-tackle her to a halt. Cress stomped off to the kitchens to complain about the serving staff's stroppy attitudes.

Tor and James, who had looked on in amusement, turned back to find Coralie and Harry engrossed in conversation about hiding places in Paris.

'I always stay at the Costes,' Harry was saying, with a slight slur.

'Mais non,' Coralie replied, placing a hand on his arm. 'It is not so discreet. It must be so terrible for you with ze press. Do you not have somebody to stay with out zere?'

'No,' he replied, a trace of little-boy-lost in his voice.

'Jesus,' James muttered under his breath.

Tor felt awkward, like an unwanted fourth point in a triangle.

'Would you like a drink? Let me get one for you,' she said hurriedly, noticing he didn't have one and thinking this would be an opportunity to escape.

'Better make it a stiff one,' he smiled wryly, embarrassed that Tor had observed his annoyance.

'I'll go to the bar,' she said, beginning to move away. 'The waitresses are shocking.'

'Don't think you're leaving me to watch their love-in,' he smiled, nodding towards Harry and Coralie. With charismatic self-assuredness, he grabbed her hand and she was deftly steered through the crowd for the second time that evening.

They found a couple of bar stools in the corner. It was a bit dark – just about the only place in the room not lit with a lantern or candle or tealight – but it was either that or stand, and Tor was feeling short in her flat sandals now. All the other women were in stacked heels and James was so tall she wouldn't hear a word he said.

He was wearing a pale blue shirt beneath a slim navy suit, and as he ordered at the bar, one hand in his trouser pocket, she saw his stomach was washboard-flat. She caught herself and quickly looked away.

He ordered them a martini each, not bothering to ask whether she liked it (she didn't, but that seemed irrelevant). They sat knee to knee. Tor fiddled with her dress, trying to pull it down, and didn't notice James surreptitiously glancing at her thighs. He cleared his throat.

'So where is your husband tonight? I never seem to see him with you.'

She tossed her hair casually. 'Hugh? Oh, he's over there.' Tor indicated her husband, lost in conversation with Mark and completely oblivious to her disappearance. 'We tend to be quite, erm, autonomous, at these kinds of things,' she smiled.

'Right. I thought maybe he was a figment of your imagination,' he said. 'You know, an imaginary friend? It's beyond me why he would be so consistently careless as to keep losing you.' His tone was jokey but his eyes were inquiring.

'He hasn't lost me,' Tor retorted. She resisted adding 'yet'.

She was keen to change the subject. 'By the way, why on earth didn't you say you were coming here when I saw you earlier?' she asked.

'Well, to be honest, I wasn't going to come. I wouldn't say Hunter and I are . . . close.'

'Oh,' Tor paused. 'But you know the party's in his honour, right?'

James laughed lightly. 'I know, it's ridiculous. I guess part of me wanted to see it with my own eyes. When I read in the papers that Cress had signed him, it seemed – unreal,' he added. 'Anyway, Coralie knew I was at school with him and when she overheard you mention it earlier, she said she wanted to go, so . . .' He held his arms up and shrugged. 'Anything for a quiet life, I guess.'

He smiled. 'Plus, it was a welcome opportunity to see you again. You look absolutely stunning. Have you ever been to Cannes?'

She giggled at their in-joke. He had a knack of making her feel as beautiful as a bird of paradise basking in a rainbow. That famous bedside manner wasn't just kept for the hospital bed. She could well imagine how it got his women into bed as well.

Feeling his eyes lift off her and alight on something else across the room, Tor followed his gaze. She saw Harry flirtatiously tracing the criss-cross straps of Coralie's dress. Coralie was standing with her back to him, laughing coquettishly over her shoulder. It looked like he was writing a message on her bare back with his finger – a game she remembered from childhood.

Tor looked back at James. His jaw had clenched and she briefly wondered whether they would brawl. Coralie was very definitely the kind of woman men fought over. He caught her looking at him, and gave a short, embarrassed smile.

He knocked back his martini and with an imperious flick of his finger, ordered another for them both. She quickly drained hers to keep up.

'I really shouldn't be surprised,' he said to her, nodding towards the errant couple.

'Oh,' Tor said, not sure whether he was referring to Harry or Coralie. 'How did you and Coralie meet? I'm guessing it wasn't through work.' She laughed, awkwardly, at his dating dilemma of meeting and treating hundreds of women, all of whom were pregnant by other men.

'No, quite.' He didn't seem to find that funny. He gave a small cough and finally looked back at her. 'Actually, it was at Bonhams. I was bidding for an oil and she was going for it as well. In the end it was just the two of us, raising our paddles in a frenzy; breaking all European records.'

'Gosh, really?'

'No, not really.' He smiled, eyes twinkling merrily again.

'Oh.' She felt abashed. She was always so gullible. 'Who won it?'

'I did, but not before she'd added another ten thousand to the price.'

'Wow.' It all sounded terribly glamorous to Tor, who couldn't imagine spending a limitless amount of money on a painting. She was just relieved not to have her card refused at the supermarket each week.

'As it was, I ended up giving it to her anyway. It seemed the best way to get her to have dinner with me.'

'Gosh,' Tor said again, simultaneously impressed and depressed that Coralie incited such extravagant passion. When she'd first met Hugh in a bar on the Fulham Road, she'd been flattered just because he'd ordered her gin and tonic with ice and lime (not lemon) and had specified Bombay Sapphire. 'So, is it serious then?'

James's eyes flitted back over to Coralie, who was now making little cat-like arches as Harry stroked her back. He paused, wondering whether she was purring too. 'No, I wouldn't say so,' he said finally. 'Put it this way, I haven't introduced her to my son.'

'I didn't know you had children.'

'Just the one, Max. He's nearly twelve now. Lives with his mother and stepfather on the east coast but I get to see him every two to three weeks. And I go up for the holidays.'

He shrugged. Tor looked at him closely. He seemed different tonight. For all his professional sang-froid and solicitous charm, she could sense a feral restlessness prowling within him. There was an edge she hadn't seen before.

The party was in full swing now. People were dancing, drinking direct from the champagne bottles, and all the restrained politeness of earlier had being replaced by a louche flirtatious mood. This was Harry Hunter's party after all. The man wasn't known for his reserve.

It was well after midnight and Tor tried to remember how much she'd had to drink.

She felt James pause, and then lean in to her. He dropped his head and didn't look at her. 'What did you mean earlier, in the shop, about Hugh leaving you? It's been bugging me all day.'

'All day?' she said playfully.

'All day.' He looked back at her intently. Her smile faded. Oh God, he was gorgeous. She swallowed hard.

'Last night, I accused Hugh of having an affair.' There, she'd said it. She waited for the sky to fall in.

Instead, James said: 'Do you really think he is?'

Tor looked at him for a long moment, as if she could find the answer in his eyes. 'I really don't know. I said afterwards I didn't but . . . I mean, it's hard to believe he'd be so reckless . . .' She paused, lost in thought. 'And he was so horrified, and so, so shocked when I said it. Furious, actually.'

'So why did you say it?'

'Well, he's been working such daft hours for the last few months, I've scarcely seen him.'

James shrugged. 'I know what that's like. It doesn't mean he's having an affair though.'

'No, but one of the mothers insinuated he was playing away, and it all just seemed to make sense. There's a feeling I can't shake. Call it female intuition.'

'Do you know who he's supposedly having the affair with?'

She nodded. 'Yes. She's very busty and divorced and rich. Every man's dream woman,' she laughed, trying to lighten the mood.

'Not this one's.'

'Oh?' She looked at him and was nearly beaten back by the heat in his eyes. 'Oh.' She swallowed hard.

'What if he is having the affair? Will you leave him? Forgive him?' She felt his leg press lightly against hers. 'Have one too?'

She tried to remember the question but she couldn't concentrate with him looking at her like that. It was too loaded. She was chicken. She was married.

She looked down at her lap, and fiddled with her fingers.

James didn't say anything. He leant forward and took her hands in his, squeezing them gently. She relaxed again. He was just being friend— Oh. He put her hands on her thighs and covered them with his. Discreetly, lightly, his fingers

73

began tracing the hem of her dress which, she realized with panic, had ridden up alarmingly high. He looked down and she knew he could see her silk knickers.

Instinctively she tried to tug the dress down but he increased the pressure on her hands, stopping her. He wanted to look. She bit her bottom lip.

She couldn't believe this was happening in a room filled with two hundred people. And yet she thanked God that every last one of them was there. They were swallowed up in the crowd. Anonymous and lost.

He leant into her and lightly, so lightly, brushed her cheek with his lips. She inclined her head towards him. He blew gently in her ear, kissed her temple. She dropped her head on his shoulder, not wanting him to stop.

'God, I've wanted you since that dinner,' he murmured. 'Did you know you kept flashing your breasts in that dress? You were driving me crazy.' He bit her gently on the earlobe. Tor, weak with longing, tried to remember how to breathe. 'And today – how did you manage to look so damned provocative in that dress and those sweet little socks?'

Tor groaned with embarrassment but he laughed gently.

'You're going to hate me for saying it –' he held her hands more firmly – 'but I really hope he is having that affair.'

Tor jerked back, tried to move away, but he was too strong.

'No.' He was insistent. 'I won't apologize for it. I want you, Tor. And I don't see that I'm going to get you any other way . . .'

She absorbed his words, battling lust with logic.

'What are we doing?' Tor whispered.

'The inevitable,' James replied.

Slowly, she raised her head to look at him, and as she did so, he kissed her full and hard on the lips. For a moment, she kissed him back and wanted with every fibre in her body for this to be a scene from her own life. But it wasn't. He was somebody else's, and so was she.

She pulled back and scanned the room to check they were still lost.

They weren't.

Hugh had found her.

Chapter Nine

Am I the kind of woman they'll fight over? she thought, as Hugh stared at her through the crowd. She couldn't bear to see the shock in his face, the hurt in his eyes. What had she done? He was the father of her children, for God's sake. How had they come to this?

She willed him to come over and claim her as his and no one else's. But without throwing so much as a punch or an insult, Hugh turned on his heel and left the room.

She watched his retreating back in disbelief. He hadn't even tried. He just couldn't be bothered.

'Hugh!'

She jumped up to chase after him but James grabbed her arm.

'Tor, don't!' he said. 'Let him calm down. He needs some space.'

'Get your hands off me!' she cried angrily, wrenching her arm away. 'What do you know about what he needs? What do you know about us at all? You don't know anything about us. You're no one. You're just . . . just . . . just the delivery man.'

James laughed reflexively, as though he'd been winded. He was used to nothing less than reverential deference about his professional skills. He delivered babies – royal babies at that – not airmail.

Tor just glowered at him, her previous passion transposed to fury in a flash. 'Keep away from me,' she hissed.

She ran out of the room, frantic to catch Hugh. There was a lift waiting and she pressed the Ground Floor button dementedly, but it didn't make the doors close any quicker.

By the time she got downstairs, she was in tears and her mascara had begun running down her cheeks. She ran towards the doors, calling for him.

'Hugh! Wait! Hugh, please! Let me explain!'

Through the glass doors she could see him striding down Kensington High Street, but as she stepped on to the pavement, she was instantly blinded by a thousand bulbs flashing as the assembled paparazzi clamoured to take her picture in the hope she might be Harry's latest totty.

'This way, love!'

'Oi! Over 'ere!'

'Give us a smile, darlin'!'

She shielded her eyes from the white glare, but by the time it subsided and she could see again, he had gone.

''Ere, you all right, love? Whassamadder?'

'Husband left without you?'

Tor sobbed. They were right. Her husband had left her.

She looked wretched, standing in the chill night air in a too-short dress, her face streaked with black tracks as though children had drawn on her. Her shoulders were heaving. She didn't know what to do. Someone passed her a slightly used tissue; another pap hailed a passing black cab.

'Where d'you need to go, love?'

She looked blankly at him.

'Where's home, love? Where d'you want the cab to take you?'

'Battersea,' she said in a small voice. 'Between the Commons.'

She clambered in and the taxi chuntered away, leaving the photographers looking after her and shaking their heads. 'These girls,' one tutted. 'Can't handle their drink.'

Then one of them noticed Harry Hunter sneaking out through the side door and climbing into his waiting Merc with a stunning girl in a peacock dress. And just like that, she was forgotten.

When she got home, Hugh had already paid the babysitter and was upstairs packing.

'You know the funny thing,' he said coolly, as he smoothed his favourite blue end-on-end shirt and tucked it into the holdall. 'I actually thought we could carry on. I thought I'd found the perfect solution.' He opened the drawer on his bedside table and picked out a clutch of condoms. He threw them in, along with his box of cufflinks.

Condoms? Tor couldn't speak. She just watched him dumbly.

'I thought we could still manage to be a real family, even though we didn't have a real marriage any more.'

He saw the confusion crossing her face.

'I mean, it's been obvious for ages sex isn't important to you. Well, not any more anyway.' He paused, trying to remember where he'd put his black belt. 'But I'd assumed it was a hormonal thing.' He laughed bitterly. 'How conceited was that? To think that it wasn't anything to do with me.'

'Hugh, I —'

'But tonight, I saw it's everything to do with me.'

She shook her head. 'No, you're wrong.'

'No! I'm not,' he shouted. Tor was stunned. She couldn't recall him ever having shouted at her. 'I saw you; I saw the look on your face,' he said coldly. 'You have never looked at me like that. You have *never* looked like you wanted to fuck me in the middle of a bar.'

He stood still for a moment, trying to regain control, then carried on packing, putting his black brogues into their dust bags.

'The fact is you don't want me any more.'

'That's not true!' she implored. 'How can you say that? You're everything to me.'

He walked over to her and put his hands heavily on her shoulders. She slumped a little beneath their weight. 'You. Don't. Want. Me,' he reiterated slowly, as though she was stupid. 'And I don't want you either.'

He may as well have slapped her. Her breath snagged. Tears stung her eyes again. His voice was so resolute, so final. He wasn't even trying to work this out.

'Let's be brutally honest, shall we? Don't you think the time has come to speak plainly for once? Because let's face it, the sex was never that good. I mean, take tonight. That was duty for you. I bet you brushed your teeth afterwards.'

Tor felt her face burn. He turned away from her and walked towards the bay window, unrolling his shirt sleeves. He looked out absently. 'You have been busy tonight. Two men in one night,' he tutted. 'What would the neighbours say about that, hmmm?'

'Hugh!'

He ignored her.

'The Yummy Mummy who wrecked her own perfect family. And with Lord White of all people. That won't do his reputation any good. He's supposed to bring families together. Not rip them apart.' Despite his utter determination not to show his hurt, Hugh couldn't keep it out of his voice.

Tor heard it and looked up at him. It gave her hope. She moved over to him and held on to his arm.

'He hasn't ripped anything, Hugh. It was just a momentary thing. He's got nothing to do with this.'

'On the contrary,' he spat. 'I think he has everything to do with it. He's our wake-up call.'

'No. No.' She shook her head. 'We were just drunk. I was feeling . . .'

'Horny?'

'No! Insecure. And it got out of hand, that's all. It was a single moment. He's nothing to do with us.'

'You're right, you're right.' He looked down at her, witheringly. 'Because there is no Us. When are you going to get it, Tor? There hasn't been an Us for a very long time.' He went to the drawers and grabbed some socks. 'There wasn't an Us long before Julia came on the scene.'

Tor looked at him. Julia?

'So I was right then,' she whispered.

'Of course,' he spat. 'Aren't you always?'

Hugh watched Tor process the revelation. He could see her incredulity – not at the confession that he'd had an affair, but (as he'd always known) that it was Julia who was her rival.

'Despite what you may think, you have a lot to thank her for,' Hugh said, as he punched some more room into the bag. 'She's made the last few months with you tolerable. If it weren't for her, I'd have gone months ago.'

'When?' she whispered.

'What's that?' he mocked, cupping a hand to his ear. 'Speak up.'

'When did it begin?'

'Eight months ago. I was playing tennis with Guy Latham

at the Harbour Club and met her at the bar afterwards. She's quite a persistent woman.'

'What do you mean?' Tor hated herself for asking. She knew he was desperate to tell her, to unburden himself of the secret, to torture her with the details.

'She was hell-bent on getting me, that's for sure. It was quite flattering really, but still I threw her off for a while. I was trying to do the Right Thing. You do remember what that is, right?' He paused. 'But then she threw that party for me.'

Tor frowned in confusion. 'Party? What party?'

'Didn't I tell you? I'm sure I told you about it.' His tone had become conversational, as though they were chatting about what to buy the children for Christmas. 'She said she wanted to introduce me to some influential contacts. And it worked.' He nodded, eyebrows raised. 'There were some council bods there – that's how I got invited to tender for the contract.' He crossed the room and pulled out a stack of various grey and navy cashmere jumpers.

'She'd got some caterers in, some musicians, really went to town on it.' He paused for a moment, as though trying to remember something. 'She was wearing a blue silky dress, like a petticoat. She wasn't wearing a bra. God knows, she needed to.' He chuckled.

Tor hugged her arms around her meagre B-cup chest. She felt freezing cold.

'But then when everybody left, and I was getting my coat, she came out of the bedroom wearing nothing. Well, nothing but a smile, actually.' He nodded at the memory, and closed his eyes, relishing it. 'And there and then, in the hallway, she unzipped my flies and went down on me.' He stopped and looked straight at her. 'And I came harder than I've ever come in my life.'

Tor felt her heart begin to crack and sank to the bed. Faced with the confession she'd been both dreading and longing for, it had never occurred to her that he'd describe it to her in all its pornographic passion. A simple admission was all she'd sought. Because then it would have just been about vague, anonymous sex. And she could compete with that – no matter what he'd just said.

But standing before him as he described the seduction – relishing the details, savouring the memory – the graphic imagery of his affair was more vivid to her than her own heartbeat, and she knew with utmost clarity there was no way back for them now. He didn't want to find a way back. He wanted to find a way with Julia, and her kiss with James had given him a 'get out of jail free' card.

'Where are you going?' she asked.

'To Julia's. She's already expecting me.'

'I'm sure.'

Hugh looked at his wife. Her tone was flat, and he could see that his words had wrecked her. His stomach tightened in despair. What the hell was he doing? He sat next to her on the edge of the bed, his head in his hands, looking like Atlas collapsing beneath the weight of the world.

He wanted to relent. Tonight had been such a bloody shock. It had never occurred to him Tor would cheat. When she'd confronted him last night, he'd panicked. He'd been awake all night trying to think of stories that would cover his tracks. And if he did have to confess, he'd assumed he'd break it off with Julia and beg forgiveness. Never in a million years had he considered it would be her indiscretion, and not his, that was splitting their family.

In his heart, he knew she was telling the truth; that whatever had happened between her and that doctor was just drunkenness. But he felt backed into a corner, tortured, by the image of her with James, their heads together, thighs apart. He'd felt like a voyeur on his own wife. He shook his head angrily and grabbed his bag.

She jumped up, shaken out of her inertia by the reality of his leaving.

'No! Hugh, wait, please! What – what shall I tell the children?' Tor asked, panic-stricken, desperate for more time.

He paused, so defiant even his tears didn't dare fall.

'This has nothing to do with them. It changes nothing. I'm still their father. No matter what.' He looked around the room, at the wedding photos whose silver frames had tarnished to copper, the lilies three days dead in the vase, balls of socks piling up in the corner, the bed still rumpled from their earlier lovemaking. Nothing had changed and everything had changed. His wife, such a vision at eight o'clock, was wretched on the floor. His children were sleeping soundly in their beds.

He took a deep breath and strode down the stairs, picking his keys up from the radiator cabinet. And then, quietly, regretfully, he closed the door on them all.

The front door clicked shut and Tor wanted to scream, but – inhibited even in raw grief – she didn't dare, in case she woke the children or titillated the neighbours. Instead, she sat on the floor at the end of the bed, hugging her knees. She held the pose. She couldn't feel her lungs breathing or her eyes blinking but she supposed they must be. The yellow numbers on the digital clock racked up, and it was nine minutes before the tears began to spill.

She knew she should get into the bed and try to sleep. But if she slept, it meant she'd wake up in another day, a new day, the first day of the rest of her life without Hugh. And she just couldn't do that. She needed to stop time, halt its progress. She could do that if she didn't go to sleep.

She wondered if he was at Julia's yet. He must be. It would only take five minutes around the common at this time of night. She imagined Julia – so happy! – naked in the bed, waiting for him. Candles lit, petals strewn, an open bottle and open legs. They were probably at it right now. Oh God. She ran to the bathroom and heaved.

He had been gone an hour when there was a knock at the door.

Tor uncurled herself from her foetal position at the base of the loo, and flew down the stairs so fast she swore her feet didn't touch the ground. He'd changed his mind. Oh God, please let him have changed his mind. They could make it work. She'd try harder. She'd be a good mother *and* a good wife. They could have make-up sex right now and she'd make him forget all about Julia McIntyre. She'd . . .

She opened the door. Two police officers were standing there, holding their hats.

'Mrs Summershill?'

Tor didn't reply.

'May we come in please?'

Chapter Ten

Even without sleep, the next day came anyway. And the day after. And the day after that. Cress moved in, despite Tor's protests that her own family needed her. 'Would that it were true,' Cress smiled bleakly. 'As far as they're concerned, I'm just on another trip.'

Tor's own parents had died a decade earlier – within months of each other – so it fell to her friends to try to pick up the pieces. Everyone pitched in. Tor and the children were saved from Cress's cooking by Kate, who came over with steaming food parcels twice a day which, although Tor could see and smell were utterly scrumptious, she was wholly unable to eat. But it did mean she didn't have to think about what to feed the children, which was a small mercy. Tor couldn't even begin to think about navigating the necessities of daily life – sleeping, eating, walking, talking.

So Kate cooked, and came over every morning to help Cress. The two women drew up a rota which saw one of them take on the washing, ironing and shopping chores, while the other dressed the children and took them to nursery or the playground. Cress went home only in the evenings to feed and bathe her own children, before coming back to sit with Kate and monitor Tor, who just rocked in silence.

Tor's shock was deep and palpable. The doctor had had

to sedate her after the police had left, and now she could only sleep when she'd had enough dopamine to knock out a horse. She was as limp as a rag doll, as pale as a moon-beam. Her usually lustrous hair hung straggly and even her lips had lost their colour. God only knew how much weight she'd lost.

She wouldn't take visitors or phone calls, and she let the sympathy cards pile up unopened. But somehow she managed to pass herself off as coping when the children were around. Then and only then, she drew upon an inner strength that no one could locate in their absence.

Telling the children they'd lost their father had been the most terrible moment of her life. Worse than hearing that Hugh had died. Worse even than having to formally iden-tify his body. His grave injuries had been internal, so the police had reassured her there wasn't anything to frighten her when she saw him. But it was precisely the ordinariness of the situation that had made it so diabolical. His body was broken, yet it had looked so athletic and strong, the sheet tracing the contours of his muscles. And although pale, he had still looked so handsome and virile. She just couldn't understand how it could possibly be that he was lying in front of her, stretched out on a gurney.

She'd stroked his hair, and flinched when her fingertips brushed his forehead, feeling his marble coolness on her skin. His features were benign but he hadn't looked like he was sleeping. He'd seemed somehow waxy, and there was definitely a lack, now. Whatever it was that had made him Hugh – his dirty laugh, the twinkle in his eye, his lacka-daisical slouch – his essence, she supposed, wasn't there any more. He'd looked like a twin of himself, identical but for a fractional difference.

Oscar, of course, was far too little to understand anything of what had happened, but to Tor's surprise, the girls hadn't cried immediately. Instead they peppered her with questions about where angels played, and how they didn't fall out of the clouds, and why couldn't they play with someone else's daddy? Tor had kept her own tears in check, searching her children's faces as if probing their souls. But their anguish only found a voice that evening, when Daddy didn't come to give them a bedtime kiss. Picking them up in her arms, she had tucked them into her bed and curled around them both like a cat, stroking their hair and kissing their temples until exhaustion rescued them from despair and they fell fast asleep on wet pillows.

But sleep barely came at all for Tor, and only when it was chemically induced. Every time she closed her eyes, she heard Hugh's parting taunts, remembered the hurt in his eyes, the scorn of his words. He had left hating her. And now that he was never coming back, the burden – guilt, anger, recriminations – was hers alone. As indeed it should be.

It was her fault he was dead. It was her actions that had driven him back out on to the street that night. If it hadn't been for her jealous infidelity, he wouldn't have packed his bags; if it hadn't been for her pathetic and persistent inadequacies as a wife, he wouldn't have had anyone to go out *to* that night. He wouldn't have been in the car, exhausted, angry, drunk and driving. He would have slept in the spare room, woken with a hangover and spent a lazy Sunday reading the papers and playing with the children. Instead he was lying cold under a sheet, and she was lying alone in their bed.

She left the funeral arrangements to Hugh's parents. They were grateful for the chance to pay homage to their son, and simply assumed she was too stricken with grief to manage it herself. But the truth was she felt she had no right to do otherwise. After all, Hugh had left her, rejected her as his wife. He wouldn't have wanted her eulogy. He would have taken her words of love and loyalty as lies, as he had that last night. Though she was the mother of his children and his wife of nine years, he had chosen Julia. He belonged to her now. To everyone else, Tor was Hugh's widow, his memory's keeper. But Tor alone knew she was a fraud.

Chapter Eleven

Kate spun round in her chair, lifting her heels off the ground and clearing four full spins before stopping squarely in front of the stone mullioned window. She was fairly expert at this now, like a ballerina ending her pirouette centre front to the audience. Though she looked like an excitable eight-year-old and it didn't do much for her ball-breaking reputation (or the chairs), it was her own particular way of disengaging and thinking through problems. Monty always joked that thank God her offices weren't open plan, or she'd never make partner.

She was beginning to wonder if she ever would anyway – spinning or not. Obviously things had been different recently – taking leave and working from home to help out with Tor and the children. But everyone knew the hours she'd put in before then, regularly pulling fourteen-hour days, working weekends, forgoing holidays and networking even at christenings. She was never off-duty. Her peptic ulcer testified to that.

She stood up and leant on the window-sill, swinging her hips from side to side and singing 'The Bare Necessities' to herself (from Marney Summershill's favourite film, which she insisted on watching daily at 'quiet time', and now Kate couldn't get the song out of her head). She watched the throngs milling about on Dean Street, the off-duty prosti-tutes covered up in jeans and denim jackets, drawing on Mayfair cigarettes and chatting in doorways; the office workers in cheap black suits heading to the corner pubs, the tourists making long-winded shortcuts from the glare of Oxford Street to the bright lights of Piccadilly Circus; and the on-trend media types diving into their private clubs for a line and a Jack Daniels.

Apart from the shock of an occasional punk's orange hair, it was a depressingly bland sea of black and grey that she looked down upon. She could be anywhere – Nice, Bruges, Milton Keynes – not London's famous Soho. But the first neon lights were switching on, casting a faint blue and red haze on to the pavements and sending an electric crackle through the air. In a few hours, these streets would be humming and teeming, with cabs' orange lights flitting like fireflies in the night.

Kate checked the large round clock that hung from the jeweller's wall just down the street. It was 6.45 p.m. She sighed. It had been a long, slow day. She watched a navy blue Maserati snake its way up the street. She was begin-ning to think cars should be her new rewards these days – there were only so many jewels a girl could own – and she liked the boomerang brake lights on the 3200GT model.

Her eyes narrowed with interest as a posse of Vespas careered up behind it, each one ejecting a passenger riding pillion, cameras at the ready. The flashbulbs started popping at the blacked-out windows before the door had even opened, but through the clamour and strobes, Kate glimpsed a composite of tumbly blond curls, chestnut sports jacket, and powerful thighs in olive moleskin jeans.

God. It couldn't be, could it?

It was. Harry Hunter flashed a devastating smile to the crowd of onlookers who had gathered so quickly she wondered whether he paid them as rent-a-crowd, before ducking into Agent Provocateur, next door to her building.

Kate couldn't help but laugh at the nerve of the man, doing his saucy shopping in full public view. The shop assistants pulled the black curtains across the windows, and the photographers dropped their cameras, getting on their mobiles, lighting up and standing around as aimlessly as the spectators, who were dithering about whether to wait or go.

The street felt eerily quiet compared to the uproar of a minute previously – everybody seemed to have lost focus. It was as though all the lights and sound had been turned off. This must be what they mean by 'star power', Kate thought.

She sat on the sill.

'Shit,' she thought, rubbing her face in her hands as she suddenly realized that he hadn't called after Cress's party. She'd been so concerned with looking after Tor, it had slipped her mind completely. Dammit!

Ordinarily, she would have chased him – she wasn't above planting an outrageous slur in the tabloids to channel her prey straight to her. Usually that, combined with a well-timed follow-up call and comforting lunch, was all it took. But more than a month had passed since the party. He wouldn't remember who on earth she was. How many women would he have met – not to say bedded too – since then?

She shook her head and reached down for her bag. She'd had enough of today. She closed her desk diary, locked her desk and shut the door. Her secretary, Camilla, motioned to her to sign a contract before she left, and as Kate scribbled away, she caught a glimpse of *OK!* magazine, showing guess-who on the cover with his latest bird.

Kate stopped and stared. She couldn't believe it.

'D'you want to take it home, Kate? I've finished with it,' said Camilla.

'Oh, actually yes. That would be great. Are you sure?'

She smiled and said goodnight, nodding to the other secretaries on the way. She strode towards the lift. All she wanted was to go home, pour a large glass of claret, run a hot bath and devour the magaz— Wallop!

She'd walked straight into a big, toned chest that smelled of apples and leather.

'Whoa! Well, hello again. Don't say I've missed you?'

Harry Hunter smiled down at her. Kate gulped, and wondered whether it would be rude to conduct the conversation rubbing her cheek against his claret cashmere jumper.

'Hunter!' she burst out, almost scoldingly. 'What are you doing here? I thought you were buying . . . buying . . .' She tried again, regaining her composure. 'I thought you were shopping.'

'Decoy. I came through the back. And I do like the way you say my name like that,' he said, eyes twinkling. 'How are you?' And before she could reply, he kissed her on both cheeks, holding her firmly by the shoulders as though she was Scarlett O'Hara in red taffeta.

'Very well, thank you,' she said stiffly, extricating herself from his grasp. 'You? I see the paparazzi are still buzzing around.'

'Oh dear,' he said. 'You saw that?'

'Who didn't?' she said tightly. 'Nice car, by the way.'

'What, that old thing?'

His smile was infectious and disarming, and his eyes never left her.

'Was it me you wanted to see?' she inquired, bringing things back up to a professional level.

'Most definitely,' he replied, with a wink that brought it straight back down again. 'Have you got time for a drink? My club's just around the corner.'

She raised her eyebrows and checked her watch. 'I'm afraid I was just off to a meeting.'

'Ah, Mrs Marfleet. Just the person I was looking for.'

Kate looked up. Nicholas Parker, the firm's senior partner, had come out of his plush office – alerted, no doubt, by his secretary, Amanda, who was every bit as canny as her boss. 'But I see you're busy. It can wait.'

'Mr Parker,' Kate said, knowing exactly what he was doing in the corridor. 'May I introduce you to Harry Hunter?'

The two men shook hands. Harry had observed Kate's deference and saw where the real power base lay. He turned on the charm.

'It's a pleasure to meet you, Mr Parker.'

'The pleasure is all ours, Mr Hunter.'

Harry laid a hand on Kate's shoulder. 'I'm very interested in securing your company's services, Mr Parker. I met Kate at a party a few weeks back and she spoke very highly of you.'

'Well, I'm delighted to hear it,' he said, basking in the compliment. Harry Hunter was the big fish he'd been angling for, for months. He couldn't believe Kate Marfleet had hooked him and said nothing of it. 'Would you like to come into my office and we'll talk privately?' He gestured towards the double doors.

'Well, actually,' Harry demurred, beaming brightly, 'Mrs

Marfleet had just agreed to accompany me to dinner, to discuss things further.' Kate went to move in protest, but his hand tightened on her shoulder. Parker looked at her – furious to be left out of the party – but he knew very well Harry Hunter's predilection for pretty things. If that was how they reeled him in, so be it.

'Marvellous. Well, Kate is one of our brightest stars. I know you'll be in safe hands.'

'I'm certainly hoping so,' Harry replied, his eyes twinkling devilishly.

Kate stood as still as a statue, her smile frozen, as they talked around her.

Harry checked his watch. 'Well, we'd best get on or they'll give our table away.' Everyone smiled politely, knowing full well Harry Hunter's table would never be given away. 'A pleasure,' he smiled, nodding to Parker, and steering Kate gently by the elbow he led her down the corridor. As they rounded the corner to the lifts, Kate looked back to see the entire typing pool congregated around Parker in the corridor. He nodded approvingly. He'd always known she'd go far.

Rather than go back through Agent Provocateur, they left through the building's back door – 'Which is an enormous shame,' Harry said mischievously, 'as I saw something on the way in which I thought would look incredible on you.'

He tried to take her arm as they crossed the back streets, but she pretended to grapple with her bag – thank God she'd grabbed the large camel Birkin today. It could act as a defensive weapon if need be. She didn't trust him.

They were there in minutes. Kate looked up at the building, amazed. She'd walked past it hundreds of times and never known it was a private members' club. The red door was so glossy she could practically do her make-up in the reflection, but there was no sign anywhere. It looked just like a private residence.

The floor inside was laid with black and white tessellated marble, and they climbed a mahogany staircase to the first floor, where an immaculate receptionist took Harry's jacket. Kate decided to keep hers on. She hoped it was true what the fashion editors said about power dressing. Her jacket would need to be a suit of armour for this dinner.

Harry signed her in, flashing the receptionist an intimate smile as he pushed the visitors' book back to her. Kate could tell by her response that he'd bedded her. She looked away in disgust. God, he was a creep.

A butler (crikey – Kate had never seen a real one before) led them up some more stairs to a large dining room, where she couldn't help but gasp. White leather button-backed booths encircled the room, with camel suede chairs set around circular tables in the centre. A giant canvas of Damien Hirst's *Butterflies* and some aboriginal art hung on the walls and a huge glass cupola was set into the roof, flooding the room with light.

They were taken to a booth in the corner – 'My favourite table,' Harry smiled – and a bottle of Krug was automatically brought over.

'Just half a glass, thank you,' Kate said.

'Tsk, I'm worried,' Harry said, shaking his head. 'I'm not a lawyer, and even I know it's against the law to have only half a glass of this stuff.'

Kate smiled sarcastically. She was annoyed. She'd been railroaded into this. Her boss had practically pimped her into this dinner and she hadn't had a chance to ring Monty and let him know where she was.

She tried to text him but she couldn't get a signal. Harry took the phone out of her hand and put it on the table. 'No mobiles allowed in here,' he smiled. 'Club rules.'

'But I just need to ring my husband – let him know where I am,' she protested.

'Probably best not to,' he said, wrinkling his nose. 'I've found husbands don't usually like knowing their wives are with me.'

Kate looked at him witheringly.

'Let's get a couple of things straight, shall we, Mr Hunter. This is business. I am sitting here only as your prospective lawyer, not your next lay.' She sniffed huffily.

He smiled calmly and let a few beats pass. 'What's the other thing?'

'Huh?'

'You said "a couple of things".'

'Oh. Did I? Yes. Well, the other thing is that – business or not – my husband has absolutely nothing to fear from a man like you.'

'Really?'

'Absolutely.'

'I'm extremely sorry to hear that,' he said, still bloody smiling, and passed her a menu.

She cast her eyes over it – she always went for the risotto – and put it back down, primly crossing her legs and clasping her hands in her lap.

'So how can I help you, Mr Hunter?'

He burst out laughing.

'Well, you can start by not calling me Mr Hunter! I feel like I'm back at school. You're like Miss Jean Brodie, sitting there. Relax, babe.' He squeezed her thigh.

She didn't smack his hand away, but regarded him coolly

for a moment before putting her mobile in her bag and snapping it shut. 'Mr Hunter, I think under the circumstances it would be advisable for you to continue this meeting with Mr Parker. We clearly aren't going to get very far.' She went to shuffle out of the booth.

'No, wait! Wait. I'm sorry. You're right. I'm being a jerk.' He spread his palms out. 'Please. I'll behave.'

He cast his eyes down to his drink. 'It's just that . . . ' He looked back at her, his eyes puppy-dog. 'I'm in a fix and I need help. It's hard to know who to trust. When I met you at the party I thought maybe I could trust you.' He looked at her. 'You're clearly very good,' he smiled, flicking his eyes down to the Tiffany étoile ring – another trophy – glittering on her finger. 'Actually, I thought you'd call me the next week and chase me on to your client list. Everybody always does that.' He frowned at her. 'But you didn't. Why?'

She looked at him. She knew he was a man to whom everything came too easily – money, success, fame, women. What he hungered for was the thrill of the chase. She decided to give him one. But on her terms.

'It's been a very busy time for us,' she shrugged casually, taking another sip of champagne.

He regarded her in turn. Her nut-brown hair tumbled on to the shoulders of her dove grey Armani trouser suit, and he couldn't stop imagining it splayed out on his white pillows, her cat-like green eyes regarding him sleepily, wantonly.

She stretched out one arm on the table and began lazily drumming her nails. 'The thing is, our books are full, Mr Hunter, and we're not really looking to take on any new clients. We need to be sure we can deliver a thorough service to our existing clients first. You're too much of a handful.'

'I am a handful,' he agreed. 'That's why I need you. And

it's why you're in business. People like me keep you in a job, Mrs Marfleet.'

'Our integrity is everything, Mr Hunter,' she said, smiling patronizingly. 'We can't afford to spread ourselves too thinly.' She shrugged, hopelessly.

'Bullshit,' he said, the smile finally fading from his lips. She was playing him. 'I've got a big problem that's going to end up being very expensive for me and very lucrative for you. I'd practically print money for you and you know it. What's the real reason?'

He looked at her, his eyes beginning to blaze. She stared at him levelly, but said nothing. After a few moments she said, 'Did you ever consider that perhaps not everything is about money, Mr Hunter?'

Clearly, he hadn't. He sat back, the frustration mounting. His jaw clenched and Kate tried not to notice how goddam handsome he looked. The domineering pose suited him.

'What is it about then?' His voice was low.

She took the magazine out of her bag and threw it down on the table. She jerked her chin towards it.

Harry didn't move. He cast his eyes over the cover and looked back at her, without picking it up. The corners of his mouth turned up.

'Don't tell me you're jealous,' he said.

Her eyebrows shot up.

'I'm disgusted,' she sneered. 'James is a friend of mine.'

'More fool you,' he sneered. He knocked back his drink, then poured himself another. 'Anyway, you can relax, because it's all over. She wasn't worth the effort.'

Kate was privately thrilled to hear Coralie dismissed, but that didn't change what he'd done to James. She remembered the tension between them at Cress's party. They clearly had history, but seducing Coralie was a low blow. She shook her head slowly. 'That doesn't make it better. It makes you even more of a shit.'

He glared at her.

'You can't speak to me like that,' he growled.

'Why not? I don't work for you yet, Mr Hunter. And I never will.'

She stood up to leave. He grabbed her wrist and held it so tightly it hurt.

'That's not your call to make.'

She pulled her wrist away and rubbed it. 'It's my call to get the hell out of here and away from you.'

'Yes it is,' he agreed. 'But I'll have Parker on the phone and firing you before you're even out the front door. If it's a matter of choosing between me and you, who do you think he'll go for?'

She stood stock still. She could see from the fire in his eyes that he'd do it.

He sat back in the booth. They both knew he'd got her. He'd guessed correctly – her job was too important to walk away from. She had nothing else to walk to.

Slowly, furiously, she sat back down again. She wasn't used to losing.

Charming in victory, he handed her her glass. 'Shall we celebrate with a toast?'

She ignored it. 'You haven't heard our terms yet, Mr Hunter. They may not be acceptable to you.'

'I'm sure they'll be fine.'

She raised an eyebrow. He was so bloody cocksure. 'Three years minimum retainer, seven hundred and fifty pounds per hour.' She had added an extra year on the retainer and £200 on the hourly rate. There was no way he'd go for it.

He didn't even blink. 'Fine. I have only one condition.'

She couldn't believe it. He was either stupid, reckless, or as unprepared to lose as she. 'Fire.'

He looked straight at her.

'I only ever want you. None of the other partners are to represent me. I am placing my trust in you, and you alone.'

She stared at him, wondering what his big secret was. In the back of her mind rattled the fear that she was sealing a pact with the devil, but these terms were too good to pass up. They guaranteed her partnership. She'd be made.

'Agreed.'

They held each other's gaze, contemplating the new relationship. Kate tried not to notice that his eyes were the same green as hers.

'Bottoms up, then,' she said finally, taking the glass from him. They drank deep, Kate feeling satisfied and glib that she'd pulled a number on him. They were even.

'There's just one other thing.'

She raised an eyebrow in suspicion.

'Let's stop with the Mr and Mrs. I'll call you Kate. You call me Hunter.'

'You don't want me to call you Harry?' she asked, baffled.

'No, I liked the way you called me Hunter in the corridor.' His eyes were dancing. 'It made me feel like a god.'

It was no good. In spite of her best efforts, she burst out laughing, and they both giggled like schoolchildren who'd sat on a whoopee cushion.

Seeing peace break out, the waiter came over and discreetly poured them each another glass.

'So,' Kate said, trying to suppress her giggles and regain some professional composure. 'What exactly is the problem?'

'Apart from the *Sun* saying I'm gay every other day?'

'I'll slap them on the wrist. Get them to stop that. They owe me a few favours.' She smoothed her trousers. Her leg still felt hot from where he'd squeezed her thigh. 'Yes, apart from that. What's the big expensive-for-you, lucrative-for-me problem?'

He took a deep breath and looked at her. 'I'm being black-mailed.'

Kate leant in, the questions rushing forward in her head, her killer instinct kicking in.

'By whom?'

'When I was teaching, I slept with one of my pupils.'

Kate didn't miss a beat.

'Only one?'

'Uh, well, no. But she's the only one who's come forward.'

'What's her name?'

'Emily Brookner.'

'How old was she at the time?'

'Fourteen.'

'When did it happen?'

'Six years ago.'

'How old were you?'

'Twenty-nine.'

'Tch.' She took stock. 'Right. Well, I'm sure you know that statutory rape carries a custodial sentence. We need to get you a criminal barrister. My role's going to have to be damage limitation. The public love a charming rogue but they've no stomach for dirty old men feeling up their daughters.'

'It wasn't quite like that . . .' he protested.

'It will be in the papers,' she countered. 'How did she contact you?'

'She sent an email to my website.'

'How much does she want?'

'One million.'

Kate whistled. 'Does she seem angry? Victimized? *Is* this about justice, do you think?'

'I don't know,' he shrugged. 'I haven't seen her since . . . since it happened.'

'Did it happen just the once?'

He shook his head.

'No.'

'How many times?'

'Countless. We were together for over six months, probably nearer to a year.'

'I see. So you wouldn't say she was traumatized by the relationship? She didn't seek counselling? Nothing came out at school?'

'No. Nobody knew anything about it. We were very careful. And she definitely wasn't traumatized. She was the one instigating everything.'

He leant back, one hand draped casually on a thigh, the other raked through his curls.

'How did the relationship end?'

'She left the school suddenly. Mid-way through term, as I remember. I think her parents sent her to a finishing school in Switzerland.'

'People still do that?'

He shrugged. 'Apparently.'

'And she's only come forward now, since your rise to fame and fortune?'

He nodded.

'So one might say she was a gold-digger, provocative, predatory . . .' Her voice trailed off. She sat still for a few moments, watching the bubbles fizz in her glass. Then the corners of her mouth tipped up and she leaned forward, placing her elbows on the table. She lowered her chin and looked up at him through her long lashes. 'She'll be twenty, twenty-one now. I'm sure she's even more – comely – now than she was then.'

Harry leaned in and looked at her, their faces so close she could feel his breath on her cheek. 'Where are you going with this?'

Kate dropped her voice. 'Well, if you were to resume the affair with her, you know – be pictured around town together, take her away, buy her a few new dresses – it would legitimize the earlier relationship and make it much harder for her to successfully argue any claim for emotional trauma. I mean, the statutory rape charge is de facto, she was under age, that's it. If she wants to take you to court, she can. But if you engage her in another relationship as a legally consenting adult, it'll be much easier for us to break her down. We can threaten to expose her as a gold-digging slut. We'll break her down so that she doesn't even want to get out of bed, much less go to court.'

Harry sat back, regarding her levelly.

'My God. You really are that good.'

Kate's eyes glinted with satisfaction, and Harry could see he wasn't the only one who enjoyed the thrill of the chase. He was desperate to get her into bed. 'You're a wildcat,' he murmured, mainly to himself. 'I can see you're going to be worth every penny.'

Chapter Twelve

Skipping up the wide shallow steps to the apartment, and singing 'King of the Swingers', Kate rounded the corner and found Cress sitting outside her front door.

'Oh, crap!' she exclaimed. 'What have I forgotten?'

'Nothing,' Cress smiled. 'I just thought we should have a summit meeting. About Tor?'

Tor – of course. Kate had been so carried away with the evening's dramatic professional progress, she'd forgotten all about her bereaved friend. She felt instantly awful about being drunk and happy. She tried to hide both.

'How is she today?'

'Well, she's kicked me out,' Cress drawled. 'Says I've got to go back to my own family. Huh!' she snorted.

'Well, that's got to be good, right?' Kate asked, rummaging in her bag for the keys. 'It's a sign she's beginning to look forward a bit. Move on.'

Cress sighed. 'She's nowhere close to moving on. She still hasn't cried yet. Don't you think that's weird? It's like she's completely in denial.'

Kate fumbled with the keys and dropped them. She hurriedly picked them up but it took three goes before she successfully got them in the lock.

'Are you pissed?' Cress asked suspiciously.

'Hmm? Well, maybe a little bit,' she said slurring, tossing her bag on to the floor and marching up the stairs to change out of her suit.

Cress gave a big sigh. She'd quite like to be drunk too. The last few weeks, looking after Tor at close quarters, had knocked the stuffing out of her. She felt toxic.

Cress took off her shoes and started the long trek towards the kitchen. Although still in Battersea, Kate and Monty were technically outside the Nappy Valley zone, being on the wrong side of the boundary road of Battersea Rise. Populated by smaller worker cottages and flats, it attracted a younger, pre-families crowd and Kate had no intention of moving over the border until she had a bump, which she said was the official Nappy Valley 'passport'.

Not that they were slumming it in this self-titled 'interim' period. Though their neighbours might have the square footage of a henhouse, she and Monty had the open-plan penthouse of an old converted school which pretty much had 360-degree views of London. The Linleys had once lived there, and it was a vast whitewashed double-height space with thirty-five-foot curtains, walnut floors and sixty-inch plasmas. The two bedrooms were upstairs on the mezzanine level and a spectacular aquarium had been fitted into the glass wall that looked down from the bedroom to the living area below. Even the fish had a view.

She went straight to the kettle and started clattering around for cups. She made an infusion of fresh mint tea – perfect for her detox and Kate's hangover.

As she walked over to the sofas, she caught sight of a Mikimoto box sitting on the coffee table. Inside were some black Tahitian pearls.

'Do you like them? I can't decide,' Kate asked, padding

downstairs in her pyjamas and wrinkling her nose. She turned on the gas fire.

'I'm not even going to justify that with an answer,' Cress said sniffily. 'It's just wrong.' But she knew what Kate's apathy about the pearls really meant. Her career wasn't enough any more. Her self-styled distraction method wasn't working.

Cress assumed a yogic position on the pristine white sofa – knees out, soles in, hands on her knees, looking like a tiny buddha – and woefully tried to find zen. Kate shuffled through the day's post, opening one important-looking letter and smiling as she read the contents.

'Where's Monty tonight?' Cress asked , in a flat monastic chant.

'Client dinner,' Kate replied. 'Same old, you know.'

'Yeah, I know what you mean,' Cress replied tonelessly, although she didn't – she was always the one who was out, not Mark. She opened one eye and regarded Kate, who was folding the letter back into the envelope. Now seemed a good time to ask. 'So, what's the latest with you guys?'

Kate took a big breath. She knew it was important to keep talking openly about the IVF; it could so easily become the elephant in the room. But it took such a monumental effort just to fix the smile to her face and keep her voice level.

'Well, round three failed too, but we're staying optimistic,' she said too brightly and too quickly, aware that she sounded as if she was reading out a press release. 'So we're just having a rest at the moment, then we're going to go for another round in October. Monty's been an absolute super-star,' she added. That bit was a lie, though she hid it well. He was now late nearly every night, and their signature lazy mornings of sleeping late, reading the papers, making love and getting crumbs in the bed had all but disappeared. Sex was fraught with tension and legs in the air. It wasn't about love or fun any more. It was about procreating. And no matter what successes they enjoyed at work, they were utter failures at that.

'Good for you,' Cress said enthusiastically, as though she was cheering on a lacrosse match, desperate not to say the wrong thing. Mark's teasing about her foot-in-mouth disease had left her paranoid. 'I'm sure each round must gear your body up a little bit more. You must get a step closer each time, right?'

'Yes, that's what I think,' nodded Kate, who didn't, and being really quite trolleyed was desperate to change the subject before drunken melancholy hit. 'So tell me, what happened with Tor today?'

Cress felt her search for calm flee for good at the mention of Tor, and she turned the meditative pose into an inner thigh stretch instead. She was much more comfortable feeling the burn than feeling the love.

'There's been a massive cock-up. On a huge fucking scale,' she sighed.

'Gosh.' Kate recoiled slightly from Cress's aggressive hyperbole.

'Hugh didn't have life insurance.'

There was a stunned silence as Kate absorbed the ramifications of the statement.

'So Tor's going to have to sell the house then,' Kate replied flatly.

'Looks like it,' Cress said. 'Their savings will only just cover the funeral costs, and about eight months of mortgage payments. It could be months – years even – before the money from his share in the business comes through.' Cress shook her head. 'I told her I'd cover her mortgage payments until she got back on her feet, but she wouldn't hear of it. You know Tor. So bloody stubborn.'

'As a mule, that one,' Kate agreed.

They sipped their tea in silence, until Cress started gagging on the string from the teabag.

'Why do I never remove the bloody bag first?' Cress said, pulling the string from between her teeth.

But Kate – deep in thought – was oblivious to Cress's histrionics.

'What do you think . . .' Kate asked slowly, an idea coming to her. 'If she won't accept charity, do you think she'd accept some work offers?'

'I don't think so, Kate. She's really not fit for going out into the big wide world yet,' Cress replied.

Kate leaned forward. 'Not for anyone else, no. But what about working for us?' She waved the envelope in her hand. 'This is the completion statement for our new house in Norfolk. What if I employed her to do it up? She could spend the summer up there, away from all the prying eyes and memories here; the children would love being next to the beach; she'd be earning without really thinking about it, and it would give her some breathing space until she decides what to do next.' Her eyes were wide. 'D'you think she'll go for it?'

'She could do.' Cress nodded. 'That could definitely work. Although you'd have to be crafty as hell about it. If she got wind you were helping her out . . .' She stopped and considered. 'How's it decorated?'

'Oh, hideous!' Kate smiled. 'We bought it off an old couple who've lived there for over fifty years. You cannot begin to imagine the tiles in the bathroom. And I'm not sure she'd walk barefoot on the carpet.'

Cress gasped, and bobbed up and down excitedly on the sofa. 'Oh! Oh! And Harry's looking for a place in LA. I could get him to commission Tor to do it up for him.'

'Will he go for that?' Kate asked, doubtful. 'He could choose anyone. He's got the pick of the decorating bunch.'

Cress dismissed her doubts. 'Trust me, Harry does whatever I ask.'

Kate smiled. She couldn't wait to tell Cress. 'Tell me, then. What's the secret to working with him? How can I get Harry Hunter under my thumb too?'

'Huh? What do you mean?'

Kate giggled and clasped her hands together, excited to be able to tell someone. Monty hadn't picked up her calls.

'Harry came to the office this evening and retained us as his libel briefs. That's why I'm half-cut, we went for dinner. We've started work with immediate effect – as you can probably well imagine,' she chuckled, nodding to Cress, whose blood had run cold. There was more to this than met the eye.

'God, I bet he keeps you busy,' Kate continued, shaking her head. 'He's got trouble written all over him. Bu-u-u-u-t landing him will guarantee I make partner!'

Unable to swallow down her excitement or drunkenness any more, Kate got up on her knees and started bouncing up and down on the sofa, jogging Cress out of her lotus position and completely thwarting once and for all her friend's futile quest for karma.

Chapter Thirteen

A week later, Kate strode across Clapham Common, eye-balling all the mothers wheeling their double buggies and exercising their bumps in the late afternoon sun. It was a glorious day. The shadows were long, rendering everyone skinny and gangly, like the mirrors in a fairground house of fun. The horse-chestnuts and beeches were full-canopied, rustling gently in the breeze, and although it was early June, the leaves retained that bright lime sappiness that showed nature was still ascending to its peak.

The grass had been freshly cut and mulched, left in messy heaps which the children jumped in and scattered by day, and which hedgehogs foraged through by night. Kate breathed deeply. She loved the smell of mown grass. It evoked some of her strongest childhood memories – racing on the sports fields at school, playing hide and seek in the spinney, camping with her parents. More than anything, though, it reminded her of the first time with Monty, lying on a scratchy car rug in a field in Shropshire. She shook her head, lost in the memories. It had hardly been worth the effort really. He'd been all fingers and thumbs and she'd ended up with appalling hay fever.

A little girl whizzed past on her bike, wobbling from side to side on the stabilizers, followed twenty seconds later by her mother, with a small baby strapped to her chest in a sling, trying to catch up. She rolled her eyes as she jogged past. 'Who'd have them, eh?' she smiled.

Kate smiled back, but the tears were still in her eyes as she rounded the corner and saw Tor sitting at their usual table at the bandstand café. She blinked hard, forcing the tears away, and checked her Tank watch. Tor was early.

She looked tiny, like a china doll, staring forlornly into space. Kate cast a glance around the playground and saw Marney scaring the pigeons. Millie and Oscar were playing in the plastic playhouse, which – despite today's fresh lime coating of bird poo – was still so bright it could be seen from space.

Even from fifty yards away, she could see the coffees steaming – a skinny latte for Tor, a decaff Americano for herself and a double espresso for Cress. Tor had her hands around the latte cup, warming herself, even though it must have been in the mid-seventies. Feeling the weight of her scrutiny, Tor looked up and saw her. She waved brightly, and Kate's heart sank. Ever since finding out about Hugh's life insurance (or lack thereof), Tor had switched out of her torpor with scary vigour. It was almost as though the grim and pressing practicality of finding ways to stay afloat financially released her from the emotional yoke of grief.

In the space of a week, she had written thank you letters to everyone who'd attended the funeral or sent cards, cooked up a month's worth of casseroles, had her hair cut and newly tinted, and bought some new jeans two sizes down.

Kate gave her a bear hug and then released her grip a bit, scared she might break. She felt so frail.

'How are you?' Kate asked gently.

'Good, actually,' Tor said briskly. 'It's not as bad as I

thought, coming out. I don't know what I was fussing about.' She rolled her eyes.

Kate nodded, putting her mobile on the table. She was expecting a call.

'And how's your week been?' Tor inquired. 'You look shattered.'

'Thanks!' She grinned wryly. 'Well, it's been an eye opener.'

Tor knew Kate was a master of understatement. This case was obviously a cracker. 'Ooh, tell me more. Give me details.'

'Well, I won't give names – naturally – but he's a premier-ship footballer, and his team colours are blue and yellow.'

Kate knew Tor was clueless about football and that this hint would yield nothing whatsoever about her client's identity.

'Hmmm, well, it's definitely not Man U because they're red and white – that I do know. West Ham? No, Wasps!'

Kate shook her head and put an affectionate hand on Tor's arm. 'They're a rugby team, you plank! God, you are shocking.'

Tor laughed and shrugged. 'Just tell me what he's been up to. Give me scandal. Some juicy titbits.'

'Well, the silly beggar got caught on camera snorting coke off a prostitute's shaved' – she searched for the right word – 'pudendum.'

'No!'

'Yes.' Kate took a sip of her coffee and watched Tor's absorption in this drama. Anything not to be absorbed in her own.

'Ewww,' she paused. 'That must have tickled. So what did you do?'

'Offered the editor a debenture at the new Wembley.'

'No!'

'Yes.'

'And make sure it's wild!'

The two women looked up. It was Cress, hollering after Greta, whom she had sent to the fishmongers over the common to buy some sea bass.

'Bet you she comes back with farmed.' Cress kissed Kate, then clutched Tor and gave her a hard hug. She drained her tepid espresso and sat down dramatically.

'Does she look better as me, than me?' Cress asked, watching Greta's retreating form. 'She wears smaller jeans, the bitch.' Everyone clocked the two women's matching skinny jeans, velvet Emma Hope trainers and white blouses.

'What's the latest?' Kate asked, raising her chin towards Greta.

'Ugh, bad to worse. I swear to God, I'm a stranger in my own home. I mean the other week, I came home to find she'd rearranged the children's bedrooms. Actually moved the furniture, can you believe it? I was looking for Orlando in the wardrobe. Of course, Mark hadn't even noticed. And then, I walked into the snug a few days ago to find them all cuddled up on the sofa watching Scooby Doo. I mean, I ask you?'

Tor nodded sympathetically at this gross breach of trust. Kate's brow furrowed.

'Um, Cress, at the very real risk of being killed by you, what exactly is the problem with Scooby Doo?'

Tor leaned in gravely. 'Ghosts under the bed, scary men in cupboards. Under-fives would never sleep again.'

'Aaaah.' Kate sat back, digesting this revelation. She felt her barren status keenly, aware of her ignorance of all the tiny nuances of raising children. 'Any others I should know about?'

Cress considered for a moment. 'Power Rangers: violent fight scenes, lurid polyester costumes. Don't get me started.'

Tor giggled at the light relief and scooped some milk foam with her finger, missing Cress and Kate's wide-eyed anxious glances to each other. They all sipped their coffee and an uncharacteristically awkward silence fell upon them.

Tor sighed loudly and looked at them both.

'What is it?' she said, sounding like a petulant teenager.

A flurry of hands folded into the table like petals, holding Tor's firmly, so that the three women were huddled together like Macbeth's witches.

'We're worried about you.' Kate said.

'Well, don't be.' Tor dismissed. 'I'm fine. Much better. Can't you see? I'm out. Look.'

'Yes. And that's so great, isn't it, Cress?'

Cress nodded furiously.

'But you seem to have gone . . . too far the other way. We're worried you're overstretching yourself.' Kate stroked her hand. 'It's still very early days, Tor. You need a lot more time.'

'I have to get it together for the children, for their sakes. Hugh wouldn't have wanted me moping about.' She snorted. 'He definitely wouldn't have wanted that.'

Cress and Kate looked at each other. Odd comment.

'Well, look.' Cress trod gently. 'We were thinking you should get away for a bit. While you can – before Marney starts school.'

'Where? Where would I go?' Tor implored.

'Why not go to our place in Norfolk?' Kate suggested tentatively.

Tor looked at her questioningly. What place?

'It's new,' she explained, quickly. 'Only just got it.'

Tor nodded, then shook her head.

'No, it's really sweet of you, Kate, but I think . . .'

'It's in Burnham Market. You love it there,' Kate interrupted. 'Just think – you can take the kids to Holkham Beach, go crabbing at the Staithe. Oh, think how they'd love it. Don't be mean.'

Tor looked at her friends, so desperate to help. They were good friends. She was so lucky to have them. But she didn't deserve them. If they knew what she'd done, they wouldn't be so sympathetic.

Cress took the pause as a good sign.

'Please – at least consider it,' she pleaded.

Tor smiled. She knew they wouldn't give in till she said what they wanted to hear. 'OK,' she conceded. 'I'll think about it.'

The table began to vibrate under their hands, and Kate lunged at her phone.

'Oh, I've been waiting for this call,' she said hurriedly. 'I must take it.'

She stood up and wandered over to the grass, trying to get a better connection.

'Kate, it's me.'

'Hello, darling.' She smiled to herself, knowing full well who it was. 'What do you fancy for supper tonight?'

'Huh? No. It's Hunter.'

'Oh. How very presumptuous of you, Hunter. Only my husband gets to ring up and say, "It's me."'

There was a low chuckle. She'd been playing all sorts of games with him since their contretemps, trying to re-establish the higher ground. God she was feisty.

'Fine.' He rang off.

Kate couldn't believe he'd hung up. She looked at the phone in disbelief. Should she ring back? He was the client, after all. She started pacing in a panic, dithering about what to do.

She needn't have worried. A minute later, it rang again.

'Kate. It's Hunter.'

She smiled.

'Yes, Hunter. What can I do for you?'

'I've done it. I've made contact with Emily. She's meeting me next week when I get back from the States.'

'Where?'

'My place.'

'Good. And you've got the digital recorder I sent over?'

'Yes.'

'Ok. Now remember, don't shy away from the subject. Do as we said – put some spin on it, refer to it as "the good old days". Phrase everything in a rose tint. Let her think it had emotional resonance for you. Lead her to believe that now she's old enough, you could have a legitimate, public relationship. Make her believe you want to get back what you had. That you've thought about her often over the years. You know, that kind of thing.'

'OK, boss.' She could hear him smiling down the phone.

'What?'

'Nothing.' He was still smiling. 'Shall I sleep with her?'

'What?'

'You heard.'

She paused.

'Well, it's got nothing to do with me,' she blustered.

'It's got everything to do with you,' he countered. 'Do you want me to?'

There was silence down the line.

'I'm thinking tactics,' he said finally. 'What were you thinking?'

'Uh, well . . .' Kate felt off-balance.

'Because if you think I'll blow it by seducing her too soon, then I'll wait. We don't want to blow our cover, do we?'

'No. Absolutely.' She started pacing and found her focus again. 'You're right. Take things slowly. Woo her. Be the perfect gentleman and show restraint. Basically be everything you're usually not on a date.'

'How would you know?'

'Well, thanks to the classy women you choose to go to bed with, your MO is well documented in black and white. It's my job to know whether what's being reported about you is lies or not.'

'You know, you're very good at this.'

'At what?'

'Honeytraps.'

'Just doing what it takes to save your sorry arse,' she said tersely.

'I'll let you know how I get on.'

He was still chuckling as the line went dead.

Cress gave Tor and the kids a lift home from the café. They pulled up outside Tor's narrow red-brick home, and Cress turned off the ignition. Tor didn't unbuckle her seat. Faced with going back into the empty house and gearing up for supper and bathtime, with no prospect of Hugh's keys in the door, her energy deserted her. She just needed a few minutes. She felt protected inside the blacked-out confines of Cress's Cayenne.

Cress sensed her energy dip. 'Do you want me to come in with you? Greta can take my lot back.'

'Bless you,' Tor smiled. 'No, I'm fine.'

They sat together quietly for a few moments, Tor's earlier conversation with Peter, Hugh's partner at Planed Spaces, banging around in her head. They were at an impasse as to what to do with Hugh's share of the business. Peter couldn't afford to buy her out – at least not until the council contract was completed and he could explore venture capital options – and she couldn't afford to wait.

Tor had felt sorry for him, of course. Hugh's death had had enormous repercussions for the business. He had been the schmoozer, Mister Charisma who'd wooed the clients (and how!) and brought in the business. Peter Golding was the technician, the backroom guy, never happier than with a protractor in one hand and a ruler in the other. Asking him to work a room and drum up new business was like asking him to pole dance for a hen party – it wasn't going to happen.

The two men had started that business from scratch, working all hours, sometimes through the night to see a job through – which had been easier for Peter than for Hugh. He wasn't married and didn't have a family at home, waiting for him. But it did mean he had an emotional attachment to the company that Hugh hadn't. It was his dream, his baby. And the idea of someone new just coming in and calling the shots horrified him.

So the only compromise they'd been able to reach was that Tor would leave it to Peter to find the new partner – that way he could get the fit he wanted. But a suitable investor could take months, even years, to find. Financial security was still nowhere near coming over her horizon.

'You should go to Norfolk, you know,' Cress said.

'Yes, I know,' Tor said, staring out of the window.

'And there's something else you should do too.'

'What's that?'

'A project,' Cress said enigmatically.

Tor looked at her in alarm. 'Oh no! I am not redesigning your office, Cress. You were a bloody nightmare last time. It is simply not possible to have a cashmere blend in an industrial grade carpet. I'm not going over it again. I'm just not. Find someone else.' Tor crossed her arms and stuck her nose in the air.

Cress laughed. 'No, no, no. It's not that. It's just that Harry's decided he needs an apartment in LA.'

'If you say so. And this involves me how?'

'He wants you to do it up for him. I told him all about you.'

'What?! Oh Cress, it's a sweet thought – but don't be daft! I can't organize that from here. For Harry Hunter? Pah.'

'Why not? All the big American companies have show-rooms in Chelsea Harbour. And it's an open budget, as you might expect. Just think what fun you'd have,' Cress schmoozed. 'It's only a short-term project. He wants it completed in time for the Oscars in February. You can do it from here and he'll pay you squillions.'

'Is that what this is about?' Tor asked, instantly suspicious.

'No!' Cress lied. 'Look,' she reasoned. 'Harry needs an LA base, because he's over there so much for the film adaptations. It's going to happen with or without you on board, but he's asked me to find someone for him, so you'd be doing *me* a favour if you'd just say yes.'

Tor looked at her through narrow eyes.

Cress sighed. 'God, you drive a hard bargain. Right. Last offer. I'll throw in Harry's mobile number as well – you can stalk him if you like.'

Tor couldn't help but laugh. Cress was so ridiculous some-times – but very persuasive.

Chapter Fourteen

The sun was glistening on the duck pond as Tor rounded the bend and headed into Burnham Market. She'd made good time from London – two and a half hours – and she was in time to take the children to lunch at the tea-rooms on the green.

She drove past the grand wisteria-clad Georgian town houses that stood like sentries at the south end of the village, boasting of its affluent farming past, and pulled up outside the bakery. Hopping out – oh, the bliss of being free from parking zones and traffic wardens – she unbuckled the children and they skipped along the pavement, deliberating on the likelihood of the tea-rooms serving hot dogs.

Tor felt light today. She had slept dreamlessly – for the first time in weeks – and woken up refreshed. It had felt like a new beginning somehow, as if the page had turned and she could move on to the next chapter.

Of course, Kate had been stunned that Tor wanted to flee to Norfolk quite so quickly – less than forty-eight hours after Kate had first mooted the idea – but she knew better than to try to stall Tor (for what, anyway?) and had couriered the key over, along with a hastily scribbled note showing how to turn on the hot water and please not to set the fire as the chimney hadn't been swept yet.

The tea-room was half full when they arrived and they bagged a big round table in the window so that the children could play I Spy. Afterwards, they popped into a small grocery shop to stock up on milk, bread, porridge, gingerbread men, honey, almond macaroons, Cheerios, orange juice, a couple of bottles of red and some washing powder. Clutching the rustly brown paper bags as though they were presents (the novelty of not carrying plastic bags), they all skipped back to the car.

They found the house easily. It was halfway up a narrow lane that twigged off from the High Street and fed into wild-flower meadows. Called The Twittens – which amused Tor enormously – the front door was painted violet, probably to complement the banks of nodding lavender which brushed up from the gravel drive to tap the windows in the breeze.

From the front, the house had a traditional Victorian brick and flint façade, with sage green painted casement windows. But as Tor went round the side to put away the bikes, she found a charming loggia that wrapped around the back, offering the perfect place to sit and look down the garden to the marshes and the sea beyond.

It was enchanting. The garden was wild and untended. Mother Nature had been given free rein here and she had taken full artistic licence. It was like an artist's palette of bright, clashing, tempting colour. Proportions were irregular, the scents heady.

High hollyhocks and delphiniums populated the meandering beds, painting the garden with brushstrokes of white, purple and pink; a white wisteria drooped heavily from the balcony, looking majestic and tragic all at once, and the lawn looked more like a wildflower meadow with poppies scattered through the shin-high grasses. Best of all, though, was the simple treehouse she could just about see in the girdle of one of the crab-apple trees, and which the children screamed to go into. Rolling her eyes and knowing that she'd never be able to deter them on this, she checked the structure was sound – that the steps weren't rickety, the wood wasn't rotten – and then left them to it, free to run and laugh and play.

She stood at the gate, watching. It looked like a scene from an E. M. Forster novel, a landscape by Manet, an ode by Keats. Her friends had been right. This place would nourish her soul. She really could learn to feel better here.

Locking the back gate, she opened the front door – which needed a fresh coat of paint when you got up close – and stepped inside. The hall was dark and poky, with original walls limed so heavily they may as well have been pebble-dashed. There were no pictures on the walls, no rugs on the floor; just a pale pink Lloyd Loom chair with an old shopping list and a copy of last year's Yellow Pages on the seat.

She threw down the car keys and, picking her way past a couple of sticky cobwebs, went through to the kitchen. It was bare. There was no fridge, the table was a child-sized one with diddy chairs arranged around it (chosen in panic by Monty because the standard adult ones were out of stock), and pristine saucepans hung from hooks suspended from the beams overhead.

That said, though, it was a bucolic delight. The floor was laid with large flagstones which had worn to a mellow patina and the solid oak freestanding units were painted in an apple green which was flaking off, only adding to its charm. Tor went and ran a hand over one of the units, which had a white enamel top. It was cool to the touch – perfect for making pastry, she sighed. She rather liked the idea of herself in a pinny, making jam and bakewell tarts. But the *pièce de résistance* had to be the glossy chocolate brown Aga that gleamed proudly against the back wall. All this place needed – except for a fridge and a decent table – was a lab stretched out in front of the Aga, whimpering in its sleep as it dreamt of chasing cats.

She opened the back door, letting the children's jubilant shrieks carry from the garden into the house and waken it up. She poked her head around the door to a small pale blue sitting room which had nothing but a washable loose-covered sofa and a glass-topped coffee table. An ancient-looking telly with stand-up aerial sat on a removals box in the corner. She sighed – getting the children to cope without Sky might be the hardest thing of all.

She walked down the corridor and climbed the creaky stairs, looking in on the bathroom – yikes! really and truly a peach suite – and smiling at the sight of the bunk beds in the spare room. Kate was so sweet, and a devoted godmother. Tor hoped so much she'd be a mother herself some day.

The master bedroom – if you could call it that – had an antique French corbeille bed which Tor recognized. Kate had bought it for her first flat, but Monty wouldn't have it in the house when they moved in together. He preferred a 'cleaner' style. Tor smiled. It looked good here. The vintage vibe worked.

The bed was dressed with white cotton sheets and some thick wool cream blankets, edged with blue stripes, which had belonged to Kate's mother at boarding school. A pea green eiderdown sprinkled with daisies nestled on top. It looked like the bed from 'The Princess and the Pea'.

Tor couldn't resist climbing on and lying down for a moment. She suddenly realized she was shattered. Moving up to Norfolk and escaping London for the summer had expended a lot of emotional energy. If she could just rest for a moment . . .

She heard the children burst into the house.

'Mummy!'

'Where are you, Mummy?'

'I'm in the bedroom!'

They thundered up the stairs and down the landing like a herd of baby elephants, jumping on the bed to join her. They loved lying down with Mummy.

They lay like that for, oooh . . . minutes, before Oscar started pleading for some juice. Tor ruffled his head and padded downstairs to the kitchen. Walking back in, she put her hands on her hips and looked around happily at the naked little house.

Time for a coffee, she felt.

She was just scanning around for a plug-in kettle – there was a whistler next to the Aga, but she hated those – when her mobile rang.

'Have I driven you away, is that it?'

She laughed. 'No.'

'Then what the fuck are you doing in Norfolk already? You said you were going to think about it. Next thing I know you've run away.'

Tor smiled. 'Cress, I have not run away. This was your flipping idea.'

'I'm coming up. Something's wrong. Kate thinks so too. She's just been on the phone.'

'Well, clearly.' Tor rolled her eyes.

'Don't roll your eyes at me, Victoria Summershill,' Cress shouted down the line. 'It's not normal to suddenly uproot yourself and your family for two months with half an hour's notice. I know when something's wrong, and I'm telling you something's wrong.'

'What, you mean besides being widowed, left with three children and pretty much broke? Of course something's wrong. Everything's wrong. Nothing's right. What further justification do I need for getting away?'

Cress sighed down the phone and it whistled down the receiver. 'I'm your friend, Tor. I'm worried about you. You don't share anything. You just keep on being superwoman. You haven't even cried, for God's sake. You've got to Let – It – Out. I'm worried you're going to make like ... like a Buddhist monk and spontaneously combust.'

'Oh, you are dramatic,' Tor dismissed. 'I'm completely fine. I've simply taken Kate up on her very kind offer a little earlier than expected.' There was an unconvinced silence. 'I promise to stay away from matches.'

'Hmm, well. I thought I might come up this weekend anyway. Keep you off the streets and all that. Mark's taking the kids camping. They're staying in some yurt in Dorset. From the looks of things it's practically got an Aga and a spa attached. He wanted to take Greta but I told him over her dead body.' She cackled mischievously.

'Cress, stay with your family. They need you. You'll have fun. You can't keep babysitting me.' Bugger. She wanted some solitude. Well, as much as you could get with three children under five.

'Yes, I can.'

'No. You can't.' Tor's voice was firm.

There was a brief pause.

'Oh, please let me come,' Cress pleaded. 'You know I'm not cut out for all that back-to-nature, sleeping under the stars crap. Oh, hang on a sec.'

Tor heard some background murmurings, then Cress came back on the line. 'I've got to go. Harry's on the other line from LA. This conversation is so not over. I'll speak to you later in the week.'

And the line went dead.

Tor sighed. Cress left her feeling exhausted at the best of times. She needed that coffee.

She went over to the Aga. It was hot! The previous owners must have left it on. 'That's so dangerous!' she muttered to herself, looking around for the dials to switch it off.

In the absence of the fridge, she unloaded everything into the pantry, which was damp and cool (although it also meant the loo rolls were soggy.) It was better that than hanging the milk in a plastic bag on the back door handle in the eighty-degree heat, though, she figured.

Having scored her cup of coffee, she began pootling around the kitchen, putting away Oscar's bottles and the vast amount of plastic tableware and paper plates she'd brought up. Although Kate and Monty had bought a job-lot of beds, sofas, tables, chairs and towels from Ikea on completion day, and the previous owners had left the curtains – though Tor sorely wished they hadn't – it was still a basic furnish. She'd need to stock up while she was here.

Taking out the ingredients from the freezer bag she'd packed in London that morning – God, it felt like days ago already – Tor threw together a spaggy bol, the children's favourite.

As part of her break with the past, Tor decided not to eat with the children at 5 p.m. She was an independent grown-up, and it was time she ate like one. She put her plate on the back of the Aga to keep warm (no microwave either) and ran the kids a warm soapy bath.

Marney and Millie were beginning to bicker. Tor knew they were approaching the witching hour, the time when Daddy's absence was most acutely felt. The excitement of the day had exhausted them anyway. She thought fast.

'Who wants to go cycling after bathtime?'

The children's jaws dropped. They never left the house after supper.

'Me!'

'Me!'

Skinny little arms shot up into the air, and twenty minutes later, their damp hair was being pushed under cycling helmets. Tor had no route or itinerary to follow. They were just going on an exploring cycle through the village and down the lanes.

The cool evening air felt delicious on their skin and the little family looked a deceptive picture of pure, unfettered happiness. Marney cycled alongside Tor without stabilizers – so proud – with Millie ahead of her with stabilizers and Oscar bouncing on the baby seat on the back of her bike. They sang 'Daisy, Daisy' at the top of their voices and gathered bunches of wild flowers (she had no idea what they were and resolved to buy a book that would teach them all) which Tor stuffed into the V of her jumper, for arranging in jam jars on the kitchen table.

They stayed out for nearly an hour, way past bedtime, and they all trudged up the stairs without needing to be asked when they got home. But the exhilaration was as short-lived as their flushed cheeks, and the tears came anyway, as the children faced the end of another day with Daddy nowhere in sight. Every sob tore at her heart. Her actions had brought this upon them. It was all her fault.

Tor snuggled up with Millie on the bottom bunk, singing

lullabies to her babies until they had fallen asleep, and she stayed with them long after their breathing had changed, listening to their gentle snores. She deliberated running a bath for herself but she feared the peach and terracotta tiles in the bathroom would give her a headache. Besides, there was nothing to do in a bath but think. And she certainly couldn't afford to do that.

So she changed into her pink flannel pyjamas (which had a sartorial age of eighty-six) and finally ate her supper on the washable sofa, with a glass of Merlot, watching TV through a fuzz of snow.

So this is how it will be, she thought resolutely. And it's fine. She had got through this first day without any major mishaps or catatonic spells.

She sat through *Coronation Street* and *EastEnders*, and was just finishing the bottle when there was a knock at the door. Puzzled – and hoping to God it wasn't Cress fresh off the M11 – she answered it.

A dazzling woman in her late sixties was standing there, with short champagne blonde hair (a colour that curiously looks cheap before sixty, and chic after it) and swathed in asymmetric linen knits. She had huge lustrous pearl globes at her ears and a languid black Labrador sitting politely at the end of a red rope lead.

'Hello.' She smiled. Her eyes twinkled kindly.

'Hello.' Tor smiled back, mortified to be standing in her pyjamas at such a respectable time of day. It was barely 8 p.m.

'I'm Henrietta Colesbrook. Are you Victoria Summershill?'

'Yes, I am.'

'I heard you were staying for a while. I just wanted to show my face in case you need anything. I live just up the lane, in the Old Rectory.'

'Gosh, that's so kind of you. Would you like to come in?' Tor motioned through to the hallway, aware that the wine bottle she was holding was conspicuously empty.

'I won't, thank you. Diggory, here' – she nodded down to the lab – 'will moult all over the carpets. Rangy mutt.' Tor thought that could only be an improvement on them. 'But here is my number – do ring, if you'd like some company or a helping hand,' she added.

Tor wondered what Kate had told her but she took the notepaper gratefully.

'There's a market in the village tomorrow – from eight a.m. till eleven. I'm on the cake stall. Do come and say hallo, won't you? You look like you could do with some feeding up and I can introduce you to some friendly locals.' She started walking down the drive. 'Tomorrow then,' she waved.

'Tomorrow. Thank you,' Tor called after her. She pushed the door shut and shrugged happily. Looking up, she caught sight of her reflection in the hallway mirror, and though she was momentarily startled to see how thin she looked, she flashed herself a winning smile.

Horrors! She gasped and clamped her hand over her mouth. The wine had stained her teeth. She looked like a bloody pirate. Oh God, what on earth must Henrietta Colesbrook have thought? Her shoulders sagged back down. How sodding typical is that, she muttered to herself.

Chapter Fifteen

They all slept late the next morning, and as Tor padded, blinking, into the sunlit kitchen, she felt a flicker of optimism waking up with her. Looking out at the pale, tendril-swept sky, she began planning adventures on the beach. A picnic, naturally. There didn't seem to be enough wind for kites, but cricket and crabbing maybe?

Filling the kettle with water and putting it on the boiling plate, she switched on the Aga and scrabbled around in the larder for the oats and honey. A big pot of porridge was just the thing to greet the children when they woke up.

Fifteen minutes later, when the children scrambled downstairs, she was rather less serene. The Aga was broken and wouldn't come on. She couldn't even make a cup of tea – which counted as one of the first signs of the Apocalypse in the Summershill household. There was nothing for it but to eat out.

The market was already doing business when they got there – the children wearing jumpers and wellies with their pyjamas – as the locals rushed to nab the best asparagus and lobster before the throngs came up from Fulham for the holidays. Tor and the children dived into the bakery and bought some warm croissants and a large carton of orange juice, before perching on a bench to tuck in.

'Victoria.'

'Mrs Colesbrook,' she cried, hurriedly wiping the orange moustache away from her top lip. 'Please, call me Tor.'

'And you must call me Hen,' she smiled. 'I thought it was you. James said it was. And these must be your children. Goodness, aren't they sweet?'

'Oh, yes. This is Marney, Millie and Oscar.' She patted them each on the head, in turn, and they all smiled, on their best behaviour. They liked the look of her. She looked kind.

'You said – James – saw us?'

'Yes, my son – he's over there.' She nodded towards the crowd. 'Oh, where's he gone now? Always gallivanting off somewhere.' She tipped her head in bemusement.

Tor felt sure she didn't know a James Colesbrook. Was he a friend of Hugh's?

'How was your first night?' Hen asked, smiling.

Tor rolled her eyes and indicated the children's attire.

'Rather better than our first morning. The Aga's broken. It was fine last night when I switched it off, but when I came down for breakfast this morning – dead as a dodo.' She shrugged.

Hen looked at her.

'You switched it off?'

Tor nodded, grabbing Millie by the collar as she made a break for freedom to the cake stall.

'Oh, you are such a dear!' Hen cried. 'Truly that is the funniest thing.' She held her arm over her stomach and belly-laughed before catching sight of Tor's face.

'Oh, I say.' Hen stopped laughing immediately. 'Oh, I am so sorry. I wasn't laughing at . . . I thought you were joking.'

She put a hand on Tor's forearm. 'It stays on all the time.

Day and night. If you've turned it off, it'll take a day or so to reheat.'

'Oh.' Tor felt this would be a good time for an earthquake to instantly strike the north Norfolk coast. 'Well, that explains it. How silly of me.' She tried not to show her mortification, but how could she not? Black teeth last night. A tramp's breakfast this morning and now the Aga disaster. Thankfully, the children were tugging on Tor's dress for her attention. Her cue to make a swift exit.

'Well, it's really so lovely to see you again,' she said, backing away. 'I expect I'll run into you, no doubt, over the next few days.'

'Oh, I'm sure,' said Hen, appalled at having embarrassed Tor so dreadfully. The poor girl had gone scarlet. 'Actually, shall we see you at the tennis?'

'The tennis?'

'At Hunstanton. It's the big tournament. It's on all week and finishes at the weekend.'

'Oh, uh . . .'

'Look, I've got some spare tickets. Why don't I pop them through your door? The children would love it, I'm sure.'

'Well, that's terrifically kind. Thank you very much,' Tor said, as Millie began pulling her away like a tugboat. 'I'll see you there, then.'

Hen was true to her word and a week's worth of member tickets were posted through the letterbox before Tor got back from the beach. They'd had a fantastic time, building sand Cinderella carriages and collecting mussels, spelling the alphabet with huge slimy strands of seaweed, and running away from the waves. Tor even managed to get the children to eat tubs of cockles and prawns for an impromptu supper, followed by ice cream cornets – with flakes! – for pudding.

They did the same the next day and the day after that, taking advantage of the fine weather, but now packing blankets, picnics and windbreaks so that they could all have lunchtime sleeps in the shade and stay out all day. The formula of non-stop play on the beach was proving highly effective at keeping the children's tears at bay, and so long as they all kept moving, Hugh's absence only really asserted itself at bedtime.

It was at bathtime on Friday that they heard the Carrera S crunch up the gravel drive. Cress had come anyway. The prospect of inhabiting a confined space with her family had clearly been too terrible to contemplate.

Tor felt herself sag. She just wanted some space, some isolation, some peace. To be some place where nobody knew her. Where she didn't have to play at being perfect or brave.

'Honey! I'm home,' Cress trilled ironically.

'We're up here,' Tor replied unenthusiastically.

Cress popped her head round the door.

'Anybody miss me?' she beamed.

'Yes. Your family probably,' Tor said flatly, passing her a sponge. 'Here, you do bathtime then. I'll get Oscar's bottle ready and start preparing supper.'

She walked past without stopping to give her a kiss in greeting. Cress realized – too late – that she'd overstepped the mark.

Tor started chopping tomatoes viciously. It had only been a week but she had escaped. She hadn't understood how liberating it would feel to be lost, to be starting afresh where nobody knew them. Already she couldn't visualize her London life and she didn't want to. The narrow streets, the traffic, the queues, the adulterous dead husband – it all seemed so far away, as if it had happened to someone else. But seeing Cress was a wake-up call. Her Londonicity – was that a word? she wondered. It should be – the way she spoke faster, louder, the very fact that she'd been Tor's bridesmaid, had Tor stressed to the roof rafters.

They ate in the garden – crayfish bought that afternoon from the wet fish stall down by the Staithe, with salad and new potatoes in dill. Tension hung in the air as heavily as the scent of the honeysuckle, but Cress tried to ignore it.

She carried the conversation, chatting about the apartment Harry had optioned in Beverly Hills, his book sales rising by twenty per cent following rumours of his Oscar nomination for the screenplay of *Scion*. But Tor wasn't interested.

'Cress,' Tor said, quietly, deliberately, during a brief pause in the flow. 'Why don't you ever spend time with your family? What's really going on?'

Cress stopped eating, and looked at her friend.

Tor wasn't smiling, there wasn't concern in her eyes. There was just detachment, scrutiny.

'Odd question,' Cress batted back, biting down on a tomato.

'Why? You feel free to ask me anything you like about my life.'

'Only because you're so bloody impossible. I've seen clams open up more than you.'

'Is Mark having an affair?'

'No! What the hell is wrong with you?'

Tor shrugged. 'I don't get it, that's all. You just seem to have this desperate need not to be around them. Travelling and working all the time, and then spending what time you do have left with me.'

'They just tend to have a better time without me, OK? I get in the way a bit and stress them out. I burn the food and put the bloody butter on the wrong toast and call them by the wrong names. I'm not good at down-time. Besides, you need me.'

'I don't actually. But I'm beginning to think you need me.'

The two women looked at each other. Tor was different. She wasn't as Cress had expected – weepy, depressed, lethargic, silent. Quite the contrary. There was no doubt the Summershill family looked transformed – each bronzed and golden from days on the beach – but there was a reckless-ness about Tor now, some sense of lack of boundaries.

'I know what this is about,' Cress said slowly as she glimpsed and recognized the fury in Tor's eyes. 'You're punishing me. I've reminded you of home, haven't I? You're furious with me because you were starting to feel better and I've made you think of Hugh, all over again. It's like I've brought him with me.'

Tor bit her lip and stared at her glass. If it had been a living object, it would have died of fright, so fierce was her glare.

'And that's OK, Tor,' Cress whispered, relieved to have got to the heart of Tor's iciness, and away from her own emotional frigidity. 'Grief has many stages; it takes many forms, you know. Punish me all you like. But I'm not going anywhere.'

Tor dropped her head. 'I'm a bitch.'

'No. You're grieving,' Cress said, stroking her hand.

Tor shook her head slowly. 'No. I'm a bitch and Hugh knew it.'

She stood up and cleared the plates, taking them into the

kitchen. Cress sat in the dusk, trying to make sense of her words.

Tor came back a few minutes later carrying a raspberry cheesecake.

'What do you mean "Hugh knew"? I don't understand.'

But the shutters had come down and Tor wouldn't be drawn. Cress was more worried now than she had been haring up the M11, but she smiled and nodded as Tor told her all about the tennis tournament they were going to tomorrow. If she was going to be any use to her friend, Cress knew she'd better keep up.

Chapter Sixteen

Cress scanned the crowds and figured there had to be well over a thousand in attendance. She couldn't believe the scene here. *Country Life* was covering it, and it was like being in a Jack Wills catalogue. Boys from Oundle and Radley (their printed sweatshirts made this a fact, rather than a well-educated guess) kicked about with floppy hair and sailing shirts and khaki cut-offs. Holding ginger beers, they nonchalantly tried to get the attention of the stunning girls with flicky hair, who mooched about in their fathers' cashmere jumpers and tiny shorts which hoicked up at the sides with D-rings and flashed even more thigh than Cress's knickers. OK, that last bit wasn't strictly true – she wore Myla G-strings. But the point was, she may as well have been Miss Havisham. The Hunstanton tennis was all about youth and flesh and warm beer. She felt ancient.

She cast a sidelong glance at Tor. She was cradling her Pimm's in her hands, seemingly relaxed, but Cress could tell there was underlying tension. Of course, it helped that the children weren't here and she wasn't constantly trying to keep hold of them in the crowds. Hen Colesbrook had proved to be a superstar and taken the children to the beach for their now customary picnic lunch. Cress was amazed at how quickly Tor had formed new habits – and new friends.

Cress liked Hen. She could see she was looking out for Tor and the two of them had insisted Tor leave the children for the day. Tor had been reluctant to let them out of her sight, but Hen quashed her concerns, and the two women had whizzed over to Hunstanton in Cress's sportster. It had been wonderful letting the wind muss their hair into bird's nests as they whizzed around the coastal road, and they'd even sung 'Boys of Summer' five times straight. For a few moments, they'd felt seventeen again – at least until they'd arrived and stood among the real teenagers.

Both women were in slim white jeans today, but Cress had teamed hers with camel driving shoes and a pale blue striped shirt; Tor was in red ballet flats and a diaphanous white blouse with splodgy red flowers on. Both were sporting huge square shades.

It was finals day and they'd missed most of the morning's match. By the time they'd found somewhere to park, there was standing room only at the back, so they'd retired to the bar, drinking weak Pimm's and looking out to sea through the telescope. After an early lunch of quiche, salad and strawberries and ice cream – what else? – the women had scored third row seats at the net for the afternoon's play. The bleachers were painted sky blue and the regulars had wisely brought cushions with them. After only ten minutes of sitting down, Cress's bony bottom ached, and she kept muttering to Tor that she wished she had one too.

Tor ignored her. She felt haunted today, anxious, as if Hugh's ghost was her shadow. She should have known this was a bad idea. It was too idle. She needed to keep moving. Keep doing stuff. The children couldn't afford to sit still, and neither could she.

Cress lifted Tor's wrist and checked her watch. The championship final was a couple of minutes off starting now. The umpire was in his seat and the bleachers were filling up quickly, the number of people fanning themselves with their orders of play spreading like a Mexican wave.

Cress leaned over to Tor.

'Have you got any suntan lotion in your bag?'

'Here.' Tor rummaged around her capacious Topshop-does-Balenciaga bag before handing her a tube of cream.

Cress applied the cream to her face and neck, still scanning the crowd, before her gaze came to rest on an exquisite woman sitting almost directly opposite in the second row. She was dressed in a coral and peach striped silk jersey polo dress that skimmed over a flawless figure, exposing tanned legs and shapely ankles. Her luxuriant nut brown hair gleamed as it absorbed the sun and her shades were – more glamorously – bigger than Cress's. They briefly made plastic eye contact before the stranger inclined her head to listen to the young boy sitting next to her.

'D'you want some water?' Tor inquired.

Cress didn't hear her. She was checking out the woman on the little boy's other side. She was less Mediterranean-looking than her companion, with a mid-brown bob and paler skin, but she had wonderful berry-red lips which rested in a natural pout, and judging by the way she had to cross her legs off-centre, she looked willowy tall.

All of a sudden, Cress got the giggles and started jabbing Tor in the side with her elbow.

Next to the pouty woman, a man in a natty ice-cream stripe linen shirt was talking animatedly to the people behind, and inadvertently sloshing his Perrier over the straw hat of the stout lady sitting next to him, who was stoically reading this week's issue of the *Field* and pretending it wasn't happening.

'Hmmm?' Tor leaned in to Cress. 'What's so funny?'

'Look. Over there,' she panted with laughter.

Tor looked over the net, to the bank of people on the other side.

'What? Who? What am I looking . . . Oh!' She caught sight of the comedy of manners. The rim of the woman's hat was beginning to bow down from the weight of the water, causing fat drips to splash on the magazine. Tor couldn't help but giggle too.

Just then, the players came on to court to start knocking up, and the crowd cheered. Everyone took their seats and the ice-cream shirted man turned to sit down.

It was James. Cress saw him at the same moment as Tor and gave a little wave.

James didn't see either of them. Seeing his bottle was empty, he had realized instantly his mistake and began solicitously brushing water off the lady's hat, which had given up the fight and sagged miserably.

Cress thought she was going to die laughing. Tor thought she was just going to die. Breathing suddenly felt difficult.

The umpire shifted in his chair. 'Quiet, please.'

Tor looked up and down the bleachers, searching for the quickest way out. She couldn't stay here. Couldn't be twenty yards away from the man who'd ruined her life with a single drunken pass. But it was impossible to get out. The bleachers were full and there was a strict 'no movement' policy when play had begun. She'd have to wait until the end of the set.

She slid down in her seat and held her order of play in front of her face. Unfortunately for her, it was a tough game. The players were well matched, neither one breaking serve, and they both played from the baseline, engaging in gruelling rallies which delighted the crowd but left Tor in a state of increasing agitation.

After twenty-five minutes, her arm was throbbing from holding the programme up so high.

'Here, let me have a look.' Cress snatched the order of play out of her hands. 'I don't even know their names.'

'No!' Tor hissed. But it was too late.

Cress jolted back as she took in Tor's strange body language. 'What's wrong?' she demanded.

Tor was now shielding her face behind her hand instead. 'Nothing.'

'It doesn't look like nothing.'

'I've just got a bit of a headache coming on.'

'Oh, well, I'm sure we can get something for it at the end of the set,' Cress reassured.

'Yup, great,' Tor said.

'First set, Mr Cavendish,' the umpire intoned.

As the players sat in their chairs, there was a cascade of movement in the bleachers as people made a dash for the loos and the bar. Tor grabbed her bag and jumped up, shuffling along the aisles as quickly as possible, treading on people's toes and bashing people with her bag.

'Sorry. I'm so sorry,' she repeated, without slowing down.

She turned at the aisle and waited for Cress to catch up.

'Crikey, that was embarrassing, Tor. You just about concussed half the row in front.'

'Oh. Whoops,' Tor said, clearly unapologetically and searching for the exit.

Cress looked at her. Tor seemed odd again. 'Come on, you,' she said. 'Let's go and say hallo to James.'

'No, absolutely not.'

'What do you mean? It's James. Let's go.'

'Leave the poor man alone, Cress,' Tor said, more severely than she'd intended. 'He's off-duty. He doesn't want to have to consort with a couple of former wombs on his day off.'

Cress looked petulant. 'I am not a womb.'

'You are to him. He'll probably only recognize you if you go up to him with your legs in stirrups.'

'Uurgh. I didn't know you could be so crude, Tor Summershill.' Cress folded her arms in a grump.

'Am I interrupting?' a deep voice enquired, hesitatingly, from behind.

Cress spun round. 'James. How are you? We were just coming to find you, weren't we, Tor?'

Tor closed her eyes in despair. She couldn't do this. She couldn't make idle chit-chat with this man who was all warm and smooth and polite, when her husband was cold in the ground.

Cress tried to gloss over her friend's rudeness.

'What on earth are you doing here? I wouldn't have thought this was your bag?' she asked.

'On the contrary. This is one of the highlights of my year. My son plays in the tournament. And I played as a boy. I always take my leave to coincide with it.' James paused. 'Hello, Tor.' She'd forgotten how deep his voice was. She realized it had been months since she'd last had a conversation with a man.

She turned round slowly.

'Tor,' he faltered. For the briefest moment they made eye contact, but that was all it took for every microscopic detail of that night to come rushing back. She started to shake.

He was stunned by how fragile she looked. She was bitterly thin.

'How are . . .'

She hit him hard across the cheek.

Everyone in the vicinity fell quiet. Even Cress was too stunned to speak. Tor was shaking violently from head to toe.

There was a long, long silence as James tried to take in everything that was happening – Tor's frailty, her trembling, and even, from beneath her huge glasses, the tears streaming down her face.

But before he could speak, she suddenly disappeared into the staring crowd, keeping low, desperate to be lost, to get away, until finally somehow, she stumbled out on to the pavement. She looked around. She didn't know where to go. There were people everywhere.

The wind coming off the sea had picked up, and it whipped her hair around before plastering the front tendrils to her cheeks. She took off her shoes and ran down the beach to the water's edge, where the crashing surf drowned out her sobs. She doubled over, clutching her arms around her waist, letting the tears come thick and fast. Then thicker and faster still. It had been eight weeks since Hugh's death and not a tear had fallen. She had calcified and been as dry as a bone. But now that the first tears had fallen, they wouldn't stop and it was like a runaway train, going faster and faster.

Cress put a hand on James's arm, mortified.

'James, are you OK?'

He nodded vaguely, but he was still looking into the crowd, trying to locate Tor. She was gone. He looked back at Cress, more focused now.

'You mustn't blame her. She's behaving really erratically

at the moment. The grief is manifesting itself quite . . . uh . . . strangely.'

'Grief?'

Cress nodded, before her hand flew up to her mouth. 'Oh my God, you mean you don't know?'

James shook his head. 'Know what?' He looked back into the crowd but Tor was still conspicuously absent. 'What's happened?' His tone was urgent.

Cress's voice got smaller. 'It's Hugh.'

James stiffened. 'What about him?'

'He died.'

'What? When?' James had gone deathly white.

'It, er . . . it was the night of the party. You know, in Kensington, for Harry. There was a traffic accident. Hugh was driving, he was over the limit.'

James stared at her for what seemed like an age, disbelieving, before suddenly breaking away and rubbing his face in his hands. It couldn't be . . . He started pacing up and down.

'I don't believe this,' he whispered, his hands on his hips. He kept looking up and searching the crowd for Tor, but she clearly wasn't coming back.

He brought his attention back to Cress.

'So – so what is she doing up here?' he asked angrily.

'Kate and I sent her up here for the summer. She wasn't coping staying in the house, so we thought a break would do her good. Plus it was a way to get her some money, without her realizing it, if you see what I mean.'

James frowned at her. 'No. I don't think I do.'

Cress paused. 'Hugh didn't have life insurance. She may have to sell the house.'

James clapped his forehead with his palm.

'I can't believe this,' he said. 'I just can't . . .'

'I'm so sorry,' Cress whispered, putting her hand on his arm. 'I didn't realize you guys were so close.'

His arms dropped to his sides, and he stood rigid. What did she know? 'Well, we're not. Not really. But it's just a dreadful thing to happen. Awful for anyone. Oh God, the children.' He shook his head.

'She's taken it really hard. Please don't be angry with her for, you know, walloping you. The grief's making her act completely out of character. I'm sure you understand?'

James nodded but said nothing. He understood more than she knew. And it wasn't irrational grief that had made her hit him.

'I've got to find her,' he said suddenly. 'She shouldn't be alone.'

'No, she shouldn't. I'll see you l—,' Cress said, starting to move.

'No. I'll go,' he interrupted sternly. 'Leave her with me.'

And before she could argue, he had disappeared into the crowd. He searched everywhere – the loos, the car park, the bar, even back at the courts. He only tracked her down when he overheard some children talking about the crying lady on the beach.

James watched her from the sea wall.

She was sitting by the water's edge, her knees tucked in to her chest, and her head pressed down, as if she was trying to be buried into herself. He could see her shoulders heaving from the road.

People were coming up to her offering help, but, too distraught even to speak, she waved them away hysterically. He felt an ache in his chest. He wanted so much to scoop her up, but he was rooted to the spot.

He had never felt so torn. She blamed him – that was clear. He still didn't know exactly what had happened that night after she'd left him, but he could guess: the show-down. Hugh storming out. He had played a big part in it all. She was right to be angry. To blame him.

He watched a man walk over to her and try to pull her up by her arm. Adrenalin coursed through his body as he saw her head shaking and her heels digging into the sand.

He could bear it no longer. Without saying a word, he ran across the beach. The man saw him race up silently, fury in his eyes. He dropped her arm and started walking off backwards, his palms held up in surrender.

'I was only trying to help,' he offered.

Without saying a word, James scooped her up like a baby and carried her back from the water's edge, setting her down in the dry sand. He put his jumper over her shoulders and sat behind her, his knees around her, enfolding her in a six-foot-two wall. He pulled her back by her shoulders so that her head rested on his chest, and slowly he smoothed her hair away from her wet cheeks, just as she had done for her babies.

She let him, but it wasn't forgiveness. He knew that. He was just the only other person in the world who knew the whole story. And right now, that made her feel a little bit less alone.

Chapter Seventeen

Harry watched Emily's pert breasts bouncing jauntily as she sat astride him, grinding away with a look of triumphant elation on her face. She had fallen for it, hook, line and sinker.

He'd given his butler, Jeremy, the night off, keen to convey an image of not having been changed by his stupendous wealth. She had to believe he was still the geography master she'd known and shagged – only with £68m in the bank.

So he had opened the door with a variant on his signature smile – charismatic, though not as cheeky as usual, with a dose of hesitancy thrown in just for good measure. But when he saw her, the smile sprang to his eyes and they twinkled with genuine delight. Standing in the dimly lit marbled lobby in a canary yellow silk dress, she looked incredible. He might have to go off-plan after all.

With a swift up-and-down, he clocked her trim waist, toned tummy and high breasts, which were fuller than he remembered. Her cheekbones were pronounced but her face was still full, in the bloom of youth. He particularly liked her rubber flip-flops – they made her ankles look delicate and, more importantly, they weren't try-hard. He was so bored of seeing vampy red-soled Louboutins next to his bed.

Her toenails weren't polished but scrubbed pink, like

seashells, and she wore a silver toe ring, like those worn by gappers on the backpacking trail. Her schoolgirl mousy brown hair had been highlighted a shimmering golden blonde – and cascaded down her back in gentle curls. Apart from a slick of lipgloss, she didn't appear to be wearing any make-up – she didn't need to.

Kate had been right. Emily had blossomed. Whatever risqué thrills she had provided at fourteen, she was now an altogether more tantalizing prospect and he liked the look of every one of her provocative and peachy-ripe twenty-one years.

'Emily.'

'Harry.'

Without kissing her, he ushered her in, watching her face as she took in the magnificent riverside penthouse. It always had the same effect. The entire back wall was glazed, drenching the room with light – and status. The view across to Chelsea was dazzlingly impressive, scanning from Chelsea Harbour in the west, past the majestic Albert Bridge, which looked as though it was bedecked with stars, over to the London Eye in the east.

The black lacquered floor had been highly glossed to create the illusion of a skin of water covering it, and bright tangerine-coloured Roche Bobois sofas, accessorized with Missoni cushions, were arranged in an arc around a vast fireplace, above which there was a strip in the ceiling for a retractable cinema screen. The walls were covered with black Chinese hand-painted silk panels by De Gournay, and a giant eight-foot buddha's head sat in the far corner. To be honest Harry had never particularly liked that piece, but it said . . . What was it the interior designer had said? Something about spirit and calm. That was it – calmer.

The kitchen was white Boffi, as highly glossed as the floor and minimal as a noodle. A pot of coq au vin was simmering in the oven, looking suitably home-made – which it was. Just not by Harry.

It was all a stark difference to the shabby housemaster's residence he'd taken her to while he was shagging her in her uniform.

Emily made her way over to the double white leather Barcelona daybed which sat in front of the huge sliding doors, her eyes resting on some annotated first drafts Harry had casually left there. He felt it struck the right note – dishevelled, hard-working, homely.

There was no need for her to know this wasn't his home. Harry didn't live here. He lived in a grand stuccoed mansion in Kensington. This was simply where he entertained. It gave people exactly what they expected of the great playboy – luxury, decadence and absolutely no intimacy whatsoever. The wardrobes were bare, save for an overnight change of clothes, and there wasn't any fresh milk in the fridge. All he kept stocked up here were bottles of Krug, condoms, some Dutch porn and spare sets of his favourite Frette bedsheets. There were a few photos dotted here and there, but only showing him with other A-listers – Bono, Julia Roberts, George Bush, Michael Caine. It was all just about the statement.

Harry handed her a glass of non-vintage champagne (certain she wouldn't notice the difference) and they walked out on to the terrace.

'I'm so glad you contacted me,' he began, referring to her letter as though it were a love note and not a demand for a million pounds. 'I didn't know how to reach you – well, not without raising suspicion.'

Emily looked at him, bemused, but said nothing.

'You know, I've always wondered about you. Wondered how you were, where you were. Who you were with.' He laughed lightly and shook his head, his curls rustling. 'I thought you might have been snapped up already, actually. Girls like you don't get left on the shelf for long.'

'My being here doesn't mean I haven't been,' she replied tartly.

'Oh, right,' he said, trying to sound like he cared. 'Who's the lucky guy?'

'You wouldn't know him,' she said dismissively.

'No. I guess not.'

They both stared out over the water. A flock of starlings was pitching and swooping around Battersea Bridge in perfect synchronicity, and the sun had dropped behind the gasworks, leaving a raspberry ripple sky in its wake.

'You look incredible.'

She said nothing. She knew she did.

'Tell me what you've been doing.'

'I've been working in PR for a few months now.'

'Do you enjoy it?'

'Seems OK,' she shrugged.

'Which accounts do you work on?'

'They're luxury brands. Nothing you'd know anything about,' she said, absolutely deadpan.

'No, you're right. Not my bag at all.' He fought back a smile.

The ice was melting. She was getting warmer. She turned to face him.

'How about you? Work seems to be going well.' Understatement was clearly her specialty.

'Yes, bumbling along. I'm working on the screenplay for

151

The Snow Leopard. And scribbling down some notes for my next book.'

'There seems to be quite a lot of talk that *Scion*'s going to be up for some Oscars.'

'Mmm.' He tried to look embarrassed, but really he was desperately excited by Hollywood's acceptance of him. The film had grossed $430m worldwide and his recent visit had been an unqualified success. They loved the 'English thang' he had going on. Stephen Fry but handsomer; Jude Law but badder.

'So how do you want to pay me, Harry? Cash or banker's draft?'

Harry spluttered on his drink.

'Bloody hell! Hold your horses! I thought we were having a nice time,' he protested.

'If you say so. But I'm not here for a good time. This is business.'

'Blackmail is not business,' he replied tersely. 'It's crime.'

'Tch. That's harsh. You should be relieved – no, *grateful* – that I'm only demanding compensation and not a custodial sentence.' She looked at him coolly. 'You broke the law, Harry – or should I say "Mr Hunter",' she said, putting on a little girl's voice.

'Don't give me that,' he flashed. 'You were the one who seduced me. You were the one who came into my class and sat there flashing your knickers.'

A thin smile hovered around her lips.

'You liked it, though, didn't you,' she said. 'I didn't see you looking away. And the look on your face that day when I didn't wear any.' Her smile was mocking. 'You couldn't clear the classroom fast enough.'

Harry turned away from her. The memory of it had made him hard.

'There's not a court in the land that would convict me,' he said, his voice low. 'I'll counter that you were provocative. Fourteen going on twenty-one.'

'The courts deal with the letter of the law, Harry – not the spirit.'

'I've got the best lawyers money can buy.'

Emily inclined her head. 'Let's hope they're worth it, then.'

Back in control in the trouser department, Harry tried another angle.

'Why are you doing this? Who's putting you up to it? I don't believe for one second this is your idea. This isn't you. It's your boyfriend, isn't it? You told him about us and he's pulling a scam to get rich quick.'

'No,' she said simply. 'It's got nothing to do with anyone else. This is about . . .' She struggled for the word. 'Justice. What you did was wrong.'

'I know it was. Don't you think I haven't beaten myself up about what I did? I have to live with the knowledge that I abused my position to be with you. But I was intoxicated by you – you drove me crazy!' That much was true. 'Not that any of that makes it right. I should have been stronger.'

He shook his head and stared at her. 'But if this was really about justice, you'd have gone to the police by now. Which tells me all you're really interested in is the money.'

'You're wrong,' she protested, but there was a slight quiver in her voice. A momentary weakness.

Harry exploited it.

153

'No. I'm not. And you know what's so bloody ridiculous? You could have had all this anyway. I wasn't the one who broke it off – who left without trace. I mean – look what I risked to be with you – my job, my reputation, my livelihood. Everything!'

She snorted.

'Clearly, it was a risk worth taking. You haven't done too badly out of your new career.'

He sighed, the poor little rich boy.

'Don't be fooled. That's brought its own problems,' he said. 'All the women I meet now are after my money or my fame. I can't trust anybody. You knew me when I was nothing – a geography teacher in a minor public school. You're one of the only people who's wanted me for me. I thought I could trust you. I couldn't believe it when I got your email.' He shook his head, betrayal etched all over his face. 'I always thought that if I ever saw you again – if I ever brought you back here – it would be as my woman. Not this.' His voice had dropped.

He let his arrows land. He could see from the tiny way she'd arched her back and lengthened her neck – just so – that she had absorbed their point. Feeling desirable, powerful and as if she was where she belonged, she turned her back to the view, resting her elbows on the glass veranda and tipping her head back to let the breeze brush her hair, her nipples hard beneath the flimsy silk.

Bravo Hunter! he thought to himself. What woman could resist that little titbit? That she could have more than a million – she could have all of it. He knew the combination of the fortune, the fizz and his hungry eyes made for a heady mix.

She turned to look at him. 'Really? You remembered me?'

Harry faced her, sensing his moment. 'Remembered you?

The memory of you tormented me. I was desperate to forget you. I was sure you'd moved on to bigger and better.'

'They don't come much bigger or better than you, Harry.' A strap had slipped off her shoulder, and the sun gleamed on her skin. He stepped towards her and slowly, teasingly, pushed the other strap off too. The sunny yellow dress fluttered to the floor, and she stood before him, in just baby blue cotton bikini pants.

Harry switched from hangdog to horny in an instant. He stared at her, openly raking his eyes all over her, taking his time, letting her wait.

When it came, it wasn't what she expected.

'Oh God! The coq!' he said, startled.

'What?' she cried, looking down at his crotch.

'The coq au vin,' he laughed. 'You always did have a dirty mind.' He winked, and, leaving her blushing and untouched on the terrace, went to take dinner out of the oven, pressing a little red button on the video recorder next to the sliding doors as he did so.

Her pert bottom was facing him as he came back out, and she was sipping her champagne, leaning on the veranda. He could hear the cheers of a crew from a passing boat as they looked up and saw her near-naked and splendid at the penthouse. She seemed to like it.

'Now where were we?' he said, sweeping her hair over her shoulder and trailing a lazy finger down her spine, over her hip bones and into her knickers. 'Oh yes. About to be deliciously legal.'

It was 8.05 a.m. when the phone rang. Kate picked it up on the second ring. She'd been at her desk for forty minutes – Monty was in Tokyo, and Camilla wouldn't be in till nearer nine, so it was a chance to catch up on some paper-work.

'Kate Marfleet.'

'Kate, it's Hunter,' whispered the voice at the other end of the line.

'Good God! I didn't know you did this time of day. Oh – don't tell me. You haven't been to bed yet.'

'Umm, strictly speaking – no.' He'd had Emily in the hot tub, the bath tub, on the island unit and the daybed. But no, he hadn't taken her to bed, yet.

'What does that mean?'

'Never mind.' He knew better than to elaborate. 'Suffice to say, Emily has been – diffused.'

Kate paused. Odd choice of words. She could tell he was hiding something from her.

'Did you use the Dictaphone?'

'No, even better.'

'What?' She was instantly suspicious.

'Video camera.'

'What the hell did you use that for?' she cried. 'What have you got – her sitting down in an interview room saying, "Yes, I'm blackmailing you?"'

'Not exactly.'

There was a brief pause.

'Oh God! You slept with her, didn't you?'

'No! I most certainly did n—' he protested feebly.

'Don't bullshit me!' Kate interrupted. 'Why did you do it? We talked about this. We agreed on the tactics to make this work. She could get you sent away, Hunter. You think that's funny?'

'No, of course I don't. But – you know – she offered herself on a plate. I could hardly turn her down. Pissing her off

156

would hardly help. Anyway, she looked good. And it had been a while since . . .'

'Since what? Thursday? Two days ago?'

'Huh? How'd you know about that?'

'Because I'm on the *News of the World*'s speed dial, that's how. Any time you're pictured with some dollybird, I get called up about it.'

'Hmm, well, that's good. They never used to do that with my old briefs. You must have them running scared.'

'Hardly,' Kate spat. 'They're ringing to know if I know their names.'

Harry chuckled, endlessly amused at getting Kate so worked up.

'So, you videoed her having sex with you. You've made a sex tape. And how exactly do you think we can use that for evidence? Unless you actually want people to see?'

She instantly regretted the remark. 'Oh, what am I saying? You probably do.'

She dropped her head in her hands.

'Look, just relax,' Harry soothed, hearing Emily coming back. 'It's all taken care of. She'll never want to go to court now. Job done – she's no longer a threat.' She heard him smirk down the line. 'You can go back to bitch-slapping the *Sun*.'

He burst out laughing as she spluttered various obscenities at him before hanging up. He tossed the phone on the floor, still chuckling, as Emily sashayed back into the bedroom, with a rapacious look in her eyes. Power – or the illusion of it – was a potent aphrodisiac.

As she straddled him, her pert breasts bouncing jauntily up and down, Harry closed his eyes with triumphant satisfaction. No, Emily Brookner had never been a threat. He'd known all along how to play her. He didn't need Kate Marfleet for sorting out a silly little tart like her. But he did need Kate Marfleet very much indeed.

And as Emily brought him off, the image of Kate's tigress eyes and pillowy lips swimming before him, he knew he needed her in more ways than one.

Chapter Eighteen

Cress's hands shook as she read the last line of the manu-script. It was sublime. Poetic, haunting, perfectly pitched. Harriet, her most trusted editor, was right. This had the legs to go all the way – to the top of the best-seller lists, and on the big award shortlists. Detectives weren't the only people who relied on hunches.

Cress hadn't been able to put it down. She'd had Rosie, her assistant, hold her calls all afternoon, and she'd switched off her mobile. She wanted to read it in peace.

She looked back at the accompanying author notes. It was entitled *The Wrong Prince*. Cress nodded her head. She liked it. But it was an anonymous pitch. There was no agent, tele-phone number or email address. Just a PO box number. Cress huffed impatiently. She wondered how long this had been sitting in the slush pile. A fortnight? Maybe more? She wanted to get to this writer before anyone else, but it looked like she'd have to do it the slow way.

She wrote a letter, saying she wanted to make an offer for the book, and asked the writer to come to the offices to discuss terms. She added her home and mobile numbers as well. She didn't want this one to get away.

There was no doubt Harry's signing to Sapphire had boosted their profile enormously. In the past few months, their daily mail bag had quadrupled, they were being wined and dined by the big agents, and now manuscripts of this calibre were landing in their laps. She couldn't believe her luck.

There was a knock at the door.

'Come in.'

It was Harriet. 'What do you think?' she asked, biting her lip.

Cress nodded solemnly, and then broke into a huge grin. 'Congratulations, Hattie. You've just found us Harry's successor.'

Harriet beamed, clasping her hands together. 'Oh, I'm so pleased! Although, who'd have ever thought we even needed one?'

'Absolutely. That man is like our own personal mint. Have you seen his latest figures?' Cress pushed a spreadsheet towards her. 'His sales are spiking again. I swear he could fill Wembley just reading the first five chapters of the new book. Pre-orders for that have already broken records. Are we still on course for a February launch?'

Harriet nodded, both as a yes to her boss's question and in appreciation of the sales numbers. They had to be good news for her bonus.

'But we've got to keep moving forwards, Hattie. There's always someone brighter and fresher coming along. And you and I both know, although we'd never publicly admit it . . .' Cress's voice dropped to a whisper, 'that he's been riding the momentum from *Scion* for too long. It's carried him for the last two titles, but if he's going to stay number one in the world, he really needs to score an ace with the new one. And we need to have a Plan B for if he doesn't.'

'*This*,' Cress said, holding the *Wrong Prince* manuscript, and slipping it into her bag for some more bedtime reading, 'is Plan B. Let's just hope this guy looks like a movie star, as well as writing like a poet. We'll start work on it tomorrow. Ask everyone to convene here at nine a.m. for the action plan.'

Harriet nodded, and Cress took the acceptance letter to the postbag herself, kissing it lightly for luck before letting it fall into the bundle of mail.

She wanted a fast turnaround on this. Tomorrow she would put Harriet on to editing the text and getting this book ready for publication. Why wait? Where were they now? July. If they could get it on the bookshelves in the next three months, there'd be time for it to hit the best-seller lists before the Christmas peak and drive up sales. There was no point holding back just to wait for the formalities to be completed. This author had come to her. So long as hers was the first publisher's acceptance letter he got, she could close the deal and start to spread the power base on her author lists – because for as long as she relied solely on Harry Hunter for profile and profits, she couldn't shake the niggling fear that Sapphire's success was built on a house of cards.

It was just after 10 p.m. when Cress pulled into the driveway, and nearly dark. She frowned to see the Golf – Greta's runabout – parked askance, and blocking the access to the front door. Rolling her eyes impatiently as she skirted round it, her Missoni dress caught on one of the giant topiaried box balls and a thread pulled.

'Shit,' she said crossly, stopping to untangle herself before the stitches unravelled. She heard laughter coming from the house and looked up.

The lights were on in the drawing room. Inside, she could see silhouettes and movement, and music was playing. Mark must have got the boys over for a game of poker, she thought, rifling around for her keys.

Unlocking the door, she dumped her bag on the mushroom velvet corner chair and was just kicking off her shoes when Greta walked through the hall, carrying a crystal decanter and wearing . . . Cress couldn't believe it! She was wearing Cress's brand-spanking-new black chiffon Alberta Ferretti dress. The halter neck revealed Greta's waifish slender arms (not a hint of bingo wings) and vanilla skin that you wanted to stroke and sniff. And though the wispy Chantilly lace hem came to Cress's knees, on Greta – whose lofty five foot nine height was mainly in her legs – it flirted around her mid-thighs tantalizingly. Her baby-blonde hair was bundled into a messy French pleat, with occasional wisps escaping, but somehow it was the precise lack of grooming that made her look all the more enticing.

Red mist descended.

'What the fuck do you think you're doing wearing my clothes and entertaining your friends?' Cress bellowed, completely unbothered about waking the kids. 'This is my house.'

Greta stood, agog.

'I'm sorry, Mrs Pelling, I tried to . . .'

'I don't give a shit what you tried to do. I don't want to hear it. How dare you walk through my house in my clothes, carrying my wine. You have ideas well and truly above your station if you think you're entitled to use this house as your own. You are an employee here! Do you hear me? You are here to work, not to play.'

'But Mrs Pelling . . .'

'I have had enough, do you hear me? I'm on to you, young lady. How dare you!' Cress hissed.

'Mr Pelling . . .'

'Oooooh, no! No, no, no!' Cress shouted. 'You think you can bat your baby blues and twist him around your little finger? Let me tell you something. My husband's got far more substance than to fall for a vacuous airhead like you. You've got nothing to offer a man like him – not conversation, not brains, not power. You are a complete nonentity, here to change nappies and cook sau—'

'I think that's enough, Cressida,' Mark said sternly.

Cress looked over. He'd come out of the drawing room and was standing in the doorway, holding a glass of wine.

'Mark!'

Cress didn't understand. What was he doing here? With Greta? Was he entertaining her? Cress's hand flew to her mouth.

'Oh my God!' she shrieked. 'You are fucking her!'

Mark marched across the hall and grabbed her roughly by the arm.

'No!' he hissed furiously. 'I am not fucking her. She was doing what you should have been doing.'

Cress looked at him blankly.

'The Bastides? The Lathams? For dinner? Ringing any bells?'

Cress felt the blood pool in her feet. Dinner with Mark's boss! How could she have forgotten?

'I've been trying to ring you all day! Why's your phone been switched off?' he demanded.

'I, uh, I was reading. I was, uh . . . Are they . . . ?' she whispered, nodding towards the drawing room.

'Yes,' he said quietly. 'They're all in there. And yes, they've heard every word you said.'

Cress felt completely, utterly and totally mortified. She stood in silence for a moment, wondering how to turn this around. 'Foot in mouth' disease strikes again, she thought wryly, knowing there was nothing else for it. She knew she had to face the music.

'OK,' she said, taking a deep breath, as she smoothed her dress and quickly patted her hair. 'I can sort this out.'

'Hang on a second,' Mark said. 'Isn't there something else you need to do first?'

Cress looked at him quizzically.

'You owe Greta an apology,' he prompted.

She gasped. She'd choke on the words first. There was no way she was going to apologize to her. Every word she'd said was true and both women knew it.

Greta was still standing in the hall, holding the decanter, her bottom lip trembling as she looked at the floor.

Cress didn't buy it for a second.

'Mark, I really don't . . .'

'If you can't apologize for the scene you've just made, and the utter slander you've just thrown at Greta, then I don't think you should come in, Cress,' Mark said, exasperated. 'Greta's been wonderful in your absence. She made a fantastic Chateaubriand with just an hour's notice and she's done you proud, getting the kids to bed, putting the house to rights and looking after our guests. I said she could pick something from your wardrobe as she was wearing a track-suit and until such time as the hostess deigned to arrive, it was only right that she should be appropriately dressed. You are in her debt.'

Cress felt herself shrink. He was adamant – and right. She closed her eyes, smarting against the shame for a moment, then crossed the hall to Greta and put a hand on her arm.

'Mark's right,' Cress said stoically. 'You've done a wonderful job, and I've been a complete harpie. It's been a . . . bad day and I took it out on you. I'm sorry.'

'Good girls,' Mark said, pleased to see harmony – and manners – restored. 'Come along then and say hallo to our guests, Cress. Greta, if you could just finish up in the kitchen, then you're clear for the night. And thank you,' he smiled, as she turned to go. 'You've been marvellous. I couldn't have managed without you.'

A look of undisguised delight crossed Greta's face, before she smiled shyly in return.

Mark walked back into the drawing room to their guests, shoulders shrugged up around his ears, his arms outstretched in embarrassed appeasement. Cress looked back at Greta, who was pulling the slide from her hair and letting it fall sexily on to her shoulders. Her shy look was now sly, and as a ripple of mirth skittered out of the drawing room a moment later – clearly at her expense – Cress saw a flash of glib satisfaction in her eyes at this latest in the line of small victories. They stared at each other in cold silence. In recognition. They both knew the gloves were off.

Chapter Nineteen

Kate held her breath as the caterer ran the palette knife around the rim of the mould, and the five-tiered rainbow jelly dropped on to the plate with a satisfying plop. Tentatively – now would not be the time to trip – Kate carried the wobbling tower through to the French grey dining room and positioned it in the middle of the table. Stepping back with relief that she had fulfilled her task without major mishap, she couldn't help but admire the party spread: iced fairy cakes were decorated with angel wings spun from a fine caramel thread; jam sandwiches had been pummelled and rolled into tiny swirls like savoury swiss rolls; cocktail sausages had been dipped in honey for a golden glaze, and a chocolate fountain was arranged with marshmallows and strawberries on the side.

The *pièce de résistance*, however, had to be the cake – a magnificent three-foot castle, complete with working draw-bridge (made from a waffle), a moat and turrets in each corner. A Barbie had been positioned in one of the towers, but was a bit too perky and smiley to look like a damsel in distress.

The occasion in question was her god-daughter Lucy Pelling's eighth birthday, and not a penny or person had been spared (Monty had muttered that voluntary conscription numbers were up). Cress had been a nightmare, delegating, shouting and throwing orders around imperiously, as though bossiness would make up for the fact she wasn't actually doing any of it herself.

A red and white striped big-top tent had been set up on the lawn, with a go-kart track laid down in the children's play area. The workmen had had to move two tonnes of woodchips before they could even get started (which Cress had failed to mention when she made the reservation), so tempers were frayed and goodwill all but gone.

Kate had arrived early, on the pretext of helping out, but her limp mood meant she was mainly a hindrance. The doorbell rang, and she shrank down in an armchair, eager to keep out of the way. The first guests had arrived but Greta wasn't back yet with the kids, which was sending Cress into apoplexy.

'God Almighty, do I have to do everything myself?' Cress shouted as she marched up the garden towards the orangery, leaving three gruff workmen trembling in her wake. 'I don't know why I bother, I really don't!'

She stomped past without seeing Kate, fluffing up her hair as she went to the door.

'Helloooo,' she trilled politely, as though she'd been calmly deadheading the begonias all morning, as five children barged past, heading straight for the garden.

'Oh cool!'

'Thass wicked man!'

Putting the door on the latch, Cress finally caught sight of Kate and, for the first time that day, really saw her. 'Well, I'm glad we've passed muster,' she smiled, coming over and sitting down next to her. She put a hand on Kate's arm. 'You look like shit,' she said warmly, taking in her friend's pallor. 'What's up?'

Kate smiled, grateful that her friend had noticed. Usually Tor would have been her proverbial shoulder, but clearly she shouldn't be burdened now. Besides, she was in Norfolk for the summer. And this wasn't something that could be discussed on the phone.

'It's . . .'

But the door burst open and Lucy ran in, eager to get to the fire-breather and go-karts. Cress instantly sprang up as Greta – who had taken the children to the Harbour Club to keep them out of the way during preparations – sashayed back in.

'I'm sorry, Mrs Pelling. I thought it was a two p.m. start,' she said, smiling sweetly, knowing full well it had been 1.30 p.m.

Cress sighed – unwilling to sour Lucy's big day – and waved one hand dismissively. 'Well, you're here now. Go and supervise the magician. I didn't check his references – check he's keeping the bunny in the hat – you know what I mean . . .'

Greta sloped off, knowing Cress was watching her. She was wearing a white playsuit that buttoned down the front and had sweet rolled-up shorts that made her legs look endless. Battered plimsolls and a scruffy ponytail kept the look easy and effortless – she knew how important it was not to look as if she was trying to be sexy in front of the mums.

Cress watched her go. She'd thought her outfit screamed 'chic' when she was getting dressed, but now she felt the narrow beige Armani pants and crisp cream shell top looked dowdy and prim by comparison.

Greta was halfway to the striped tent when they both heard a cry. Cress saw her first. Felicity had tripped on a tree root in the orchard and was clutching her knee. She started running down the lawn to her baby, but just as she got past the big top, stopped suddenly, like a frozen statue.

'Greta!' Felicity wailed, the tears falling piteously. 'Greta!'

Mark was standing thirty feet away, talking to the other dads, in navy shorts and a pale pink polo shirt. He had seen both women react, but Greta had got there first, full of concern and smothering the little girl with kisses and cuddles.

He looked back to Cress, who had turned on her heel and was heading back towards the house. He felt a stab of pity for his wife, who always seemed to be there at the wrong time, or that little bit too late.

Mark walked towards his daughter, who had calmed down and was now just enjoying the cuddles. Greta was crouched down, with Felicity sitting on her lap, her arms wrapped tightly around Greta's neck.

'Hush, baby,' she soothed. 'Is OK. Greta make it all better. Let me see.'

She saw Mark approach and started to look up, but with Felicity on her lap too she lost balance and toppled over – rather dramatically – gangly arms and legs akimbo. She wasn't wearing any knickers.

There was a brief pause before he spoke.

'Are you OK, darling?' He picked up Felicity as Greta scrambled her long legs back together and stood up. 'Who's my brave girl then?'

'Daddy!' Felicity cried, thrilled to have her father's undivided attention.

'I think she'll be OK,' Greta said, smiling and demure again. Vixen to virgin in the bat of an eye.

'Yes, thank you, Greta,' Mark said, without making eye

contact. And he turned and left with his daughter in his arms.

Greta stared after him, as Mark walked over to Monty. He put Felicity down affectionately and she scampered off to play, right as rain.

'I think you might be in there, Pelling,' Monty ribbed, having seen Greta's forlorn face as Mark left.

'Mmm, because she's going to be interested in an old duffer like me,' Mark deflected, self-deprecatingly. He knew he was a good catch – looking better with age, and with a high net worth. But he had Cress. She was all he'd ever wanted. He'd never looked at anyone since meeting her – though there had been plenty of opportunity – and he'd be damned if he was going to start now. Even if there was a knickerless nanny in his house, dammit.

'D'you see the match on Wednesday?'

Harry Hunter had arrived – Cress's invitation had been not so much a request as an order – and was standing on the other side of the not-so-big-top, listening. He was feeling ridiculous sneaking a fag against the striped canopy. Cress didn't want the children seeing him smoke: 'You're a role model, Harry'; 'They'll think it's cool', yada, yada . . . He might be an international player in the jet-set, but Cress had a particular knack of making him feel like a naughty schoolboy who'd been caught out. Which, let's face it, he had.

Of course, everyone bought the charade. The chummy phone calls, the dear little gifts here, or another party there as sales broke yet more barriers. In fact, he was convinced even Cress bought it. Blackmail wasn't her bag; she was much more of a Chanel girl. She'd simply been given an opportunity, and grabbed it. He couldn't really blame her. He'd have done the same. Correction – *had* done the same.

But however sweet she was to him, it didn't take away the fact that he was her puppet, and she had him well and truly dancing to her tune. She'd even made him pay his own advance to come over to Sapphire, for Chrissakes. She couldn't afford anywhere near the going rate to bring Harry on board, and if they were going to get it past Harry's agent, his accountants and the industry rags, he needed to cover his tracks. She'd shown an admirable lack of mercy that he almost respected. She didn't just want to sign him and his future work, including his film work; she wanted his entire back catalogue as well. After all, she'd purred, it was *Scion* that had brought about their partnership. All in all, he'd had to pay her £3m to make the move look legitimate, and there hadn't been a moment since when it hadn't pissed him off to hell.

He sucked on the cigarette viciously, before beating it to death on the ground. There had to be a way out of this bloody awful mess. She was tough, yes, but he'd faced down badder boys than her.

He just needed to get hold of the whole picture, and it certainly wasn't with Cress. A couple of weeks after signing with her, he'd received a copy of *Scion* with the heading page scrawled: '*These words hereafter thy tormentors be.*'

It was *Richard II*, but he doubted Cress knew that. Nobody who loved Shakespeare built a career publishing sex blogs. Besides, she had him under her thumb now, had done ever since she'd stopped him getting on that plane to New York. There was no need for her to threaten him further. It had to have come from someone else, the person who'd given her the information about Brendan Hillier in the first place. They were the real threat.

So he was biding his time. Waiting, watching, getting to know her world, her fault lines. Everybody had a fatal weakness, and thanks to her bullying tactics getting him here today, she had just revealed hers. If he hadn't been hiding behind the tent like a sniper, he'd never have seen how her child called for the nanny and not her. Nor would he have seen how the nanny – stunning on any day of the week – had opened her legs for Cress's husband. Mark had walked away for now. But for how long could any man resist a woman like her?

Harry looked round at the delightful scene of children skipping, chasing and shrieking with laughter, parents relaxing, old friends catching up. This might be Battersea at its apotheosis, but it was his idea of hell. Thirty-plus eight-year-olds stuffing themselves with E numbers until they were so high the only thing that would bring them back down was Ritalin. He couldn't believe he'd left Emily naked in bed and wanting more, for this.

Cress had gathered everyone around and was leading them in singing 'Happy Birthday' out of key. The fire-breather was standing next to the cake, poised to blow a dramatic flame over the top of it – which worked well until Barbie's hair caught fire. Harry creased up, half expecting Ken to pitch up in a dinky-car fire engine.

And then he saw something that wiped the smile clean off his face. Kate was standing in a corner, talking to that bloke who'd teased Mark – her husband, he assumed. Harry looked at him. He looked familiar somehow, a face from the past. He wasn't that tall – maybe five foot ten – stocky build, sandy hair. But as the man moved his head, Hunter caught sight of a small but distinctive scar running down his neck, below his left ear. Maybe they'd met at the party in Kensington? Whatever. It would come to him.

He looked back at Kate. She was wearing capri jeans cut off at the knee and a white knitted top which was cut away at the shoulders to reveal enviably toned arms. Her hair was freshly washed, but unstyled, and she was free of her usual trophy jewels. Harry had never seen her off-duty before. He had grown used to her big bags and sharp suits and ball-busting rocks. Looking at her now, so soft and unaggressive, it was hard to believe she made her living squaring up for battles with the *Sun* or the *News of the World* or *OK!* magazine.

He watched them talk. Their body language was brittle. Kate had her arms across her stomach, her head down. Monty was half turned away from her, a closed look on his face as he shook his head. They spoke like that for a couple of minutes, before Monty put his drink on the wall and walked off.

Harry watched Kate move into the house. Quickly, he glanced round the garden – Cress was flapping about, terrified the vision of perfection she'd conjured for her eldest child was going to be burned to the ground. The no-knickers nanny was looking more wholesome than muesli, with the three-year-old on her shoulders, plaiting her hair. Monty had joined the dads, who had resumed their positions around the drinks table and were getting quietly pissed on lager and Pimm's. For once, no one was watching.

He moved stealthily into the house. It's cool, shaded quietness contrasted with the glaring noise in the garden, and as his eyes adjusted to the dim, he quickly darted in and out of rooms – the kitchen, drawing room, dining room, cinema room, loo, utility. Nothing. His hand rested on the curved rail of the staircase and he looked up the elegant flight. She must be up there.

Not bothering to take his ever-so-slightly muddy shoes off, he felt a childish satisfaction at the grubby imprints he left behind him. As he got to the top, he saw that the landing was impressive, an extravagant waste of space that could have comfortably accommodated at least five 'London doubles'. An eighteenth-century daybed, upholstered in a thick coral and white stripe silk, sat regally beneath a large round window at one end of the landing, and opposite a pair of densely patterned six-foot Chinese urns at the other.

All the doors were closed, except for one set of double doors. He walked towards it and looked in. The room was vast – the size of the landing at least – double aspect, with a Chesney stone fireplace against one wall. The walls had been covered with an elegant pale blue Nina Campbell wallpaper, and a button-backed cream chaise sat in front of the window. The bed was an emperor-sized four-poster festooned with monogrammed pillows, and a huge antique walnut blanket box ran along its base.

So this was where his gaoler slept.

Kate had kicked off her ballet pumps and was sitting cross-legged on the bed, her face obscured behind a sheet of glossy hair.

'Are you stalking me?' he inquired, his eyes laughing. 'Because you know I've got one bitch of a lawyer who'll slap you down if you . . . Hey, hey, hey . . . What's the matter?'

She was in floods of tears, her eyes so puffy even her eyebrows had gone red. He crossed the room and sat down next to her, giving her his pristine handkerchief. 'No. Really.' She shrugged and blew her nose noisily.

'It's all right. You keep it,' he smiled when she went to hand it back. 'I only use them once and throw them away anyway.'

He didn't put his arm round her, but his weight on the soft mattress meant she dipped towards him anyway, and their legs pressed together.

He waited for her breathing to become regular again.

'Do you want to talk about it?'

She shook her head.

'Don't blame you,' he said, nodding. 'I'm pretty crap with . . . this kind of thing.' There was another little silence.

'Awful, in fact. People have, in the past, paid me to keep my counsel.' He tailed off.

He inhaled, as though ready to say something, then blew out his cheeks. 'Was it wrong to take their money, d'you think? Bear in mind, I was on a teacher's salary back then. Could hardly buy a bottle of Dom for what I used to bring home in a week.' He shook his head. 'Shocking.'

She started to laugh, then began crying harder.

'Bugger. I'm ballsing up. The thing is – you're distracting me. Making me nervous. I can only really cope with you when you're laughing at me or shouting, or being witheringly sarcastic,' he said in a low voice. 'I'm not used to you being all . . . well . . . womanly.' He put a hand on her knee and she jumped. He immediately withdrew.

'Hey, no! No. I'm not trying anything on. Really. I'm just trying to be a friend. You always do so much for me. I'm trying to return the favour.'

'You pay me a lot of money to do so much for you,' Kate said wryly. 'Don't think it's out of the goodness of my heart.'

He smiled. She was back.

'I wouldn't dare,' he said.

She gave a big sigh, a bigger sniff, and her shoulders dropped heavily.

'Oh dear,' she said, smiling ruefully.

'Oh dear,' he mirrored back.

They looked at each other.

'I thought you had the perfect life,' he said. 'The big job, the loving husband, ME! Game, set and match. What could be wrong in that set-up?' He couldn't resist pushing back a strand of hair which had clung to her wet cheek.

'No baby.'

'Oh.' He sat quietly for a moment, digesting this revelation. He'd never guessed she was the maternal type. She did the killer-lawyer thing so well.

'Husband doesn't want any, then?'

'If only it were that easy. We uh – can't. There's no medical reason why. Everything works. But we've been trying for four years and . . . nothing.'

'What about IVF?'

'Been there, done that. We've just finished our third round, but it failed.' Her voice wobbled.

'Shit. Sorry to hear that.' She looked up at him, fleetingly, acknowledging his effort to have an 'emotional' conversation. Harry swallowed hard. All the tears had left her eyes red-rimmed, but it made her irises blaze like emeralds. She had absolutely no idea, but she had probably never looked more beautiful in her life. He was mesmerized.

'So, uh, what are you going to do now?'

Kate looked back at her hands. 'I want to try again. To keep going. But Monty—' she shook her head. 'He thinks we should leave it there. Says it's getting too hard. We always agreed we'd stop if it didn't happen after three rounds. But now that we're here, I can't give up. I just can't.' Her voice broke and the tears began flowing again.

This time Harry did put his arm around her and she

dropped her head against him – relieved to have found her shoulder at last.

'That's my Kate,' he said, the bass of his voice rumbling next to her ear. 'Ever the fighter.'

Chapter Twenty

Diggory lay curled around the plinth of the Aga, trying to outgloss the enamel with his sleek coat, and occasionally twitching his nose for signs of supper. He had learned over the course of the last month that this was the plum spot for rich pickings. Though the children didn't engage in food fights as such, they may as well have done, given the amount of food that ended up on the floor. And so lying prone, and keeping one eye firmly on the floor beneath the children's chairs, the old dog had mastered a new trick.

Every afternoon, at 4.30, he faithfully trotted down the lane from the Old Rectory to The Twittens. The children left the back door open for him and he would bound in, tail wagging, eyes bright, ready for their excitable welcome. You would never guess they were London kids now. A month previously they'd cowered in his presence as though he were a wolf; now they hung off his neck and ruffled his tummy like farmers' children.

Today he had Hen in tow, which made him rather sulky as she was bound to curb his hoovering instincts. She had settled herself easily at the table (Tor had found an old pippy oak table at the Salvation Army shop which had scrubbed up beautifully), which reduced his chances of an amuse-bouche before dinner to practically nil.

Hen was restless, laying one hand on top of the other, and then switching, before swapping back again. Tor didn't notice. She had her back to her, in companionable silence, and was wiping down the worktops. She'd perfected her baking (as she'd promised herself), and a batch of apricot cookies was baking in the Aga, making Diggory drool like a drunk.

The kettle whistled, and as Tor prepared some piping hot tea Hen couldn't hold it in any longer.

'I was talking to Rhianna Weston yesterday,' she said casually, examining her impeccable nails.

'Hmm, have I met her?' Tor asked distractedly, pulling the cookies out. 'I seem to recognize the name.'

'Oh, yes, you've definitely met,' Hen smiled, her eyes offset by her cornflower blue cashmere twinset. 'The head at the primary. Light brown curly bob, short, voluptuous. Always dresses like it's 1954.'

Tor smiled as she arranged the cookies on the wire rack. 'God, yes! She's a riot. I saw her coming out of the butcher's once wearing a pillbox.'

Hen shook her head and laughed. Tor knew many of the faces in the village now. They had accepted her readily and welcomed her into the community with a warmth and generosity she'd never encountered before. Privately, she suspected her widow status meant she got sympathy votes where once she would have had suspicion, but with Hen Colesbrook on her side as well, taking her to coffee mornings, toddler groups and even a book club (though she hadn't yet managed to get her to the WI), she had soon become one of the best-connected people in the village.

'Yes. We were just chatting about the school. Did you know they're being nominated as a beacon school?'

'Oh? What is that exactly?' asked Tor, surreptitiously tossing a cookie to Diggory, before bringing the piled-high plate to the table.

'It's formal recognition of consistently achieving levels of excellence. A very big deal.'

'Gosh, how wonderful! Honestly! How lucky are the children who get to grow up here?' she asked rhetorically. 'A childhood spent on some of the best beaches in Britain and now a flagship school as well.'

'Yes, well, that's what I was thinking,' Hen murmured, before biting into a warm, unguent cookie.

Tor put the tea-cups down on the table. Impromptu tea breaks like this had become habitual, and she looked forward to hearing Hen's operatic shouts of 'Anybody home?'

They had become close quickly, and with the age gap and Tor's own parents dead, there had been a natural inclination to fall into a surrogate mother-daughter relationship. Tor felt strangely unjudged and relaxed with Hen, and they shared a similar sense of humour, quite often laughing uproariously. But still, there were limits, and though they had never touched upon Hugh, Tor knew Kate must have briefed her fully, for Hen never pried for details. Tor liked that Hen allowed her to deal with her grief privately and didn't try to bully her into emotional showdowns, unlike Cress (who, though sincere, was misguided).

'What do you think of this for curtain material?' Tor asked, pulling up a banner of vintage ticking, which she'd placed on the seat of a chair earlier. 'I got it on eBay for a song. I thought it would look rather lovely in the bathroom?'

'How very original. I think Kate will love that,' Hen smiled warmly, running the fabric between her hands. She'd been a house model for Christian Dior in the fifties, before marrying her first husband, and had exquisite, and well-informed, taste herself.

'You know, you have such a strong eye, Tor. You really should do something professionally. There are far too many people out there with appalling taste. They really do need to be saved from themselves. You may even qualify for some kind of grant. I mean, it would practically be a public service.'

'Oh no. I wouldn't know where to start.'

'Nonsense. Start here! Do up this place.' Hen spread her palms wide, indicating the cottage. Tor had been systematically turning it into a home, a small rug here, a car blanket there, flowers in jam jars in the windows, the children's artwork on the walls. It wasn't chic yet, nor refined. But it had a feeling, a personality that was beginning to take shape.

'Well, you know,' Tor said slowly, 'I was thinking of doing some bits and bobs round about – you know, as a way of saying thank you to Kate and Monty for letting us stay here. It's just so unbelievably generous.'

'Have you decided when you're going back?'

Tor shrugged and looked down at her nails, which were badly bitten. In most other ways, she appeared to have turned a corner. The daily walks and plays on the beach had left her skin glowing and scrubbed – as though the salty breeze itself exfoliated her. For the first time in nearly three months, she had colour in her cheeks again, and there was some volume in her hair. Her new passion for home baking – she felt a deep-rooted need to nourish her family – meant she'd put on five pounds, and although still slender, she'd lost that shockingly gaunt look which had haunted her features. But her nails, bitten so far down as to reveal the angry red top of the nail bed, betrayed the guilt and anxieties that plagued her at night, when she lay alone in the dark without her husband.

'Kate's been forwarding my post up here. Marney's term is due to start in three weeks. I just . . . Oh God, Hen, I just don't know what to do. The fees are astronomical. I don't think I can afford to send her now, but I daren't give up her place. We had to fight tooth and nail, practically from birth, to get it.' She paused, her voice dropped. 'And . . . and . . .'

'What is it?' Hen prompted.

'It's Hugh. He really wanted a private education for the children. I feel I'll be going against his wishes if I don't send her . . .'

Hen leaned forward and placed a comforting hand over Tor's. 'He would understand that your reality is quite, quite different now – at least for the moment. And anyway, any decision you make now wouldn't have to stand for ever. She's only four. Maybe you could send her to prep in a few years, once your business gets going.'

'Business?' Tor asked. 'Oh, that,' she said warily, realizing just how serious Hen was about the interior design idea.

'You should consider it, Tor. You could work from home, work your own hours. And I know you'd do well. Didn't you say that Hunter fellow had bought the Hollywood apartment now?'

Tor nodded.

'So that will be another string to your bow,' Hen encouraged. 'That's two already and you're not even trying yet.' She leant in and whispered, full of mischief. 'I know for a fact that Mo Rawlins has a wallpaper in the drawing room so hideous even the cockroaches die of fright.' She sighed. 'And I really must get round to redoing the library. I haven't touched it since George died.'

George, Hen's husband, had died five years earlier. He'd been a literary agent, so there were literally thousands of books stuffed on to bookshelves, stacked up in towers on the floor and piled high on the many reading desks dotted around the house. Hen kept fretting about the woodworm that was rife in the library and bringing the original Regency bookcases to a state of near-collapse, but she seemed incapable of making any kind of decision that would change how things had been when George was alive. Although she was an independent woman in so many ways, with a thumping social life, Tor often felt her grief was only just below the surface. The wound was still raw and unhealed, and Tor wondered whether other people could see the same loss in her.

She tried to focus her mind on the reality of setting up her own business. It was true – there would be few start-up costs and overheads would be low if she worked from home; she could fit her hours around the children.

'Oh, Hen, you make it sound so easy,' she said finally. 'But setting up my own business doesn't solve the school situation. I won't have the money in time. There's only three weeks till the beginning of term and I'll never get her in anywhere else now. All the places went two years ago. You have no idea how crazy Battersea is.'

'So don't send her there. Send her here.'

Tor looked up sharply.

'What?'

'Yes, they've got a place left. Rhianna told me. It's yours if you want it.'

Tor gawped but couldn't say anything. Her mind was a blur. Stay in Norfolk? She had never considered leaving London. It was in her DNA. She was an urban animal.

Obviously, in the early weeks after Hugh's death, it had been cathartic to escape. To get away from their old life. But she loved London – she loved the bustle, the vibe, the shops, the commons, Big Ben. OK, she didn't love the pigeons or the noisy taxis chuntering down her road at three in the morning, or the traffic, or the congestion charge, or the sadistic traffic wardens on her street, or having the children charging round on their bikes precariously near to the roads, or the dark, narrow houses, or the gardens which were smaller than most people's downstairs loos . . .

She stopped. There seemed to be quite a lot she didn't like, now that she thought about it.

But no! She shook her head. What was she thinking? Had she completely lost her mind? She didn't want to stay in Norfolk and actually set up a life here. There was no doubt she loved it here, but this was only ever supposed to have been a holiday, a break, a chance to get away.

Just because the thought of returning to London made her chest hurt didn't mean it would always feel like that. That was just nerves, right? She had friends there, a life. The memories stabbed her now, but in time she'd be able to smile back at the friendly faces on the mummy runs and not see them as the ghosts of Christmas past. Wouldn't she?

Hen raised her eyebrows, as though reading the tumult in her mind. 'It's at least worth a look, don't you think? Beacon school; rounders on the beach; packed lunches in the dunes. Forget Battersea's waiting lists. If all that came in a glossy prospectus, you'd sign up first and conceive later.'

Tor hid her smile behind her cup of tea, blowing on it carefully, as though snuffing out a candle. Hen was right.

'Well,' she said finally. 'I guess it can't hurt to have a look.'

In the background, Diggory – satisfied that a stealth mission beneath the table wasn't required in the children's absence – gave a long lazy snuffle and, befitting his status as the man of the house, began to snore.

Chapter Twenty-one

'I've just seen Gordon Ramsay bump-parking his Ferrari outside the Hoste Arms,' Kate whispered tipsily as she rejoined Tor at the bar. Tonight was the grand unveiling of Rick Stein's newest venture, his north Norfolk answer to Padstow.

'I know. His wife's just over there, talking to Jools Oliver,' she murmured back, as a clutch of Jennifer's Diary regulars wafted past. Kate had come up for the weekend, after Monty had announced he was staying in the office to catch up with his paperwork and emails. Again.

The whole town had collaborated to celebrate the launch. Bunting was strung up between the horse-chestnuts, leaflets were taped to every window in the high street, and the premises on either side of the restaurant had even been repainted in complementary whispers of willow. The pretty bowed windows flanking the front door had herbs planted in the flower-boxes, sending aromatic wafts along on the sea breeze and enticing pedestrians inside.

'It's not your average provincial backwater, is it?' Kate asked rhetorically, draining her glass. 'I'm so glad we bought up here when we did. The launch of this place is going to push property prices even higher,' she said excitedly.

Tor watched her, trying not to feel jealous of her success.

Kate had had a fringe cut into her hair – which brought intense focus to her fabulous eyes – and she'd swapped her signature diamonds for some bold green glass jumbo-sized beads. Her white wrap dress was neither try-hard, nor showy, yet draped over her supple curves she still managed effortlessly to attract admiring glances from all the men.

A woman in her prime, Tor thought. Although they were both the same age, thirty-two, she didn't put herself in that bracket any more. She'd had her babies. She'd had her marriage. Her time had passed. Babies and grief had aged her, and she felt invisible in this throng of bustling twenty-somethings all looking over their shoulders for the photographer who'd take their pictures and put them on the front page, or the man who'd walk in and change their lives.

Expecting some tepid wine and a few cheese biscuits – she could have kicked herself; what on earth had she been thinking? – Tor had left her jeans on and borrowed one of Hen's Dior jackets from her days as a house model. With narrow arms and a sharp waist, it punched above its weight, but still, the most effort she'd put in was washing her hair. A summer spent at the beach had bleached the mousey blonde tones almost white around her face, and the back sections now glistened like sand.

Kate was knocking back her drinks and greeting most of the people there like old friends (many of whom were, to be fair) and Tor slipped back into being the 'new girl' again. Kate had been coming up to Burnham Market ever since she'd been with Monty, so for over fifteen years. His family had had a holiday home here, but given that they used it for every Christmas, Easter and Summer holiday, when he came back from boarding school, he regarded it more as home than Shropshire where the family 'officially' lived.

Kate gave a little gasp and her eyes twinkled. 'Bloody hell. That sly old dog'.

'Who is?' Tor tried to follow her gaze.

'James White,' she said, nodding towards the door. 'Look – he's with Amelia Abingdon. Now how the devil did he pull her? No wonder there's so many photographers here.'

Tor smiled weakly as her brain tried to process how on earth James had ended up with an A-list star like Amelia Abingdon on his arm. Like Keira Knightley and Rachel Weisz before her, she was the latest Brit to hit the big time in Hollywood, making her name on a small-budget film that had caught the public mood and mushroomed into the biggest-grossing British film of last summer. She had refused the big-bucks blockbusters that flooded in, choosing instead to do a worthy stint at the Old Vic playing Viola in *Twelfth Night* before striking box-office gold again with an acclaimed portrayal of the Duchess of Argyll – she of the pearls and headless lover scandal – which was being spoken about as an Oscar-winning performance.

Her Snow White beauty of long brown hair, apple-round cheeks and red lips that suggested she was only ever five minutes after a kiss not only meant she had her pick of the scripts, but also her pick of the men. And it would appear that of all the men in all of the world, she had chosen James.

Kate and Tor watched the beautiful couple and laughed as they were snared by Henry Rowlins, a terrific bore and significant landowner in the area who – because his fields butted up to the Earl of Norfolk's land – conveyed himself as one of the grandees of the north Norfolk social scene.

James was listening politely, but Tor could see from the

way his mouth kept twitching that his patience was running out.

'Ha, ha!' Kate giggled, letting the alcohol wash over her. 'Look at James. He looks bored rigid. Just wait till I tell Hunter that James has trumped him by pulling Amelia Abingdon. Coralie who? Eh, eh?' She jabbed her elbow playfully into Tor's side.

Tor looked at her blankly. This was the first she'd heard of Harry stealing Coralie from James.

Kate laughed, barely drawing breath. 'I do love teasing him. He's such an awful tart. I call him the man-whore – drives him nuts! But really, what does he expect? He thinks he can have any woman he wants. No, really, he does,' she emphasized, seemingly oblivious to the fact that Tor wasn't actually contradicting her. She wrinkled her nose, head tipped to one side. 'I'll give him credit though, he's not all that bad. There is another side to him too. I mean, he's not a cartoon character, for God's sake!'

Tor wondered whether Kate even knew she was still there, or whether she was just talking entirely to herself.

'. . . I'm only just beginning to see it, of course, but do you know? I do think he's actually quite lonely. I suppose that level of fame might be quite isolating, when you think about it. In fact I really must speak to Cress about it. She'll know more than me.'

She leaned in, swaying a little. 'Having said that,' she said in a low voice. 'I have noticed she's always quite cagey when I try to bring up Hunter with her. I mean, obviously we've both got confidentiality contracts so we're not going to go into any deee-tails, but as old friends you'd think we'd have a bit more of a laugh about him. I mean, we're both working with one of the biggest icons in the world, you know? It's another bond, you'd think.' She sighed. 'But you know Cress – so competitive. It's probably put her nose out of joint that she has to share him with me.'

'Yes, probably,' Tor said quietly, feeling terribly mundane not to be partaking in their power Olympics.

James and Amelia had made their excuses and left Henry Rowlins and were making their way over. Tor felt her stomach tighten.

She hadn't seen James since that day on the beach. There had been an understanding between them then, an instinct, which had comforted her for the first and only time since Hugh's death. But now, with several weeks between them and a Hollywood actress by his side, she felt exposed.

He'd read her correctly and known not to exploit her tears on the beach, so he hadn't called. She didn't want his friendship – or wasn't ready for it, he didn't know which. Maybe too much had happened now for them to ever get past it, for what connected them to each other also estranged them from each other. It was an impossible situation, their shared secret.

'Ooh, how gorgeous to see you,' Kate squealed, betraying her drunkenness all at once. James grinned at her, his eyebrows raised in amusement.

He looked over at Tor, the smile remaining on his face but his eyes searching hers for an indication as to her emotions. She betrayed nothing. Amelia Abingdon wasn't the only actress in the room.

'Hello, James,' she said politely, nodding her head but not leaning in to kiss.

'Amelia, may I introduce you to Kate Marfleet, an old family friend —'

'Hey! Less of the old!' Kate interrupted

'And Victoria Summershill.'

Amelia smiled graciously at them both. God, she was other-worldly. She looked younger than she did on screen, with teeth that seemed unnaturally white. A waiter came over with a tray of edamame beans and stood by their little group. Amelia daintily picked a couple. Tor did the same.

'These are super. Do you know Rick?' Amelia inquired.

'Mmm, not so much,' Kate slurred a bit.

Amelia looked at Tor. She had learnt to carry the conversation until people relaxed and forgot 'who she was'.

'Liar. We don't know him at all,' Tor said, embarrassed. 'We're just here for the free food.'

Amelia laughed, liking Tor's candour. 'Me too. What do you do?'

Tor was just about to reply that she was a housewife when she stopped herself. She wasn't anyone's wife any more.

'Tor's an interior designer,' Kate said proudly before Tor could say, 'Stay-at-home mother.' Tor had mooted Hen's proposal about setting up her own company over lunch and Kate had gone wild for the idea, instantly commissioning Tor to do up The Twittens. Tor had tried to protest. She had wanted to negotiate doing up the house in lieu of rent, at least until she had some money coming in and she could find somewhere of their own to move into. But Kate wouldn't hear of it. Said she and Monty were far too busy with work to be up before next summer and that she couldn't possibly cope with the house in the state it was in. Tor would be doing *her* an enormous favour if she'd accept the commission.

There had been no moving her. Kate was absolutely set on the idea, and so, just that day, Summershill Interiors had been born.

'Oh really?' Amelia said. 'What's your signature look?'

'Um, well, I . . . gosh, I don't know how to sum it up. Am I going to need a catchphrase?' Tor asked, looking at Kate for reassurance, but Kate's gaze was glassy. She'd have to bluff this on her own.

'Well, I guess I'm more interested in giving rooms, houses, a feeling than a look. I want them to look like homes, not show homes.'

Kate kicked her in the ankle. 'Say about your rules,' she said bossily.

Tor looked at her. 'My rules?'

Kate looked dead ahead.

'Uh, yes. Well, I . . . uh, always try to have a . . . um, little bit of black somewhere – be it a trim on a lampshade, or a cushion on the sofa; it's great for adding definition and focus.' She looked to Kate for reassurance – or ideas. No use.

'And I'm a greater believer in – um, defying scale. There's nothing wrong with putting big pieces in a small space. It's more a question of editing clutter.'

'You forgot something,' Kate drawled.

'I did? What's that?' Tor asked, panic-stricken.

'No china figurines. You hate those,' Kate said.

'Yes. Yes, I do,' Tor burst out laughing. 'No excuse for them, ever.'

'Oh yes, me too. Aren't they ghastly?' Amelia joined in, so relieved to have people relaxed with her.

James watched them. Tor looked beautiful – dressed casually in just jeans and a jacket, she made everyone else look overdressed and tarty by comparison. Even Amelia, whose aubergine Vivienne Westwood dress had looked drop-dead glamorous in front of the paparazzi, now looked rather *de trop*.

Tor had put on a little bit of weight since the tennis and her hair suited her so light. She had a light tan that made her eyes dance and her giant freckles were adorable, as though she'd dotted herself with a brown felt tip.

'Tor's really very good,' he chipped in, to Amelia. 'You'd love what she does.'

He felt the weight of Tor and Kate's scrutiny, both of them knowing full well he had no idea how good she was. But he was just so glad to hear Tor was setting up her own business and moving on. He'd been desperately worried about her after learning from Cress that Hugh didn't have life insurance. If he could get Amelia to commission her, it would be a flying start for Tor's business.

'Really? Because obviously I'll be needing . . .' Amelia looked back at Tor. 'I'd love to see your work. Do you have a website?'

'Not yet,' Kate interjected, her antennae alert again to Tor telling the truth. 'It's being rejigged. It kept crashing, it was just getting too many hits.'

'Really?' Amelia asked, impressed. 'Well, that's great. Are you taking on any new commissions at the moment?'

'Hmm, well,' Kate shook her head gravely, every inch Tor's manager. 'She's got a couple of projects to do here, and then you're doing up Harry Hunter's place in LA, aren't you?' Kate asked rhetorically, eager to namedrop.

'Harry Hunter? Really?' James asked, looking agitated.

Tor shifted from side to side, embarrassed that Kate was being so indiscreet. 'Well, yes.'

'You sound busy for the foreseeable, then,' Amelia said.

'Well, there's a bit of a deadline on the LA job, isn't there, Tor?' Kate said. 'But after that you're freer.'

'Oh?' Amelia had an eyebrow raised.

'He wants it done by February,' Tor explained.

'Oscar time. Does he know something we don't?' Amelia smiled.

Tor shrugged, not remotely *au fait* with Hollywood's award season.

'You'll need to watch yourself with him,' Amelia said, smiling, in a confiding tone. 'He's quite the Lothario.'

'You're telling me!' Kate screeched. 'Honestly, the things I've had to squash.' She leant in to Amelia. 'I'm his lawyer. Owwww!'

Tor had kicked her ankle, this time. Kate couldn't afford to be so indiscreet, even in Norfolk. It was time to shut up.

'Are you?' James asked, frowning. 'I didn't know that.'

'Oh yes,' Kate said, feeling terribly important.

'It looks like we've all got stories to tell about him,' Amelia smiled. 'Maybe you will too, Tor.'

'Well,' James said, quickly. 'I really don't think Tor is going to be distracted by a womanizer like —'

'Man-whore,' Kate interrupted.

James looked at her, utterly perplexed and losing his train of thought.

'A man-whore? Where do you get these words?' he asked Kate, as Amelia snorted with laughter. She was having a great time.

'Well, I'd love to meet up with you at a later date and go over some ideas,' she said, when she'd recovered. 'I've just bought a place in Pimlico but I don't really know where to begin with it. And being away on location such a lot makes it difficult to get started. I need someone who can run the project while I'm gone. Would you be interested in having a look?'

Tor shrugged, not sure whether to be overjoyed that her

fledgling business had just been commissioned by Amelia Abingdon, or whether to be dejected over having to work with James's new lover. Her pride wanted her to reject Amelia's request and keep well away from both of them, but she knew there was no way she could turn down an opportunity like this. She hadn't even picked up her spade and she'd struck gold.

'Sure,' she said.

'Do you have a card?' Amelia inquired.

'Um, no. Not on me,' Tor bluffed. 'I wasn't expecting to get any commissions tonight.' At least that bit was true.

'That's OK. I'm away filming in Cairo for the next few months, but James can give you my number when I'm back next in the UK.'

'Sure,' Tor said, looking at him, and wondering why, even with a girlfriend like Amelia Abingdon, his eyes always seemed to scorch her.

Chapter Twenty-two

'Rosie! Is there another bloody postal strike?' Cress hollered through from her office.

'No!' Rosie hollered back.

'And you're quite sure we're getting all our post?' Cress hollered again.

'Yes!' Rosie sighed and looked around her. How could you doubt it? Four sackloads of manuscripts were coming through every day and were stacked in piles around her ankles, ready to sort through and send out to the editors. If only they could lose some; everyone was snowed under.

'Can you just check with everyone again – Oh, you're there.' Cress lowered her voice and looked at Rosie, standing in the doorway. 'I just don't understand why we haven't heard anything. It's been two weeks. That reply has to be somewhere. You've checked everyone's voicemail?'

'Everyone's,' Rosie said solemnly. That had not gone down well with the staff.

'And no one's had a rejection letter? No "Thanks, I'm so flattered but regrettably have decided to sign with"... blah, blah, blah?'

'Nope.' Rosie shook her mousy brown ringlets. Those letters were very few and far between. And anyway, no one would have dared overlook it. Cress had called a staff meeting the morning after first reading the manuscript, pulling all the most senior staff off their projects – getting the chief sub working on the copy, the art director designing the jacket. All the editors had put in calls to trusted agents, putting out feelers to try to establish whether anyone recognized the plot or any of the characters – anything that might yield a name. Cress had – hugely prematurely – even spoken to a scout in Holly-wood, sketching out the preliminary details, and although she hadn't yet released the manuscript to him (though God only knows, she was sorely tempted) he was already excited about the big screen prospects and raring to go.

All the wheels were in motion, all the hard stuff done. She just needed one thing: the sodding author. Someone to come and shake her hand, sign on the dotted line, and drink some fizz. Hell, that was usually the easy part. So what was going on? Why the silence? There was no rejection letter. No acceptance call. Nothing. It was all very odd.

Cress twiddled with the silver Mont Blanc on her desk. There had to be a logical explanation for it. Why send in a masterpiece and then disappear? Maybe he was on holiday? Or had moved? Or what if – what if he had never received Cress's letter at all? She could always write another letter but ... bloody hell, she didn't have time for another two weeks of waiting. She had taken a huge gamble, stalling all her other projects to give this the green light. Time was money. She couldn't afford to lose weeks chasing this, only for the author to remain stubbornly unknown and unfound.

Cress stood up and started pacing, her heels stabbing the parquet flooring. What a bloody farce. She needed to track this author down.

'Rosie!' Cress hollered again. 'How do PO box numbers work?'

There was a pause as Rosie scuttled back in.

'Um. You pay for the PO box number and it gets directed to your actual address. I think. Shall I check?'

'Would you? I need to know whether it goes to an actual address, or whether it gets delivered to a little mail drop place and it gets picked up there.'

'OK, I'll find out. And do you want some tea?'

'You're a star.'

Cress had cleared four emails when Rosie came back into the room, carrying a mug of tea and an armful of paperwork. 'Just got this from the mail room,' she said, carefully placing the mug on Cress's desk before handing over a pamphlet. 'I was wrong. Royal Mail hold it at your local delivery office and you pick it up from there.'

'Shit, that's not very helpful,' Cress muttered. 'What have I got to do? A stakeout? What's the postcode?'

'SW6 2PR.' Rosie knew it off by heart.

'Fulham,' Cress said to herself. 'And I don't suppose anyone in the mail room has contacts with anyone in Fulham's sorting office?'

'It's not likely,' Rosie shrugged, 'But I'll ask. You never know.'

'Yes, do. Thanks, Rosie. Tell them there'll be a bonus for them if they come up trumps,' Cress said distractedly.

'OK. And the first edit's been done on this now,' Rosie added, placing a thick manuscript on the desk. 'There's a few consistency questions for the author, but overall, Harriet says she barely had to touch it. She's got it in at four hundred and sixty-four pages, which marketing say they can cost at twelve ninety-nine.'

Cress picked up the weighty tome, running a manicured finger over the bold black lettering, as though it had been die-stamped on milled paper.

'The Wrong Prince.'
Anonymous.

She smiled. Nobody else in the building realized the extent to which the words within these pages translated into treasure: securing their jobs and guaranteeing her lifelong financial security. With Harry Hunter *and* this author on her list, the venture capitalists would start banging down her door and she'd have done it.

Her gamble would have worked. So she hadn't 'done the right thing' – as asked – but it would have been worth hanging on to him. He who dares wins, and all that.

'Thanks. I'll get my notes back to you.'

She put down the title page. Rosie was almost at the door when she felt ice in the air.

'What the fuck is this?' Cress's tone was stony.

Rosie faltered and looked back. Cress was holding up page two.

'Er, well, that's the dedication page.'

'I know that! Where did you get it from?'

'It was in with the original manuscript. Why? Is something wrong?'

Cress looked down at the bold black print. How could she have missed it?

It read: *'For Brendan Hillier.'*

Yes, something was definitely wrong.

Chapter Twenty-three

The letter, printed on ivory and embellished with an ornate crest, lay on the bed, floating up with each of Harry's jubilant thrusts, fluttering back down beneath Emily's ecstatic sighs, before finally slipping to the floor as the bed trembled with their mutual climax.

'You are one fine filly, Miss Brookner,' he said, rolling off her and jumping up. Emily watched him snatch a towel off the back of the chair and march into the shower.

She stretched out silkily on the sheets, feeling them smooth away beneath her. Her eyes ran around the room, clocking the Cartier carriage clock, the Asprey crystal schooner that he used as a paperweight, that strange Buddha's head thing. Everything was familiar to her now. It was becoming home. She'd slept here with him every night since their reunion dinner, although he was exasperated by her refusal to accompany him to public events or go out to restaurants or clubs with him.

'Why?' he kept asking. 'I want to show you off to the world.'

'I'm not ready,' she kept telling him. The round-the-clock presence of the paparazzi meant she'd be exposed within a day. 'My parents would recognize you, and I haven't told them – how can I? Anyway, people from school might ask questions, or remember things and put two and two together,' she'd warn. So they kept things under wraps. 'Only for a while,' Harry kept saying. But she made sure he always came home to her every night. She knew better than to let a man like him out of her sights for too long.

She heard the water turn off. He sauntered back in, naked and lightly towelling his hair, before shaking out his curls like a golden retriever after a long, muddy walk.

'Why exactly is this invitation so special?' Emily asked, bemused, as she extended a balletic leg into the air. 'You get invited to speak at events all the time. And you never accept any of them. What's so great about this?'

'Are you kidding? It's the Oxford Union. No one turns them down. It's the ultimate accolade. The stamp of credibility, babe.'

His eyes ran down the length of her leg.

'I think the world knows you've made it, Harry,' she smiled.

'The critics would disagree with you,' he said, his eyes darkening. 'They've mauled the last two books. They treat me like some kind of one-trick wonder. It fucking pisses me off.'

Emily brought up her other leg so that both were in the air, then she slowly opened them wide and looked straight at him, between them.

'Well, as long as your fans adore you,' she purred. 'That's all that matters.'

He dropped his towel and crossed the room. Standing between her legs, with an impressive hard-on between his, he grabbed her ankles.

'Come with me,' he said, his voice thick.

Emily shook her head.

'What? To listen to you lecture a load of spotty teenagers?

I don't think so. That's not what I call showing a girl a good time.'

'I always show you a good time,' he said, rubbing his thumbs around her ankle bones, his voice fading as he dropped his head and took a perfectly unmanicured toe in his mouth.

Her eyes closed with heady pleasure as he sucked on it, before running the tip of his tongue along the arch of her foot and down her calf, to the weak spot behind her knee. Her leg bent involuntarily and he dropped to his knees, moving oh-so-slowly, nibbling and teasing her inner thigh with fleeting kisses which were so close to where she wanted them to be, and yet not quite close enough.

He let her luxuriate in the exquisite agony of not having what she desired.

'Are you having a good time now?' he murmured.

'Yes, yes,' she said, her fists clenching, barely able to speak.

'And you'll come with me?'

'Yes, yes, I'll come,' she panted, grabbing his curls.

And sure enough, three minutes later, she did.

Twenty minutes after that – and another cold shower – he was whizzing over Chelsea Bridge in his favourite car, the blue Maserati, the one Kate had said she liked. He liked taunting her with it.

Emily stood, naked, on the balcony and watched him go. She was something of a pin-up to the local boatmen now, and would saucily wave back when they called up to her appreciatively. Harry kept joking that rents on the house-boats opposite had quadrupled since she'd moved in.

She saw the sun glisten on his hair, trying to match the

gold that gleamed from him. He was a rare catch, an incredible lover. She knew she was a lucky girl.

But not lucky enough.

She turned back into the apartment and wondered where to try next. The bookshelves had yielded nothing, there was no safe on the walls, in the wardrobe or inside the desk. There was no loft hatch into the ceiling. She'd even looked for trapdoors beneath the rugs. All she'd found in the bedside cupboards was some coke and a stash of porn mags, plus an interesting collection of home-made sex videos. She'd watched most of them, but although she'd seen two major Hollywood actresses, a clutch of socialites, some schoolgirls still in their Knightsbridge uniforms – and now knew his entire sexual repertoire – she appeared to have gone unrecorded. She didn't know whether to be insulted or not.

She sat on the corner of the bed and sighed. It was like looking for a needle in a haystack. He had homes all over the world – it could be in New York, Gstaad, the Bahamas. Or what if he had a safety deposit box? With his wealth, he probably had all manner of . . .

Absent-mindedly admiring her taut reflection in the floor-to-ceiling mirror opposite, her eye caught sight of the letter peeking out from beneath the bed, next to her foot. She bent down and picked it up. She read it slowly, word for word, and then read it again.

'Oxford Union . . . debate . . . celebrity . . . new religion . . . November 18th . . .'

And then she saw it. What she'd been looking for.

It was addressed to him personally. But not here. The address was Langdale Gardens, Kensington.

And suddenly the personal vacuum in this impressive, awe-inspiring bachelor pad made sense: the impersonal starry photos, the absence of family mementoes, the matchy-matchy trophy antiques chosen for him by a personal shopper – this wasn't where he lived. It was where he partied – his shag pile, she thought wryly.

She smiled and tossed herself back on to the rumpled silky sheets, the letter wafting dreamily back to the floor.

She was on to him.

Kate was reading the *Mirror* at an outside table at Oriel in Sloane Square when she heard Harry pull up. She didn't need to look up to know it was him. She knew perfectly well that he revved the V8s just that little bit harder when he saw her.

She kept reading, knowing it would wind him up to arrive unnoticed (well, by her anyway). There was a minute's pause as he gathered his jacket and sunglasses, and surreptitiously checked his appearance. Then she could tell by the clamour of teenagers and Chelsea blondes suddenly teetering along the pavement for autographs that he had got out of the car. She kept reading. It was eight minutes before he made the ten-yard swagger to the table.

'Would you prefer to go inside?' she said, looking at the shiny tips of his oxblood brogues. Slowly she raised her eyes to meet his. He was grinning at her.

He enjoyed their games immensely.

'I think we'd better. It might be a Health and Safety issue if we don't.'

Kate rolled her eyes as she picked up her bag.

'Gosh, how dreadful it must be to know that you're risking the very lives of your fans, every time you pop out for lunch,' she said deadpan, motioning to the Maitre d' for a table at the back.

The restaurant went quiet as they glided through, and Kate couldn't help but feel a thrill at being so envied by every woman in there for lunching with Harry Hunter. She shimmied into the chair he held out for her, putting her briefcase on the floor next to her feet and picking up a copy of the menu.

'She'll have the chicken risotto. I'll have the fillet steak, rare. And bring up a bottle of Pétrus,' he said, all before he'd sat down.

He looked over at Kate, whose eyebrows were up on the ceiling.

'Actually, I feel like the snapper today,' she said contrarily. She didn't want the fish at all, but she'd be damned if she'd let him predict her.

He looked at her, his eyes dancing with amusement.

'No you don't.'

'Yes I do. I'll have the snapper,' she said smugly to the waiter.

Harry reached into his pocket and took out a fifty.

'That's for bringing my partner the risotto.' He was not a man used to being contradicted.

The waiter inclined his head and left them together. Kate closed her mouth, aware she looked like she was catching flies.

'Partner?' she inquired, changing tack. 'What? As in business?'

'As in crime,' he smiled winningly.

'You're the only criminal here,' she retorted.

'Not necessarily. I'd say it's a crime you won't let me pay for lunch.'

'This is a business meeting. We pay.'

'But I'd like to buy you lunch. Let's make it social.'

'Let's not,' she said witheringly. 'And don't worry. We'll bill the cost back to you somewhere down the line,' she smirked.

'You can't blame me for wanting to get to know you a bit better. We work so closely together. And anyway – I've been thinking about you a lot since Cress's kid's party.'

'Her name's Lucy,' Kate said, trying to change the focus of his point. She was shocked that he'd brought it up. Now that there were chinks in her armour – Monty, hiding from the exhaustive IVF arguments, had practically moved into the office – she had to be on her guard. She couldn't afford to get into a situation where she shared genuine intimacy with Harry.

'. . . And I'm fine, thank you. A random moment of weakness. But you were very sweet. It shan't be forgotten,' she smiled patronizingly. 'I shall be sure to put in extra hours being cruel to the *Sun* on your behalf this week.'

He couldn't help but smile. She was expert at deflection.

'Is Monty coming to the cricket this weekend?' he asked, sitting back in his chair, watching her reaction. A charity cricket match – an annual event – was being played at a schoolfriend's estate in Cornwall. The Old Etonian team played the locals, followed by a lavish party that night. Harry was underwriting this year's do, and had brought *Tatler* on board, ostensibly to promote the chosen charity but in reality they'd promised him the cover, an eight-page spread and gratuitous references to his new book.

Kate looked at him. 'Of course. Why wouldn't he? He's looking forward to it enormously.'

Harry gave a tight smile. 'Good. I'd like to get to know him better. Maybe he can give me some tips on handling you.'

He smiled boyishly.

Kate rolled her eyes and tried not think about him handling her.

'D'you want me to pick you up? I'm choppering down.'

'We're good, thanks. Shall we get down to business?'

Harry leaned in. 'I thought you'd never —' He was cut short by her stern look. 'Absolutely.'

'What's up with Emily?' she asked. 'I have yet to see a single picture of her with you.'

Harry shook his head.

'I know. I can't get her to go out with me.'

Kate tilted her head to the side.

'Aaah, what millions teenage boys would pay to hear those words coming from you.'

'What I mean is – I can't get her out of bed. She just wants to stay in the whole time.'

Kate nodded sarcastically.

'It must be terrible,' she said.

The waiter arrived with their bottle, just as Harry narrowed his eyes at her. He inspected it, swilled it around his glass and took in the bouquet. 'That's fine,' he nodded to the waiter.

They waited for him to leave.

'Well, you need to get her out of the house soon. It can't be that difficult, surely? Has she said anything else about money or courts recently?'

Harry shook his head.

'No. It's all gone very quiet on that front. She wants to shag, not sue. She seems very satisfied with what she's got.'

'I'm sure she does. But the trick is keeping her satisfied, Hunter. Are you sure you can do that? Or are you running out of tricks? You don't usually play a long game. And for as long as you don't have any public evidence of a legitimate relationship between the two of you, she can still take you to court. I can't believe I'm going to say this, but I actually want to see you in the redtops.'

Harry watched her. He found her intensity, her focus, absorbing. He realized she was waiting for him to respond.

'She keeps banging on about her parents not knowing.' He rolled his eyes. 'But the Oxford Union have invited me to address them in a couple of months. At the very least, she's said she'll go with me to that.' He looked for signs that she was impressed by this honour.

There were none.

'Well, I hope so, Hunter. Because otherwise your only saving grace is going to be playing that sex tape to a jury. And you'd better be as impressive between the sheets as all your kiss-and-tells say you are.'

'Oh, I am,' he smiled. 'Don't you believe everything you read?'

'Never.' She caught the waiter's eye and he came back to the table. 'Waiter, let's be clear. *I'm* paying. And I'm having the snapper.'

Chapter Twenty-four

Watching from the window, Cress bet that the curvy brunette wearing the sunray-pleated skirt wished she'd chosen her white jeans instead, as the rotor blades from their landing helicopter whirled the air around her and whipped her skirt over her pretty head.

There was a roar of appreciation for her pert brown bottom and skimpy pink thong from inside the clubhouse, and ten seconds later Cress burst out laughing as she watched the girl's amorous boyfriend dash out of the pavilion and start chasing her across the square.

It was 1.20 p.m. and she and Tor were late. Unexpected fog had delayed their departure, but Harry – who had come down the day before and sent the chopper back for them – had ensured that their party started early in the VIP lounge with a couple of bottles of Cristal.

The co-pilot jumped out athletically, long before the blades came to a stop, and helped Tor and Cress down, just as a welcoming party rushed over the grass to greet them.

Tor looked around her. The cricket pitch was immaculate – even after choppers had been landing on it all day long – and bordered on all sides by a deer park. She searched for a sixteen-point stag to complete the vision of perfection, but none was forthcoming. Given the noise, though, she supposed she couldn't blame them for hiding.

She went to grab her bag, but someone picked it up for her.

'Tor! You're looking as lovely as ever.'

She looked up. Guy Latham.

She felt herself stiffen. Though she didn't know whether or not he knew about Hugh and Julia's affair, he'd introduced them. He'd started it all off.

'How are you, Guy?' she shouted over the din. 'I didn't know you were going to be here.'

'Ah, you know me,' he smiled. 'Hang around everywhere – like a bad smell.'

Don't you just, she thought.

He walked her up to the clubhouse. Glazed double doors led into a large open-plan room with a kitchen and two dressing rooms leading off it. A veranda ran the length of the building and it had been freshly painted white – no doubt in anticipation of the photographers this weekend. *Tatler* was covering the match for its November issue.

There must have been over eighty people gathered there, but she couldn't see the trees for the wood and no individual faces jumped out at her.

'Here. Let me.' Guy dropped her bag and barged through the scrum, getting her an iced and very minty Pimm's from the trestle table. She sipped it gratefully. It was baking today. It might be the first weekend in September, but it was a scorcher.

'Is Laetitia here?' she asked politely, hoping she wasn't.

'Over there,' he nodded. 'Tish!' he called.

Laetitia turned, hitting just the right WASP note in khaki linen, her face falling ever so slightly, though the smile stayed on, when she saw Tor. She nodded her head in greeting and gave a little wave from across the room, but she made no effort to move. Tor realized instantly that she wasn't important or impressive enough to warrant that.

A shadow fell across her and she looked up into a blazing halo.

'You probably don't remember me,' Harry smiled assuredly. 'I'm Harry Hunter. We met at Cress's party earlier in the summer.'

Tor didn't know whether to laugh or cry. Laugh at the supreme irony of Harry Hunter being remotely forgettable; or cry at the fact that the night she'd first met him – exactly seventy-eight days ago – was the night her husband had died. Not that he knew that.

'Hello again, Harry,' she smiled, offering a hand. 'I'm Tor Summershill. I'm your —'

'I know exactly who you are. Cress has told me everything. You're the woman who's going to bring taste into my life.'

Tor smiled at him, quizzically.

'Well, I guess so, yes.'

'And I believe her. I must say you do look very, very tasty,' he smiled wickedly.

Oh. My. God, Tor thought. Harry Hunter's flirting with me.

'Jesus, mate.' Guy jabbed him in the ribs with a sharp elbow. 'Do you ever turn it off? You're like a leaky tap with that stuff.'

Harry laughed. 'Just playing to type,' he grinned. 'I don't want to let anyone down. They have such deliciously low expectations of me.'

'Anyway,' he said more seriously, looking back to Tor, 'we

shall definitely have to get together and spank – I mean, thrash – out the finer details of the project before tomorrow.'

'Harry,' Cress said, joining the group and kissing him on both cheeks. 'You're behaving yourself, I trust.'

'Yes, Mummy,' he smiled.

Cress rolled her eyes and looked at Tor.

'Shall we go and find our rooms?'

Tor nodded quickly, eager to get away.

'See you later,' she smiled.

'You can be sure of it,' Harry said, watching her go, his eyes travelling down her slender back and toned rump. He had a good feeling about this weekend.

A golf cart took them up the lane from the pavilion, winding around the glorious grounds, before turning into a clearing and pulling up outside the Lodge. The building was humble compared to the grand scale of the main house, which Tor had googled online the day before. That came with Doric columns, Adam fireplaces and a Capability Brown landscape. But still, the hunting lodge was larger than your average country house. It had an oversized roof with eaves cut in, and was rendered with a dark brown clapboarding that, had it been painted pale blue, would have looked perfectly at home on the Hamptons coastline.

The front door sat centrally in the building, with gigantic stone hunting dogs on either side. They walked in. Despite the late summer heat, it was cool and dark. The floor was laid with stone flags and an impressive fireplace took pride of place in the hall. The sixteen-pointers Tor had looked for earlier in the park were clearly all here and not frolicking in the grass, their heads lined along the wall and up the stair-case, which divided like a candelabra.

To the left of the hall were rows upon rows of welly sticks, hooded with pairs of dark green Hunters in every size. Off to the right was a large partner's desk with a Lalique vase of garden roses and a red leather visitors' book open on it.

Cress signed it first with a flourishing hand, then Tor, her signature looking tremulous and shaky by comparison. She couldn't help but feel intimidated by all the shabby grandeur.

'Come on,' Cress said, consulting the paperwork Harry had given her. 'We're sharing. Our room's this way.'

They bounded up the stairs and down the corridor, which was lined with a dark green damask, passing five or six doors before Cress stopped.

'This is ours,' she said.

A brass plaque on the door read 'Turlington'.

Cress unlocked the door with a heavy-looking key and they stepped in. The floor was covered with a rust and grey tartan rug, mainly obscured by the double bed on the other side of the room, and two wing chairs were arranged around a fireplace. A door on the same wall as the bed led through to an en-suite.

'Home sweet home,' Cress sighed.

'Is Kate here yet?' Tor asked, lugging her bag on to the bed.

'No. She and Monty are coming down after lunch. She had to go into the office first.'

'They'll be ages if they're driving down after lunch.'

'They're not driving,' Cress said lightly. 'Harry's sent his helicopter back for them.'

'Gosh. He's very . . . generous with it, isn't he?' Tor said. She'd never been in a helicopter before today, and had been thrilled and terrified at the prospect in equal measure.

'Oh yes, he's quite the benevolent billionaire. Anyway, he can afford it,' Cress said.

'I guess.' Tor flopped on the bed, arms outstretched. 'There seem to be lots of families and wives here. I should have brought the children. Why didn't you bring Mark and the kids?'

Cress was bending over a handsome set of Georgian drawers, putting away her clothes.

'Ugh, what a hideous thought. This is work, Tor. I can't have the kids running around everywhere. And Mark wouldn't come down without them, you know what he's like. The weekend's the only time he really gets to be with them. But that's fine.' She stood up and shrugged. 'It's only twenty-four hours. They'll survive without me.'

Tor worried that was probably precisely the problem.

There was a knock at the door.

'Come in,' Cress said.

It was the porter who'd driven them up.

'The match is starting in twenty minutes. Would you like me to drive you back?' he inquired.

'Oh, yes please. Can you wait for ten while we quickly freshen up?'

He nodded his assent and they took it in turns using the bathroom, changing into fresh clothes. Cress shrugged on a short navy piqué tennis dress; Tor stepped into a red-and-blue-printed jersey dress with fluted cap sleeves and shirring at the shoulders that pulled open the front and made her breasts look full and peachy – for once.

As they trundled back down through the trees, Tor glimpsed a herd of fallow deer, well away from the cricket pavilion. Just as well, she thought. Cricket balls could do serious damage. She wondered whether any of the heads on the wall at the Lodge came to be there from sustaining grave cricketing injuries, rather than lead shot.

A group of green-and-white-striped deckchairs had been opened out in front of the veranda, looking like a flotilla of yachts in Cowes harbour, and were gradually filling up with lithe, tanned bodies.

Cress and Tor grabbed another drink each and sat down. The men had changed into their whites and were standing in a gaggle on the pitch, tossing a coin.

'I know everyone goes on about men in uniform,' Cress murmured, 'but give me a bloke in cricket whites any day of the week.'

The OEs won the toss and opted to bowl first. Harry, naturally, was the fast bowler. Tor felt sorry for the batsman stepping up to him. Stocky, with a tummy that protruded over the waistband of his trousers, a ruddy complexion and a handlebar moustache, he was as far from the glistening, hard-muscled Adonis hurling a ball at 90 m.p.h. at him as it was possible to be.

She looked around at the other guests. Laetitia Latham was still holding court, talking to two brunettes whom Tor vaguely recognized.

'Cress, do you know the women Laetitia's talking to? They seem familiar to me.'

Cress twisted in her chair.

'Umm, mmmm. I know what you mean. But I can't place them off the top of my head. Give me a few minutes. It'll come to me.'

They watched the action on the pitch. Despite the batsman's inferior presentation, he proved a formidable player and managed thirty-two runs before Harry bowled a yorker that caught him LBW.

The second batsman – same belly, rough hands and a receding hairline – walked on to polite, slightly patronizing applause which died when he promptly hit a huge six off the first ball. His second sliced deep to cow corner and had the OEs running like billy-o to stop him before he ran a third.

A player in the deep cast an impressive flat throw that covered the outfield, and was caught by Guy Latham at the bowler's end to stop the runs.

'Thank God for that!' Cress said. 'We'll be out here all night if they carry on scoring runs like that.'

Tor shaded her eyes and tried to see the deep fielder more clearly.

'It was the tennis,' Cress whispered.

'Huh?' Tor said, not paying the least bit attention.

'Yep, definitely. I remember her glasses.'

Tor turned and looked at her. Cress widened her eyes and looked at Tor as though she were an idiot.

'You asked me who those women were? They were sitting next to James White at the tennis.'

'Oh. Were they?'

'Right before you slugged him,' Cress wanted to add, but didn't.

Tor looked over at the two women. They were still chatting to Laetitia. A couple of young boys were chucking a cricket ball at each other nearby.

'I wonder if one of them is his girlfriend,' Cress hissed. 'Now that Coralie's out of the pictu—'

'They aren't,' Tor said tersely.

Cress shifted in her seat and looked at her.

'How do you know they're not?' she frowned.

'Because Kate and I saw him in Burnham a couple of weeks ago. He's with Amelia Abingdon.'

Cress's jaw dropped.

'No!'

'Yes.'

'No!'

'Sly old dog.'

'That's just what I said.'

They both looked up. Kate was standing in front of them, looking achingly glamorous in a floppy chocolate wide-brimmed hat and white linen palazzo pants.

'You're here,' Tor cried.

'We didn't hear you,' Cress said. 'Where's the chopper?'

Kate inclined her head. 'Up at the main house. Well, we couldn't very well interrupt play, could we?'

They all kissed their hellos, and Kate sank down into the chair next to Tor, as Monty jogged over with a drink for her.

'Hi girls,' he said.

'Are you playing?' Cress asked absently.

'No!' he crossed his fingers one over the other in the sign of the cross. 'I didn't go to Eton, foul fiend.'

Cress laughed.

'Sorry, hon. Forgot. Try not to feel inferior.'

'Thanks,' he said, bashfully. 'So what's going on? What's the score?'

'No idea! And who bloody cares?' Cress said. 'I was just finding out that James White has scored with Amelia Abingdon.'

'Amelia?' Monty said questioningly. 'No way. They . . .' A cricket ball whistled past, narrowly avoiding his head. 'Hey! What's the bloody idea?'

The ball hit the strut of the pavilion behind him and trickled back to his feet. He turned around and picked it up, just as the two young boys ran over.

'We're so sorry, sir,' said the younger, dark-haired one. 'We didn't . . . Uncle Monty! It's you!'

'Max!' Monty said, picking the boy up and spinning him around. He put him down and gave the older boy – probably sixteen or so – a solid handshake. 'How are you, Billy?'

'Very well, thanks, sir,' Billy nodded. Tor admired his manners.

'Are your mothers here?' Monty asked, looking around, his eyes coming to rest upon them as he said it. 'Lily! Anna!' he called over.

The two brunettes both broke into wide smiles when they saw him and skittered over, leaving Laetitia alone.

Kate got up as elegantly as she could manage from the deckchair and greeted the two women with friendly kisses. It was hard to know which one to look at first. One was a lissom five foot ten in a silk tea dress, the other had dynamite curves and a glossy tan. They made a formidable pair.

Monty stood there with a heavy hand on each of the boys' shoulders.

'You realize your boys damn near killed me with a cricket ball just now,' he teased.

The taller brunette looked at Billy scoldingly. 'Don't tell me you missed, Billy. How long have we been practising for? I told you, you may only get one shot.' She looked back at Monty with a wicked look in her eye and winked.

They all guffawed.

'Charming!' Monty said, ruffling Billy's hair.

There was a sudden rush of activity as gallon teapots and platters of cucumber sandwiches were brought out on to the tables. It was tea-time. The players jogged over, jostling the group slightly as they tramped through to the dressing rooms to take off the hot, heavy kit.

'Cress, Tor,' Monty said after they'd passed. 'I'd like you to meet Anna – who is Max's mother – and Lily – who is Billy's mother. Ladies, Cress and Tor are friends from London.'

The two brunettes smiled. 'There is actually more to us than being the boys' mothers,' Lily said dryly.

'I'm sure,' Tor smiled back, as they shook hands. 'We get it all the time too.'

Monty groaned. 'Urgh. Mothers' etiquette. I can't do anything right.'

'Once you accept that, you're halfway to a quieter life,' said a voice behind them. They all turned. 'I see everybody's already met.'

James was standing there, his cap in hand and raking a hand through his dark hair. His cheeks were flushed and his sweaty shirt, streaked with red, was clinging to him in the heat.

'Daddy!' Max cried. 'You did such a great throw. It was awesome.'

'Yeah,' Billy agreed. 'It was wicked, Uncle Jamie. Can we do some practice later?'

'We'll see,' James smiled, looking up from the boys and locking eyes with Tor. He shrugged, indicating his dishevelled appearance.

'I would kiss you hello, but I fear it would be a far less pleasurable experience for you, than for me.' He looked at the group, trying to include them all in the comment, before finding his gaze magnetically brought back to Tor again.

'Uh, so . . . sorry! Sorry!' Cress said, waving her hands in the air. 'Run me through this again. Max is your son, James. And Anna, you are Max's mum, so that means you are . . .' She looked over at Anna, who was busy watching James and Tor. She had seen the look he'd given her.

'Anna is my, er – my ex-wife,' James said awkwardly. 'And Billy is my nephew. And Lily here is my little sister.'

'And so is your husband playing?' Cress asked Lily.

Lily shifted position. 'No. He didn't go to Eton.'

'Ha! Monty neither,' Cress snorted. 'They can form a rival gang.'

Tor couldn't help but sneak a look at Anna, and was surprised to find her already staring back. So she was the ex-wife. She knew she'd recognized her. She'd seen her photographed with him in society magazines a few years back.

Anna tipped her beautiful head to one side. 'Do you live in London?' she asked, her voice as silky and mellifluous as a negligée.

'Not any more. We've just moved to north Norfolk.'

'How interesting. That's where we are. Where are you exactly?'

'Burnham Market.'

Anna smiled quietly. 'We're in Burnham Overy Thorpe.' The two women weren't more than three miles from each other, but Tor could feel that an invitation to coffee would not be forthcoming.

'Gosh,' Tor said, struggling for something to say. 'There's a super pub there, isn't there?'

'Yes,' Anna smiled tightly. 'But we don't go there. My husband and I.' Tor felt chastened. Of course she didn't. She didn't look like a pub sort of woman.

Tor decided to follow Cress's lead. 'Is your husband here? Your new one, I mean?' Christ! That had come out wrong.

Anna looked at her coolly. 'He's coming back from the States. He'll be here tonight. And your husband – is he here?'

A piercing silence fell over the group. Cress, Kate, Monty,

James – all of them hesitated over whether to speak for Tor, or let her say it herself.

Tor got in first.

'No. He's not . . . My husband is . . . he died, a few months ago.' She managed to keep her voice consistent, although she couldn't maintain eye contact.

Ever alert to her friend's distress, Cress stepped in to divert sole attention from Tor.

'So, boys – which one of you can show me how to do a proper serve?'

'A serve? But we don't have any tennis balls here,' Max replied earnestly.

'That's OK. We can use this cricket ball.'

Billy laughed. 'You'll break your wrist trying to serve with that.'

'I don't think so, Billy. I'm a tough old bird. Just ask your uncle. Monty – give us a hand, would you?'

Chapter Twenty-five

The day beat on under the hot blue sky. The women lathered themselves with suntan lotion and made like onions, gradually peeling off layers; the men stood around drinking beer and either reddened or tanned before Cress's eyes, depending upon their colouring. James was one of the brown ones; poor Monty was not. His hair was cut in such a close crop; Kate kept trying to rub spots of cream into his scalp but he seemed irritated by her fussing and moved away to chat to the players.

The OEs had bowled the Locals out for two hundred and nine; and after tea, they swapped sides, so that all but two of the OEs were constantly in the bar. Cress reckoned that was why they'd chosen to bat last – nothing to do with strategy and knowing what you were running against.

The ambient noise level was steadily increasing as the beer took hold, and she saw a few couples randomly straggling off for various mini-breaks before casually returning twenty minutes later. She wondered what Mark and the kids were up to. He'd said he was going to take them to Richmond Park for a picnic – said they'd think of her if they bagged a deer. Ha bloody ha.

Cress's mobile rang and she moved away from the group to get better reception. Nobody noticed. Lily and Kate were catching up on last summer on the beach in Norfolk, and Anna and Tor were now getting on famously, discussing the local schools and where to go for the best langoustines and who stocked Joseph. Everything but James, in fact.

'Yes?' Cress yelled into the receiver.

'Cress? It's Rosie.'

'Yes, Rosie?'

'Sorry to bother you on the weekend, but we've had a development.'

Cress pressed the phone closer to her ear. 'Go on,' she urged.

'Joe in the post room has got a mate who works from Fulham. He's not in the sorting office, he works in the special deliveries section, but he's managed to get some info for us.'

'Go on, go on,' Cress said, stalking the grounds like a ghillie.

'Well, it seems the address given is not actually a Royal Mail PO box number. It's a private company. He thought it looked like one from a place called the Box Shop. They're based in Fulham too, just off the Munster Road. I've got a number. Do you want it?'

'Yes, but give it to me slowly. I'm in the middle of grass. Not a fucking biro in sight. I'll have to punch it direct into my phone.'

She took down the number, one digit at a time.

'Thanks, Rosie. I don't know what I'd do without you. And tell Joe, on the QT, there'll be a thirty per cent mark-up in his take-home next month. I'll speak to accounts on Monday.'

'Sure thing. Have fun.'

Cress hung up and looked back at the party. She'd

wandered several hundred yards away already, and decided to go for a walk. She needed to think about her next move. She had to close in on this author, find out who he was and find out the nature of his relationship with Brendan Hillier. Was the dedication page in *The Wrong Prince* some kind of threat? Was the author letting her know they knew about her and Harry Hunter? Because if it was, those three words on that page had changed everything, changing its status from the book that could save Sapphire to the book that could take them down. After all, she hadn't done what she was supposed to with Harry. She'd been greedy, gone for the money, looked the gift horse in the mouth. She could be implicated with him. She had to find out who was behind this new book before he made his next move.

She walked along the pitch boundary towards a copse, lost in thought and kicking stray pine cones through the dusty grass, instantly regretting it when a needle rolled into her thong sandals and pricked her toes.

'Ow-ow-ow-ow,' she said, hobbling for a couple of steps, before sitting in a heap on the ground and kicking off the shoe.

'May I assist this damsel in distress?' came a bemused voice.

Cress looked up and saw Harry leaning against a tree, a cigarette dangling insolently between his fingers. He looked like a splendid Robert Redford in *The Great Gatsby* in his kit.

'What are you doing here, Harry? Aren't you up in a minute?'

'Well, I certainly could be,' he smirked, stubbing out the cigarette beneath his foot and sitting himself next to her.

Cress glared at him. They hadn't flirted once since she'd brought up Brendan Hillier. He used sex to corroborate his dominance, and as soon as he'd lost his power over her they had settled into an almost familial role play.

Until now. His eyes ran over her face hungrily, and he pushed a hand through her hair, cupping her cheek. He was huge compared to her, his hands like bear paws, his breath warm against her cheek. He leaned in and kissed her mouth.

'What the hell are you doing?' she demanded, pulling back.

His eyes danced. 'Well. You know those four children you've got?' he smiled. 'This was how they happened.'

He started kissing her neck, his hand moving down to her bare thighs, pushing up the hem of her dress.

'Get off, Harry. Just stop it,' she cried, smacking his hand away and trying to pull away from him.

Barely noticing her protests, he scooped her arms away from beneath her and cradled her down on the ground. He pinned a leg over hers and, with his elbow on the floor, rested his head in his hand.

'Come on, why not?' he said, smiling down at her. 'You know we'd have fun. We were always supposed to – let's be honest. We both wanted it.'

'I did not!'

'You were one little signature away from going into that hotel bedroom with me.'

'It was never going to happen, Harry. I would always have played my trump card if it had come to that.' She pushed him roughly away and sat up. She saw the fire blaze in his eyes. 'I would never cheat on my husband. And certainly not with someone like you.'

'How very noble of you,' Harry muttered under his breath, taking another cigarette from his shirt pocket. 'The thing is,

Cress, do you think your husband returns that particular compliment of fidelity?'

Cress stalled. 'What are you talking about?'

'I'm talking about your husband and the very pretty nanny.'

'Oh, don't be idiotic. That's such a fucking cliché.'

'Doesn't mean it's not true, though,' he said into his cupped hand as he lit another cigarette. He took a drag and exhaled slowly, looking at her through hooded eyes. 'I saw more than enough at Lucy's party.'

Cress watched him, looking for a sign, a muscle twitch, anything that would show he was lying, bluffing her. There was nothing.

'What did you see?' she said quietly.

'I saw that your nanny doesn't like wearing panties. And I saw Mark see it too. Why's he not here by the way?'

'The idea of forty-eight hours with tossers like you didn't really appeal. He's spending the weekend with the kids.'

'Oh yes. Quality time is it? And how about the nanny? Is she *filling in* in your absence?'

'She doesn't work weekends,' Cress said, but her voice lacked edge. He was too close to the bone.

'You sure about that?'

'Fuck off, Hunter,' she said turning away from him.

'Just trying to be a friend,' he said.

'We are not friends,' she spat back.

He sighed. 'You're quite right of course. We're not even business partners. Not in the legitimate sense, anyway.'

'Oh, you want to talk about being legit? That's rich!' she laughed bitterly. 'And anyway, has it really been so bad being signed to me? Has your career nose-dived? Are you in the doldrums? Have the sales bombed? The screenplay talks died? No! I've delivered everything I said I would. Everything I promised you. I've been good to my word.'

'Technically, yes,' he said coolly, almost bored. 'But I suppose it just comes down to the stigma of being signed to a *nobody*. I mean, everybody laughs at you. They call you the Blog Dog – did you know that? Without me, you are nothing. Without me, you have no company. If I go, you go bust.'

'If you go, you go straight to jail, mate,' she hissed. 'And don't be so sure Sapphire relies on you. I'm about to sign someone who'll blow you into obscurity. You'll be lucky to get your name in the Yellow Pages once they're out. And let me tell you, then you'll need to worry.' She jabbed a finger at him. 'You'd better start thinking about what comes after you're disposable. Because you are, Harry! And then what do you think I should do with the information I've got, once you're no longer printing money for me, hmmm?'

Cress stood there, shaking violently, as red in the face as Harry was white. She had said too much, gone too far, threatened him outright.

Harry twitched and shook out a hand which was being burned by the cigarette he'd left smouldering between his fingers. His eyes seared into her.

'Hallo, Hunter!'

Peter Temple, the chap whose family owned Carliffey, the estate in which they were playing, ran up. 'There you are. I've been looking all over.'

He took in the stand-off.

'Ah – sticky wicket?'

Harry turned and looked at him, slapping him on the back.

'Sticky something, if you get my meaning. But keep it to yourself, mate, she's married – doesn't want it getting out.'

Cress flinched. What the hell was he doing?

Peter smiled reassuringly at them both. Same old Harry.

'Of course. Well, the photographer's here. He's asking after you. Wants a shot of the captain in all his glory.'

'And who can blame him?' Harry smiled expansively. He turned to Cress. 'Come on, darling, I'll give you a lift. Your little legs must be tired out.' And before she could so much as gasp, he hoisted her over his shoulder and carried her in a fireman's lift out of the woods and all the way back to the clubhouse, smacking her bottom as they neared and eliciting uproarious cheers from the crowd.

'*Tatler*'s readers will love that,' he whispered to her as he put her down, right in front of the photographer, and kissed her passionately on the mouth.

Cress, who moments earlier had felt hot with the humiliation, grew cold as she realized his game. She looked over to her friends, who were still sitting in the deckchairs, staring open-mouthed in disbelief. She thought she'd never seen them – Tor, James, Monty, Kate, particularly Kate – look so angry.

James stayed at the crease for ten overs, eventually being run out for seventy-six. He waved his bat in salute to the crowd cheering him as he strode off, and kept his eyes dead ahead as he passed Harry gambolling on.

'Good innings, Dad,' Max said, falling into step with his father.

'Didn't embarrass you too much then?' James asked, smiling, stopping at the deckchairs and untying the pads from his thighs.

'Nah. It was all good,' Max said, bouncing the cricket ball from one hand to the other. 'D'you fancy a swim? Mum says we can't go in without an adult.'

James paused, weighing it up.

'I guess we could . . . Oh no!' he shrugged. 'I haven't brought any trunks.'

'I packed your Norfolk ones for you,' Anna said quietly. 'They're in with Max's.'

Tor flicked her eyes quietly between the former couple, unduly irritated by this act of marital consideration.

'Oh go on, Uncle Jamie. Please!' Billy begged.

James laughed.

'Come on then. Monty – d'you fancy it?'

Monty looked at Kate questioningly.

'Yes, I packed yours,' she said wearily. 'They're in the room. And put some sun cream on.'

'Great. I'll see you up there,' Monty said, striding off towards the Lodge.

'Ladies?' James asked, looking at the girls, who were fanning themselves with glossy magazines.

Kate and Lily looked at each other and shrugged. 'Yes, why not?'

Tor could think of plenty of reasons why not – cellulite, jiggly thighs, no pedicure and two weeks from a wax, for starters.

'Come on,' Kate said, taking her by the wrist. 'And you, Anna. You're looking a bit pale. You could do with topping up that tan.'

Anna laughed, resignedly.

They all hopped into two golf carts, with Billy and Max bagging the wheel in each. James jumped in next to Tor, his arm draped around the back of the leather bench. He smiled easily at her.

'Right. Let's go,' he shouted, slapping the back of the front seat, and the two boys revved the carts, racing each other back to the Lodge at a grand speed of 6 m.p.h.

Max won, although it was irrelevant. James had got what he wanted, which was to sit next to Tor and feel her hair tickle his neck as they bumped along the lane.

They all discharged into the Lodge with threats that the last one in the pool was a squashed banana, and Tor shrieked as Billy, Max and James chased her up the stairs and down the corridor.

James caught her, laying his hands on her narrow waist just as she got to her door.

'Turlington,' he read, one arm propped on the door frame. 'So this is where you are,' he said.

'Where are you?' she asked casually, her heart pounding like a jackhammer, and not strictly because of the fifty-yard sprint.

'Evesham, two doors down,' he said.

'Oh!' She took a deep breath. 'Is Amelia coming down later?' she asked lightly.

James frowned slightly.

'Amelia? Er, no. She's in Cairo. Do you want to speak to her about . . . ?'

'No, no. I was just wondering. I'd, er, better change then,' she smiled.

'See you in a bit,' he smiled, taking his arm away and standing up straight.

She slid into the room, suppressing a teenage urge to shriek again, and turned around to face the bed. Cress had come back to the room for a rest after Harry's 'high jinks', as she'd called them, but Tor didn't buy it. She knew Cress better than to think she'd cheated on Mark, but she was intrigued to press her on what had really happened.

Cress wasn't there. Tor walked through to the bathroom – it was empty.

'Cress?' Tor asked, with her hands on her hips.

There was a letter on the mantelpiece, written on Carliffey Estate paper and addressed to her. Tor knew even before she'd read it what it would say.

Darling T,

Can't be arsed to stay here a second longer. Missing the family. Sorry to leave you in the lurch. Send my apologies to all except Hunter. Give him the bird from me and tell him he's a wanker.

Kisses

C.

Tor sighed and folded the letter back into the envelope. Whatever happened, it must have been bad to send Cress back to the bosom of her family. Not much made her run.

She grabbed a red and white polka-dot bikini from the bag and climbed into it, slipping a chiffon kaftan over the top, eminently grateful she'd only had a liquid lunch. Anna, Lily and Kate were gathered in the hall waiting for her when she came out.

'Cress has gone home,' Tor said before anyone could ask. 'Missing the family.'

'What a shame,' Anna said.

'How sweet,' Lily said at the same time.

Kate shot Tor a quizzical look. She knew Cress better than that.

They walked barefoot over the camomile grass, up the lawns in the direction of the main house, and as they rounded a densely planted hedge, which provided both shade and a windbreak, they all gasped at the vision of opulence. The pool was Olympic-sized, with a springboard at the deep end. Steps ran the width of it at the shallow end, and yellow tiles lined the interior, creating dazzling emerald green water. The boys were already in, playing a fiercely contested water polo tournament – James and Max versus Monty and Billy – although no one was keeping score.

The girls billowed out the fluffy towels and arranged themselves on the steamers, fussing with sunglasses, magazines, suntan lotion, the direction of the sun, straps and hairbands.

Tor, who spent eight minutes flapping about, spotted a pitcher of lemon barley only once she'd sat down. She eyed it greedily. The heat, combined with the all-day drinking, had done her no favours and she was parched. She'd already taken off her kaftan and she felt insecure at the prospect of walking around in her itsy-bitsy number. Still . . . everyone was busy reading, dozing and playing. They weren't going to be interested in what she was doing.

She got up and padded over to the table, instantly feeling six pairs of eyes swivel round and follow her.

'Um, does anyone else fancy a drink?'

'Thought you'd never ask,' they chorused.

'I'll go and get some more ice,' said Lily, whose lounger was nearest to the poolhouse and in direct sight of an ice bucket.

'Is there a loo in there?' Kate asked, following her.

Tor stood at the table, pouring and serving for the girls, then placing the other tumblers on a tray and carrying them over to the water's edge.

'Here you are,' she said, kneeling down slowly and trying not to spill the drinks.

Billy and Max went off to practise their dives, but Monty and James swam over, resting on their forearms at the side. With his hair wet, Tor could see that Monty's scalp was clearly burning in the sun. His skin looked scrubbed pink and as shiny as a button. James, on the other hand, had dipped under the water just before he got to the wall, surfacing with his hair pushed back from his face, and looking as sleek as a seal.

'Thanks,' he said, taking a tumbler and grinning up at her.

'Yeah, thanks, Tor,' Monty said.

'Pleasure,' she smiled. 'Um, Monty do you want me to get you some lotion? I've got a waterproof one in my bag somewhere . . .'

'Don't bother!' Kate called from inside the poolhouse. 'He won't be told. Just leave him to it. A nasty dose of sunstroke should be enough to warn him off for next time.'

Monty rolled his eyes and sank beneath the water, still holding his glass.

Tor giggled and shook her head.

'Come on, let's carry on, boys,' Monty called when he resurfaced, placing his glass on the side and swimming to the centre with the ball.

Tor stood up and was just going to walk back to her chair when she heard a long, leery wolf-whistle.

She jumped, startled, and saw Harry Hunter fifty yards away, striding up the lawn to the pool area, pulling off his cricket shirt as he went.

'My god, woman, you look even tastier with your clothes off than you do with them on. And you were streets ahead then,' he said, smiling wolfishly and heading straight for her.

Tor took a step back. 'Hunter' was the word. That man was a predator.

'What are you doing here so soon, Hunter? I'd have thought you'd be on the crease till sundown,' she heard James mock.

Harry looked down and saw his old foe, along with Monty and the boys, in the water. With a quick sweep, he spotted James's glamorous ex lounging around the poolside. He hadn't seen any of them from further down the lawn and had thought he'd spotted an opening with Tor. She was vulnerable, easy prey, he could tell. And Christ almighty, he just wanted to feast right now. His run-in with Cress had left him incandescent and his mood hadn't improved when he'd caught Kate bounding off with White and his friends in the golf carts – the distraction of her departure had seen him bowled out for a duck.

He looked back at James. Even this place wasn't big enough for the two of them. Monty was treading water and tossing the ball casually above the waterline. Harry caught sight of the scar below his ear again. Why did he know him?

Billy raised his hand to receive the ball, utterly uninterested in this adult banter, and Monty threw it to him. They chucked the ball a few times and Max swam over, turning the game into 'Piggy in the Middle'.

'Oh, hello. How's it going, Hunter?' Kate asked, walking out through the doors of the poolhouse. She'd missed his approach to Tor.

Harry's eyes took in her figure in the imposing aquamarine halterneck swimsuit, instantly overwriting the visual impression Tor had made in her bikini. Had Monty not been underwater, he would have punched Harry square in the jaw for looking at his wife in that way.

But Monty was underwater, and anyway, everyone's attention was immediately diverted by a sudden clatter. Lily had followed Kate out of the poolhouse, and the silver ice bucket she had been holding was lying on the floor.

Visibly pale, she stood rooted to the spot staring at Harry, before finally regaining her poise, and without a word, walking over to the pool's edge.

Tor figured he had that effect on people a lot. He was Harry Hunter. And here he was, shirtless and sexy. It was an overwhelming experience.

'Monty,' Lily said bossily, holding out a tube of sunblock. 'Put this on or your wife's going to divorce you on the grounds of irreconcilable pinkness.'

Monty grinned, and Harry watched him swim over obediently and start applying the lotion to his head.

He remembered. They'd had a thing. Monty had been sniffing around her years back.

'Are they still winning?' Kate asked, picking up the ice from the floor and wondering why Harry looked so cross. She'd noticed he hadn't brought Emily along.

'Looks like it,' James smirked.

'White's right, for once. I'm a shit captain. And anyway, everyone's bollocksed,' Harry said, taking his shoes and socks off.

He walked up to the diving board and, without any preamble, executed a brilliant splashless dive, surfacing in between James and Monty. He intercepted the ball mid-air and pounded it over to Billy, before dipping down and swimming the rest of the length underwater.

He pulled himself out of the water by his arms, his trousers dripping wet and clinging to his thighs, just as the *Tatler* photographer jumped out of the bushes and took the shot. 'You're not a fucking paparazzo,' Harry snarled under his breath. 'Ask nicely when you want my picture.'

The photographer nodded silently and backed off.

Harry turned back to the group. 'Anyway, I shan't interrupt. I can see you're all playing happy families, and nobody likes a gooseberry, do they, Kate?' He paused for a beat. 'I'm going to take a shower. Care to join me?'

And without waiting for her answer, leaving his clothes discarded around the lawn, he sauntered back to the Lodge.

Monty gawped like a fish at his retreating back.

'What did he say? Did I just hear right?' Monty looked incredulously at James, then at Kate, then back at James. 'Did he actually stand there in front of me and invite my wife to shower with him?'

'Oh, do shut up, Monty,' Kate snapped. 'Of course he didn't mean it. He's saying it to wind you up. It's what he thinks we expect him to say.'

She watched Harry disappear out of sight. Tor came up and stood next to her.

'What the hell was that all about?' she whispered.

'I don't know,' Kate said pensively. 'He's a bloody sore loser. But that was ripe even by his standards.'

'What's he going on about gooseberries for?'

'Your guess is as good as mine.'

'I think something happened with Cress earlier,' Tor whispered again.

'What? Really? You think they . . . '

'No, no,' Tor dismissed. 'Nothing like that. She wouldn't. But I think something's gone on between them. It's not like her to leave early.'

'No, it's not. I should probably go and talk to him,' Kate said.

'Mmm. He'll listen to you. But I'd give him a chance to cool down. Catch him after dinner. He looks pretty dangerous to be around at the moment.'

Kate snorted. 'That man's dangerous in his sleep.'

Chapter Twenty-six

Everyone had agreed to meet in the drawing room at eight, but Tor felt nervous at the prospect of walking in on her own, now that Cress had gone. She stood on the edge of the bed, trying to get a full-length view of herself in the face mirror. She'd gone for the ivory satin Dolce & Gabbana dress adorned with crimson poppies – the one she'd told Cress gave you fabulous boobs. God knows, after all the weight loss following Hugh's death, she needed as much help as she could get.

She was just getting the last hairpin into position when she heard laughter in the hallway. She let it pass her door, then tiptoed across the room and looked out. A couple she didn't recognize were heading down to the drawing room.

'What are you doing?' Kate asked, looking amused by her cloak-and-dagger act.

Tor smiled sheepishly. 'Looking for you?'

She opened the door wider and Kate ambled into the room. She looked killer. She had on a peach silk strapless column dress with a high split that flashed her thighs, but her auburn hair swung around her shoulders freely and she was in flat white beaded thong sandals.

'Oh God – am I overdone?' Tor asked, her hands rushing to her updo and then just as quickly down to her high heels.

'You sound like a Christmas turkey,' Kate laughed. 'And no. You look gorgeous.'

'You're sure?'

'Positive.'

'Where's Monty?' Tor asked, realizing he wasn't with Kate.

Kate rolled her eyes. 'Oh, don't!' she said crossly. 'He's delirious. Heatstroke.' She shook her head. 'Didn't I say? I mean, I did, didn't I? I spent all day warning him, but no – why listen to me? I'm only the wife.'

'Oh dear,' Tor said. 'Does he need a doctor?'

'Nope,' Kate said, looking out of the window and across the endless acres. 'I gave him some paracetamol and he's conked out.'

Tor grabbed her evening bag. 'Come on. I'm ravenous, aren't you?' she asked, linking her arm through Kate's, and they walked down the corridor together.

'Have you seen Harry yet?' Tor asked in a low voice as they entered the drawing room.

Kate shook her head. 'Been too busy dealing with my sick husband. I'll corner him after dinner.'

The gathering before them looked suitably glamorous, as befitted the grand surroundings. Candles had been lit on every surface and densely cushioned sofas pouffed and plumped up to within an inch of their lives. A silver and rasp-berry coloured silk Persian rug was pinned to the floor by the elegant legs of the Chippendale cabinets and the row of French doors was swung open to reveal a torchlit terrace.

Although the local team had left after beers in the club-house, other halves and non-playing Old Boys who hadn't made it in time for the match had pitched up and swelled the numbers to over a hundred, and Tor was pleased she'd made a reasonable effort for the first time in a long time.

She cast her eyes around the room. Everyone glittered with sun-lightened hair and pearly white teeth, the men looking dashing in bespoke black tie, the women catching the light with sequinned dresses and some pretty impressive jewels. She could see Harry in the middle, with a coterie of stunning girls hanging on to his every word. The chaps didn't seem to mind. Much like with the Prince of Wales, she mused, mixing with Harry Hunter bestowed a golden cachet that exceeded the ignominy of possibly being cuckolded by him.

Champagne buckets were placed conveniently at the arm of every sofa, and a console table had a pyramid of 'Josephine's breast' champagne glasses balanced on it.

'Here, allow me,' James said, joining them at the table as they giggled over Kate's dare of trying to jiggle a glass out from the bottom.

Grabbing a magnum from the nearest bucket, he poured them each a breastful of fizz – which naturally didn't bubble over the top – and led them over to where Anna and Lily were standing. A distinguished-looking grey-haired man with glasses and a rock hard –'squash twice a week' – torso was standing with his arm around Anna.

'Tor, Kate, this is John Brightling, Anna's husband,' James said quickly.

'Pleased to meet you,' Tor said, shaking his hand.

'We heard you'd be here tonight,' Kate said. 'You've been in the States, I hear?'

'Yes. I have a clinic in Palm Beach. I go over twice a month.' He had an odd, mid-Atlantic accent.

'Palm Beach?' Kate said. 'You must be in plastics then?'

'Yes. Good guess,' he laughed lightly.

Kate looked around the room at the legion of highly bred,

high-maintenance women. 'I hope you've brought lots of your cards with you. You've got a captive market here tonight.'

John smiled, nodding.

'Where are the boys?' Tor asked, looking around for Max and Billy.

Lily shook her head. 'They're playing Playstation in their room. A roomful of grown-ups standing around talking can't compete with the attractions of Gran Turismo.'

'Fair enough,' Tor said.

'Where's Monty?' James inquired.

Kate sniffed indignantly. 'Heatstroke.'

James frowned. 'That can be nasty. D'you want me to check on him?'

'Nope. He's fine. He's sleeping now.'

'Well, let me know if I can help. I am a doctor.'

'You've never been any use to me up till now, James,' she smiled dryly.

He inclined his glass towards her. 'Touché.'

A gong sounded and everybody was called to sit for dinner.

Tor was alarmed to find she was seated between Harry and Peter Temple, the weekend's host – an icon and an aristocrat? What would she talk about? But she needn't have worried. Peter proved to be an experienced dinner party host and absorbed her over the main course with stories and anecdotes about the big house.

Now he in turn was being kept amused (despite Cress's empty chair next to him) by Etienne St Clair, an Eton crony two chairs away, who was winding up Kate with his rhetoric on primogeniture. Kate caught Tor's eye and widened hers in horror at the relic she was stuck with. Tor suppressed a giggle.

'So did you see my shortlist for what I want in the apartment?' she heard Harry ask.

Tor turned and found him alarmingly close.

'Uh, yes. I did,' she smiled, trying to move back a bit. 'You don't actually want a real fire in there, do you?'

Harry was resting his chin on his hand and smiling at her, amused. 'I most certainly do. I like the atmosphere a fire creates. And don't put in air-con. I can't be doing with refrigerated air. If I need to cool down I'll hire a bikini-clad punkawallah.' He paused. 'You know, you do look awfully fine in yours, I don't suppose you'd be int—?'

Tor smacked his hand playfully. She was getting the measure of him, she thought.

'I am not going to be your punkawallah,' she giggled.

'What will you be then?' he said, leaning in to her so that his face was inches from hers.

'Your interior designer,' she said coolly, matching his gaze.

'How dull. You could be so much more, you know,' he said tracing a lazy finger over her hand. 'God, your hands are tiny,' he remarked.

'And your ego's huge,' she said cheekily. She was having fun. She couldn't believe Harry Hunter was her plaything.

'Along with other things, yes.'

Tor laughed. 'You really are a teenager trapped in a man's body.'

'A god's body, don't you mean? Have you seen my six-pack?' And he tore open his shirt, buttons popping everywhere as he grabbed Tor's hand and ran it suggestively over his carved stomach. Everybody cheered and Tor looked around, giggling and embarrassed.

She rolled her eyes in mock exasperation and pulled her hand away, sitting back to allow a white-jacketed waiter to clear the plates. They'd had lobster bisque, rack of lamb and buttermilk bavarois, and she'd successfully managed to eat hers without slopping it all over her dress. Another hurdle cleared.

She looked around the room. Laetitia Latham was in social Siberia, her resplendent black Roland Mouret dress lost and unnoticed in the farthest reaches of the room. She looked up and caught Tor's eye, waving cheerily as though they were best friends. Tor smiled back, aware her currency had risen as Harry's right-hand companion.

The bottles on all the tables were being emptied and replenished at an astonishing rate – the waiters practically running to and from the cellars – and the low hum of conversation had risen to a jarring decibel, pierced by shrieks of drunken laughter and more braying than Tor had ever heard outside of a dressage event. She felt pretty tipsy herself. Harry had kept her and Kate's glasses full all evening so she'd had no idea how much she'd had to drink.

She wondered where the loos were – being a private house, there were no illuminated signs to help her out – and she twisted round to have a look.

She caught sight of table sixteen behind her, only two tables away. Lily was sitting back in her chair, looking bored, Monty's chair beside her glaringly empty. John Brightling was holding up his pretty companion's face, examining it for a Botox consult. Tor recognized her as the girl in the pleated skirt from earlier. Anna hadn't noticed her husband's absorption in another woman's lips. She was laughing coquettishly at something James had said to her, and Tor felt irritated, again, by the super-friendliness of the former couple.

Everyone was beginning to get up and table-hop. When Tor turned back, Kate had disappeared and Harry was talking to a beautiful redhead who was bending down to talk to him and affording him far-reaching views of her splendid cleavage.

Tor decided to hunt down the loos before her tummy started sticking out, but the full effect of the evening's drinking hit her as she stood up, and she picked her way slowly through the pushed-out chairs.

A number of people were leaning against the walls in the hall, a few more were sitting on the stairs drinking brandy, and from a room far off, Tor heard some music strike up.

She wandered down a corridor, trying not to look up at the stuffed heads above her. She found them haunting at the best of times, but now, in the dim light, they were downright creepy.

She tried a few doors, but two were locked and one was a store cupboard. She sighed. It would just be easier to use the bathroom in her room. She wandered back along the corridor, trailing one hand along the wall.

'Excuse me, excuse me,' Tor smiled, tiptoeing past the groups on the stairs as daintily as she could, and trying not to look as alone as she suddenly felt. Cress had bolted and Kate had disappeared. There was no one really here for her to be with. Certainly no Hugh. Never him again.

She broke into a trot up the stairs and dashed to her door. She hadn't bothered to lock it. No one did. It was considered bad form – this wasn't a hotel – and she let herself in, jigging about a bit as she tried to slither her dress up her hips. It was no good. The dress was too tight, or she was too drunk. One or the other. Or maybe both. She unzipped it and hopped out, leaving it in a puddle on the floor as she dashed into the bathroom.

As she washed her hands, she looked at her reflection in

the mirror. Her hair was beginning to go limp and her blusher had worn off, although her lips were stained red by the wine and looked like she'd been snogging for hours. She quickly checked her teeth, remembering her first meeting with Hen. They were still frosty white, thank God. They were obviously drinking good stuff tonight.

She went and stood at the window, not really noticing the rain that had begun to fall. She didn't want to put her dress back on or reapply her make-up or fix her hair. She wanted a bath. She wanted to sleep. She wanted her children. And she wanted her husband.

No one would notice if she slipped away. Tor turned on the taps and took off her knickers, immediately climbing into the tub and letting the water fill up around her. She liked her baths extra hot.

She ran it up to the overflow and lay there, eyes closed, feeling the sweat trickle down her neck and shoulders. The room was filled with steam, the mirror misted, and she hoped she was sweating some of the alcohol out of her system. Tomorrow was going to be painful otherwise. She managed twenty minutes before the heat became unbearable and she stood up, grabbing a towel from the rack.

She had just managed to wrap it round her when the colours in the room pixillated and drained to black and white. And then just to black.

James was sitting on the bed when he heard the thump.

'Tor!' he shouted, rushing into the bathroom and finding her slumped on the floor. Immediately he scooped her up and carried her through to the bedroom, laying her out on the bed and putting some pillows beneath her feet. He sat on the bed next to her, rubbing her hands.

'Tor, Tor, can you hear me?'

Tor's eyelids fluttered and slowly she opened them. He watched her as she focused, pushing her gently back on the bed as she frowned and tried to sit up.

'What happened?' she asked.

'I think you fainted,' he smiled, though there was concern in his eyes. 'Has it ever happened before?'

'A couple of times. I have low blood pressure,' she said.

'Mmm, that did look like a pretty hot bath. I could scarcely see you for all the steam in there. I half expected to find a couple of fat hairy Turkish men in there with you.' He grinned at her, while holding her wrist between his fingers and thumb and checking her pulse.

'I should be so lucky,' she smiled back, thinking how gorgeous he looked in black tie. He had long since taken his jacket off, and his top button was undone, his tie hanging loosely.

He pushed her damp hair away from her face. 'Your colour's returning,' he said gently. 'Not that it looks like it ever left your legs,' he joked.

She looked down and giggled. They were bright red, brighter than Monty's scalp.

'You should see my bottom, then. That's always the worst.'

'I'd love to.'

Their laughter faded as they looked at each other.

'What were you doing here?' she said quietly.

'I came to look for you. I couldn't see you downstairs and I was starting to worry.' He smiled. 'And with good reason, it turns out. You clearly can't be trusted on your own.'

'What would have happened to me if you hadn't been there? Could I have died?' she asked teasingly.

He laughed. 'No. You didn't bump your head – luckily. But you would have woken up awfully wet.'

246

Tor bit her lip. 'Well, you're not helping on that score, doctor,' she said quietly, scarcely able to believe she had the nerve to say it out loud.

His eyes roamed hers as he hesitated. Had she really said it? And then he was doing it anyway, kissing her hard, urgently, bruising her with passion.

Tor ran her hands around the back of his head, entwining her fingers in his hair, keeping him on her. He teased her with his tongue, sucking gently on her lower lip, before moving his mouth off hers and inching down her neck.

Tor gasped for breath, from pleasure, untying her towel with one hand so that she lay naked beneath him. He pulled away and looked at her, his eyes clouded with lust. He had waited so l—

She reached up under his arms and pulled him down again, hooking her legs around him to bring him on top of her. He shifted on to both elbows and she pushed herself up into him, wanting his weight, his hardness, feeling his tux against her bare skin.

She writhed against him, wanting more, and he kissed her mouth again, before suddenly pushing himself up. He kept his eyes on her as he fiddled with his cuffs. Tor sat up and swung herself on to his lap, straddling him as she nibbled his ear and deftly unbuttoned his shirt with her hands. He moaned as she opened his shirt and pressed her breasts against his chest, kissing his neck wetly and running her hands through his hair. She had never been so turned on in her life. It had never been like this with . . .

'Tor,' he said, arching away a little and trying to look at her. She ignored him. 'Tor, Tor, wait. I don't think . . .'

'Don't think,' she whispered into his neck, her hands fluttering down to his flies. 'Don't think.'

'We must, Tor.' He grabbed her wrists, trying to stop her while he still had the self-control. 'We must. It's too soon. You're not ready for this.'

Tor stared at him, incredulous.

'I'm not ready? *I'm* not? Can you see me here, James? Can you feel me? Can you smell me? I've never been more ready.'

'No, no,' he shook his head, lifting her off his lap and getting up from the bed. 'I don't mean – I mean, you're not ready emotionally. You'd regret this. You'd hate me if we did this.'

'No. I wouldn't. Really, I wouldn't. I promise. Please – come back here.' She held her hands out to him, but he turned away.

He paced the floor, rubbing his face in his hands, his shirt open. Tor saw what her hands had just felt. His broad shoulders, the toned chest, her eyes moving along the scruff of dark hair that tapered into a narrow line down his stomach.

He dropped his hands to his sides and faced her, his resolve deserting him as he took her in again. She was sitting on the bed with her knees together, her feet splayed out to the sides. He had never understood how women could sit comfortably like that. Her breasts were small but firm, her waist tight, her eyes beseeching. He couldn't believe he was doing this.

He closed his eyes and shook his head. He had to do this. He began buttoning up his shirt.

'Tor, this is hard enough for me to do . . . Let's just take a bit of time out from this. I don't . . .'

'It's Amelia, isn't it?' Tor said angrily. 'It's nothing to do with me at all.'

'What? No!' he said. 'No, she's got nothing to do with any of this. Why would she?'

'Yeah, right,' Tor snorted derisively, scrambling off the bed and stepping into her dress. 'Be a man, James! This has all been a game to you, hasn't it? You said that night you'd get me any way you could. And now that you have, you can't even be bothered to see it through.'

'Tor, no! You've got this all wrong. You are the only woman I want. I just think we should wait. You've been through a lot!'

'Yes! I have, James! And I've been through it all on my own. And I'm tired of being on my own. So right now, I just want to be with someone. Even if it's just for tonight.' She pulled the zip up angrily, and pushed her feet into her shoes.

'Where are you going?' he asked hurriedly.

'Back to the party. What does it look like? You may not want me, James, but I know for a fact that Harry does.'

She started for the door.

'No!'

He said it so fiercely she stopped dead in her tracks.

'You are not going to him!' he growled. 'That man is . . . He doesn't care about you – he doesn't care about anyone.'

Tor looked at him witheringly. 'Don't be melodramatic, James.'

James crossed the room and put a hand against the door. 'I said, you are not going to him.'

She looked at him and saw the fury, the jealousy blazing all over his face. What was going on? Why wouldn't he . . . ? She began to cry. She hid her face in her hands and sobbed.

James moved away from the door and wrapped his arms around her, holding her head against his chest and whispering into her hair.

'I'm so sorry, I'm so sorry,' he whispered, over and over and over, until eventually he ran out of words. He tilted her head up with his hands and looked down at her tear-streaked face. Her eyes, staring back at him, looked like luminous pools and he couldn't do the right thing any longer. He began kissing her again, pushing her backwards, walking her back until she came to the chest of drawers and stumbled back on it, still kissing him, over and over.

He slid his hands up her thighs, expertly easing her dress over her hips. With one hand he undid his flies, pushing himself into her, feeling her ankles clasp around him, her buttocks tighten as she took him, all of him, her breath quick against his ear as they rocked together. And then he heard her moan build, her muscles clamp and the sweet rush of air as she exhaled and they released together. He dropped his head on to her shoulder and bit it gently. She was his.

Chapter Twenty-seven

Unlike Tor, Kate had actually managed to find the loos. She'd had quite enough of pompous old duffers for one night and was sitting sideways on the loo, her legs up against the cubicle wall, listening to groups of women coming in, sniffing and then leaving again. No one ever flushed. 'Whatever can they be doing?' she thought ironically, inspecting her nails.

She'd been upstairs to check on Monty, but lying next to him hadn't been an enticing proposition. He had looked like a nightlight, his sunburn glowing like embers in the dark, and the medicine (combined with the day's drinking) had knocked him out cold.

She frowned to herself as she picked at a hangnail and wondered what to do next. Tor and Harry had sloped off and she couldn't find either of them anywh— She stiffened as the thought suddenly came to her: they couldn't be together, could they? Harry had flirted outrageously with Tor at dinner.

No, no. She dismissed the idea, slumping back. Tor wouldn't. But she was sure Harry was trying to piss her off – first Cress and now Tor. He seemed to be on a mission this weekend.

She heard the door swing open too hard and hit the back

wall. Kate rolled her eyes. She just wanted a little peace. It was here or lying next to her snoring, pink shrimp of a husband.

'. . . such a bore. I seriously considered drowning myself in the bisque. All he can talk about are the bloodlines. I know that horse's family tree better than my own.'

'Mmmm.'

The door of the cubicle next to her slotted shut and Kate tried to shut her ears to the tinkle.

'I must say, I'd have thought twice about coming if I'd known Harry was going to be here,' the woman at the basin called out. 'Did you know he was coming this year?'

Kate's ears pricked up.

'No. No idea at all. Jamie hadn't told me he was going to be here.'

'I'm not sure he even knew, actually. He'd have been the first to blackball him.' Kate could tell by the way the woman's voice was slightly stretched that she was reapplying her mascara. 'Typical of Harry, though – buying his way in. Did you know he's paid for it all this year?'

'Doesn't surprise me. He's always flashing his cash to muscle in.'

There was a pause as the woman switched eyes.

'And what's all this business about it being covered by *Tatler*? Next year will be shocking. Everyone will want to come. Before you know it, Moët will be sponsoring it and Mahiki will have a tent.'

'It's the photographer that's driving me crazy, Anna. He's snooping around all over the place, practically jumping out of bushes. I caught him up by the pool earlier. I mean, what does he think he's looking for? It's a charity cricket match, for heaven's sake.'

'Where there's Harry, there's scandal, Lily.'

'Talking of which, my heart stopped when he mentioned happy families. He said it right to Kate, did you see?'

Kate felt her throat go dry.

'Yes, but I don't think he meant anything by it though. I mean – if Monty doesn't know, and Jamie is the soul of discretion, how could he possibly know? It was just a figure of speech.'

The loo next to Kate flushed – for once. The door opened and the voices dropped as the two women stood next to each other again. Kate got up and stood next to the door, straining to hear over the rushing water.

'It was a bit too close for comfort, Anna.'

'I know. Did Billy hear it?'

Kate heard the taps turning and one of the women washed her hands.

'I don't think so. He hasn't said anything. But even if he had overheard, I don't think he'd have twigged. He's not looking for it. And Monty's hidden in plain sight, so to speak. We see them every year. There's no reason for Billy to think . . .'

Kate heard the door open, the voices retreating, '. . . other than a family friend . . .'

Kate stood against the door, tears streaming silently down her cheeks, the pieces in the jigsaw falling into place. Of course, she had known about Lily and Monty. It had all been years ago. Sixteen years ago. They'd just had a short break, before university, a few months at most. But five minutes was all it took.

Harry had been right. Kate was the gooseberry fool.

James rolled Tor on to her back. She was laughing, her head thrown back and her long white neck exposed as he tickled her beneath the sheet, and felt her body wriggle against him.

It had been one of the most glorious hours of his life and he was determined never to get out of bed from this woman again. They would be like John and Yoko and stage a lie-in. Let the world come to them.

He released her from his grip and looked down at her lying stretched out like a slender Venus de Milo beneath him. He held up the sheet, making her blush as he took her all in, raking his eyes over her every bit as lustily as he had with his tongue just minutes before.

'Please never get dressed again,' he grinned, beginning to inch his way down the bed. 'It's over-rated. And actually – it doesn't suit you. You look so . . .' he kissed her tummy, 'so . . .' again – 'so much better like this . . .'

He grabbed her hip bone between his teeth, and she was just beginning to wind her fingers through his hair again when the door burst open.

'Jesus Christ!' he said, springing up and finding himself starkers in front of Kate.

Kate stood there, tramlines of tears carving up her beautiful face. She'd come to find her friend, her shoulder to cry on. She couldn't go to Monty, not yet.

But she was completely unprepared for the scene before her and she swayed a little – literally reeled – from the shock of it.

'You have *got* to be kidding me,' she said finally.

Tor sat up, the sheet clutched around her, feeling like a teenager busted by her parents. James grabbed the bath towel still lying on the edge of the bed and wrapped it around his hips.

'Kate – what's happened?' Tor asked, taking in Kate's

blazing green eyes and red cheeks. Even her neck was wet, the tears racing each other like raindrops down a window, nestling in the hollow of her collarbone.

Kate ignored her. Whatever had prompted her to barge into the room was by-the-by now. Standing before the lovers romping in bed, she was a dog with a new bone.

'How could you sleep with *him*?' Kate demanded, looking at Tor.

Tor didn't know what to say – why was she so angry at her and James? She looked from Kate to James and back to Kate again.

'She was always going to sleep with me,' James said calmly and with utter authority, as though directing a student nurse in theatre. 'We're together. It was never not going to happen.'

Tor looked at him, not sure whether to be flattered or annoyed by his confidence on the matter. She was that predictable, was she?

'Not that it's got anything to do with you, Kate. It's private,' he said, picking up his trousers and putting them on. 'What's happened? Why are you here?'

Kate glared at him, new tears budding. She went to speak, then stopped herself and turned away again. She couldn't seem to face him. She looked at Tor again instead, determined not to be deterred.

'I'm interested to know why – when you're now free to take your pick of all the good men out there – why exactly you would choose a lying shit like James White?'

Tor's mouth dropped. 'Kate!'

'I beg your pardon?' James said coldly. 'And what have I done to warrant that?'

'Oh, I don't know, James,' Kate said, whirling around to face him, fury finally overriding shock. 'Why don't we go and ask your sister? Maybe she can enlighten us. I'm sure there are many things she'd like to tell me. Or shall we save her the bother? Is there anything you'd like to share with me perhaps?'

James stood rigid, his jaw locked. So Kate knew. His brain whirred, trying to establish how it had got out. Who could have told her? Not Lily. Not Anna. Billy didn't kn— Harry's comment flashed in front of him.

Her anger flared as she saw him take stock, no doubt trying to cover their tracks, planning, scheming a new set of lies.

'Why didn't you tell me?' she shouted. 'You were supposed to be my friend. You all were – you, Lily, Anna. And what about Monty? He doesn't even know? How could you be his friend and not even tell him that he has a son! What kind of family are you? What about poor Billy?'

She turned away and walked to the wall, leaning against it for support.

'A son?' Tor watched them both – Kate standing limply, like a rag doll who'd lost her stuffing, trying to catch her breath, her thoughts. James, pale and silent.

'It wasn't for me to tell, Kate,' he said quietly, finally. 'I am so sorry. I didn't agree with it, but . . .'

Kate couldn't bear to hear his excuses. Their justification.

'Don't give me that crap! You've had a ringside seat watching us try to have a family. We've spoken more to you about it than anyone. We confided in you. Trusted your advice. And all the time, you knew he was a father and you kept it from him.'

'Kate, it wasn't that simple. By the time Lily found out, Monty was already back with you. It was clear they had no future. She was trying to do the right thing.'

'The right thing? The right thing? For whom? Certainly not for Billy! You've let him spend the first sixteen years of his life without a father, when he was actually there all the time. How exactly do you think he's going to react to the knowledge that you not only lied to him, but maintained this elaborate deception for every single year of his life? How can he ever trust any of you again?'

James crossed the room and put a hand on her arm.

'Kate. I thought I was helping. I tried to do the best thing under the circumstances.'

'Was there a grand plan in place to ever reveal the truth? Or were we all just going to rub along in blissful ignorance?'

'It had to be Lily's decision. She . . .'

'He had the right to know, James! From the day she found out, he had that right,' she said, fresh tears bursting through. 'We all did. But this changes everything now. Everything! Don't you see? Monty's a father. He's got what we've always wanted. Our impossible dream. Except that he doesn't need me to have it. He doesn't need me at all any more.'

Tor gasped. 'No, Kate,' she said quickly, realizing her friend's thought process, remembering the couple's tetchiness with each other, lonely drunkenness, the sarcastic asides. 'I know this is an awful shock – but it doesn't mean it will change anything between . . .'

Kate shook her head wildly, not wanting to hear platitudes, hope. Fucking hope. For all the good it ever did her. She jerked her arm away from James and fled the room, slamming the door behind her, the backdraught swinging a portrait precariously away from the wall for a few seconds.

James came and sat on the bed. 'Shit,' he said, running his hands through his hair, his elbows resting on his knees.

Tor watched the picture settle back on its hook, trying to

take in the full ramifications of what had just unfolded. Billy. James lying to Monty year after year. Just this afternoon, he'd cajoled him into playing water polo with them. Put them on the same team . . .

And then suddenly she remembered. She felt a deathly chill blanket her body as some deeply buried words floated up from her brain, taunting her, warning her. A message from the grave.

'He said that,' she whispered. 'He warned me about this.'

James looked at her. She was staring into space, ghostly white, that last night flooding her mind.

'Who did? Who said what?' He leant in to her and started rubbing her arm. She felt so cold.

'He said that you were supposed to bring families together, not rip them apart. But you don't. You destroy families. First mine. Now Kate's.'

James absorbed her words. 'Tor, no! It's not like that! Who said that? You can't think . . .'

But she got up silently from the bed, leaving the sheet behind her, and unselfconscious, unembarrassed, uncaring, walked across the room.

She stopped at the bathroom door.

'I want you to go now.'

'Tor, please. Let's just talk about this.'

She looked at him. 'There is nothing for us to say to each other. Just stay away from me. I can't be around someone like you.'

And she shut the door, climbing straight back into the chill bath and turning on the hot taps. Not because she cared about the cold water. But she'd be damned if she was going to let him hear her cry.

*

'Just get dressed and go,' Harry snarled at the redhead, rolling away from her and pulling on his trousers. His day was not getting any better. First Cress, then Kate fannying about with White of all people, and now even her. She had a rack you could eat your dinner off, and she still couldn't make it work for him. His head was screwed.

He heard her sniff as she grabbed her shoes – Louboutins again, he might have known – and burst through the doors into the drenched night. He lit a cigarette and waited for her to disappear before walking to the door himself. He inhaled a drag deeply and looked out, watching the stair-rods shattering the mirror-calm of the pool's surface. He felt tempted to dive in. He'd always enjoyed the perverse pleasure of swimming in the rain. Like him, it was so deliciously contrary.

He stared into the night. He was at an impasse. The fight with Cress had bothered him more than he cared to admit. After months of playing sweet, she'd bared her teeth, and she wasn't the pushover he'd assumed. He needed to find an angle on her – and fast.

He flicked the cigarette butt into the water, just as a door opened at the Lodge and a cone of light spilled on to the lawn. A figure ran through it and into the black. It was a woman, though he couldn't make out who, more was the pity. She had great legs.

She had gathered her skirt in her hands and was flying athletically down the grass towards the cricket pavilion, before turning abruptly and racing towards the poolhouse instead. Harry straightened up. The evening might be salvageable after all.

She stopped running before she got there, falling to her hands on the terrace and staggering to a lounger by the water.

Even fifty yards away, her sobs were audible above the rain, her breath ragged and heavy.

Her profile was towards him and Harry took in her full heaving breasts, long elegant back and taut stomach. Her gown was wet through and practically sheer, her hair clinging like a helmet to her head. His heart rate quickened but he said nothing. Didn't stir. He let the minutes pass as he watched her breathing slow, her head drop, the tears wane.

Sensing someone's eyes on her, Kate looked up. She saw Harry leaning against the doorway, his hair flopping forward towards those thick lashes. How long had he been there? He was wearing just his dinner trousers, his feet and chest bare. Kate didn't know why, nor did she care. She wasn't interested in asking questions. She just knew she'd found an answer.

They stared at each other through the rain, neither one sure who was the predator, until she stood up and faced him square on. She tipped back her head, smoothing her hair back from her face, before bringing her hands over to the zip and slowly – so slowly – sliding it down. She held the dress up, watching his eyes, waiting for the look to cross his face that would say he didn't believe she'd do it. And when it did, as she'd known it would, she let it drop insolently – just like that – a cloud of silk at her ankles. She side-stepped out of it and hooked it with one ankle, kicking it into the water. And then she just stood there, naked and glorious in front of him, daring him to come up to her, touch her, take her.

What the redhead couldn't manage with a D-cup and two sex toys, Kate had achieved with nothing but defiance. He walked towards her. He should have known it would be this way, on her terms. She was never going to surrender.

Chapter Twenty-eight

It was just after midnight when Cress put her key in the lock. The house was dark and hot and silent. She kicked off her shoes and tiptoed quickly over the cool marble floor, anticipating the alarm pips. They didn't come.

Cress checked the keypad. The alarm hadn't been set. She frowned. Mark usually part-set it at night. She stared at it for a moment, before wondering if . . . Harry! She ran into the study, her heart hammering. But everything was untouched.

She closed her eyes and tried to calm down. She was deliriously tired. Mark had just forgotten, that was all. Bachelor inertia.

She padded into the kitchen. She kept the lights off – it was a full moon and she liked the moody silverstreams of light poking in from the orangery.

A half-drunk bottle of Cab Sauv was sitting on the island, with a smeared glass next to it. More bachelor inertia. She grabbed a sparkling crystal glass from the cupboard and poured herself a large measure. Without bothering to inhale the bouquet, she took a deep slug of the wine – God, she was shattered; she'd been driving for six hours – and carried the bottle through to the orangery, where she curled up on her favourite armchair and looked out to the night garden.

For the first time, Cress noticed that summer was nearly over – the leaves had begun to turn and some were already blowing gently across the lawn. Most of the beds were colourless, their bounty buried for another year, although a few hydrangeas bracketed the garden with blue and lilac notes.

She could hear an owl in one of the bigger trees, though she couldn't see it for love nor money. She saw a russet fox creep out from behind the bare peony bed, sniffing in the wind for tonight's supper. He looked well fed and healthy. A sly one, she thought. She watched his stealthy progress as he picked his way across the garden, trotting quickly when he was exposed on the lawn, then stopping and looking about suspiciously from the relative camouflage of an apple tree at the top of the orchard. Confident the coast was clear, he broke cover and was stalking over the grass with something approaching machismo when a sudden noise or movement startled him and he skipped sideways, his head low, ears pricked, looking for the source.

Cress watched, intrigued by nature at work. Or rather, at play. For there, behind the pear tree thirty yards down the garden, shadows were moving. She leant out of the chair and squinted, trying to make out what they were, but the tree obscured her view.

The fox was less interested in deciphering the situation than in getting the hell away from it, and it galloped over to the boundary fence, dipping beneath a partly broken-off section of panelling and disappearing from sight.

Cress blinked at the dusk. She was sure it wasn't another animal, even though the sounds coming from the pear tree suggested as much. The shape was moving but then split, the sapphire blue sky leaping between the inky silhouettes.

The shadows stood up and moved around the tree looking

for a suitable spot, before conjoining again and carrying on as before. Cress inhaled sharply as she realized what she was seeing. The couple's bare skin gleamed like alabaster as they inched into the moonbeams, and when one of the figures tipped back its head, her blonde hair streamed down like weeping willow to a pond. She was facing the tree, her arms braced against a branch, her breasts bouncing rhythmically.

Cress stiffened, flooded with outrage that this was happening in her own garden. What if one of the children was to see? Or the neighbours? She got up, in a fury, and rushed into the kitchen to turn on the switch for the outdoor lights. She hesitated as she tried to remember which one was which. The lighting system, inside and out, was state of the art but it still didn't mean she knew how to use it. She was determined to stop their little peepshow once and for all.

But then something else occurred to her. Something better. Even Mark wouldn't tolerate this. It was what she'd been waiting for – the sackable offence. Finally, Little Miss Perfect had strayed and now she could get rid of her. Out of their lives, for good.

Cress skipped silently up the stairs and across the landing. The door was ajar and she peeked in, already anticipating her husband's comforting shape beneath the blankets, his pillow pushed up against the headboard, one long leg thrown out as he slowly and customarily overheated.

Except that he wasn't there. He was standing at the window. And the curtains were wide, wide open.

'I wonder if I can stain it?' Harry asked idly, twiddling a strawberry in Kate's belly-button. 'Then you'll look like you're studded with rubies and you can join my harem. You do belly-dance, I take it?'

He laughed as Kate whacked him over the head with a cushion.

'Thought not. You're just not that kind of girl,' he said, popping the strawberry in her mouth and pulling himself on top of her again, pinning her arms above her head. 'But then you're not like any girl I've ever met. And I've met a few.'

He kissed her deeply, feeling hungry for her all over again. He couldn't seem to get enough of her. She'd been everything he predicted – wanton, athletic, fierce and demanding. His match.

'I guess I should have believed what I read after all,' she laughed, pulling away for air. 'You're insatiable.'

'You can't say you weren't warned,' he said, running a finger down her nose.

'I need more . . .' she raised her eyebrows provocatively, watching the smile creep on to his lips. 'Water. I don't want to get drunk and let you have your wicked way with me.'

'If you don't consider everything we've just done to be wicked, then you really are my dream woman,' he said, kissing her hard, before reluctantly getting up and crossing the room to the fridge. For an impromptu seduction, they'd done pretty well: the poolhouse boasted piles and piles of towels and blankets, and a basket of strawberries, a hand of bananas and an unopened bottle of Bollinger had kept their energy levels up for their twilight tryst.

Harry poured her a glass of water and watched as she got up from the sofa and walked over to the doors, looking out at the dawn, which was already burning the sky into hot coral. She stretched easily, like a cat, and he admired her physique. She was so unlike his usual cadaverous conquests. Her body was strong, responsive, ripe. Well, in all but one capacity. Which reminded him . . .

He walked up behind her and handed her the glass, sweeping her hair away with a hand to kiss the back of her neck. 'So. Are you going to tell me what happened last night? Or just leaving me to assume that you couldn't resist my legendary charms a second longer?'

He put a hand on her chin and turned her face to him, kissing her lightly on the mouth. He drew back, his eyes twinkling. But tears were standing on guard in Kate's, her bottom lip trembling.

'Hey, hey,' he said, drawing her in to him and enfolding her in his warm chest. He walked her over to the sofa and sat her on his lap, smoothing her hair rhythmically as the tears dropped and she recounted the overheard conversation in the loos.

'If you hadn't made the comment about playing happy families,' she hiccupped. 'We'd still be none the wiser. How much longer would it have gone on for? Months? Years? Forever?'

Harry shook his head. 'I'm so sorry. I thought you knew. I never would have said it if I'd thought for a moment you didn't. It was just a flippant comment.' He kissed her shoulder. 'It just made me see red. After seeing your distress at Lucy's – and then to watch them flaunting their family in front of you like that, playing "father and son" in the water, while you had to look on and swallow it . . .'

Kate nodded, looking back on the previous day's merriment with fresh eyes, new anger. What about all the holidays they'd shared with them? The Christmases? And now the cottage in Burnham Market – bought at their hearty encouragement.

'I feel so betrayed by them. By the entire family. How could they keep us so close to them? I'm Billy's godmother, for God's sake. What kind of family are they?'

'One I keep well away from,' Harry said darkly. 'They've brought me nothing but misery.'

Kate looked at him, remembering the animosity she'd seen between the two men at every encounter.

'What do you mean?'

There was a pause and Harry dropped his head.

'White made my life a misery at Eton,' he said. 'My father was a beak there – a Latin master. It meant I was entitled to go there too. But White's a snob, always hung with the aristo crowd. Never saw me as a fully paid-up member. Said I got in through the back door. That kind of thing. '

'Go on.'

'White was in the same house as me. And our fathers were good friends – had gone to Cambridge together – so it became quite usual for me to go and stay with them all in the holidays. My mother died when I was fourteen and Pa often used to go on sabbaticals after term ended, so I'd stay with them over Easter and some of the summer.'

'So what changed?' Kate prompted.

'I had a fling with Lily. Nothing serious. Just a one-time thing but they all totally flipped. Banged on about boundaries and honour. They're big on honour in that family. They take their royal connection pretty seriously.' He paused. 'Anyway, they booted me out, and ever since then, I've been in the deep freeze.'

Kate smiled. 'Well, I can't say I blame him entirely. You do seem to have a track record for going off with his women.' Harry looked at her. 'Coralie?'

'Oh, her! Right.' He shrugged and chuckled. 'Well, what can I say? He may find them first but it's hardly my fault if they end up choosing me when there's a choice.'

Kate rolled her eyes. 'God, you're a conceited pig.'

He reached an arm out and started massaging her neck. 'You never had a thing with him, did you?'

She raised an eyebrow, amused. 'Why? Would it make me more attractive to you if I had?'

'No. You couldn't possibly be more irresistible to me.' He paused. 'But did you?'

She giggled. 'No. He's spent far too much time examining my bits to see me as anything other than a medical conundrum.' She sniffed. 'Besides, I was very happily married at the time. Wasn't looking.'

'Well, I promise you one thing. I too intend to spend a very long time examining your bits, because the only conundrum I have is why I can't get enough of you.' His hand drifted down between her thighs and began to explore, expertly, exquisitely.

'Mmmmmm.' She tipped her head back, eyes closed, as she felt the tip of his tongue at the base of her throat.

'It's obviously not a hard and fast rule though,' she mumbled.

'What isn't?'

'Not seeing his patients as sexual beings.'

'What do you mean?'

But Kate couldn't answer. He had started doing something with his thumb that made it very hard to concentrate.

When she didn't answer, he took the thumb away and looked at her, his eyes inquisitive.

'Huh? Why've you stopped?' she gasped.

'Are you saying he sleeps with his patients?'

'What? Oh no! God, no!' she laughed. 'That would be one helluvan allegation to make.'

'So what did you mean then?'

'Last night, I walked in on him and Tor – a *former* patient.

I found them in bed together. It was just after I had found out about Billy. I needed to talk to someone and . . . well, I interrupted them. *In flagrante delicto*, as your father would no doubt say.' She winked.

Harry's mind raced. James White and the pretty little interiors girl. Well, well. He hadn't predicted that. He looked back at Kate.

'Do you think it's been going on for long?'

Kate shrugged. 'I don't know. I doubt it. Tor's not the kind of woman to have an affair.'

Harry looked at her, his eyes aflame. 'There's no such thing as a woman who doesn't cheat.'

Kate gasped. 'You bloody misogynist!' she cried, slapping his arm.

He grabbed her wrist and held it fast. 'Well, answer me this. Up until last night, did you think you would?'

She looked at him, lost for words. He was hurting her wrist a bit and his intensity was unsettling. He loosened the grip and pressed her wrist between his lips.

'I'm not trying to call anyone names,' he said quietly. 'I'm just saying, none of us is immune to temptation. Not even your prim friend.'

'Tor's not prim. She just happened to have the perfect marriage. There's no way she would have cheated on Hugh when he was alive. And she probably only slept with James because she was drunk and lonely, and he was a shoulder to cry on. I'll bet they're both regretting it this morning.'

He kissed the palm of her hand, his previous focus gone.

'I'm sure you're right. About Tor, anyway. But don't be fooled by James. Lord White isn't quite as honourable as he likes everyone to think. He's every bit as capable as me at doing whatever it takes to get what he wants.' He smiled. 'It's what makes him such a worthy opponent.'

Kate looked at him. 'You actually enjoy warring with him, don't you?'

Harry looked at her, his eyes hooded and dancing.

'Of course. I don't believe that it's love that makes the world go round, Kate. It's hate that drives us forward. It makes us try to get away from things, to change things. You can never be complacent with hate. Love just makes you lazy and takes your eye off the ball.'

'That's unbelievably cynical.'

Harry shrugged. 'It's the truth, though no one else will dare say it. But I'm not interested in living my life by tired old clichés. I accept life for what it is and squeeze what I need from it. I'm not looking for reconciliation or forgiveness from the Whites. I'm where I am now largely because of events which have happened between me and that family.'

'Sleeping with Lily, you mean?'

'That was the springboard, yes. It was the catalyst for the feud. They threw me out and I had to sink or swim. So I swam, and became an icon in the process. And that's pissed them off no end, ever since. It isn't "just" that I should be unrepentant or successful following my grievous transgression. Make no mistake, James is after me. And he won't stop. Not until he's satisfied he's broken me.'

Kate put her hands out in puzzlement. 'Won't stop what? I don't understand. What is it he's doing to you?'

Harry looked at her, one hand idly cupping her naked breast. The moment couldn't be more perfect. 'He's blackmailing me.'

*

Kate jumped up in shock.

'Don't be ridiculous!' she cried. 'James wouldn't do a thing like that!'

'Wouldn't he? You don't think he's capable of deception? Even in light of his lies to you and Monty?' Harry shrugged. 'I'm not going to try and convince you of anything Kate. It's my problem. I'll sort it out.'

Kate stalked the room, her hands rubbing her temples, trying to make her brain work. 'But why? What does he want? Not money surely? James is minted.'

'No. This isn't about money. Revenge? Honour? Who knows? He won't admit to anything.'

'So if he's not getting money out of you, then what?'

'Power.'

Kate stared at him.

'He's got Cressida in his pocket.'

'Cressida? Cress, your publisher?'

'Cress, my publisher. Your friend.' He watched her closely. 'So you didn't know, then?'

'Of course I didn't!' she cried indignantly. 'Why on earth would I?'

She seemed genuine.

Kate turned her back to him and looked out at the grounds. Her dress was still floating in the pool. She couldn't believe her friend was being implicated in this mess.

She turned back and leaned against the back of a chair, her arms folded but beneath rather than across her breasts, causing them to swell pleasingly. Her long legs were crossed at the ankles and her chin had tipped up, making her look haughty and austere. It was a pose he had seen her strike many times in her starched pinstripes, and the sight of her doing it now, butt naked, made him instantly hard again.

270

'Tell me everything,' she demanded.

'When we were at Eton, a boy in our house died. Fell off the roof of the boarding house. There was a route where the buildings were close enough for you to jump between the Brewhouse Gallery and Baldwin's Bec, our house. After lights out, we'd stuff our beds with clothes and scramble out of the windows and on to the roof. It was an initiation thing.

'Anyway, one night, I was going up with another boy, Hillier, who hadn't done it before. He was supposed to follow my path. No one knew we were going, but White saw me as we climbed on to the guttering. He said Hillier was too young and that he'd get a beak if we didn't come down. I just ignored him. I knew he wouldn't rat on us. But he did.' Harry's mouth set in a bitter line. 'We were nearly round when I saw some of the lights come on in the dorm. I knew we had to get back and pretend we'd been in the loos. So I rushed ahead, thinking he could keep up. All I could think was – if I was rusticated, it could hurt my father's career. Next thing, I heard a scream and . . .' His hands had gone to his ears, as though he could still hear it, twenty years later.

He stood still, staring at his feet. 'I never told anyone I had been up there with him. And neither did White, surprisingly. I think he felt guilty that his dobbing may have played a part in Hillier's fall. We never even talked to each other about it. It was our shared secret. I thought we'd go to our graves with it.'

'But what has this got to do with Cress?'

'When my contract was up for grabs, she contacted me saying she'd go public about Hillier unless I signed with her. The only way she could possibly have known about him was through White. She was his patient too, right?'

Kate nodded.

'So it looks like he keeps in touch with his patients – former or otherwise – for all sorts of reasons.'

Kate nodded, but didn't speak. She was absorbing his words, trying to re-cast the James of old in this new mould which had been poured in the past twelve hours. As for Cress, well – she'd known she was ambitious, but this was beyond the pale. She didn't know whether to hate her friend for being so unscrupulous, or whether to admire her balls for blackmailing one of the biggest icons in the world.

'And you didn't mention this before – when we were discussing the issue of blackmail – because . . . ?'

'Because with my reputation, shagging a girl four months before her fifteenth birthday probably isn't that surprising. But being on the roof when a boy fell to his death? I don't think the public could forgive that. Even though I had no direct hand in it, White was right. I never should have let him come up there with me. And anyway, it's not like White's trying to expose me. He's not extorting me. He's just shackled me. It's control by proxy.'

Kate felt her anger steadily rise at James's self-righteousness and arrogance. She'd had enough of him.

'But that's not fair! It was an accident. He has no right to use this over you, just because he's angry you slept with Lily,' Kate said indignantly.

Harry shrugged.

She picked up his crumpled dinner shirt and slung it on. She had to get back to the Lodge before Monty woke up.

'Well,' she said, regaining her calm. 'Let's keep it between us for now. We'll find a way out of this.'

Harry walked over to her. 'You're probably right.' A wolfish grin crossed his face. 'I'm coming to realize you usually are.'

Kate grinned back, as she buttoned up. 'Damn right, baby.'

Then, 'I need to get back,' she said defensively, recognizing the hungry look in his eyes.

There was a long silence as they both thought about her going back to her sleeping husband.

'What are you going to do?' he asked, twiddling with her buttons.

She looked down, shaking her head.

'Tell him about Billy – obviously. He deserves to know. But after that, I don't know. Things aren't good at the moment . . . If he wants to be involved with Billy I'll understand. But . . .' Her arms dropped to her sides, the cuffs flopping several inches past her hands. 'But I don't know if I'll be able to stay around. Like you said, I don't think I can bear to watch him play happy families.'

She opened the doors and stood on the terrace, feeling the heat already pulsing off the sun. He came up behind her and put his hands under the shirt, kissing her neck.

'I don't want you to go,' he murmured.

She turned around to face him and put her arms around his neck, kissing him lustily.

'I have to,' she whispered. 'I'll call you.' And she ran fleetingly on tiptoes up the dewy clover lawn.

She didn't see the photographer returning from a dawn shoot in the deer park. The editor wanted lots of background shots to build up atmosphere and give an insider's view of what it was to be on the inside of this gilded circle, to capture Harry Hunter at play. But as he stood behind the oak and let the shutter click, taking frame after frame after frame, he knew he was delivering so much more than that. Harry Hunter was playing all right – the lucky bastard – and it had nothing to do with the evocative sound of leather on willow.

Chapter Twenty-nine

Cress was sleeping fitfully on the embattled green leather chesterfield when Rosie came in, jingling a large ring of keys.

'What on earth are you doing here?' she cried in amazement. Of all the things she'd never expected to see . . . Cress's hair had mussed itself into an impressive beehive that a dedicated hour of backcombing and a can of hairspray wouldn't have been able to achieve, and mascara had dripped off her lashes and mixed with her tears to create a crazy-paving effect. 'You're supposed to be in Cornwall.'

Cress blinked hard a couple of times, trying to work out why her assistant was standing in her bedroom. It only took a New York second to remember.

'I wanted to come in and get ahead. Can't let another bloody week pass without making some headway,' she said briskly, her hands automatically going to smooth her swingy helmet of hair and finding that birds had nested there in the night instead.

She grabbed a mirror out of her desk and looked at herself. She looked like Boadicea off the battlefield – and she felt it too. Her body was stiff from sleeping on the sofa, and she stretched, trying to release the kinks. She pursed her lips and looked at Rosie with raised eyebrows, her fingers laced together in a business-like fashion, trying to feel more dignified than she looked.

'And what exactly are you doing here on a Sunday morning?' Deflection as defence seemed a good option, until she'd worked out a cover story.

Rosie shrugged. 'I usually work Sundays now. It's the only way to keep on top of the paperwork. That post bag is on steroids.'

Cress looked at her, amazed. She'd had no idea.

'Why didn't you tell me?' she asked.

'It never came up. D'you fancy some coffee?'

Cress took in her assistant's loyalty, bright green shrunken T-shirt and baggy carpenter jeans.

'Excellent idea. Thanks.'

'I'll pop down to Gino's. Back in a sec.'

She bounded off and Cress looked at herself in the mirror again. She looked like a cracked china doll who was beginning to fall to pieces. And she did feel damaged.

But she wasn't broken yet. Irrationally, what she felt most of all was grateful. Grateful that Mark hadn't heard her backtrack last night, flee down the stairs and go back out to the hire car. Grateful that he hadn't rumbled her, rumbling him. Because then they would have had to have some terrible confrontation, with all her weakness and failings, her neglect, her absence being flung at her.

And she couldn't cope with that just now. Not with Harry beginning to challenge their status quo, and the complications with the *Wrong Prince* author.

Mark wasn't expecting her home until today anyway, so that gave her time to think. After all, he hadn't technically been unfaithful, he'd just been watching. And it could just have been an unfortunate coincidence. He'd probably heard something in the garden and gone to investigate, and just happened to see them – like she had. He may only have been standing there five seconds. Who knew?

He deserved the benefit of the doubt, she decided, grabbing her make-up from the weekend's overnight bag and scrabbling around for the make-up remover.

By the time Rosie returned with a macchiato for herself and a double espresso for her boss, steel was running through Cress's veins again and she was sitting with her bare, pedicured feet up on the desk, with an immaculately made-up face and wearing an YSL purple silk toga, clasped at one shoulder by a cluster of pearls. Even her defiant hair had slipped back into silky subservience.

'Wow!' Rosie exclaimed, relieved to see her boss back to her usual controlled self. Something had clearly gone very wrong the night before and Rosie wasn't buying her story for one second. 'You look incredible. What a difference ten minutes and a couture dress makes.'

'Hmm? Oh you mean this?' She pinched an inch of the buttery fabric. 'Yes. It was the only thing left in my bag that didn't stink of deer.'

She was holding the manuscript of *The Wrong Prince* in her hands.

'We need to get on to the Box Shop.'

'Already done it,' Rosie smiled, watching Cress's surprise pop over her face. 'I went in yesterday, after I spoke to you. It's pretty near to where I live anyway. I'm in Parsons Green, so it was no bother.'

'And?'

'And it turns out my room-mate from uni is their branch manager.'

Rosie smiled at her boss's expression. She passed over a piece of paper.

'Forty-three Felden Street,' Cress read. 'There's no name?'

'No. Client doesn't have to supply one. It's one of the perks of using a private company apparently. More privacy.'

'Oh, great!' Cress slumped back in the chair.

'We've still got the address though. I'll go round now if you like and knock on some doors. You go home and see Mark and the kids, and I'll give you a call if I come up trumps.'

Cress didn't need to consider the offer.

'No, no. Not necessary, I'll catch them later. This is too important. We'll go together.'

And with that, she picked up the keys for the hire car – an azure-blue Seat, all that had been available in the depths of Truro late on a Saturday afternoon in high season – and slipped on her thong sandals, looking a ridiculously glamorous creature at 10.49 a.m. on a Sunday morning.

Within minutes the Seat's bright blue nose poked out on to the New Kings Road, where the flower sellers promised never to sell carnations, gerberas, gypsophila or gladioli, and where the charity shops looked like Bond Street on sale. Cress waited for an opening as the black cabs and red buses and yellow lambos streamed by, no one even thinking to let her itty-bitty blue car out into the flow.

Cress idly watched the pedestrian buzz – teenage girls in denim minis and Uggs here, continental women in expensive paisley scarfs there. Unlike Nappy Valley, where almost everyone belonged to a nuclear family unit, this area was a melting pot of personalities and types and generations: ambitious city boys buying their first flat with their bonuses; students renting in bedsits; pensioners trying to do a weekly shop on a budget of £38 per week, then shuffling back to their £2m three-storey homes they'd owned since the sixties and bought for £1,500.

After four minutes, a kind cabbie took pity on her and let her out, and with a hundred-yard sprint and two right turns, they swung into Felden Street. Cress had driven by the end of the road hundreds of times, but she'd never had reason to turn in here. It was populated with lots of tall narrow houses with pretty paned windows and ice-cream-coloured stucco walls. The gardens were well tended and mostly mature, being generally too small to convert into off-street parking spaces. Cress idled along, counting down the numbers. Fifty-nine, fifty-seven, fifty-five, fifty-three, forty-nine, forty-seven, forty-five, forty-three. Aha. There it was.

It was an innocuous-looking building. It didn't have the tonal splash of the pinks melding into lilacs, melding into blues, further up the street. Rather, it was putty-coloured pebbledash, with a varnished pine door and plastic double-glazing. The garden had been concreted over, but there was no car parked on it, simply an unruly collection of bins, most of which had lost their lids. A strip of doorbells ran down the side of the front door.

Cress cheered up. Whoever lived here wasn't rich. They needed money. They needed her.

With characteristic cheek, Cress swung the little car into the drive – she'd be damned if she was going to swell the mayor's coffers any more than she had to – knocking over a couple of the bins as she struggled without her parking sensors.

She and Rosie got out and walked up to the front door. There were no names next to the bells.

Cress rang one at random.

A minute passed. She tried another. Nothing.

They pressed all five bells, but still nothing.

Cress took a couple of steps back and looked up at the building. It faced her blankly. No curtains twitched and all were open.

They were just opening the door of the little blue car when they heard the sound of a deadbolt being pushed back behind the pine door. They paused, mid-action, and waited for it to open. When it did, they found themselves face to face with a tiny, very lined little woman with eyes as small as a shrew's. She wore a headscarf over her hair, which made her look like a Hungarian doll, and she was wearing a polyester house-coat, decorated with lime and pink flowers.

'Hello,' Cress said in a patronizing tone, clasping her hands together in front of her as though she was about to burst into song. 'I wonder if we could trouble you for a moment.'

The little woman's eyes narrowed to pinpricks, looking like full stops on a crumpled piece of paper. She didn't trust the effete manners of her neighbours. They only ever extended to plummy-voiced freeholders, and certainly not to immi-grant labourers living in dingy bedsits. The postcode was the only thing they shared in common.

'We're looking for somebody . . .'

'No, no, I know nothing,' the old woman said immedi-ately, shaking her head and going to shut the door. 'Leave alone.'

'No, wait, please. We're looking for a writer.'

The woman stopped closing the door, and although she didn't open it wide, she held it in place. She was listening.

'We want to offer him a deal. Lots of money. We want to help him.'

'No know writer.'

'Are you sure? Brendan Hillier?'

'No Brendan here.'

'You're absolutely sure about that?'

'I sure.'

'Right.' Cress sagged. She shook her head wearily. They were wasting their time. 'Sorry for troubling you,' she said. 'Let's go.'

'Is Bridget,' came the voice at the door.

Cress whirled around. 'I'm sorry?'

'Is no Brendan Hillier. Is Bridget Hillier.'

'Bridget Hillier? Is she here?'

'Never see her.'

Christ – give me a break, Cress thought.

Then an idea struck her. She clasped her hands piously together again.

'I don't suppose you would be so kind as to let us have a look at her mail tray, would you?'

The door started to close again.

'I'd make it worth your while,' she said hurriedly, reaching for her bag. She realized suddenly how incongruous she must look, wearing a cocktail dress in the middle of a Sunday morning and offering a little old lady a bribe. 'I just want to see if a letter I wrote has arrived.' She shrugged with what she hoped came across as innocence – not an easy look for her to pull off – and held out a £20 note.

The little old lady could move surprisingly fast when the mood took her, and she snatched the note before opening the door sullenly.

'Thank you,' Cress said.

A row of plastic boxes sat on a shelf just inside the door,

each one marked with A, B, C or D. The C box was over-flowing, and as Cress looked around, she saw that an overflow pile had begun to rise in a corner on the floor.

Most of the post had company postmarks, so she was able to identify the senders without opening the mail – Carphone Warehouse, BT, London Electricity, DVLA, HM Customs, Pure cashmere catalogues, Coco de Mer brochures, the White Company – but precious little had a hand-written envelope, and Cress's letter wasn't in the pile.

Cress sat on her knees, her silk dress snagging slightly on the seagrass floor. She smiled up wearily at the little old woman, who had folded her arms across her low-slung bosom and was tapping her foot impatiently. Twenty pounds didn't buy more than a few minutes on the parking meters round here, much less for rifling through people's mail.

Cress reached up to the shelf to pull herself to standing, and as she did so, she noticed a separate bundle of mail that had been stacked away from the others.

'What's this?' she asked. 'Who does this belong to?'

The old lady shrugged impatiently. 'Nobody know. No name. Eez pest.'

Cress looked at the address: PO Box 598.

'That's it!' she cried, faltering as she saw how many there were. 'Those are my letters! Oh, I'm so pleased! I thought we'd lost them for good.'

The old lady frowned at her.

'Letters?' Rosie said. 'Don't you mean . . .'

'Precisely,' Cress said quickly. 'Well, we may as well take them back if they're just sitting there. They contain confidential information,' she said confidingly to the old lady, who was looking increasingly sceptical.

'And of course, we must thank you – again –' she said, handing over another twenty, 'for being so kind as to assist us.'

The old lady smiled at last. 'Eez pleasure.'

Cress pushed the bundle of letters into her bag and they went back to the car.

'Bridget never here,' said the old lady, the bribe loosening her tongue like liquor. 'But her daughter some time.'

'Really? I don't suppose you'd happen to know her name.'

'Eez Amelie.'

'Amelie?' Amelie Hillier. Finally, she was getting somewhere. 'Thank you! Thank you very much,' she smiled.

She had two new names. She had her competitors' letters. She knew she was closing in on her man.

Chapter Thirty

England whizzed past the window, but Tor saw none of it. Not the magnificent stained-glass windows of Ely cathedral glinting in the morning sun, nor the centuries-old trees of Thetford Forest shedding their summer coats, nor the ancient walls of the Sandringham estate standing as proud as any soldier, nor the imperious and splendid colleges of Cambridge bleaching in the sunshine. She didn't notice how the winding coast roads, dusted with sand and tickled by reeds, gave way to marshy fens, and then to traffic lights and dual carriageways, or how the sudden rush of chimneys introducing London's outer boundaries sat on the rooftops, smokeless and decorative.

The unopened copy of *The Times* sat on the vinyl-topped table. She hadn't got past the front page. She hadn't needed to. Global disasters couldn't compete with the implosion of her world, yet again.

Her eyes flickered down and she took in Amelia's emerald satin dress again, the way it lifted her swollen bosom, how those clever little pleats beneath the bust-line created just enough fabric to accommodate that teeny hint of bump, without adding inches to her hips.

James photographed well, she thought, what she could see of him. He was half cropped out, but he looked bemused, hanging back a bit to let the photographers get their shot of the star, his eyes down, but his mouth in a wide smile, an insouciant hand in his pocket.

Tor had long been of the opinion that most men couldn't carry off black tie. They looked like schoolboys in their first suit, too starched and aware of what they were wearing. But he looked good in it, wearing it with all the ease of pyjamas. He was buttoned up, showing off the jacket's immaculate cut, but all Tor saw was the spread of his shoulders, and remembered how the barathea had rippled beneath her fingers that night.

Three months. That was what Amelia would have been when they'd gone to bed. Had he known? Surely he must have. She'd always known she was pregnant by seven weeks . . . He had to have known. It was his bloody job to know. He couldn't *not* have known.

She felt the tears threaten but she sniffed quickly, trying to pull herself together. Not that it mattered. The first class carriage, bought for a £5 upgrade offer, was practically empty. The commuters were already at their desks and the only other passenger was an elderly man in checked golfing trousers and a trilby, doing the crossword and stuck on 15 across.

She dropped her head back against the headrest and closed her eyes, letting the banished memories from that night, only two weeks ago, flood her senses, flushing her cheeks with shame and – she hated herself for it but it didn't change the bloody fact – desire.

He'd known but he'd still pursued her. When she'd said she was going to Harry, he'd actually barred the door. He simply couldn't countenance losing out to Harry Hunter. Not again. Harry had stolen Coralie from him – wasn't that what Kate had said? He'd seduced her just for the principle of getting in first. There was no greater turn-on than winning to these alpha males.

She lifted her head sharply and looked, unseeing again, out of the window. He was detestable. The lowest of the low. A liar and a cheat. And that wasn't even bringing up what he'd done to Kate and Monty. Or Hugh. Clearly, he was a man who couldn't bear to lose, whatever the costs, whatever the consequences. She felt the hate and the fury flash around her blood. She hated him. She really did. She really, really hated him . . . She took a deep breath and tried to capture the moment. She was going to hold on to this feeling and sustain it and be inured to him once and for all. Because she hated him.

She was on page three before she realized that the train had actually stopped and she was in King's Cross. The man in the trilby had long gone. She grabbed her empty Gladstone bag and smacked the paper down on the table. She didn't need that trash.

The lock was stiff, but, falling straight back into old habits, she pulled the door in a little, before turning the key. It gave easily then and she pushed heroically against the door and stumbled into the hall. The post was shin-deep. She sighed – another bad sign. Kate had volunteered to check the house weekly, forwarding bills and important-looking post to Tor in Burnham Market, but she clearly hadn't been around for a while.

Tor hadn't heard from her. Nor had Cress. In fact, no one had. The fall-out from the revelation about Billy had been catastrophic. The Marfleets had separated immediately, with Kate apparently refusing to speak to Monty or try counselling. By the time Monty got back from Cornwall (she'd hijacked Harry's chopper, much to his amusement), she'd shut the door on their marriage and moved into a hotel. He hadn't seen her since.

From what Cress had heard from Mark, he was in pieces, oscillating crazily between frantic anxiety about Kate, fury at Lily and James's deception, and hesitant joy that Billy was his son. He'd taken some time off work to try to sort his head out, but Billy was already back at Wellington and refusing to take calls from anyone – including his mother – and Lily was equally uncommunicative. She was belligerently unrepentant that she had kept Monty so near and yet so far from his own son, and appeared to be oblivious to everyone's distress, except her own.

Tor had tried ringing countless times on Kate's mobile but it always went to voicemail, and none of her messages were ever returned or acknowledged. Kate clearly felt Tor had sided with the Whites, despite her messages to the contrary. She had been found guilty by association.

She didn't know what to do. Kate was notorious for being in control, detached. She was scary at the best of times. Monty always used to joke that only the dumb psychopaths killed; the best ones became lawyers. But now that she'd cut herself loose from her old life – her childhood sweetheart, her old friends, her home – who knew what the rules were, or how best to approach her? Cress counselled giving her time and space, so they were giving that idea a trial run, but it was hard not to keep picking up the phone and leaving more plaintive messages.

Tor stood in the hallway and looked around, feeling her family's own distinctive smell creep around her like a shawl. A thick layer of dust had covered the radiator cover, and the

Patek Philippe bowl on top sat like a modern day still-life, with crinkly, yellowing Waitrose receipts, some coppers and a spare set of keys for the Mini inside.

Tor handled the keys of the car Hugh had died in. The car insurance money had come through the previous week – enough to help pay a year's worth of school fees. Her mind had increasingly begun to wander to a return to London. She wasn't sure she could carry on living in The Twittens, given the change in circumstances with the Marfleets.

Monty had been very sweet, of course. When she'd spoken to him the previous week – checking how he was getting on – she'd raised moving out, but he had insisted their troubles had nothing to do with her (Kate obviously hadn't mentioned finding Tor in bed with James) and that she must stay there as long as she liked.

But she felt awkward. Her fling with James, if it ever got out, would be considered to compromise her loyalty. How could she accept their hospitality, knowing she'd bedded the man at the root of their break-up? It might have been different if Kate was talking to her, but given that the friendship appeared to be in meltdown, as well as the marriage, she didn't want to cause yet further opprobrium.

Anyway, the end was in sight for the Twittens project. Since returning from Cornwall, she'd cast James out of her thoughts by putting her head down and working like a demon, trying to finish the projects she'd started and mobilize some cashflow. She'd begun the Twittens job two and a half months ago, but her need to fill her head with something other than James White meant she'd achieved nearly as much in the last fortnight as she had over the entire summer. But with Marney now at school, Millie at nursery, Hen unofficial nanny to Oscar and her mobile switched off

– enabling her to be as adept at avoiding James's calls as Kate was at avoiding hers – all that remained now was to do the drawing room and kitchen. Once they were completed, it would be difficult to justify staying on.

She walked down the hallway into the kitchen, trailing her hand – habitually – along the dado rail. The pictures of the children stuck with magnets to the fridge looked outdated already – they had grown up so quickly this summer, more quickly than they ever would again – and Tor ran her fingers over their glossy, chubby faces.

She looked around her beloved old kitchen. The rainbow-striped oilcloth on the table hadn't been wiped down properly and there were rings from where the girls' smoothies had dripped; a bunch of ranunculus roses had dried in the vase, their fragile silhouettes only a breath away from collapsing into a powdery heap; some mismatched cups and two Marks & Spencer plates were still out on the draining board, and the girls' drawings she'd sellotaped to the walls had begun to curl up at the bottom. Her eyes came to rest on the framed photo-collage of Tor and Hugh taken in those heady years before the children came along, when life was a constant stream of weddings and parties and lie-ins. They looked so young, so in love.

She inhaled deeply at the scene. It was like being Goldilocks and walking into the bears' house. Everything seemed . . . suspended. Not tidied away, or packed up. Just abandoned, as they waited for the porridge to cool.

She went to the sink and let the water run for a minute or so, before filling up the kettle and making some black coffee. She usually liked it milky, but today it suited her black. She needed something bitter. Truth be told, she could have done with a straight whisky. A few drops scalded her hands and she realized they were shaking. She stood at the window and looked out to the garden. It was completely overgrown and the grass was practically knee-high, just as it had been at The Twittens when they first arrived. How quickly things revert to being wild, she thought to herself.

She had felt the temptation herself – an irresistible pull to just let everything collapse into its feral state. But she couldn't. Not with the children. Hugh might have died, but she didn't have the time to fall apart. Not yet – anyway. She still had to do the weekly shopping, the nightly baths, find new schools and pay the bills. It wasn't love that made her world go round. It was children.

She sipped the coffee and went into the drawing room. Piles of unmade-up removal boxes stood propped against the wall. She hardly knew where to begin. She'd always known today was going to be tough. But this . . . this was worse than she'd thought. Stepping back into her old skin, even for just an afternoon, was stultifying.

She had managed only three weeks here after Hugh's death, before fleeing. Twenty-four days of lying in bed, not sleeping. Twenty-four days of sitting at the table, not eating; twenty-four days of shivering in cashmere in the heatwave. She had fled like an asylum seeker, looking for safety and refuge. And in Norfolk she had found it. The physical space she'd put between her family and her old life had been balm to their loss. It had been so much easier to start a new life than rebuild their old one. It had spared them the agony of constant stimulus, memories, reminders of Hugh.

He was everywhere here. A pair of his shoes – the brown suede brogues – poked out from beneath the tapestried ottoman, his comb was on top of the mantelpiece, the drawings for the council offices he'd been looking through just before Cress's party had been stacked on top of some of Marney's comics.

Tor dropped her head and tried to breathe through the pain of each and every stabbing reminder of this life interrupted. But it was no good. Bravery didn't make her feel any better – only other people. She slid down the wall and began to cry.

The tears were relentless, harsh and double-edged. They weren't just for Hugh. She had come to accept his death. It didn't surprise her any more. She didn't expect to wake up and find him lying next to her, warm and floppy and a heavy hand across her hip. She had let him go.

But not his words. That vicious showdown which should have been nothing more than a bad fight had become their swansong, superseding the whole nine years of happy marriage that went before it. His accusations that their happy family was a charade tainted their history, soured her memories and through his death had become the defining statement of their marriage. Their happiness had been real for her, but that didn't seem to count. He had had the last words. They were the ones that stood.

By the time her tears abated, her coffee was cold, but she had no stomach for it any more. Blankly, she started picking up the toys, collecting up the photos, gathering together the DVDs and packing away everything that had characterized their life there. The estate agent had said just to leave the bare bones – the furniture, cutlery, kitchen equipment and so on. They'd take a full inventory before the tenants arrived the following week. The new occupants had taken a year-long let, but with a six-month break clause. Tor had insisted upon that. She wanted the freedom to pick up where they left off – just in case they ever could.

She emptied the room and climbed the stairs, going through the children's bedrooms, absorbing the love in them from the memory bank of bedtime cuddles, tickles on the changing mat, stories on the nursing chair. She sat in them for a long time, the sound of their giggles, the splashing at bathtime, the hushed lullabys and all the glorious noises that had filled this house and given it spirit, swimming in her head; all of it trying to be heard above the death mask of guilt and recriminations and accusations; trying to reassure her that they had been happy. He was wrong, he was wrong, he was wrong, he was wrong . . .

Tor walked into the master bedroom and opened the wardrobes, packing everything into the hanging boxes the moving company had left out for her. She and Cress had co-rented a space in Big Yellow Storage together after all, and Cress had arranged to come over with the delivery men this afternoon to take it all away. Personally, Tor couldn't see how there'd be any room for Cress's stuff by the time she had finished packing up the house, but Cress was adamant she only really needed it for old paperwork and her Christmas stash (she'd already bought most of her presents, even though it was only the third week in September).

Tor folded the flaps on the last of her boxes, and looked over at Hugh's section. His shirts were still hanging, colour-coded, on the top rail; the ties dangling limply through the hangers. She started moving quickly, trying to stay ahead of her own emotions, folding his shirts, rolling his boxers and socks, and putting the shoes back in their dust bags – everything he hadn't had a chance to take with him that last night – as though she was just packing for a holiday. But before she could catch herself, she sniffed at his jumpers, trying to capture his smell one last time. It had faded already. What she wouldn't give to bottle his scent.

Fat tears were still tumbling down her cheeks, but these ones were silent and better behaved. She came to the suits – that navy one which was always slightly too wide in the shoulder; the grey flannel with the pleated trousers she'd never liked; that ghastly chalk stripe that he'd bought in a sale and she'd banned him from ever wearing. And then she got to his dinner suit. It wasn't bespoke, not as smart as James's, not a midnight blue Savile Row cut, but a drabber off-the-rack black, which he had still always looked so handsome in; he was another man who'd worn black tie well. She thought about Oscar and decided to keep the DJ, along with Hugh's favourite grey suit – his only made-to-measure – his cashmere-blend overcoat and a collection of seven-fold silk ties they'd bought in Venice before Marney was born.

That was it. His essence, edited. This was what Oscar would have to remember his father by. Looking down at the paltry bag, she hoped it was enough. But how could it ever be? No matter how much her heart tried to convince her head, it still felt like her fault.

Chapter Thirty-one

Kate's phone had stopped ringing but she was too happy to care. It had been four days now since Tor had left her last whining message, six since Cress's. None from Lily or James, of course. And as for Monty, well – his calls, which had been every twenty minutes, had dropped back to twice a day. They all seemed to be getting the message, at last. You could train dogs faster, she'd laughed, with Harry.

The past few weeks had been fabulous. They'd barely got out of bed. She had called in to the office and block-booked scores of off-site meetings with Mr Hunter. The other partners didn't care – so long as she was billing him and keeping the star client happy.

If only they knew, she thought to herself. He's fucking delirious.

She swung her legs out of bed and walked to the window. It was 10.40 a.m. and London was wide awake. The cabbies were honking their horns, red buses were belching out black fumes and everyone was busy, distracted, late, disengaged. She sighed with contentment at the scene of urban bliss beneath her. There wasn't a buggy or bump in sight. She felt more relaxed than she had in years. How could it have taken her so long to realize that she was living the wrong life? Married to a man she should have left dumped as a teenager, a man whom Mother Nature had clearly been saying wasn't her biological mate. And living on the fringes of Nappy Valley, overlooking all the other people who were living the life she should have had. How could Monty have been so insensitive keeping her there, so blind to her pain?

She knew now that there was so much more to life than babies and coffee mornings. Harry had shown her that. He'd taken her into a London she didn't even know existed. A London where a spontaneous supper was at San Lorenzo and a swim was at the RAC, where a morning's sightseeing was in Getty's helicopter (the only one licensed to fly over the City), and where the red-brick walls of the mansions in Holland Park camouflaged not just Old Masters but the hard-partying antics of the young elite.

She'd met so many new people, made so many new friends – all of them in the papers, of course, and the partners were practically wetting themselves at the prospect of all the new business she was bringing their way, as she casually name-dropped in meetings. It wasn't just her personal life in the ascendant. So too was her career. She'd never done less work in her life, but she was making the Old Boys motto work for her: it isn't what you know, but who.

No one knew anything of her marriage break-up, so they didn't think too much about the change in her appearance – the mane lopped into a layered bob and the chic flowing Armani suits replaced by tight, tight Gucci.

Harry had just adored taking her shopping. She had been his plaything out of bed, as well as in, letting him choose everything for her. It had been delicious relinquishing all control for once. His car had crawled along Sloane Street and they'd jumped out in dark glasses, making furtive fifty-yard dashes into Versace for bum-skimming babydolls,

Alberta Ferretti for demure 'work function' chiffons, Gina for fuck-me boots and Dolce & Gabbana for corset dresses she could barely get on before he'd take them off her again. He'd made a private visit to Myla and come back with the sauciest demi-tasse bras, whalebone corsets and minuscule thongs she'd ever seen, and he'd even bought her a black satin French maid's outfit, which, had Monty ever brought it home, she'd have knocked him out cold.

Life had become a whirl of glamour and cocktails and whitened teeth and dirty sex. There were several parties a night, and they were all over each other behind closed doors, but in public the wall came down and she networked as his lawyer, taking great pains not to appear remotely intimate or personal. It didn't take long for her to realize that the colder she was with him in public, the more it drove him wild. So it became their little game. Foreplay. To see them at some events was to think there was a cold war. But it was a different matter in the back of the car on the way home, and she'd given up worrying about what Christophe, his driver, saw. Harry had long paid him a fat bonus for his discretion.

She padded into the bathroom and turned on the shower, trying to push back down the wave of nausea that rose in her throat. Her body was dog-tired – bed wasn't for sleeping in these days – and there was no doubt the hard partying was beginning to tell. It was getting harder and harder to get up in the mornings, and there were bags on the bags under her eyes.

She was due in the office at eleven, but Harry had put her up in his club so she was only a two-minute walk away. She had loads of time to soak, recover and shake off last night, before facing the world for another day.

She felt the hot water run over her face, over her shoulders and down her back, feeling the warmth spread around her body. She stayed under the hot stream for a luxuriant five extra minutes – today's hangover was spectacularly bad – before turning the water off and wrapping the enormous bath sheet around her. She went over to the wardrobe and stood huddled in front of the groaning rails, feeling bewildered by the choice. She'd never thought the six-star lifestyle could be so exhausting. Where to start?

It was 11.10 a.m. when she wiggled down the corridor in the Vivienne Westwood navy pinstripe hobble skirt.

'Sorry, Camilla. Nightmare on the Northern Line again,' she said briskly, putting her new chocolate crocodile Kelly on her secretary's desk and picking up the files from her tray. 'What've I got?'

'A new client is waiting for you in the Red Room.'

'Great, thanks. Send through some coffee, would you?'

She unlocked her office door and put down her bag, pausing to give it an admiring stroke – Harry had leapfrogged the two-year waiting list in just four days – before picking up her laptop and walking slowly to the conference room. She just couldn't move any faster in this skirt, dammit. God help her if there was a fire. She'd have to ask Nicholas Parker to give her a fireman's lift out of the building.

She opened the door, the charming smile she'd spread across her face fading fast as she saw her client.

She shut the door behind her, quickly.

'What are you doing here?' she hissed.

'Isn't it obvious?' Monty said. 'How else did you expect me to get hold of you? You won't return my calls. No one's heard from you. I have no idea where you're staying.'

He stared at her. He couldn't believe how good she looked. She'd had her hair cut and she'd dropped a few pounds. And that suit – he'd never seen her in anything so slinky. Especially not for work.

'Where are you staying?' he frowned.

'That's none of your business,' she clipped. She couldn't believe how dreadful he looked. He'd lost a colossal amount of weight and seemed to have aged eight years. His sandy-blond hair had started to grey, as though the pigmentation was draining out of him, as if he was being slowly washed away.

'You can't stay here, Monty. I've got another appointment in ten min— ' she checked her watch. 'No, in five minutes. I'm running late. This isn't the time or the place.'

'Then when is? How am I expected to reach you?'

'You're not. My lawyers will contact you with all the relevant paperwork.'

She couldn't look at him. He was ruining her day.

'The paperw— ' His mouth dropped open. 'What paperwork? What are you saying?'

'You know exactly what I'm saying. There's no point in us pretending any longer. It's over. It has been for a long time.'

'For Christ's sake, Kate! Be reasonable,' he pleaded. 'This isn't my fault. It's all as much a surprise to me as it is to you.'

'Yup. Bit of a difference though. You get the consolation prize of being a daddy. Me? I'm the same as I ever was.'

'But I don't want this without you.'

'You are a father. I'm not a mother. I can't do this with you. Not like this.'

Monty dropped his face in his hands and turned away.

How had everything turned out like this? He still couldn't take it in. Lily's lies. James's complicity. Billy his son. And now Kate – carefree, unconcerned. Gone.

'The marriage was failing anyway, Monts,' she said quietly. 'Deep down, you know that. We weren't going to make it. It was too hard.'

He turned back to face her. For all her cold words, she looked tiny at the other side of the table. He moved around it, taking her hands in his.

'Kate, you don't mean any of this. You know I have nothing without you. It's always been about you. Ever since we were kids.'

'Not for fifteen crucial minutes though, hey?' She slid her hands out of his and backed away.

'Kate, I was eighteen! I was trying to do what I thought I ought to be doing – playing the field, sowing my oats. But it wasn't what I wanted. Even then, when I was just one giant hormone.'

Kate shrugged and perched on the edge of the table. 'Maybe,' she said. 'But you know what? This is what I want now. Because I'm having a ball.' She saw the incredulity cross his face. 'No, really. There is actually an upside of not having kids – freedom. Hedonism. Time. Cash. You don't get any of that with babies, you know. But you and I – we didn't appreciate it. We didn't realize what we had. We didn't go out and take drugs and have sex in the park. We stayed in and went to bed early, as though there really was a baby in the next room and we couldn't get a babysitter. We tried to live both lives and ended up having neither.'

She slapped a hand down on the table and began to laugh. 'I mean – what the fuck were we doing, Monty, living childless in the middle of Nappy Valley?' She tipped her head back and laughed at their own ridiculousness.

Monty watched her. This euphoria, this anti-kids rhetoric. Where was it coming from? What was making her so damned happy?

She heard the elevators ping open and wiggled off the table. He watched her move. She seemed so sexual. Sexed up.

Christ – was she seeing someone?

'That'll be my next client,' she said, smiling patiently. Patronizingly. As though the breakdown of their marriage was nothing more than paperwork she wanted to clear off her desk.

'So that's it?' he asked.

'I'll be in touch about the division of assets. I suggest we each draw up a list and then meet again to discuss it. There's no need for this to be anything other than amicable.'

She opened the door and walked through it. He followed after her, his mouth open, his heart in his boots.

'I'll be right with you,' he heard her saying. He looked up and found Harry Hunter, in a blue open-necked shirt, navy cashmere tank and jeans, sitting on the leather sofa, arms splayed out wide across the top, an ankle resting casually on his knee.

'I'm happy to wait for you,' Harry smiled back at her.

Monty looked at Kate. Her cheeks had flushed a little, and her body language seemed to have become . . . coquettish, somehow.

Oh no, not a crush on Harry Hunter, he despaired. She didn't stand a chance. He felt so protective of her, seeing her single and tough and all on her own in the big bad world, with cocky bastards like Harry looking for an easy lay.

'Monty,' Harry acknowledged, getting up from the sofa and offering a hand.

'Harry,' Monty said, shaking back, unaware of Harry's role in the Cornwall debacle.

'I'm not sure what the right thing is to say in these situations. But I hear you're a father,' Harry said. 'Congratulations?'

Monty's smile froze.

'Very kind of you, Harry,' he said, looking back to Kate. 'I'll see you later,' he said, trying to keep their marriage woes private from Harry and hoping desperately she'd come to her senses and walk back through their front door.

He walked into the lifts and pressed to go down, watching her walk slowly back to her office – she clearly couldn't walk in such a daft skirt – to where Harry was waiting.

'He won't, will he?' Harry murmured into her neck, once she'd locked her door.

She sighed as she felt his hands travel up and down her body. 'Of course not,' she breathed.

'Good. Because I was planning something special for us tonight. I've told Emily I'm in Bristol accepting an honorary degree.' He chuckled at the deception. He still hadn't managed to get her to go out in public with him. Camerashy wasn't the word. She was perfectly happy playing wife, holed up in the riverside apartment and waiting for him to come home. And frankly, since getting it on with Kate in Cornwall, he'd lost all momentum in trying to get her to do anything at all. It suited him fine if she wanted to stay there.

At Kate's behest, he'd spent the previous night with Emily – so that he didn't arouse her suspicion that anyone else was on the scene – but even the prospect of her impressive sexual gymnastics didn't hold their usual thrill, and it was 10 p.m.

before he rocked in. She was sulking, of course, but it only took two orgasms in twenty minutes for all to be forgiven, and she had ordered in truffle risotto from San Lorenzo for supper, whereupon they collapsed on the sofa and he hadn't had to deal with her for the rest of the night. Job done.

For one night anyway. Kate wouldn't go public with him, nor let him dump Emily until he had secured paparazzo proof of his relationship with her first. Kate kept warning him that Emily could be very dangerous, but it pissed him off. It was pointless having one woman in one apartment, and another at his club, and both of them a secret.

'Where are you taking me?' Kate asked, moaning a little as he unbuttoned her jacket and found her wearing just the cupless bra underneath.

'Here. On the desk. Twice,' he smiled, eyes dancing.

She giggled helplessly. But he wasn't lying.

Chapter Thirty-two

Fat clouds plodded across the sky, and Cress shivered on her recliner as she watched Greta push the children on the swings in the garden and play around the very tree where she'd shagged her boyfriend.

'Hon, can you pass my jumper?' she asked, looking over at Mark, who was reading the paper – or supposed to be. His eyes were on Greta too.

She looked back down again quickly. Nearly a month had passed since she'd found him at the window, and she was only just blagging her way through it. She was sleeping in the spare room, blaming a noisy radiator for keeping her awake at night, but she knew Mark wasn't buying it. They hadn't had sex since she'd come back from Cornwall – it was the longest time they'd ever gone without each other – and she could tell he was increasingly frustrated, snapping at the kids and spending long hours in the gym in the basement, knocking the bejesus out of the punchbag.

They had tried a few times, to be fair. She wasn't withholding out of spite. But just as her body had started to respond to his touch, the image of him watching Greta had replayed itself in her mind and she had pulled away angrily, frigidly. Did she measure up? Could her body, which had borne four children, match up to Greta's tight, springy figure?

She watched her nanny do delicate ballet-runs across the lawn like a gazelle, closely followed by Flick copying her, her arms above her head in a very dodgy first position. Not a hope. Cress didn't fancy her chances against Greta in a tutu.

She looked back at the paperwork on her lap – her signature green ink scrawled all over the drafts. There was precious little progress on that front either, despite Rosie suspending all her PA duties to investigate further. It had turned out Brendan Hillier was dead – had been for quite a long time actually: August 1989, so at least that ruled him out as the *Wrong Prince* author. Rosie had managed to establish that the deeds to the flat had passed to this woman, Bridget Hillier, although they still didn't know who she was. Sister? Aunt? Cousin? Mother? And searches on Amelie Hillier were still bringing up nothing.

Poor Rosie was searching every public record office she could think of, but the backlogs for each were several weeks long and seemingly even a cash incentive couldn't leapfrog you to the front. Cress was tempted to just park Rosie in a camper-van outside the flat and wait for one of the Hilliers to return. So what if it freaked out the neighbours?

She handled the thick bundle of letters, now tied together with string, which she'd taken from the Felden Street flat. Seven publishing houses had come back with offers to publish. Seven! Whoever this author was, if he ever got hold of these letters, he could command a bidding war that would price Sapphire out of the market. Despite the company's paper value, and the bank's goodwill, there would be a cash-flow crisis if talks went beyond a certain ceiling.

Too cold to stay outside any longer, she got up and went into the house. The phone was ringing. She picked it up, cradling it on one shoulder while she peered into the larder cupboard for some nibbles.

'Yes?' she said brusquely, spying a packet of dried apple rings.

'Mrs Pelling? It's Mrs Beevor, from Littlington Hall.'

Lucy's headmistress? What did she want? Cress felt herself tense. It was either money, or help at the Christmas Fayre. Please God, let it be money.

'How can I help you, Mrs Beevor?'

'I was ringing to inquire whether there was a particular reason you didn't attend Lucy's parents' evening on Thursday? We had you down for the 7.20 p.m. slot and I know several of Lucy's teachers were keen to speak to you.'

Parents' evening? This was the first she'd heard of it.

'I'm sorry, Mrs Beevor. I had no idea parents' evening had even been on.'

'We sent the letters home in the book bags.'

'Hang on a moment, could you? I'll just consult the diary.' Cress went into the study and brought back the family diary, a big brown leather desk-bound volume in which she and Mark wrote down their various schedules on a daily basis, and Greta added in the children's appointments – play dates, dental appointments, events at school and so on. Cress couldn't imagine not consulting it. It was a habit as regular as brushing her teeth.

As she walked back into the kitchen, she looked out into the garden. The game had ended in tears, with Felicity crying and Orlando looking sheepish. Mark was holding her in his arms as Greta played peekaboo – or was it Happy Families? – from behind his arm to make her laugh. She was holding his bicep, standing so close, and Cress could see that her hair was tickling Mark's neck, her breasts brushing his arm.

Felicity was in fits, though. She wondered whether both levels of Greta's play were having the desired effect.

'Mrs Pelling?'

She looked quickly back down.

'Um . . . where was I? Oh yes, let me see . . . Thursday . . . what was the date? . . . Oh, here it is. Thursday the twenty-seventh. I'm quite sure . . . oh!'

There it was. Written in Greta's distinctive European hand. 'Parents' Evening, Littlington, Prep Block, Room 17, 7.20 p.m.' She was sure it hadn't been there on Thursday morning. She remembered checking because she'd had a hair appointment and couldn't remember the time.

'Well, I don't know what to say, Mrs Beevor. It's written here, plain as day, but I just don't know how I managed to miss it.' There was a stiff silence as Kathleen Beevor took in Cress's weak excuse. Cress was well known among the teachers and other parents for her hands-off approach to parenting – she never did the school run, and had missed last year's nativity and sports day – and Kathleen had long suspected it was the root of Lucy's increasingly troublesome behaviour.

Still, she had three children at the school, and one more to come up. Her termly fees were significant, so it wouldn't do to kick her into touch. Besides, everybody knew Cressida Pelling was Harry Hunter's publisher. Although she rarely graced the school grounds, there was a palpable buzz of excitement among the mothers at the gates and the admin staff in the office when she did stride in. Kathleen was biding her time before angling for Harry to do a reading at the school. The Board of Governors would lap it up.

'Well, we all lead such busy lives, don't we? Shall we reschedule another time? Lucy's teachers do feel we need to meet as a matter of urgency.'

She touched briefly on the topic of concern, and they arranged a date for the following week. Cress put the phone down, stunned, wondering how on earth she was going to tell Mark not only that they'd missed this key event in their daughter's school career, but that their eldest child was also the class bully.

She looked back at Greta's original diary entry. She didn't understand how she could have missed it. Unless . . . a thought struck her . . . unless Greta had entered it *after* the event.

Cress narrowed her eyes. It had to have been that. Another petty sabotage. She and Mark had argued only the previous morning when she'd realized her Perretti gold bone cuff was missing and had suggested asking Greta point-blank if she'd taken it. Mark had hit the roof. He'd said if Cress was going to get rid of her, she'd need a rock-solid charge and not some jealous hunch. It had occurred to Cress to ask Mark why he would think she was jealous of Greta – did she have reason to be? But she had left it.

She closed the diary and put it back on the desk in the study. She needed some air, and anyway, the phone call had reminded her of something she needed to deal with. If she popped out now, no one would even notice she'd gone. She walked over to the bookcase next to the fireplace and ran her manicured hand along the spines of a collection of tall leather volumes, looking for the join. When her fingers found it, she pushed down firmly and the dummy door swung back, revealing the gunmetal grey safe.

She deftly entered the code and felt the door click open. Ignoring the pillarbox red leather Asprey boxes, and the formally waxed wills, she reached down to the glossy Littlington Hall prospectus lying on the floor of the safe.

She sank down into the chair and opened it up. There, in the back cover, was an innocuous brown envelope, with Strictly Private and Confidential stamped twice, boasting that its contents were more important than they looked.

My, hadn't that proved to be the case.

Whoever had sent it had taken no chances. Cress's name had been printed, rather than hand-written, and it had been hand-delivered. The porters hadn't been able to give a description of the courier – Sapphire shared the building (and postal depot) with four other companies – as most of them made the drop with their motorcycle helmets still on.

She peered inside the envelope, just to reassure herself it was still there, and clasped it to her chest. It had been an enormous risk leaving it in the safe – Mark could have chanced upon it many times. But he hadn't really been her main concern. It was Harry Hunter she didn't trust. With his money, there were plenty of avenues open to him for making sure he got what he wanted. When the alarm hadn't been set the night she'd come back from Cornwall, she'd thought . . .

But she'd thought wrong. Over-estimated Harry Hunter and under-estimated the nanny on that occasion. Anyway, she didn't want to think back to that night. What did it matter now? There could be room for only one thing in her mind – getting this evidence out of the house.

Chapter Thirty-three

She wasn't stupid. Or certainly not as stupid as she looked, anyway. The blonde hair and habitual bra-lessness could be deceptive, but she knew what was going on. The doors of the elevator trilled open and she saw the resident clique of photographers sitting on their mopeds outside. She pushed open the door and they rushed forwards, camera poised. With her red beret, tight jeans and navy-striped jumper, she was every inch Harry's type. Posh Totty done up as Miss October.

''Ere, you don't know when Mr Hunter's gonna be home, do you, love?'

'What?' Emily gasped. 'Harry Hunter lives here? Ohmigod! You are kidding me! I had no idea. Which apartment's he in?'

They dropped back with disappointment. 'The penthouse,' they said wearily. He had been around here less and less recently. She wasn't the only one with her suspicions.

'Oh yes. Of course,' she giggled. 'I guess he would be, wouldn't he? No wonder I haven't seen him. My studio's practically in the boiler room.' She wrinkled her nose as though it was a dingy bedsit on the Old Kent Road, even though the smallest studios in the building still commanded upwards of £500,000.

They nodded, already bored – it looked like another no-show today.

'Hey, I don't suppose I could give you my number to pass on to him – you know, when you see him?'

'He doesn't really stop to chat, if you get my drift,' one of them said.

'Oh, yes, I see.' She shrugged. 'Well, you can't blame a girl for trying, right?' And she skipped down the steps and towards Chelsea Bridge, her brown vintage satchel swinging on her shoulder, her hair catching the breeze.

If she was more intelligent than she looked, she also looked more beautiful than she felt. Harry hadn't been near her for weeks. The stream of excuses had been endless – pre-production meetings in LA, research trips for the next title, awards ceremonies, book readings, nightclub launches, chat shows, boutique openings, honorary degree ceremonies. He'd even stopped in his endless quest of trying to get her to go out to places with him. She kept telling him she wanted respect, but what she really needed was more time.

She inhaled deeply as she strode over the arc of the bridge, lost in thought and oblivious to the double-takes and honking car horns. She'd been making herself indispensable, giving him all the things the other women didn't even get a chance to try: cooking his meals, giving him packed lunches when he went off to write in the British Library (the only place he could work); ironing his shirts and shagging him senseless.

And it had been working. Jeremy, his butler, had said she'd put him out of a job (not with the last bit, clearly), and even he had raised his eyebrows at this relationship's unusual endurance. So when Emily had asked him to give her a key to the Kensington house so that she could surprise him for his upcoming birthday, he had broken his employer's cardinal rule and given it to her – a gold-dipped one! The very fact that she even knew about it told Jeremy that Mr Hunter had discussed it with her – a most unusual step. That in itself was tacit approval.

But Emily wasn't really going there to arrange a birthday surprise. Something – or someone – had changed it all, and she knew she needed to protect herself. Time was running out. Emily was living in his apartment, but he'd spent less than a week with her there in the past month. All the other nights, he'd stayed at his club. It was 'more centrally located', he kept saying. But he scarcely made up for it when he was with her – just a few weeks ago he'd been like a lifer let loose in a brothel, practically chasing her from room to room. Now? Well, she'd never have believed he could be so . . . polite, sexually.

The fact was, she didn't share his life, only his bed. He hadn't even mentioned Kensington to her. As far as he was concerned, she didn't even know it existed. Despite her best efforts to be more than the others – to stand out – she was still nothing more than his illicit thrill. And now he was slipping away from her.

A rickety Routemaster coughed phlegmatically next to her, its route impeded by the solid chain of traffic, and she jumped on, gripping the smeared handrail tightly as she climbed the steps to the top and took a seat right at the front.

She looked down from her perch and watched London dance in its new autumn colours. Ginger leaves chased each other along the pavements, leaving the stripped trees to gently shiver against the streaky skies. The sun had lost its power but none of its personality, and it threw long shadows on the ground and shimmering sparkles on the water as pedestrians ambled by, enjoying the new-season feeling of being cosy and wrapped up.

The journey took nearly forty minutes – Chelsea, South Ken, Gloucester Road – but Emily was in no rush.

She jumped off at Kensington High Street and started walking up Church Street, moving past the boutique windows without even glancing at all the temptations they had to offer. She wove deftly through the crowds, coming to a small, cobbled one-way lane with a deli on the corner and scores of office workers queuing from the counter and out the door.

She strode on until the lane opened out suddenly into a leafy square surrounded on all sides by grand red-brick mansions with ornate mullioned windows and shiny black double doors. But she didn't stop. She walked through it, and turned right up the hill, heading towards Notting Hill and Holland Park, where the houses were bigger still. Here the houses were rendered Regency and set well back from the road, with magnolia trees still in bloom – as though Nature had reserved this little nicety just for this tiny, wealthy pocket – and imposing electric gates keeping out the riff-raff.

Harry's pile was set right on the crest of the hill and she could already tell that the rooms at the top would be afforded the most commanding views of London. And to think she'd thought those were the USP of the riverside apartment . . .

She stood at the keypad by the entrance gate and entered the code Jeremy had given her. P-U-S-S-Y. She sighed at the predictability of it all. There was a momentary pause and then the solid black gates silently, smoothly, swung open.

She gasped at the sight before her. The garden was like a mini Versailles, with clipped, trimmed, practically brushed box hedges planted in curves and symmetrical sweeps around the lawn. A twinkling granite path led up to the steps where, at the top, sat the biggest lemon trees she had ever seen. To the far side sat Harry's favourite car, the blue Maserati, and the Range Rover.

She climbed the steps and rang the bell. No one answered. Jeremy had said as much. Harry had sent the housekeeping staff on to Verbier to get the chalet ready for his winter sojourn, but still – it didn't hurt to double-check.

Taking the key out of her pocket, her heart galloping, she opened the heavy door and stepped into the hallway, looking around for the control pad.

One.

Two.

Three . . .

Jeremy had said it was just behind the Magritte. She hadn't asked for further details, expecting a single impressive spotlit painting on the wall. Tada!

But looking at the museum-standard gallery stretching out in front of her, she couldn't tell the Magritte from the Manet or the Hirst, or the Freud or all the others either.

Four.

Five.

Six.

Seven . . .

She shut the door and walked quickly down the corridor, scanning the perimeter of each painting. Jeremy had said she'd only have twenty seconds to disengage the alarm before police helicopters and an armed response unit would be scrambled.

Eleven.

Twelve.

Thirteen . . .

Where was it? Where was it?

Fifteen.

Sixteen.

She was beginning to properly panic when she suddenly saw the glint of the LCD display. She ran over and swiped the card Jeremy had given her, beads of sweat popping up at her brow. She looked at the numbers. The pips had stopped at nineteen.

Emily leant against the wall and tried to gather her wits. She had come in legitimately, she told herself. She had done nothing wrong. She was just at her boyfriend's house. There was just one thing she needed to get and then she could go again. No big deal.

She walked through the hallway into the kitchen, her boots tapping on the marble floor. It wasn't as she'd imagined at all. She'd supposed he'd have more of the sleek, minimal bachelor style he had going on in the riverside apartment, but this was heavier, warmer. Triple-thickness granite worktops encircled the room, dissecting mahogany Clive Christian cabinetry, with imported antique delft tiles lining the walls. She counted a wine fridge, three sinks, four ovens.

The drawing room was even more impressive, the size of Claridge's ballroom, but with fewer chandeliers and better parquet.

She wondered where to start. The house was huge, far bigger than she'd imagined, and it could be anywhere. She checked the library – more mahogany cabinetry, lots of Tiffany reading lamps and a Stubbs on the wall, but no sign of what she wanted. It wasn't in the apartment. It had to be here.

She went through the bedrooms – all twelve of them immaculately left, as though ready to accommodate any unexpected visits by large parties such as the European Commission, say or the Olympic Federation – but nothing.

She found Harry's room right at the very top of the building and accessed by a private lift system. It had to be his. It was unlike anything she'd ever seen before. The room was round, housed in a tower not visible from the street, with curved glass walls encasing it on all sides. It was like being in the lamp room of a lighthouse. A telescope stood in the middle of the room, and she could see that the roof folded back like an observatory, so that he could watch the stars – or his more delectable neighbours.

The eight-foot bed had clearly been custom built and was carved in walnut, the footboard housing a flat-screen TV that slid up at the touch of a button. There was no art or curtains hanging on the glass walls, just London pulsing around him in concentric ripples. She stood at the wall and looked down over the smart slated rooftops and realized he really was the king of the castle. Master of all he surveyed. His wealth, success, achievement and power surpassed anything she had imagined. She realized she had done well to hold on to him this long.

Emily walked across the room into the bathroom and dressing room, and opened the wall of tobacco leather-faced wardrobes. Rails and rails of tweed jackets, cord jackets, linen and seersucker blazers hung there, just waiting to be chosen, each hanger lined with tissue paper and the shoulders covered with muslin. There was scarcely a suit to be seen. His shirts were bespoke, preferring a cutaway collar and double cuffs, and the stacks of cashmere jumpers looked like a Pantone colour chart.

She went to close the door when she noticed one of the cubbyholes wasn't filled with jumpers but front-faced. There was no handle, but when she pressed against it, a door sprang open.

Eureka! A laptop was inside, on idle, sitting on top of a plastic Fortnum's bag. She peered inside at the yellowing papers. She gave a little, sad smile. She couldn't resist dropping to her knees and booting up the laptop.

God, it was so fast. Hers took half a day to get going. Almost instantly it requested a password. She tried 'Harry'.

No.

Hunter?

No.

What about Harold? Was he a Harold? Apparently not.

What could it be? 'Pussy' didn't work, nor Maserati.

And then it occurred to her. What had brought him all this? She typed in 'Scion'.

Bingo. She was in. She scanned through the emails and then the movies. It didn't take long to find the file she was looking for. She felt her heart break a little as she saw it. A small part of her had hoped that she wouldn't find this, that coming here today would prove nothing more than paranoia. But as she pressed return and their first night of raw, dirty, insatiable sex popped up on the screen, he confirmed her hunch. It wasn't enough that he was trying to use the paparazzi as his witnesses. He was going to use this to blackmail her back too. She'd suspected as much when she'd found his homemade collection in the apartment. Why should she have been the only one to get away?

She watched their beautiful bodies on the screen, dispassionately. But she couldn't stomach more than a minute of it before inserting the USB flashdrive into the port and transferring the file. She sat on the floor while it saved down, her heart pounding with pain and relief. Then she took out the flashdrive and deleted the file.

She'd done it. She was in the clear. She had got what she'd

come for *and* covered her back in the process. But where did it leave them? How could she stay with him after this? Because she still wanted to, in spite of everything.

She logged off, put the memory stick into her satchel, grabbed the Fortnum's bag and stood up. She took one last look at the room, the intimate sanctuary she knew he was never going to bring her to. She turned to walk away, but something caught her eye. A twinkle.

What was that by the bed? Something was winking at her in the carpet. She walked over and picked up an earring. It was beautiful. A heart-shaped emerald surrounded by diamonds. A love token.

She dropped the earring back to the floor and looked around with fresh eyes. She hadn't thought to look for the other woman here. Even though she'd suspected as much, she'd assumed she was the one who had her feet under the table. She thought the nearest anyone got was the apartment she'd appropriated.

She walked back into the bathroom and looked in the Smallbone cabinet. There wasn't much – a Guerlain moisturizer, some Clinique lipstick, Lancôme mascara, Chanel powder – but it was enough. She checked the other wardrobe and found a few Marchesa gowns and some Dolce & Gabbana suits hanging there too. An Hermès whip was propped up in the corner.

Whoever she was, she had eclipsed Emily's efforts by quite some distance. If anyone was playing the wife, it was she. Emily was nothing more than the mistress.

She gulped as hot tears of humiliation ran down her cheeks, everything so clear now. He was out of her league, always had been. She was just a child playing with the grown-ups. It had all been a game to him. Just a frisky, kinky game. She had meant nothing after all.

She got into the lift and pressed to go down, wiping her tears away angrily. He had played her for a fool. Taken her at face value, the dumb blonde.

She ran down the spiral staircase, her hands clasping the handrail as she tried to see through the tears, down one floor, then another and then the other, until eventually, dizzy and breathless, she reached the marble hall.

She stood at the Magritte, wanting to punch it out of its frame and shock him the way he'd shocked her. But she'd never be so reckless. Revenge was a dish best served cold. She knew that better than anyone.

She leant an arm against the wall and tried to think clearly. She couldn't go back to the apartment. It would be tonight of all nights that Harry would come back, full of charm and sexual mischief, treating her like his best girl in the world.

She swiped the card over the alarm and the pips started to beep, and she fled to the door as hurriedly as when she'd first come in. She'd go back to her flat. She needed space to collect herself. To regroup. Think how best to play this.

Emily shut the enormous doors behind her and stumbled down the steps, out of the gate. It had started to rain. She felt a desperate need to get back to her own flat and hide. She checked her purse. She only had ten quid on her, but at this time of day, traffic would still be quite light and she could be home in under ten minutes. An orange light beamed over the top of the hill, and she flagged it down, passing off the tears as raindrops.

She collapsed, sobbing, on to the leather seat and began rummaging in her satchel. It had been so long since she'd gone home, at least four months – did she even have the keys on her? Don't say she'd have to go back to Battersea after . . . Her shaking hands found them. Thank God.

Roadworks in South Ken held them up and it took over fifteen minutes to get to the flat, so she only had enough to tip the cabbie thirty pence. She hiccupped apologetically and tried to explain, but he drove off without a word of thanks. What would she have said anyway? 'I'm sorry, but I'm Harry Hunter's girlfriend. I'm not used to carrying cash.' It sounded ridiculous. It was ridiculous.

It was raining hard now, the sky ominously dark, thunder rumbling in the distance, and she ran to the door, holding her bag above her head. She fiddled about with the keys, trying to fit the key in the lock, but the rain was cold and stinging on her back. By the time she did get it in, she was wet through, her bag sodden.

She shut the door behind her and leant against it, momentarily shocked out of her tears by the state of the shabby hall. She'd become so used to Harry's master of the universe opulence, she'd completely forgotten how – well, how tiny this little flat was. Still, it had always been a useful bolthole and her parents – who never used it – were signing over the deeds into her name, as her twenty-first birthday present. All her friends already had impressive apartments in South Ken and mews houses in Chelsea, and this somewhat undermined her party scene status as one of the gorgeous new girls about town, but it wasn't bad for a freebie – and at least she was on the property ladder.

She wiped her nose on her sleeve and checked the post. There was a horrendous amount, spilling on to the floor, most of it covered with dusty and muddy footprints, caused as the other residents trod over it on their way out and in. She actually couldn't believe they hadn't bagged it all up and chucked it away. She scooped up as big an armful as she could manage and staggered up the stairs. She'd have to come back down for the rest in a minute.

She unlocked the door, her satchel hanging from the crook of her elbow, her jeans clinging to her thighs, and pushed it open with her bottom. She tried to put the letters down on the table but they just slid over, the polythene wrappers of all the catalogues giving momentum so that they ended up in a heap on the floor.

She sighed and went back down to get the rest, just dropping it carelessly on to the kitchen floor when she got back. She pulled off her boots and beret, and walked through the tiny hallway into the bedroom, feeling her body begin to recover from the shock of the day's discoveries as she found sanctuary in her little flat. The whole thing probably only measured 800 square feet, and it was far from grand, but she loved it. The first thing she'd done when she'd moved back from Switzerland was to paint everything celadon and have white louvred shutters fitted to the windows. The floorboards beneath the old rotten sisal flooring had proved to be pretty decent – if a little draughty in winter – so she'd stained them with a dark varnish and thrown down some sumptuous sheepskin rugs. But it was the view that she loved best of all. It was pretty, not impressive like Harry's status skylines, but overlooking the well-kept gardens and hardwood conservatories of her flush neighbours, and she had loved looking out at it when she'd been working on her tiny terrace in the spring, sitting at her small round blue table, feeling like Audrey Hepburn in Gregory Peck's apartment in *Roman Holiday*.

She peeled off her jeans, slapping her thighs, which were bright red from the wet. She walked through to the bathroom – which was so small she hadn't been able to get a full-length bath in, and so had fitted a semi-upright slipper bath instead – and opened the taps, pouring in lashings of her favourite Benefit bath oil. She moved quickly around her little home, closing the shutters, putting a frozen pizza in the oven, and putting on the gas fire in the little sitting room so that it could heat up and the tell-tale blue flame would have disappeared by the time she came to sit down.

She switched on her computer and let the emails download while she soaked in the tub with a couple of bottles of Merlot – suitably dusty from several months on the worktop. It worked a treat, soothing her frazzled nerves into languid torpor, and by the time she slipped on her PJs and sat eating pizza slices on the sofa, the discovery that her boyfriend had both forgotten to dump her and was planning at some point to blackmail her had begun to seem like a distant, bad dream.

She channel-hopped between her only five channels, working her way slowly through the tower of mail. She couldn't believe how much unsolicited rubbish came through, and eighty per cent of it she chucked without even opening. There were a few letters from schoolfriends living in New York and Paris – her finishing school had impressed upon them the importance of maintaining friendships through written correspondence – and there was a bundle of cheques from her parents for her monthly allowance.

She realized with sudden alarm that she'd better get to the bank tomorrow. All her bills would have left her account through direct debit, and she needed to get these funds in quickly before things started to bounce. She took another slug of wine, her head beginning to spin. She hadn't had to think about any of this with Harry. She'd just forgotten about all of it. Left it without a backward glance. With him, life was limitless, pampered, catered, every whim realized. Whatever you wanted, it just happened.

She filed through the rest of the post, disappointment barging past drunken fog as she realized that what she'd been hoping for wasn't here. She'd known the odds had been long from the start, but she'd worked so hard, tirelessly for months, sleeping at odd hours, and eating erratically. And for what? Some romantic notion of honour.

She staggered over to the computer and saw with despair that she had 894 new messages. Without bothering to look at them, she fired off a couple of new ones, letting neglected friends know she was 'back in town' and not dead and rotting in her flat.

She slumped back on the sofa as her mobile began to ring. Lethargically she picked it up and checked the caller.

It was Harry. Of course it was.

Her heart didn't bother to quicken. It was too late now. So late. She let the phone drop from her hand, and slid down the sofa until she was lying flat out and surrendering to fast, fast sleep.

It was mid-morning before she retrieved the message. She'd spent most of the early hours running fresh baths, climbing back into bed and with her head down the loo. But even the Alka-Seltzer couldn't perk her up as much as the shock and puzzlement in Harry's voice that she wasn't at home. Where was she? Ring back, baby.

By the time she'd slept off the worst of the hangover and managed to keep down a cup of tea, he had left three more. Her heart soared higher with each. He still wanted her. Or needed her. Whichever, it didn't matter. Because as bad as her hangover was, she had still woken to a pain in her heart that hurt far more than her head.

Chapter Thirty-four

'Oh, what now?' Cress muttered to herself crossly as she hurtled round the one-way gyratory system. Rosie had been ringing practically non-stop since she'd left the office, but she couldn't pick up. She'd left her bluetooth at home and there was a police car in front of her. She already had six points on her licence. She couldn't afford any more – it would have to wait until she got home.

This is what happens when you try to get away early, she thought, as she accelerated up Trinity Road, slowing down just in time for the speed camera before swinging into the residential tree-lined avenues which fed off to her street.

She turned the corner into her road and – Christ, it was bedlam! There must have been an incident, she thought, her hands gripping the wheel as she got nearer to the crowd jostling in the road.

'What's going on?' she asked, pulling alongside a man in his early twenties, wearing bum-fluff on his chin and a khaki parka.

He turned and looked at her.

'It's her!'

The entire crowd turned as one, like a shoal of fish, and in seconds had engulfed the car, flashbulbs popping in her face, microphones thrust towards her.

'Have you got any comment to make?'

'What?' she cried, flustered by the onslaught. 'What do you mean? I don't know what you're talking about!'

She panicked and tried to press the button for the window to scroll up, but she pressed the wrong one and the back window opened instead. Someone reached their arm in and tried to lift the door lock, trying to get into the car.

'Get out! Stop it! What the hell do you think you're doing?' she screamed, managing to close the window up again. She started pressing on the horn, trying to get the crowd away from the car, as her neighbours poured out of their houses to see what was causing the commotion.

With one arm up against her face, trying to shield her eyes from the glare, she inched forward, eventually managing to crawl, sobbing, into her driveway. Cress sat there for a moment, too terrified to get out, petrified of the swarm that would engulf her as soon as she stepped out.

She tried to calm down. She was only twenty yards from her front door. Nothing could happen to her here. She hurriedly wiped away the tears and took several deep breaths, feeling an angry calm descend. She could do this.

She fished her house keys out of her bag and opened the door. As she'd feared, they rushed forward, but she turned sharply to face them and they stopped abruptly.

'This is private property!' she shouted, stalking towards them, diminutive but menacing. 'And I will prosecute any one of you bastards who is still standing on my drive in the next five seconds.'

They rushed back again, recognizing from her tone, authority and massive house that her threats were real. But they didn't disperse, merely regrouped on the pavement.

'How long's it been going on, Cressida?'

'Does your husband know?'

'Any comment?'

Cress turned on her heel and stamped up the drive, hoping to look more frightening than frightened. She let herself into the house and slammed the door firmly behind her. No comment.

She dropped her bags at her feet and breathed into her hands, trying to calm herself again, the adrenalin coursing through her like a Ferrari in Monaco. What the hell had that been about? She'd never been so scared in her life.

She looked up. The house was stony quiet.

'Greta!'

Nothing.

She walked straight into the study. She needed a stiff drink.

Mark was sitting at the desk, a half-empty glass of brandy in front of him, his head in his hands.

'Oh God, Mark! Mark!' She ran over to him and threw her arms around his neck. 'You'll never guess what's just happened. I've just been doorstepped! There's all these reporters out there. Loads of them. Didn't you see? Can't you hear them?'

'Yes, I heard,' he said calmly, holding out his brandy to her. 'You'll be needing this, I imagine.'

She was too distracted by his answer to notice the drink.

'Wha— What? What do you mean you heard? Why didn't you do something? For God's sake. Have you seen them?'

'Yes. I had just the same thing. They're just as interested in me too. Unsurprisingly.'

'What do you mean? Oh my God, where are the kids?'

'They're at the Harbour Club. I've asked Greta to keep them there until that lot clear off. Here, take this.' He motioned the drink towards her.

She took the drink and gulped half of it down. It burned her throat and she gave a little involuntary shudder, walking over to the reading chair by the fireplace. Mark walked around and sat facing her on the edge of the desk, as though interviewing a graduate.

'What's going on?' she asked, taking in his posture and uncharacteristic detachment.

'That's what we all want to know,' he said. 'Them and me.' He thrust a rolled-up magazine into her hand. 'Care to explain?'

She looked down at the glossy cover shot of Harry Hunter pulling himself half-dressed in cricket whites out of a stunning Olympic pool. His shoulders were broadly muscled, his stomach as chiselled as his jaw. His eyes were blazing and a stray blond curl had fallen forward. It was a magnificent shot. A defining image. Iconic.

'Holy cow!' Cress said, smiling as she took it all in. 'Great cover! God, you've got to hand it to him – he really knows how to turn it on!' She flicked her eyes up at Mark. 'This will single-handedly boost his sales, you mark my words.'

She folded with laughter as she suddenly caught sight of the *Tatler* cover line: 'The Lonely Lover'.

'Yeah, right!' she snorted, shaking her head. 'They have got to be kidding.' She flicked through the magazine, looking for the article that accompanied the image.

Things had settled back into a courteous rapprochement since that hideous weekend, Harry sending her an incredible spray of yellow roses and a Tiffany bracelet by way of apology the very next day. She had kept the roses but returned the bracelet; they both knew neither had forgiven nor forgotten.

She found it on the centre spread, and Mark watched the

smile fade from her face as she saw their hook for the piece. Another holding image of Harry – this time actually playing cricket and looking every inch the classic English gentleman – was on the left-hand page, but facing it, the page had been quartered. In the top left quadrant was an image of Harry carrying Cress triumphantly – and seemingly post-coitally – out of the woods; next to it was an image of Tor sitting next to Harry at dinner. He was wearing black tie, but with his shirt ripped open, Tor's hands all over his torso. She had her head tipped back and was laughing, looking like the belle of the ball; in the bottom left was a picture of Harry necking a busty redhead, whom Cress didn't know. And then, in the bottom right – Christ, Cress couldn't believe it – was a picture of Kate and Harry down by the poolhouse. He was wearing just his dinner trousers, she was wearing just a shirt – his shirt. They were only talking, but it was clear the relationship was anything other than business.

Cress looked up at Mark, speechless.

'Read it,' he said sharply.

She looked straight back down again. The strapline read: 'The Heartbroken Hero'. She frowned. Hey? She read on, her hands beginning to tremble as she married the article's insinuation with the images.

'You're kidding, right? You don't actually think that I am the married woman he's in love with?'

Mark shrugged. 'Why not? According to that, one of you has got to be. He is clearly quoted as saying the love of his life was down there with him in Cornwall. Why not you? It actually makes a lot of sense.'

'Mark! Don't be idiotic! You know Harry's not in love with anyone but himself . . .'

'You've barely looked at me since Cornwall,' he cut in.

327

'You certainly haven't touched me. You're detached, cold, absent. Gone, really, in every way. It's hard to see why you do actually come back to us each night. The children are in bed, you despise Greta – who does a great job of looking after your children for you – and you're sleeping in the spare room. Why shouldn't it be you?'

'Why shouldn't it be me? Why shouldn't it be me? I'll tell you why,' she said, her voice rising with her temper. 'Because everything I do, I do for you and our family. The hours I work, the stresses I take, I do it all in the hope that one day, in the not too distant future, I will be able to make us financially secure and we can retire and be together all the time.'

'Right! Because I don't make enough to support you, is that it? We're doing so badly on my banker's salary that we need you to sail in and save the day?'

'No! You know I don't mean that. This is not a reflection on you, Mark.' She walked over to him. 'But the sky is the limit for Sapphire – for us! – now that I've signed Harry Hunter.'

'Mmmm, I'm glad you brought that up, actually, because I've been wondering for quite some time now exactly how you got him to sign with you. I mean, let's be honest, Cress. You weren't exactly a front-runner in the race. You'd only been going for eight years. It's nothing! So how did you land him, huh? How *exactly* did you get him to sign on the dotted line?'

Cress faltered. 'I – I just did what everybody else did. I pitched and I got him on merit. He liked our background, said we were forward-thinking, dynamic. The future of publishing. I said we could give him the global reach he needed, that we'd actively develop his Hollywood career . . . you know all this!'

'Oh, I know it all right. I just don't buy it, Cress. You're hiding something. You have been for a long time. And now these photos, these rumours, come out in the national press, and you expect me to believe your flimsy tale? What exactly were you doing in the woods with him anyway? Why is he parading you around like his goddam trophy?'

'We – we just went for a walk. We were talking shop. That was all. I promise.'

'Bullshit! I don't believe you!' he shouted. 'And nor will anyone else. Do you think they will?' He motioned towards the reporters outside. 'Do you think that they will buy – for one second – your flannel about going for a walk in the woods with Harry Hunter to discuss business? Do me a favour.' He drained his drink and slammed it down on the desk, making Cress jump. 'Why don't you just do us all a favour and do what you've been trying to do all along. Go! Go, so that lot out there will fuck off and your children can get back into their own home and not be scared half to death. Just go and don't bother coming back. I suspect we'll scarcely notice the difference anyhow.'

Cress watched in horror as he marched out, her marriage, her family, her life being crushed beneath every step. There was nothing more she could say to convince him. Not unless she told him the whole truth. And she couldn't do that. Not yet. She couldn't afford for anyone – not even her own beloved husband – to know that she was blackmailing Harry.

She looked at the magazine spread out on the desk, the lustrous photos depicting a world so glamorous, so beautiful, so spirited. So rotten to its core.

And then she suddenly realized . . . Tor! She picked up the phone on the desk and hurriedly rang the number. She wasn't the only one whose life would be falling apart from this.

Chapter Thirty-five

Harry told Christophe to get the Range Rover ready. The flashbulbs couldn't penetrate the blacked-out windows, and he needed something more anonymous today. This wasn't the time for the Harry Hunter roadshow.

He checked his Patek Philippe and strode the marble floor impatiently. Why did women always take so bloody long? She'd already changed outfits four times. You'd have thought they were going to a Paris couture show.

He walked over to the intercom and tapped the button for the bedroom. 'Kate, we have got to go,' he said. 'Anyone would think you didn't want to go.'

'I nearly don't,' she said softly, behind him.

He turned around. She had gone back to her original choice after all, the camel-coloured Amanda Wakeley shift dress with matching long shearling coat. She looked incredible, tawny and supple.

He kissed her on the mouth. 'What do you mean?' he said, combing her hair back from her face, so that he could see her cheekbones.

She gave a small shrug. 'It's been so exciting keeping it as our little secret. Now, we're going to share it and . . . I don't know. I guess I've just enjoyed being in our little bubble.'

'I know. I don't get to have many secrets these days.' He kissed her again. 'Come on. The car's ready.'

They walked out and climbed into the back of the car. She looked back at the house as the gates opened and they swept out of the drive. She could scarcely believe the way her life had changed since the summer. She had only stayed at the club a month before he'd moved her into his home. It had been pointless them camping out in her room, he'd said, when he had a perfectly adequate place in Kensington.

And so they had set up home together – after a fashion. She didn't need to do any of the cooking or the cleaning or the shopping. He'd recalled his staff from Verbier to do that. She just worked and made love and slept, and he wrote and made love and slept too – except for the days when he had to 'check in' at the Chelsea apartment.

There had been a brief hiccup when Emily had gone AWOL for a few days and Harry had been frantic, thinking he'd blown it. She'd come back fairly quickly though, having let her hair down with her girlfriends, but Kate had urged him to stay with Emily until he was completely sure she was back under his thumb. It was nearly two weeks before he did come back, and even though he'd gone at her insistence, it had been harder for her to accept than she'd let on.

They needed resolution to the whole situation, and soon. It couldn't drag on. Not now. She just kept telling herself that the debate at the Oxford Union was tomorrow night. The place would be absolutely crawling with press. Emily had promised him faithfully she would go and he was holding her to it – he needed her support, he'd told her.

Kate looked out of the window at all the ordinary people walking by, some trying to peer into the car and see who was lucky enough to be living the life those tinted windows protected.

If only they knew. The past fortnight had been awful. The *Tatler* story had well and truly put the cat among the pigeons, and her name – along with Cress's, Tor's and Marina's, the busty redhead – was now synonymous with Harry's.

Luckily for her, she had convinced Nicholas Parker that if there was any inappropriate relationship with Harry, it was that he had been a friend and confidant while her marriage was breaking down. Accordingly, the full might of Moreton Parker had swung behind her. Even if Parker hadn't bought it, there was no way he was going to let this story compromise the professional integrity of his company – and not a publication had dared point the finger directly at Kate, no matter how incriminating the photo had been.

Instead, all eyes were on Cress, who – fortunately for the lovers and to Harry's great glee – had moved out of the family home immediately following the exposé, adding further weight to the claims that she was Harry's paramour.

Kate didn't feel too bad about it. As Harry had said, it took the heat off them, and there must have been cracks in the marriage for a while, as he'd personally seen Mark cosying up to Greta at Lucy's birthday party. Besides, she kept reminding herself, look what Cress was doing to him.

The car cruised through Hyde Park, emerging on to Park Lane and being swallowed up in the indigenous fleets of limos and blacked-out 4 x 4s that patrolled the routes outside the premier hotels. Christophe changed lanes smoothly, overtaking the other cars without causing offence or eliciting the usual hand gestures reserved for luxury cars.

Confident they weren't being followed – a few cryptic soundbites from a forlorn Harry had been enough to ensure that most of the paparazzi were still trailing his pack of women – they snaked through the back streets of Mayfair before turning north towards Baker Street. They slipped up Green Street and made a sharp right and then a left, cruising out on to Harley Street.

Kate closed her eyes and tried to stop the tears welling again. She'd been emotional for days now, amusing and frustrating Harry in equal turn. He couldn't understand what a long journey it had been for her to get here. Six years and eighteen minutes.

Just a few Mercedes were parked on the wide street, the engines ticking over, the drivers wearing shades and shifty looks as their passengers darted in and out of cosmetic, fertility, psychiatric and sexual dysfunction clinics.

Christophe purred past, coming to a stop outside number thirty-five, a York stone building with Palladian columns and wide steps.

Harry turned to Kate.

'Are you ready?' he said, placing a hot hand on her knee. She nodded.

'Put your glasses on,' he said, as Christophe came round to open the door.

They put their heads down and rushed inside the building, the game having lost its allure in the past few weeks.

The reception area was austere, stark white marble lining the floor and walls, making Kate feel chilly. She pulled her coat around her, glad she'd plumped for the sheepskin.

'May I help you?' the receptionist asked.

'Mrs . . . Miss Miller to see Mr Fallon. Three p.m.' She stumbled on the words, her brain unused to her own maiden name. But it was important to protect Harry's identity. And anyway it wasn't right to use Monty's name any more.

'Thank you, Miss Miller. I'm afraid Mr Fallon has been called away on an emergency. Are you happy to see one of the other consultants?'

Kate nodded. Fallon was a friend of Harry's so she'd booked him, but truth be told, she didn't care who she saw. Anyone in a white coat would do.

'If I could ask you to fill in this questionnaire please, and hand it back here before you see the doctor. You'll be called in five minutes.'

She took a seat and started filling it in on her own. Harry was still standing just inside the main doors, trying not to be seen by the other patients. With all the heat on him at the moment, this was the worst possible place to be spotted.

She handed it back to the receptionist, who consulted her screen. The initials VIP had been added next to Kate's name. She couldn't be kept waiting.

'Thank you, Miss Miller. If you'd like to go into room five – just follow the corridor down to the left – the doctor will join you in a moment.'

Kate nodded again and walked slowly down the corridor, trying not to skip. She inclined her head slightly as she passed the doors and Harry dashed into room five just as the receptionist got up from her desk and walked to the photocopier behind her.

'It never could be straightforward with you, could it?' she giggled, sitting on the bed, as he closed the door. They'd made it.

'You'd be bored if it was,' he said, though he looked uneasy.

'Come here,' she said, holding out her hands. 'There's no need to look so worried.'

'I'm not worried,' he said nonchalantly. 'I'm just convinced a pap's going to jump out from behind the monitor.' And he checked behind it, just to make sure. 'Anyway, I haven't done this before. I don't know what to expect.'

'Well, they're not going to do anything to you, if that's what you're worried about. You've done your bit.'

Kate regarded him, an amused smile on her lips.

'Actually, it is strange, though, that there haven't been any paternity claims against you. God knows there's been enough opportunity. You've hardly been discriminating.'

He looked at her. 'You know, you don't come out too well from that statement.'

She smiled cockily, her green eyes locking with his. 'The others don't bother me. I know I rock your world.'

He kissed her, feeling instantly randy. Their sex life had dwindled to practically zero since she'd found out – she was terrified of doing anything that might threaten the pregnancy – and he had found himself increasingly drawn back to Emily's arms . . . and legs.

The door opened and they pulled apart.

'Hello, Miss Miller, I'm . . .' The doctor's voice faded away. There was a charged silence.

'Well,' Harry said finally. 'There's no need for introductions. Where's Fallon?'

James was dumbfounded, looking between Harry and Kate and back again, her notes in his hands.

Harry crossed the room and snatched them from him. 'You won't be needing those,' he spat. 'And I don't think I need to remind you that everything you've read in there is strictly confidential.'

James looked at Kate. Was it true?

For a split second, her eyes told him so, but she couldn't hold his gaze and she looked away.

'Mr Fallon has been called away. I'm taking his clinic this afternoon,' he said eventually.

'Where's Fallon gone?' Harry demanded. 'He assured me he'd be here. Don't tell me he's playing fucking golf.'

'No. He's not playing golf,' James said, more calmly than he felt. 'One of his patients has been diagnosed with an ectopic pregnancy. He's in theatre.'

'Couldn't someone else deal with it?'

James looked sharply at him. 'No! They couldn't! His patient could die. He has a responsibility to be there for her.'

Harry snorted in contempt, his lip curled in a sneer. Didn't they know who he was?

'Come on, Kate,' he said, taking her sharply by the elbow. 'We'll have to do this another time.'

'But Harry . . .' she protested. 'What about the scan? I need to know everything's all right. I can't wait for another day . . . I can't.'

'Of course you can. The baby will still be there tomorrow. We'll get Fallon to come over to the house.'

James shook his head, enraged by Harry's arrogance. He really did think he could have whatever he wanted.

'If you want the scan, it'll have to be here,' James said flatly.

He looked at Kate. 'This is an awkward situation, Kate, for all of us, but I'm happy to do it for you, if you want me to. I know how important this . . .'

'Oh, quit with the Dr Kildare routine, White! Nobody wants to hear it,' Harry snapped, stalking the room. He looked over at Kate, who hadn't moved and was still on the bed. He knew she wouldn't go until this was done.

'Well, there must be someone else in this bloody clinic who can do it?'

James stared at him. 'No. I'm the only consultant on duty. And given Kate's history, she should be seen by me.'

Kate reached up to Harry, clutching his arm. 'Please, baby. I need to know. Let's just do it.' A look came into her eyes. 'As soon as we know everything's OK, we can – you know – get back to normal.'

Harry knew just what she was talking about. That was certainly worth half an hour in White's company. 'OK,' he relented. 'If it'll make you happy.'

James switched on the machine and sat down, lights flashing, fan humming, as he squeezed a tube of jelly and warmed it in his hands before rubbing it on Kate's still-flat tummy.

He checked the notes, his eyebrows shooting up.

'So, it's eleven weeks since the first day of your last menstrual period?'

Kate nodded.

There was a pause.

'It happened quickly then,' he said blankly, looking at the screen.

'Not all men are created equal, White. You know that,' Harry quipped.

Kate saw James clench his jaw as he ran the ultrasound in figures of eight over her tummy.

'Does Monty know?' he asked, still keeping his voice flat.

Kate stiffened.

'I don't want to talk about it,' she said. 'It's none of his business any more.'

James nodded, just as he found the perfect tiny heart, its rapid beats like the fluttering wings of a butterfly.

He turned to look at them both. 'Well, congratulations. It looks like you're going to be one happy family.'

Chapter Thirty-six

Cress braced herself, and hoped the pilot had more control of this plane than she had of her life. She looked at all the other first class passengers and wondered whether their success had come at such a high price.

It had been eight days since she'd last seen the children. She'd spoken to them all on the phone, but only when Greta didn't get there first and let it go over to answerphone. As for Mark, he was communicating with her only by text, now convinced that she was sleeping with Harry, as the papers published new and more incriminating photos of the two of them in the woods every day.

Harry had only stoked the fire further when he gave the press a comment that was supposedly beseeching them to call off the search. 'I will say only this,' he had said forlornly on the steps of his club. 'She is my sexual match, my intellectual match, my dream woman. But she is someone else's. Your speculation is pointless. I'll never marry now. Please. Leave us both alone.'

Obviously, that riddle had had the desired effect and driven the press into frenzies. Everyone had a view. Kate, Cress, Tor and Marina (the redhead) – the Harry Hunter Four – had become minor celebrities as the press ran profiles on each woman, whipping up a national debate trying to discover which of the women had stolen Harry's heart.

Tor hadn't come out well, being condemned for throwing off her widow's weeds so soon and cavorting at glamorous parties with the playboy set.

Kate's hard-won reputation as a top libel lawyer had taken a bit of a beating too. The picture of them at the poolhouse was damning evidence of a tryst, but she was married in name only. The divorce was going through, which wasn't what Harry Hunter had said in the interview, claiming he'd never marry because the only woman he wanted was lost to another man.

Marina had been discarded almost from the off. She collected husbands like they were Jimmy Choos, and the *Mirror* had run a kiss-and-tell by a masseur who claimed to have enjoyed a holiday romance with her, while she honeymooned with her third and latest husband, the jockey Luke Matthews. If Harry Hunter really wanted her, it wasn't her marriage that was keeping them apart.

Which left Cress, with her rock-solid marriage and four children flashing like beacons in the storm. Not that she'd been there to watch. After putting the phone down to Tor, she'd packed a suitcase and caught the first flight to LA, burying herself in meetings by day and hitting the hotel minibar by night.

Her bill had come in at over $7000 – the accountants would go spare – but she'd blag it. You couldn't put a price on oblivion when your world was going tits up. Anyway, that was nothing compared to the money that she was throwing at the problem now.

Her BlackBerry buzzed and she picked it up. It was from Rosie.

Eureka! Email contact! Wrong Prince author wants to know if u liked bk? Duh! Won't meet. Only email. Have emailed contract 2 him. Gd to go.

Cress's heart galloped. He'd made contact? He actually wanted to publish? She couldn't believe it. She'd been so sure she was being sabotaged, that the connection to Brendan Hillier was a tacit threat for her involvement with Harry's deceit.

She took a deep breath and tried to focus. Stop being paranoid. There was no time to lose. It was mid-November already. The book was already copy-edited, proof-read and the jacket designed. If he signed by the end of the day, they could start the presses tomorrow and get the first shipment of the books in the shops within three weeks. It meant he wouldn't have time to approve the edit, but if he wanted any kind of shot at getting on the best-seller list for Christmas, they couldn't afford to wait. It was time to start fanning the hype.

She stared out of the window at the other planes parking, the lights flashing on luggage carts, the cubed Arrivals buildings which looked as if they'd been built from Lego.

The BlackBerry sat silent – but so full of promise – in her hand.

Come on!

She'd been waiting days now. She'd expected something sooner than this.

Even the imminent prospect of signing the *Prince* author and gold-plating Sapphire's fortunes and reputation would be pointless if she didn't get a breakthrough soon. Harry had outdone himself this time. She'd been so anxious to protect her professional investments – so sure that was where he'd strike – it hadn't occurred to her he'd target her family.

He'd nearly obliterated them – forced her out of her home, out of the country even. But she saw now that he'd done her a favour. For the first time she'd realized that without Mark, without the children, Sapphire's success meant nothing. She didn't want any of it. She only wanted them back. And she'd come back to get them.

The BlackBerry buzzed again. Finally.

'**The eagle has landed!**' Cress felt a shot of adrenalin ricochet through her body, as she clicked on the accompanying jpeg.

Her jaw dropped in disbelief.

Bingo!

She sniffed as the cabin crew turned the doors to manual, and she reached for her oversized shades. She felt the eyes of the other passengers settle on her as she moved towards the steps – taking in her Michael Kors khaki cashmere poloneck, the narrow taupe skirt and boots. So she was the one . . .

Cress let them scrutinize her, judge her, knowing that at least one of them would be on their mobile to the tabloids as soon as they hit the baggage halls. She wanted them to. She wanted Harry to know she was back in town, she wanted everyone to know. Because tonight, they would all know the truth.

Tor carried the children's bedding down to the utility room and put on another load. It was the third time this week that Marney had woken up wet. She'd never had problems staying dry at night before, but now Tor was having to restrict her evening milk and had bought a potty to leave beside her bed. Tor shook her head as she turned the dial. She'd known this was a move too far.

Much as the children loved staying with 'Granny Hen',

the covert relocation – achieved by trekking unseen across the adjoining meadow at the back – had unsettled them all. The boisterous packs of photographers outside The Twittens had scared the children and, as well as Marney's wet nights, Millie had started having nightmares too.

Tor walked back into the kitchen and picked up her coffee cup. All because of one stupid, unguarded moment. An innocent flirtation she hadn't even instigated.

She picked up the phone and tried Cress's mobile again. It connected.

'Babe!' Cress said down the line. 'How are you?'

'I'm OK. I was getting worried. I haven't been able to get hold of you for over a week.'

'Yuh, I know, sorry. I was in LA. I've just landed. I had some meetings out there to start negotiations on an original screenplay deal for Harry.'

'You're still working for him, after all he's done? He's stitched us up like kippers!'

Cress chortled. 'He's my cash cow, Tor. But don't you worry – this won't be forgotten. I'm striking back, for both of us.'

Tor had no doubt she would. Cressida Pelling hadn't founded an international company by following coffee-morning etiquette.

'Where are you, anyway? It doesn't sound as if you're in the office.'

'No, I'm in the car, going up to Oxford. Harry's speaking there tonight.'

'Right,' Tor said, sipping her coffee.

'How about you?'

'Well, we've been hiding out at Hen's for the past week. I haven't left the house; Hen's doing all the school runs.

Everyone in the village is being really sweet and telling the press to bugger off back to London. There's still a few of them left, but I'm hoping we'll be able to go back in the next few days.'

Cress tutted. 'God, I am so sorry, hon. It is ridiculous it's come to this.'

'I just cannot believe Harry lives with this on a daily basis.'

'Oh, don't feel sorry for him! He knows how to play the game – that's precisely what this is to him. And most of the time, it serves his purposes.'

'Most?'

'It isn't always going to go his way.'

'How do you think Kate's doing? I tried ringing her but she's changed her number.'

'Oh, I should imagine Kate's just peachy.' Cress couldn't keep the sarcasm out of her voice.

'What do you mean?'

'Well, has it not struck you as odd that she's come out of this without a scratch – even though the photo of her in his shirt was the most incriminating of all?'

There was a pause as Tor saw Cress's point.

'Well, yes, it is a bit strange I guess. But let's face it, it's not as if she can have any control over that.'

'Really? You don't think so? She deals with these newspapers all day every day. They're her bread and butter. Judging by that photo, she'd certainly *been* with him. And that's more than you or I had, Tor.'

'I guess,' Tor faltered.

'She could have made this go away a long time ago, if she'd wanted to. She's with him Tor, did you know that?'

Tor gasped and shook her head down the line, too shocked to speak.

'It serves her purpose to keep us in the frame. It keeps the heat off her.'

There was a pause. 'Well, you know these things better than me,' Tor said diplomatically, not wanting to face up to the bald truth of Kate's disloyalty. She changed the subject. 'By the way, I spoke to Mark earlier in the week, when I was trying to get hold of you. Is – is everything OK with you guys? I thought he seemed pretty stressed.'

'Yes, well, he has been. The papers have had their fun, let's face it. You know and I know that nothing's going on with Harry, but the papers can put a spin on a picture with just a clever caption. It's all about the power of suggestion, isn't it? He's actually gone and believed the hype, the silly bugger, but it's all going to be OK now. I've finally got what I need to convince him.'

'Which is?'

'Mmm, I can't say yet,' Cress said enigmatically, aware her driver was listening. 'But just make sure you get the papers tomorrow.'

'OK,' Tor said slowly, and suspiciously. She revelled in the vicarious thrills of Cressida Pelling's unscrupulousness. They'd forged their friendship on the even playing fields of Bristol University, and Tor loved hearing these snippets about the glamour and power play of life beyond children. 'I'd stopped buying them, but I'll get Hen to pick them up tomorrow.'

'All right babe,' Cress said distractedly as she read the *Mirror*'s latest portrayal of Tor as a social-climbing yummy mummy. Someone had sold an ancient picture of her draped around a handsome rugger bugger at a university ball. 'I've got to hit the phones before I get to Oxford. Let's speak tomorrow, OK?'

'OK.'

Chapter Thirty-seven

Chandos Matlock looked out from his ivory tower, one hand pushing back his raven-black hair, the other jammed casually into his trouser pocket.

'It's bloody marvellous! A freaking media circus out there. Why did we never ask him before?'

'Because he's a shit writer?' Freddie Tulliver replied, putting down his first edition copy of *Life at Blandings* and watching Chandos's wiry frame at the window.

Chandos strode across the room and sank down on to the worn velvet sofa. He got some Rizla and tobacco out of his pocket and started rolling up.

'Doesn't matter. Not in this day and age. It's all about the cult of celebrity; talent doesn't come into it.' He gummed the Rizla and looked over at his room-mate. 'Which is just as well for you.'

He ducked, as Freddie chucked a cushion across the room. Just because he was the fifth generation of Tullivers to go up to Oxford didn't mean he hadn't got there on merit.

'I still can't believe you got him,' Freddie said, shaking his head. 'Jammy bastard.'

'I always said it was worth a shot. Nobody's above having their vanity flattered. Even the mighty Harry Hunter.' He took a deep drag, before blowing out rings. 'In fact, him most of all.'

'What do you mean?' asked Freddie, standing up and taking the roll-ups from the table.

Chandos shrugged. 'You can tell in all his interviews he's completely paranoid about not being taken seriously. All his recent reviews have been vicious – the literati can't stand him – he's only what he is because he gets the female vote.'

'That's not true. The first book was fucking A! I read it twice. And I've seen it on your shelf too, you pretentious tosser.'

Chandos blew out a cloud of smoke. 'All right. But he's a one-trick pony.'

Freddie leaned forward and flicked through *The Times*, pushing it across the table.

'Well, he's no donkey. Look at that – the shortlist for the Oscar nominations has been announced. He's in the frame for Best Adapted Screenplay.'

Chandos scanned the article.

'So that's what's fanned the flames for tonight,' he said, getting up and walking back to the window, watching the media scrum below. 'God, talk about getting miles to the gallon. He's gone a bloody long way on the little talent he has.'

'How do you rate his chances tonight?'

Chandos snorted and shook his head. 'Not good. The pretty boy's going to be annihilated.'

He stubbed out his cigarette and stood up, smoothing down his jacket – tweed, in honour of the guest.

'How do I look?'

Freddie suppressed a sigh of appreciation. He looked incredible but he'd die rather than admit it. 'As good as you ever will.'

346

'Then let the games begin,' Chandos said, grabbing his papers and marching out the door.

Emily sat beside Harry in the car, her palms sweating, her dress too short. She'd gone for a black knitted beatnik style with grey ribbed tights and red flats, hoping to strike a naïve Left Bank note. Sorbonne chic in Oxford.

'Are you sure this is OK?' she asked him.

Harry tuned back in and looked at her.

'Stunning,' he said. 'Although you could ditch those bloody tights. How am I supposed to get anywhere near you in those things?' He started pinging the waistband through her dress, and she slid down the seat, laughing and wriggling frantically.

She slid away from his grasp on the slippery leather seat and looked out at the city she knew so well. An ex was reading law at Balliol and she'd spent many hedonistic weekends here – at least until she'd caught him in bed with his tutor.

Not that she could throw stones. Look at the glasshouse she now lived in – double height and with river views.

She stole a glance at her upgraded lover, who had slipped back into pensive silence. A pile of papers sat on his lap and his lips were moving as he recited his speech. He had put on a burgundy velvet jacket with pale pink shirt, and his hair was longer than usual, lending him an unkempt, bookish air.

She smiled to herself. Her coquettish ploy had worked, her mystery rival long since kicked into touch. Ever since she'd played hard to get, lying low at her flat for a few days and being photographed partying with her girlfriends, he'd been all over her like a rash. If she'd thought the sex was good before, now it had gone through the roof, and he was as reluctant as she to leave the apartment. She knew a proposal couldn't be far off. That would solve everything. He was already talking about spending Christmas in Verbier, the New Year in Sandy Lane and then LA, getting ready for the Oscars. He kept saying it was as good as his, but she knew his bursts of bravado just camouflaged his nerves. It meant more to him than he was willing to let on. Acceptance always seemed to be so important to him.

Magdalen, Teddy Hall, Queen's, All Souls, University . . . The ancient, rain-washed walls of the colleges rushed past each other seamlessly, confusing tourists until they were walking around in circles with upside-down maps, while knowing students darted in and out of old oak doors that were set at odd heights in the walls and gates.

She saw a trio of girls walking along and laughing together, their books tied in a college affectation with string, their knitted beanies and pea coats keeping out the autumn chill. And for a brief moment, it crossed Emily's mind that she'd left this world of privileged, youthful academia too quickly, leapfrogging straight from gauche black tie summer balls to the full-on global glamour of the Oscars.

She stiffened again, at the thought. Harry kept joking that if she thought standing in front of the domestic press tonight was nerve-racking, just wait till February 23rd.

'The eyes of the world really will be on you then, sexpot,' he'd laughed, as he'd pushed her over the desk for another quickie.

Christophe pulled off the high street and slipped the wrong way up a small one-way lane – he was Harry Hunter's driver; the laws of the Highway Code didn't apply to him. All the little backstreets were made narrower still by rows of boneshakers propped against the walls and he snaked the over-sized car around the tight corners effortlessly, until he came out into Frewin Court.

Even through the blacked-out windows, the sudden light pollution was staggering as the hordes of photographers – who'd arranged themselves in tiers on the steps, like the pappers at the end of a catwalk – tested their flashes and light stops.

Emily squeezed her hands together and took a deep breath. There'd been no getting out of this. He had met her halfway, coming round to her way of thinking that hiding their relationship was the best way of protecting it. Shielding her with the *Tatler* scandal had been a stroke of genius.

But tonight – the time had come to blow her cover and support her man in front of the whole world.

The night sky glowed white as Christophe opened the door and they stepped out, holding hands, the cameras frenziedly taking their picture for tomorrow's headlines. She could just see it: 'Harry in Love!'

'Just relax,' he said, dropping her clammy hand and waving to the crowd jostling behind the police barriers. 'It's me they want.'

Emily watched him walk across the street to the fans, signing autographs on books, OU tickets and – she craned to see – a boob! One woman had hoicked up her top and Harry was laughing, taking his time with that one, indulging her horseplay.

Emily stood alone on the steps, wondering whether to join him, get back in the car, or move into the building. Most of the snappers had trained their lenses on Harry's walkabout, but a few stray bulbs popped in her direction and she tried to assume a pose that looked supportive and – well, cool.

She felt a hand on her shoulder.

'You always did know how to make an entrance,' said a deep voice. She turned and found herself reflected in soot-black eyes.

'Chandos!' she exclaimed. 'What on earth are you doing here?'

He took in her too-bright smile and scared expression. She'd looked like a deer in headlights standing alone in front of all those photographers. And as for those coltish legs . . .

'I'm heading up this gig. I'm the OU President now,' he said casually, hoping it would impress her.

'God, that's great!' she said. 'I'm so glad to see you.'

'That's a relief. I wasn't sure if we were still . . . friends. Could've been embarrassing in front of the world's press if you were still pissed off . . .'

Emily tipped her head to one side and smiled. 'All in the past. We've both moved on.'

'And how,' he said, a light touch of sarcasm hovering around the edges. 'Although I accept I am a hard act to follow.'

Emily laughed.

'Been together long?' he asked.

She shrugged. 'Over six months now. We're living together actually.'

'Is that so?'

Emily nodded, keeping her eyes on Harry. 'But we're – you know – keeping it on the QT.'

'Right,' Chandos said slowly. 'So the whole *Tatler* debacle . . . ?'

She smiled, cunningly. 'All a ruse to keep the press's attention elsewhere. I mean, those women are his publisher, lawyer and interior decorator, for heaven's sake.' She shook her head despairingly. 'Honestly, people will believe anything they read in the papers.'

Harry was still pressing the flesh when Cress's car pulled up. She had expected a crowd, but this was ridiculous. It was more like a West End premiere.

She stepped out, and there was a moment of crystal silence before the sky fell in and stars started exploding all around her. Dazzled by the response, she stood stock still in her best Victoria Beckham pose, waiting for the flashes to abate so that she could find her way to the steps.

Christ, it was cold! What had she been thinking? Just because it was still warm in LA in November . . . would the goosebumps show up in the pictures?

She moved slowly up the steps. The armpit-to-knee Spanx control underwear she was wearing underneath the grey flannel strapless dress gave her a sensational silhouette, but she felt like a coil ready to spring and not entirely in control of her limbs.

Some students, a beautiful couple, were standing on the steps talking, ready to meet and greet. She held out a hand.

'Hello. I'm Cressida Pelling. Harry's long-suffering publisher.'

Chandos shook it firmly. 'You certainly are,' he said cheekily. 'I'm Chandos Matlock, President of the Oxford Union, and this is Emily Brookner.'

Cress looked vaguely at the pretty girl. 'Pleased to meet you.' She looked back at Chandos, nodding her head towards Harry. 'Has he been here long?'

'Ten minutes or so.'

Cress nodded. 'He'll be winding it up in a moment or two then. Is the debate still scheduled for nine o'clock?'

Chandos nodded. 'All the other speakers are here. We're good to go.'

Cress nodded, keeping her tummy sucked in and the photographers on her best side. 'That's great.'

'Cress,' came the honeyed voice in her ear she'd been expecting.

'Harry,' she cooed back, kissing him lightly on each cheek and letting the papers get their picture. She kept her hands on his shoulders, keeping him close. 'How have you been? You've scarcely been off the front page.'

Harry laughed lightly, wrong-footed by her willingness to be caught so close to him.

'Nor you, Cress.'

She shrugged happily. 'It's true what they say. "Any publicity is good publicity." Your sales have spiked again.'

'Always nice to hear. I don't want to get low on socks.'

'Well, quite.'

'And I understand you've been in LA?' Harry said. A little light phone flirtation with Rosie and he'd got it out of her that Cress had left the country on the first flight.

'Oh yes, yes,' she said lightly. 'Beavering away on your behalf, Harry. Dreamworks are very keen to sign you.'

'I hope you weren't working too hard,' he said insincerely.

'I have to be honest – it was more like a holiday out there. It was all lobster salad and yoga on the beach. You made it easy for me – Tinseltown's really in your thrall.'

Harry nodded, watching her closely. Her tone was skippy, her eyes steady. She'd lost some weight, but that wasn't a great surprise after a trip to LA. (There was, no doubt, a pair of trophy Size Zero jeans packed somewhere in her bags.) She wasn't letting anything at all slip, but the fall-out for her had to have been catastrophic. The papers had crucified her. It had been intense even by his standards. He'd barely been able to juggle Kate – who was becoming more neurotic and shapeless by the day – and Emily, whom he'd only managed to silence from ceaseless questioning about the other women by keeping her permanently in bed.

Emily and Chandos looked on, unaware of the bedrock of subtext that was loaded into every question and answer.

'Shall we?' Harry said, gesturing towards the debating hall.

Cress smiled, and he held out an arm for her to hold on to as they went up the steps, leaving Emily to go up with Chandos.

Cress felt triumphant as they got to the top, knowing she'd called his bluff. He hadn't expected her to come here tonight, but she'd faced him down. And that was just for starters.

The room was alive with conversation and colour, banks of red leather benches ranked along each wall like a mini Parliament – or its training ground. It was like being back at Hunstanton, an ode to youth – a hothouse of beauty, confidence, invincibility and freshly washed hair.

A deafening cheer went up as Harry entered the room, looking every inch the Bond-figure with his irresistible international glamour, year-round tan and surrounded by his posse of glamorous alleged lovers. One for every mood, it seemed.

Harry raised his hand in salute and the huzzahs! grew louder still, but Emily caught a distinct rumble of discord whistling along the belly of the opposition crowd. Not everybody here was a fan.

Harry crossed the floor to greet his opponent – the

Archbishop of York – and Chandos showed Emily and Cress to their front-row seats, just next to Harry's rostrum. Kate was already sitting there, one ear glued to her mobile.

She looked up, her eyes widening with surprise, but she held up a hand – silencing Cress before she could even speak – as she continued her call, putting one finger in her ear.

'. . . Let me make this absolutely clear to you, Mr Pryce, I am not in the habit of letting grubby little editors like you sully the . . . well, then it shall be my very great pleasure to personally make calls to every single agent in London telling them about . . . rest assured I have their ear . . . If you think the short-term gain outweighs the long-term game then you're . . . If you go to press with that story, I'll have an injunction slapped on you by midnight and a defamatory writ served by breakfast . . . Uh-huh . . . You do that.'

She hung up and put her phone away, her eyes settling coldly on Cress.

'I didn't expect to see you here,' Cress said levelly.

'Why wouldn't I be? It'll be a heated debate, things will be said, rumours can start. It's my job to put a lid on them before they even get that far.'

'That's funny. I was beginning to think your job was starting the rumours, not squashing them,' Cress said lightly, settling herself on the chair and talking across Emily who was sitting between them. 'My, but the past few weeks have been fun, haven't they? Harry really caused some collateral damage this time.' She looked at Kate. 'But what am I saying? You were at the heart of it too . . . Tell me, how the devil did you manage to get away so lightly?' She held up a hand. 'No, let me guess: they never touch their own, right? You called in a few favours, pulled a few strings?' She rested an elbow on her lap, looking over at Kate, her eyebrows raised in unfriendly conspiracy.

Emily shifted on her seat uncomfortably.

'Excuse me, won't you?' Kate said curtly, standing up and walking over to Harry, who was standing talking to the Opposition speakers.

Cress watched her go, her eagle eyes noticing the way Kate's trousers strained slightly at the waistband.

Cress shifted in her seat, looking around the sea of faces and wondering whether there was anywhere she could get a drink. She really didn't fancy sitting through – what was the debate? She checked the sheet: This House believes that Celebrity is the new Religion. Hardly Socrates! Where did they think up this stuff?

She smoothed her dress over her tummy and checked her watch.

Nine fifteen p.m.

Good, Cress thought. The later this went on, the better.

She fidgeted about, wrapping one leg around the other like a corkscrew, taking care she hid her cellulite, before becoming aware of the long, skinny legs of the pretty student still sitting next to her.

She tried to be polite – to pass the time – and turned to face her slightly. 'What did you say your name was again? I'm terrible with names.'

'Emily Brookner.'

'I'm Cressida Pelling.'

'Yes, I know,' Emily smiled. 'You're Harry's publisher.'

'Publisher, mind, not lover,' Cress sniffed haughtily. 'Don't believe what the rags tell you.'

'Oh no, I know you're not!' she said with searing conviction.

Cress looked at her. At least someone in the country believed her.

She smiled. 'So what are you reading?'

Emily paused. 'Um, well – I've just finished *East of Eden*.'

Cress burst out laughing.

'No! No!' she said, amused. 'I meant your subject – what are you reading for your degree? PPE, English, Law?'

'Oh, oh, I see,' Emily said, cringing with embarrassment. 'I thought you meant . . .' Her voice faded away. 'Well, I'm not actually a student here.'

Cress's eyebrows shot up.

'Oh, I'm sorry. I assumed . . .' Cress looked over towards Chandos, who was shuffling papers importantly at his desk.

'No, Chandos is just an old friend. I'm here with Harry.'

'Ah.' Cress nodded benignly – tonight's totty.

Chandos brought the gavel down on the desk three times and brought the hall to order.

The buzz of conversation died instantly, and Harry and Kate sauntered back over, taking their seats. Kate started fiddling about officiously with her text messages.

'My honourable Lords, Ladies and Gentlemen,' he began.

This must be what it's like in the House of Lords, Cress thought to herself, looking around at the lofty environs and the sea of college scarves. There's probably as many titles here as there.

Chandos introduced the speakers, the crowd booing and yelling by turns, already whipped into a frenzy by Harry's stellar presence and floppy hair.

Harry was up first, and the hall fell silent as he took the floor.

He took a deep breath. This was it. Time to get some respect.

His voice resounded around the room. 'John Lennon hit a collective nerve when he famously said that the Beatles were more famous than Jesus. It caused a scandal at the time, but forty years on, can we really say he was wrong? Jesus has had over two thousand years to build his fanbase – and yet every Sunday, his throng dwindles in churches across the country, while Lennon's songs are still played on radio stations every day, all over the world.

'What Christians found so intolerable about Lennon's remark was not the idea that Jesus should be eclipsed by a mere mortal – after all, both men stood for the same messages of love, hope and peace – but that that mortal should be a celebrity. Had he been an artist, a computer programmer, or – better still – a carpenter, Lennon's wry remarks may have had a shot at credibility. But a celebrity as a moral heavy-weight? Well, not in his lifetime.

'But what about in ours? The school of thought that celebrities have no moral compass, that they are somehow devoid of morality . . .'

'Well, you are!' shouted a wag from the back.

Harry raised his eyebrows but let it pass.

'. . . Is, uh, beginning to fade. The fact is, that now – in the twentieth century . . .'

'Try again!' someone piped up, to much laughter.

'Now, in the twenty-first century . . .'

'Hurrah! Give the man an A level!'

Harry clenched his jaw and tried again. Fuck these little smart-arses for patronizing him. 'Now, in the twenty-first century, we live in an empirical age where . . .'

'That's a big word for such a pretty boy!'

'. . . Where there is simply no tolerance any more for unsubstantiated dogma. In this day and age, Fact is king. Logic and reason – the progeny of Science – underlie everything we believe in now. Creationism can't compete with the Big Bang . . .'

'Nor yours, Harry! From what I keep reading, yours is the biggest bang of the lot!'

The roof lifted with laughter, whilst Harry clenched the rostrum, flushed red with anger.

'. . . Adam and Eve are just a fanciful fairy tale to the real story of Evolution. And it's in the wake of cold, hard fact – which has systematically taken away our belief in religion's hollow promises of miracles and redemption – that celebrity has taken on a new role, new depth . . .'

The three women sat together, watching him, the various spokes in the Harry Hunter machine.

Kate's phone kept vibrating, giving her something to do with her hands and silently elevating her status as indispensable. Cress got her BlackBerry out of her bag and started checking her own texts too. She'd be damned if she was going to lose face to Kate. Not after what she'd done.

There was an update from Rosie.

B. Hillier not on Elect. Reg. No trace of Am. Hillier.

She stared at it. Did she even need to pursue this quest any longer? The *Wrong Prince* author had signed the contract this afternoon. The presses were now running and it would soon be printing money for Sapphire; the first quarter of the book was being drip-fed to the bloggers, copies had been sent to the critics and the omnipotent Richard and Judy book club, and her film scout would find the story sitting in his inbox when LA woke up in four hours' time – Cress expected a film deal by the end of the week. This book would be her insurance policy against any fall-out from Harry; she could feel it.

And yet she still couldn't relax about it. The author's continuing insistence upon anonymity bothered her. Only her senior legal adviser knew his name – divulged in a separate affidavit – and it made her worry that this author wanted to hide his identity not so much from the greater public, but specifically from *her*. It had to be tied in with the chilling Hillier connection. She knew she had to keep investigating.

She looked back at the text. If Bridget wasn't on the electoral register here, did it suggest she was foreign; or maybe that she lived abroad? Perhaps she had married and Amelie had been born abroad – that was why there was no trace of her on the birth register?

She shifted position. The seats were narrow, and her circulatory system was already compressed enough in the control underwear. Her left glute was going to sleep. She shook out her leg, her mobile flying off her lap as she did so.

'Shit!' she hissed, as it clattered on to the stone floor, at Kate's feet.

Harry lost his place in his speech as he looked around, and Kate shot her a withering look.

'Apologies,' she said, shrugging. 'Accident!'

Kate leant down and picked up the phone, the text flashing past her eyes as she handed it back. *Hillier?* So Harry had been right. Cress was in on it.

'Thanks,' Cress said, taking it without looking at her. She gunned off a message to Rosie – oblivious to the fact it was 9.30 at night – telling her to look in Europe for Bridget and Amelie Hillier. Amelie – that was French, right? Try France, or – where else did they speak French? – Belgium? Switzerland? Luxembourg?

Kate's phone rang silently and she picked it up without saying hello. 'Mmm', 'mmm', 'mmmm', she breathed, before clicking off.

Cress's text was still bothering her but she sat back in her seat, trying to relax and not feel so ruffled by the fact that Emily was infinitely more luscious than she had ever realized. She'd be gone after tonight anyway. She'd turned up on Harry's arm in front of 200 photographers. Someone was bound to have caught the two of them together. They only needed one shot.

Imperceptibly she slid her eyes sideways, taking in her rival's retroussé nose and upturned mouth, her lashes as thick as bullion and creamy hair. Emily was completely wrapped up in Harry's speech, nodding occasionally and smiling supportively at his ridiculous arguments, which Kate knew were bound to result in a flurry of hate mail from religious fundamentalists. That was all she needed – Harry Hunter with a fatwah!

Kate could see that Emily had fallen hook, line and sinker for him. She just hoped tonight's public witnesses and the back-up sex tape would be all it took to encourage her to make a clean getaway. Kate wasn't entirely convinced that Harry would be so easily able to untangle himself from this stunning girl by himself.

She dropped her phone into her bag and swept her hair away from her face, gazing up at the ornate frescoed ceiling, not noticing Emily's own return scrutiny as the heart-shaped emerald earrings twinkled beneath the chandeliers and betrayed her best-kept secret.

Chapter Thirty-eight

Feeling the weight of her stare, Kate looked back. But Emily still couldn't take her eyes off her. Her rival was revealed; she was here and she was so, so untouchable. Just look at her. Those almond-shaped green eyes – just like Harry's – the glossy 'power' hair, the aura of importance emanating from her like perfume. Emily knew she didn't stand a chance. She was nobody.

The two women stared at each other, the tears building in Emily's eyes as she knew that it was finally over.

Kate said nothing, but she realized instinctively that Emily had guessed. She frowned a little, trying to work out what had given the game away – a look between her and Harry? A touch?

Not that it would matter. She could see defeat in the younger girl's eyes. She wouldn't have to worry about her hanging around after all. She was going to be out of there like a greyhound at the gate.

Kate gave a small victorious smile, tipping her chin slightly in acknowledgement, before turning back to Harry and joining in with the polite, tepid applause as he sat down.

Suddenly, Emily felt a hand upon hers, dragging her up from her seat and pulling her along the benches to a room at the back.

'Chandos! What are you doing?' she hissed, as she skittered past Harry, her long legs knock-kneed and tangled. Harry looked up, alarmed, as she sped past, but Kate's slight shake of the head kept him in his seat.

A chorus of wolf-whistles and shouts of approval at their apparent tryst echoed around the benches. The Archbishop of York looked on sternly, but didn't falter.

Chandos shut the door behind them.

'Chandos!' she spluttered, throwing her hands feebly up into the air. 'You can't just ... what the hell do you think you're doing, dragging me in here in front of everybody, like some wench?'

Chandos wiped his hair away from his face and looked at her, concerned. 'You looked as if you were going to pass out,' he stuttered. 'You just suddenly went as white as a sheet. I've never seen anything like it. I thought you might need some water or air or something.'

Emily stared at him, shaking, her colour well and truly returned. 'I don't need any bloody water, thank you very much.'

He paused. 'A valedictory glass of wine then, perhaps?' he asked, motioning towards the bottle on the desk.

Emily looked away, exasperated. 'If this is some seduction technique you've found works a treat on the new undergraduates, I'm afraid you're going to find it gets short shrift from me.'

Chandos shook his head. 'I'm not trying to seduce you, Emily. Apart from the fact that you're with one of the most legendary playboys in the western world – which makes it quite hard, even for me, to compete – I think it's hardly my place to start doing a number on you ... not after what I did.'

'Oh, don't beat yourself up about it,' Emily said dismissively, beginning to calm down and feeling really quite relieved to be away from Harry and Kate, after all. She walked over to the table and picked up a glass.

Chandos poured one for her, and then another for himself.

'My betrayal didn't break you, then,' he said theatrically, stealing a glance at her.

'Why? Was it supposed to?' she asked, archly.

'No, of course not. But – I guess my ego would like to know you didn't just walk away without a backward glance.'

Emily tipped her head to one side. 'Your ego?'

He shrugged and gave a boyish grin. 'I was gutted when you left. I'd no idea you meant so much to me. Not until after you'd gone, anyway. And then seeing you here tonight. With him.' He took a slug of wine. 'I mean – of all the people – why does it have to be him? It hardly lets anyone else in with a chance.'

Emily smiled, in spite of herself. 'So you did bring me in here to seduce me,' she said. She snorted derisively. 'Trust me, Chandos. That's the last thing I want.'

'But it may be the very thing you need,' Chandos said assuredly.

She perched on the edge of the desk and took a deep breath.

'Well, I guess I am back on the market,' she said contrarily. She felt no desire to be predictable. Pliable. Not now. 'I'm a free agent, I can do as I please.'

'Huh?' Chandos stared at her quizzically. 'But you just told me outside on the steps that you're living with Harry.'

'What's the matter? Do you only want me if I'm Harry's, is that it? You want the accolade of sleeping with his bird?'

Chandos frowned. 'No, of course not. I'm delighted you're

not with him. But – I'm lost.' He shrugged. 'I don't under-stand what's just happened in the last fifty minutes that's meant you and Harry are no longer together.'

Emily inhaled deeply. 'Let's just say, some new informa-tion has come to light.'

Chandos frowned at her.

'He's been fucking another woman,' she said brightly. 'And I've just had the pleasure of meeting her.' She shook her head, matter-of-factly. 'There's no way I can compete.' She put her glass down and he saw her hands tremble, even though her voice was defiant.

'Oh, baby,' Chandos said, advancing towards her. 'What are you talking about? No one can hold a candle to you.'

'No,' she said flatly. 'It's only been a game to him. I started out holding all the cards but he's just been playing me. I've been an idiot. I let my heart rule my head.'

'It's his loss, Emily. He's the fucking loser. Just like I was.' He stroked her hair. 'But I'd do anything . . . anything to have you back. I was desperate to make it up to you. But I didn't know where to find you. You just disappeared.'

There was thunderous applause from the other side of the door, as Harry's opponent emerged the clear victor.

Emily looked at him, confused, feeling a tiny lock begin to turn inside her, threatening to spill out all the emotions she'd buried away. It hadn't crossed her mind she'd bump into him tonight. His infidelity had tossed her world upside down – she had drunk when she should have eaten, worked when she should have slept, cried when she should have laughed – and it had taken her so long to get over him. And now he was standing here, stroking her, adding more compli-cations to her world, trying to catch her off-balance, when in the next room . . .

She pulled away roughly. 'Do you really think I'd go straight from his betrayal, back to you? I already know *you're* a cheating bastard,' she said harshly, wiping away the stray tear that had fallen. 'You're all the bloody same, the lot of you. I should have known that this is always how it's going to end.'

She poured herself another glass and downed it. 'But it's my own fault. You treat me this way because I let you.'

She put the glass on the table and walked to the tall window. She watched all the photographers standing smoking and chatting outside. 'But not any more. I didn't come here to get back with you. Just like I didn't get back with Harry to fall in love with him.'

'Back with him? You were with him before?'

But her voice was remote, distracted. 'It was supposed to be business.'

'Business?' Chandos's voice rose an octave. What did that mean?

'He made me fall for him all over again and I lost sight of the fact that he was only ever a means to an end.' She turned and walked back to him, with renewed focus.

She stood in front of him, her hands on his arms. 'Thanks for this pep talk, Chandos. It was just what I needed.' She stood on tiptoe and kissed him, her tongue tracing his lip suggestively. She winked. 'For old time's sake.'

Then she ran to the door and fled down the long hallowed hall, her hair streaming like ribbons behind her.

'Emily, wait!' Chandos called, placing his glass on the table and running after her.

But she was nimble and light and got to the main doors quickly. As she opened them, the night was bright white again, as though an alien spaceship was landing on the

365

cobbled street outside, but she could instinctively feel that something much more ominous than that was happening.

The crowd was at fever pitch and it was almost impossible to move in the glare of the flashbulbs. Emily shielded her eyes and inched her way around the gaggle surrounding Harry and Kate. Everyone was calling out, pushing this way and that, and she could see Kate crying as Harry tried to cut a swathe towards the car.

Emily looked for an exit point, but suddenly the crowd pushed back and her ankle turned on the edge of the step. She felt herself fall, and she screamed. She'd be crushed in the mêlée.

Chandos lunged forwards, catching her in his arms easily. But he didn't put her down. He bundled her on to the back of his Vespa and bombed through the back streets to somewhere safe, away from Harry Hunter.

Cress reached her car and looked back at the cluster on the steps. No one was interested in her any more. The truth was out. It was like seeing a bomb explode in slow motion – Harry's arms held up defensively in front of his face, Kate at his side clutching her red Kelly bag protectively to her stomach, just like Princess Grace fifty years before. The two of them frozen in time as the bulbs flashed, and the late edition of the *Evening Standard* was waved like a flag, and one question was repeated over and over like a Buddhist mantra: 'When's the baby due, Harry? When's the baby due?'

Chapter Thirty-nine

Emily felt the kisses on her neck, and she stretched languorously, her body waking up in the most heavenly way.

'Mmmmmmm,' she said, rolling off her tummy, her arms above her head.

'Good morning, lover,' said an unfamiliar voice.

She opened her eyes in alarm and found herself reflected – again – in those black pools.

'Chandos!' She sat bolt upright and looked around at the student room. Where the hell was she? What had happened? She brought her hands to her temples. 'Oh my God. What's happened to my head?'

Chandos picked up the empty bottle of Absolut. 'This?'

'What – did you hit me with it?' she groaned. 'Owwww.'

He laughed and she heard a kettle come to the boil. 'Some hair of the dog will sort you out,' he smiled, the smile fading as Emily visibly paled at the thought, her hands flying to her mouth. 'The bathroom's that way!' he said, pointing to a flimsy door.

She ran across the room, her trim little figure an absolute delight to watch. She managed to slam the door behind her and he chuckled to himself as he heard a chorus of approval in the hallway. It was ten minutes before she came back in, a hand towel held in front of her.

'You didn't tell me it was a communal bathroom,' she said glumly, too hungover to be mortified, her skin deathly white, her eyes sunken and black-rimmed. Even the goth look suited her, he thought to himself. God, he'd missed her.

'There wasn't really time,' he shrugged. 'And just think – you've made their day, and made me look like the biggest stud since – well, Harry Hunter! Here, this'll make you feel better,' he said, handing her a cup of builder's.

He walked over to the back of the door and handed her a navy piped dressing-gown. 'Put this on. You'll catch your death if you carry on parading naked – not to mention I might die of overexcitement.'

She put it on, her mind beginning to wake up, a flash of images playing like a cine film in her mind – silent, jerky, a bit too fast.

'How are you feeling?' Chandos asked quietly.

She raised her eyes to his.

'Idiotic; humiliated; like my head's going to fall off.'

Chandos nodded.

'Are those today's papers?' she said, nodding towards a pile on the coffee table.

'Oh no, no,' he said jumping up and tidying them away. 'They're old.'

'It's OK,' she said, getting up and taking them off him. 'It really is. I can take it.'

She looked down at the front cover of *The Times*. It had been like walking into an ambush. Cress was nowhere to be seen, but then she didn't need to be. She was exonerated, yesterday's news. The picture showed the real love story –

Kate in tears, her arm across her belly; Harry's jaw set –
already sore from the intellectual thrashing he'd just received
– as he looked hatefully into the white ether.

At the corner of the picture, barely visible, was Chandos,
holding Emily in his arms. He had saved her from national
humiliation, peeling her away from the crowd as Kate and
Harry bundled forwards into the Range Rover, plonking her
on the back of his moped and whizzing her around the tiny
amber lanes to his digs.

'Thank you,' she said.

'For what?'

'For everything. You saved me countless times last
night.'

'Anything for the beautiful lady,' he said, in a dreadful
Italian accent. 'Besides, I owed you some chivalry. After
behaving like such a dick before . . . What are you going to
do?' he asked.

Emily sighed deeply and closed her eyes. The press knew
who she was now – Harry had been pictured with Emily on
the way in; Kate on the way out. They weren't going to leave
her alone until they'd got what they wanted – a picture, a
soundbite, an interview.

She got up – the dressing-gown falling open as she did
so, causing Chandos's pulse to skyrocket – and checked her
mobile. The voicemail was full. It had already begun.

She turned to face Chandos. 'I'm going to face the music,'
she said finally.

'Promise me you won't do anything rash,' he said.

'Trust me. There'll be nothing rash about it. It's all very
well thought out,' she replied cryptically.

Chandos frowned – what did she mean? – as he watched
her shrug off the dressing-gown unselfconsciously and slip

her dress over her head. He admired how she went from sex-bomb to sweet gawky ingénue with just one movement. He knew she was leaving him.

'What's the time, do you know?' she said, smoothing up her tights.

'Nearly ten. Why?'

'I need to catch a train back to London. I've got an appointment.'

'Well, the next train is at 10.45.' He paused, his brain in overdrive. 'But I need to go into town too. Let me drive you.'

Her chin dipped in amusement.

'Chandos, I am not being driven down the M40 on a moped!'

'I wouldn't expect you to be. The Vespa's just for lectures. I use this for mileage.' And he clicked his keys. She heard the beep outside and went to the window. A shiny gunmetal grey Vantage was parked beneath.

'That'll do, I guess,' she said, smiling, slipping her feet into her Cinderella shoes. 'Come on then. "Home, James! And don't spare the horsepower!"'

He didn't. They were in Battersea and lunching by the river by noon.

'So what now?' Chandos asked ambiguously.

'Well, I've got to see my solicitor,' she said, draining her prosecco.

'Sounds fun,' he said, disappointed she hadn't taken the hint and pursued a conversation about 'them'.

Emily checked her watch. 'I've got forty minutes before my appointment,' she said. 'Do you think . . .'

'There's time for a quickie?' he winked. 'Always.'

She smacked his hand playfully. Last night had just been

drunkenness and shock and old times' sake. He knew that, right?

'Do you think you could drop me round to the apartment? It's just round the corner and I want to pick up my things.'

'Won't Hunter be there?'

She shook her head. 'No. He's probably left the country for a bit. One of the perks of having your own jet,' she added carelessly.

'It'll be besieged with reporters.'

'I know. But I've already been outed. And anyway, I've done nothing wrong.' She smiled defiantly.

'Let's go then.'

They hopped back into the car and purred around the corner. Sure enough, there were nearly a hundred people standing on the pavement opposite, cameras set up on tripods, Dictaphones held at the ready.

'Shit! Where should I park?' Chandos asked, suddenly worried about his car's bodywork being used for crowd control.

'It's OK,' Emily said calmly. 'There's an underground car park. Just bear left.'

He steered towards the dip and there was a sudden frenzy of activity as they were spotted in the not-so-inconspicuous motor. Emily felt acutely aware she was still in last night's clothes, and she grabbed Chandos's jacket and held it over her head, dipping down in her seat below the window line.

She heard the whirr-click of the cameras above the mushroom-silk lining – and smelled Chandos's sandalwood scent beneath it – but she'd denied them a clean shot, and they were on to private property and out of reach in a few moments. She was determined she wasn't going to be the victim in this. Harry had confused her, distracted her from her real purpose, but she was back on track now. She was going to do it her way.

They travelled up in the penthouse's private lift, and her heart stammered as she put her key in the lock. Would Jeremy be here? Would he be under orders to throw her out? Would Harry have changed the locks already?

But her fears were unfounded. The apartment was pristine and untouched, ready for the next stream of blondes to fall through the door.

Chandos tried not to be impressed by the cinema screen, and really hard not to be jealous of the view. Most of all, he tried hard not to imagine Emily in here, naked, with Harry on that big round bed.

He watched her move through the space with the casual indifference that comes from familiarity, picking out her clothes from the wardrobes and drawers. He noticed there were no photos of the two of them together. It all seemed to be 'Harry with . . .'

She pulled out a pair of jeans and a blue marled cashmere sweater and put them on with some boots. Fresh clothes for a fresh day. Her fresh start.

It only took fifteen minutes to pack. She really hadn't taken up so very much of his space, of his life.

'Let's go then,' she shrugged easily.

'You're not upset?' Chandos asked, expecting her to burst into tears at any moment. Not many women would leave Harry Hunter without a backward glance.

She shook her head. Learning that Harry was going to become a father had changed everything. A baby was involved, and she wasn't even going to try to fight for him.

But that didn't mean she wasn't going to fight. She had another call to make.

It was simply Harry's tough luck that when she'd woken up in Chandos's bed this morning, the pain in her head had been worse than the pain in her heart.

Chapter Forty

Greta was stirring a casserole when Cress walked into the kitchen, freshly showered and changed into her favourite khaki cashmere tracksuit. The afternoon's reunion with the children had been the stuff of her dreams, and for once it seemed her absence really had made their hearts grow fonder.

'Mmm, smells good,' Cress said generously, walking over and peering inside the pot. 'I don't know how you do it, Greta. I'm such a disaster in the kitchen.'

Greta shrugged. 'Yes, the children say so.'

Cress smiled to herself. Tact must be lost in translation, she thought.

She took a breath for patience. 'Anyway, I want to thank you for holding the fort here while I've been away. It's been a tough couple of weeks, and I know it must have been hard on you. We'll sort out a bonus to reflect the extra workload,' she said, reaching for a wine glass.

Greta stole a sideways look at Cress. 'Thank you, Mrs Pelling,' she said quietly.

'And by way of saying thanks, you can have an extended Christmas break. Why don't you go back and see your family in Sweden? We'll pay for your flights.'

Greta's face fell. So that was it. She was being booted out.

This wasn't a reward; Cress was making sure she was well out of the way while she cosied back up to Mark.

Greta bit her lip and carried on stirring the casserole. The past eight days had been wonderful. Mark had complimented her on everything – her cooking, her housekeeping, the way she dressed the children, played with them. For the first few nights he'd come home drunk and refused to eat, but she'd quickly managed to get him to come in and eat with her every night instead, polishing off bottles of red or vodka together. They'd found they laughed easily together and there was no doubting the sexual tension. She'd seen him watch her from the window that night – for a fraction of a second, she'd held his gaze – and she knew he thought about it. She still wore his shirt in bed, and one night, when they'd been sitting on the sofa together, he'd dropped his head on to her shoulder, his hand gently stroking her waist, his thumb just an inch from her breast. 'You're so lovely,' he'd mumbled, as he fell asleep.

She knew he couldn't resist for much longer. His romantic ideals about Cress were falling away. He was realizing Cress wasn't interested in any of them – just her big-shot career.

But now – now the furore with Harry Hunter had switched to that friend of hers, Kate, and Cress had barged back into their lives.

Greta's hand gripped the spoon with resentment. Cress didn't deserve him.

'In the meantime, take the rest of the evening off,' Cress continued, oblivious. 'You've done more than enough here.'

Greta nodded and went reluctantly upstairs, but she didn't go to her room. She sat on the chaise on the landing and waited for Mark's return. She wanted to hear this. She might be out of sight, but she wasn't out of her mind.

*

It was 11.30 p.m. when the lock in the door turned and Mark came in. Cress heard him hang his coat on the stair-post and walk down the hallway to the kitchen, loosening his tie. She was sitting cross-legged on the island, her favourite spot.

'Hello,' she said softly, not a hint of 'where-the-hell-have-you-been' in her voice.

Mark stared at her – taking in her sparkling complexion and super-blonded LA hair – as she handed him a glass.

'Care to join me?' she asked casually, appealingly.

Mark took it, but his face was far from pleased. He looked shattered.

'You're back then,' he said, stating the obvious.

'Seems so,' she nodded.

'When did you get back?' he asked, taking a deep swill, but keeping his eyes on her.

'This afternoon.'

'No, I meant when did you get back into the country?' A note of irritation punched the words.

'Yesterday lunchtime.' Cress swallowed uneasily. His tone was more interrogating than welcoming.

'But you thought you'd wait till today to come back.'

'I had to go up to Oxford. To sort things out.'

'Before seeing us?'

'If I'd come back yesterday, you wouldn't have let me through the door. You would have still thought I was with Harry. I had to show you I was innocent first.' Why was he being so combative? Had he seen the papers?

He shrugged. 'We haven't heard from you for days. I had no idea what to tell the children.'

'What? You didn't get my messages?'

Mark shrugged as he took off his tie.

'But I've been leaving messages three times a day,' she said.

'Not on this answerphone you haven't.'

Cress looked at him. 'That doesn't make sense!' she exclaimed. 'I've been — ' The penny dropped. 'Greta!' she said bitterly. 'She must have wiped them.'

'Oh, don't start on that again,' Mark said contemptuously. 'You've not been back five minutes and already you're laying into her. She's held this family together in your absence. She's been incredible.'

'Incredible? Really? That's high praise,' Cress said evenly.

'Praise that's well deserved. Nothing more.'

'Why do you always have to defend her?'

'Because you're nothing short of a bitch to her, that's why, and the children happen to adore her. I'm not having you disrupt their lives just because you're jealous of yet another nanny who does a better job of mothering your children than you.'

He couldn't have hurt her more if he'd slapped her. He could see it written all over her face, as vividly as any hand-print. He swallowed and turned away.

'Anyway, how did you intend to "prove your innocence"?' he asked sarcastically, leaning against the worktop.

She tried again. 'With the photos – the ones of Harry and Kate coming out of the baby clinic,' she said. 'You must have seen them?'

His eyes narrowed. 'Oh, I've seen them all right. It just didn't occur to me you were behind them.'

'Is that a problem? The photos clearly prove that the woman Harry is involved with is Kate, not me.'

'So you shopped Kate to save yourself.'

Cress laughed. 'Oh my God, Mark! What exactly is it you

want me to do? Let you carry on thinking I'm sleeping with Harry? Or let the two of them get away with their manipulation of the press and using me as their fall guy?'

'Don't be so melodramatic. Kate would never do that.'

'Oh, right, right. It's just a coincidence that there's been a resounding silence around her involvement in all this; it's just a coincidence that she happens to have a huge amount of contacts and clout in this industry.'

Cress heard her voice rise. 'If you want to talk about betrayal, Mark, why don't you consider not only why the press came after me and Tor, but also why she let them perform character assassinations on her two supposed best friends. I mean, you want betrayal? Think about poor Tor. She's a widow only six months and the entire British nation think she's a gold-digger after Harry's fortune. I'll bet she's coping really well with that!'

Mark turned away from her stream of rhetoric.

'Make no mistake, Mark,' she said to his back. 'Kate pulled the strings! She protected herself, knowing that by doing so she was dropping us in it. She's not the innocent in this. She has completely lost the plot since finding out about Monty's boy. I mean, she won't speak to any of us – not you, me, Tor, Monty. None of us. We've all been dropped like hot potatoes. The Kate that's having Harry's baby is *not* the Kate we knew. I owe her nothing!'

Mark walked over to the window, his cheeks flushed with anger. 'Your arrogance is incredible. You have no idea of the damage you've done! I've just come from seeing Monty – he's a bloody mess!'

'Well, of course he is!' Cress said, palms outstretched. 'But you can't blame that on me? It's his wife carrying Harry's baby.'

'Yes, but look how he found out. Because of you.'

'It was Kate's responsibility to tell him! I can't believe she didn't bother!'

Mark put his hands on his hips, his body rigid with frustration and resentment.

'Why are you looking at me like that?' she cried.

He shook his head. 'You just always have to be right, don't you? Always the winner.'

Cress jumped off the island. 'I should have known this was pointless. I can't do right for doing wrong. I don't know what more I can do.'

Mark strode across the room and grabbed her arms. 'I *know* there's something going on with you and Hunter. Ever since you signed him, you've been blowing hot and cold with me. At first you got all relaxed and sexy and didn't care about hair or your make-up; you were all over me like a rash. Then you went off to Cornwall with him, and came back giving me the "I've got a headache" routine, just as pictures emerged of the two of you frolicking in woodland in the national press. What the hell do you expect me to think?'

The baby monitor in the corner started flashing red and Felicity's distinctive bawl echoed through the kitchen.

'Now look what you've done!' Mark said furiously.

'Me?' Cress said, incredulously.

Mark stared at her.

'I'll go,' Cress said, but he wheeled around and stopped her dead in her tracks.

'No. You won't. I'll deal with it,' he said, and he stalked out of the room, leaving her redundant and guilty. She stood staring after him, trembling violently, trying to take in the scale of his fury and resentment with her.

She heard the door open in Felicity's room, and the kisses he gave her as he settled her back to sleep. She heard the rustle of sheets and the door closing again, little baby snores whistling softly, popping up as green lights.

Cress waited. She slowly finished her drink, trying to calm down and work out what it was he wanted from her.

Five minutes passed. Seven. Twelve. Everything was silent upstairs. Was he not even bothering to come back down? She turned off the lights, climbed the stairs and walked into their room. Mark was in bed, his clothes in a heap on the floor, his back turned to the door. The curtains were drawn.

'Mark?' she whispered, but he didn't reply, even though she could tell from the sound of his breathing that he wasn't asleep. His message was clear. She was still in the spare room.

Cress walked – dejected and rejected – across the landing, not noticing the light peeking out from under the door to Greta's room. She grabbed a bundle of sheets to make up the bed, just as Greta came out into the hallway looking like Heidi in an oversized nightshirt and floppy bedsocks.

'Goodnight, Mrs Pelling,' Greta said, walking towards the bathroom, a satisfied little smile playing on her lips as she remembered something her mother had always told her. Separate beds only ever mean one thing: separate lives.

Chapter Forty-one

Tor shivered as she got the children out of their car seats, pulling her moth-nibbled cashmere cardigan around her. It was her latest 'find' at the local charity shop. Burnham was such an affluent area, it didn't seem quite so bad to be buying hand-me-downs when they were Ralph Lauren, Max Mara and Caramel. She kept telling herself she was 'doing' Vintage. It's all just a matter of perception – and a boil wash.

Buying second-hand clothes was her latest money-saving scheme. The savings they'd been living on had dwindled, and if it was an ordinary month, she would have just over one month's reserves left. But it wasn't ordinary. Christmas was two weeks away and Tor was becoming paralysed with blind panic at the prospect of financing a Christmas with less than £300. She defied anyone to find an organic turkey for less than £40.

But this Christmas had to be special. It had to be! It was their first without Hugh. She had to make up for that, somehow. It had to glitter and shine and make her children's eyes widen in wonder. Because Christmas was what children remembered – Christmas and birthdays – and they would always remember, never be able to forget, this one.

The tiny profit she made on renting out the London house

went straight back into a contingency fund, and although Monty had sent her an initial – and very generous – cheque for cashflow purposes so that she could hire labourers, buy furniture and paints and fabrics, she had no intention of invoicing him for her own fee. With the divorce going through, the poor man's world was somewhere down by his ankles.

She kicked open the front door and the children flooded in, Millie tripping over Marney's book bag, Oscar heading straight for the biscuit tin, Marney calling out for Diggory (Tor had had a dog flap put into the back door and they regularly found him pressed against the Aga, eagerly awaiting their return and Oscar's pilgrimage to the biscuits).

Tor picked up the pile of post on the floor and walked down the hall to unlock the back door, shuffling through it disinterestedly. Nothing ever arrived except bills.

Except today. She looked down at a tacky, 1970s shot of the Pyramids, with tourists on camels and cloaked in hyper-tans and beige safari suits. She turned the postcard over.

Dear Tor,

 I shall be back in the UK next week and would love to meet up with you to discuss my refurb. I am having a baby in February so need to add a nursery to the spec. Could you call James to get my number? Sorry for being evasive – unfortunately, I have to keep it top secret.

 Speak soon,

 Best Regards,

 AA

Tor swallowed, her face red hot. James! Could she call James? Could she call James! No, she bloody well could not! How could he be so insensitive? After everything that had happened between them, how could he possibly let Amelia commission her to decorate their baby's room? What was wrong with the man? Jesus!

Tor flung the postcard on the table. She'd ring James over her dead body.

She looked down furiously at the remaining post. Another Boden catalogue? She dropped it in the bin and looked at the last letter. It was handwritten.

She filled the kettle and opened the letter, feeling a jolt of shock as she saw the Planed Spaces logo in the top right corner.

Tor's hands trembled as she read it. Did this mean – did this mean Christmas was back on? She grabbed the phone and punched in the numbers, still knowing them off by heart.

A clipped voice picked up.

'Peter? Peter, it's Tor!'

The voice warmed. 'Tor! You got my letter?'

'I can't believe it. Is it really worth that much?'

'It's all true! Are you pleased?'

Tor shrieked with excitement.

'That's a yes, then!' he laughed. There was a pause and he cleared his throat.

'How are you all, anyway?'

'Getting through it,' Tor replied. 'You?'

'We miss him badly, Tor. It's not the same without him.' His voice was choked.

'I know. Nothing will ever be the same without him,' Tor said, struggling to reassure him. She was increasingly finding that she was the comforter now. She'd lived with the loss day in day out, to the point where it was getting hard to remember what it had felt like to be *with* Hugh any more.

His absence had become her reality, her normality, but for everyone else it was something to remember, an adjustment.

'You're sure about selling?'

'Oh, I would love more than anything to be able to hold on to Hugh's share, if only to keep it as an investment for the children. To be able to keep that part of his life for them. But I can't. I thought I was going to have to cancel Christmas.'

Tor heard him nod down the line. 'I understand. Well, I reckon we can get this wrapped up before Christmas. The investor's pretty keen to seal the deal.'

'And this investor – you're sure he's the right person?'

'Absolutely. He's rock solid, and he's coming in as a sleeping partner, which suits me down to the ground.'

'Well then, it's your baby now. Get the paperwork to me as soon as possible, and I'll sign.'

'OK. ' He paused. 'I'm really pleased this has worked out so well, Tor.'

'Me too, Peter.'

'I'll courier everything up to you.'

Tor put the phone down and sighed happily, shutting her eyes and clasping her hands beneath her chin. Serendipity! She couldn't believe that in the space of ten minutes she had gone from impoverished to prosperous.

She poured a large splash of brandy into her coffee. Why the heck not? Fortune had intervened when she'd least expected it. After months of rain, finally they had their silver lining.

Chapter Forty-two

Kate burrowed her toes deeper into the pink Barbadian sand. It was so finely milled it was like lying on icing sugar, emanating a gentle warmth like those electric blankets her granny had always tucked around her in bed when she was a little girl.

She was about as far away now from her grandmother's sweet humble cottage, nestled in the Irish heather, as it was possible to get. She stretched her neck and looked behind her at Harry's extravagant plantation house. Three storeys high and faced with sunny blue clapboard, a wooden veranda skirted the perimeter, populated with a density of swing seats that made it hard to ever remain upright for more than a five-yard stretch.

Not that they ever did anyway. Harry's lust for her remained unabated, even though her pregnancy hormones meant she had the libido of a stone.

She looked back out to sea, watching the speedboat the paparazzi had moored 500 yards out bobbing gently on the azure water. There was no point in hiding from them any more. Their telephoto lenses were so powerful that if she yawned they could probably see what she'd had for breakfast. The game was well and truly up.

It was time to accept that this was how life would be from

now on. Even on Christmas Day they were on duty, recording her. The exposure in Oxford had just been the start. They'd got hold of photos of her as a girl in Shropshire, at university in Durham, at law school in York, partying with her friends. Not an area or age of her life was out of bounds – as Harry's lover and the mother of his unborn child, she was public property. It seemed the British public had a right to know who she'd slept with as a teenager and where she had her hair done and what she was eating on her pregnancy diet.

But she didn't really care for herself. None of this was a surprise. She dealt with the media for her living – she was simply on the other side of the fence now. No, it was Monty she was worried about. As if he hadn't been emasculated enough, their infertility problems had been recorded in microscopic detail.

Kate's eyes narrowed as she saw another boat pull up and drop anchor, her stomach tight as she played out in her mind the scene of Monty finding out about Harry and the baby. She should have rung, written, seen him, sent a message in a bloody bottle. Anything! Anything rather than read about it in the papers. He'd never forgive her, and she didn't blame him. It was unforgivable. She'd never have thought she was capable of hurting him like that. But then, she'd never have thought she was capable of anything that constituted her life now.

She wrapped her aquamarine chiffon sarong around her and stood up, her little belly tight and neat, swaddled in a giraffe-print swimsuit, tortoiseshell shades and with a floppy chocolate hat keeping the sun off.

She walked slowly up the rosy-pink bank towards the house. Harry wasn't back yet. He'd gone for an early morning dive and wouldn't get back till just before lunch. They were having roast turkey with all the trimmings, although Kate couldn't think of anything worse in this heat.

'Mary, I'm just popping into town,' Kate called to the housekeeper as she stood in the hallway, reapplying some suntan lotion.

'Yes, madam,' Mary said, popping out of the dining room, where she'd been dusting.

'Is there anything you need me to get while I'm out?' she asked absently.

'No, madam.'

'Right, OK. Well, I'll be back in an hour or so.'

'Yes, madam,' Mary said, watching after her curiously. Harry was a big star out here. He stayed here every Christmas, and this new girlfriend wasn't at all what she was used to.

Kate put the keys in the Mini Moke and turned on the ignition. The white leather bucket seats gleamed in the sun and she felt their heat sear into the backs of her thighs.

She roared down the long drive, the gravel spraying up behind her wheels. The house sat in thirty acres of land, and she loved flooring it down the long drive to the pineapple-topped gates, dodging coconuts as they dropped from the lofty palm trees.

She pulled out on to the narrow dusty road and felt the wind stream over her skin and lift her hair, the shadows cast by the banyan trees flickering over her. It was freedom – of sorts.

She kept her eyes on the road, not bothering to clock the other manses on this millionaires' row, but more concerned with avoiding locals swerving dangerously on their bikes. As she got nearer into town and the big houses made way for tiny shanty huts, bleached billboards advertising sun lotion and fizzy drinks and ice creams peppered the road-sides, with little trestle tables selling fresh strawberries and coconut milk for two bucks.

The streets were empty. It was eleven o'clock on Christmas Day and everybody was at church. Judging by the horrendous parking, most of the congregation had been late and just abandoned their cars in the road, rather than bothering to manoeuvre them to the kerb.

Kate drove through the town slowly, the turquoise sea peeking periodically around the sides of the small buildings, trying to entice her back to its warm waters. She found a free spot, carelessly parked the car – well, when in Rome – and sat on the bonnet. She looked out to the horizon. She could just see the photographers' boat past the promontory – they had no idea she'd gone yet – and her eyes narrowed as she looked for Harry's dive boat. He was out there somewhere, under that heavy sea. Peaceful, floating, like their bab— She felt a kick!

She couldn't believe it. The first kick, the very first. It was really happening. She was having a baby! Kate threw back her head and laughed loudly all to herself like a crazy woman, her shoulders shaking.

Even though she'd weed on seven pregnancy sticks and seen Mr Fallon fortnightly and had already had four scans, her head hadn't been able to get past the theoretical stage. She had seen that she was pregnant, she had been told that she was pregnant. But she hadn't really felt pregnant. Or at least, not the happy pregnant she'd always imagined. Frankly, she'd spent the first trimester of this pregnancy completely terrified. She used to fantasize about the way she would tell Monty when the line went blue, about the party they would throw to tell their family and friends, the neat designer bump and no weight-gain that would have everyone so jealous, the excitement of going on maternity leave.

But it hadn't been like that. Exhilaration hadn't been the first emotion to flood her brain when the little blue line appeared in the window. It had been so early in her relationship with Harry; they were still devouring each other, wanton and insatiable. It had been the first time in years she had had sex without thinking about making a baby. This relationship wasn't supposed to have been for keeps. She had been trying to run away, not settle down.

As for Harry, well, he'd taken it better than she'd anticipated. There had been a moment when . . . a look on his face that had been hard to forget, even after he'd recovered and said all the right things. It was a look that had stayed with her, so that even though he patted her tummy and made the phone calls to the right doctors, she found herself trying to act as though she wasn't really pregnant at all – pretending she wasn't too coma-tired to go to another party, swallowing back the retches as he sipped his aromatic espressos and tucked into cornflakes (even just looking at the box made her heave), and acquiring a habit of wearing negligées in bed to show off her budding bosom and hide her spreading waist.

Up till now, she had tried to minimize the impact of the pregnancy on their relationship – trying to show him that things between them didn't have to change, but now, with the baby beginning to intrude – quite literally – upon them, she didn't want to keep pretending. She wanted to rejoice and celebrate it and dwell on it and show off. Because it was everything she had ever wanted.

She slid off the bonnet and walked around to the back of the car, catching sight of a little girl skipping towards her as she picked up her bag.

Kate straightened up to watch her. She couldn't have been any older than five, her hair in bunches, her green cotton piqué dress ballooning with air at each jump.

Becoming aware of the rich lady's scrutiny, the little girl looked up and stumbled.

'Oh, I'm sorry,' Kate said. 'I didn't mean to put you off. It's just you're such a terribly good skipper. I couldn't help but watch.'

The little girl looked at her, unsure, her skipping rope dangling by her side.

'Merry Christmas?' Kate offered limply.

The little girl kept on staring.

'Where are your family?'

The little girl pointed to the church.

'Aren't you supposed to be in there with them?'

She shrugged, and twiddled with the rope.

'Did Father Christmas bring you any presents?'

The little girl nodded again.

'What did he get you?'

She held up the rope. Kate could see that the wooden handles had been fashioned as frogs and painted green.

'Wow. You must have been a very good girl for Father Christmas to give you that.'

The little girl nodded and took a couple of tentative steps forward. She held up the rope for Kate to examine, and Kate admired it enthusiastically.

'Is there a baby in your belly?' the little girl asked finally.

'There is.'

'Can I touch it?'

Kate nodded and the little girl placed a tiny hot hand on her belly.

'It feels all hard.'

Kate smiled.

'What is it?'

Kate crouched down low and looked the little girl in the eyes. She had had an eighteen-week scan with Alex Fallon, to check everything was OK before she flew out, and he'd been fairly certain of the sex. 'Although there are never any guarantees at this stage. It's still hard to tell,' he'd said, covering all his bases. Harry hadn't wanted to find out, preferring to wait until the birth, but Kate had been absolutely busting to tell somebody.

'Well, you mustn't tell anybody,' she said. 'Because it's a big secret. OK?'

The little girl nodded.

'It's a baby girl.'

The little girl gasped and clapped her hand over her mouth, and Kate giggled. It felt so good to share it with somebody. She hadn't realized she was so lonely. Once upon a time, she would have been having this conversation with the girls over a coffee at the bandstand café. Now here she was in a swimsuit on Christmas Day, confiding in a pre-schooler.

'What you goin' to call her?' the little girl asked breath-lessly, her brown eyes wide.

'Well, I'm not really sure yet, but I like Ottilie. What do you think?'

The little girl nodded. 'Ollity. That's pretty.'

Kate smiled and stood up. 'Yes, I think so. Now I've just got to convince her daddy. He prefers Erin.'

'Me don't like that,' the little girl said decisively.

Kate wrinkled her nose. 'Me either.'

The little girl picked up her rope. 'I got to go now.'

'OK. Well, it was lovely meeting you,' she said as the girl skipped off unceremoniously.

Kate smiled and turned back towards the shops and beach stalls. She wanted to get Harry some whimsical stocking-fillers, even though she knew the only thing he wanted to fill in stockings was her.

She didn't see the little girl stop at the hibiscus bush and put her hand out for the $10 she'd been promised.

When she got back, Harry was swimming butterfly lengths in the buff. She sat down next to the pool and dangled her legs in the water, waiting for him to notice her.

It didn't take long. For all the splashing above the water, he could see her scarlet toenails clearly underwater and swam over.

'I thought you'd left me,' he grinned, looking up at her.

'Considered it,' she said, smiling archly. 'But I thought I'd wait until after you'd given me my Christmas present.'

'Sweet girl,' he said, his eyes falling down to her breasts, which were barely contained by the swimsuit.

'I take it you brought a fish back for supper?'

''Course. Hammerhead shark. It's sitting on ice in the kitchen.'

She kicked some water at him. 'Smart-arse.' She sighed and stretched. 'Oh, it's too hot, Hunter! How can we be expected to eat roast turkey in this heat?'

'I'm sorry, darling. Is paradise too much for you?'

She narrowed her eyes. 'You know the saying "bun in the oven"? Well, I'm the sodding oven. I can't cool down.'

''Course you can. Get in here with me.'

She arched an eyebrow and leant back on her elbows, watching that curl right at the front of his forehead beginning to dry and flop forward into its customary place. 'If you think I'm getting into the water with you, you can think again. I know exactly what'll happen.'

'I don't know what you mean,' he said, amused and un-deterred.

'I see that lot haven't moved,' she said, nodding towards the speedboat. 'Bloody morons, all of them. I mean, what are they waiting for? What do they think is going to happen?'

Harry said nothing, but reached up out of the water, artfully pulling one of the strands of her halterneck so that the bow came away and the swimsuit rolled down to her waist.

'Well, something along the lines of that, I should imagine,' he winked, as Kate's eyes widened in horror and her hands flew up to cover her modesty.

'Harry! You bastard!' she shrieked. 'What'd you do that for?'

'You'd better get in here, hadn't you,' he laughed. 'Or the *National Enquirer* will have their next cover.' And he picked her up and brought her down into the water, holding her in the relative safety of his arms.

'You are unbelievable,' she giggled as he rolled the swim-suit the rest of the way down. 'What you'll do to get your own way.'

'Machiavelli's my hero,' he mumbled, burying his face in her cleavage. 'I find the end always justifies the means.'

Chapter Forty-three

It was the low whirr of the fan that woke her up, a sure sign she'd had a sufficiency of sleep. Kate rolled over and checked the Asprey carriage clock sitting by the bed.

10.24 a.m.

Uuugh. What was wrong with her? The more she slept, the more she wanted to sleep. She hadn't had this many lie-ins since she was a teenager.

As usual, Harry was already up. He liked to go for 6 a.m. runs on the beach, before anyone – particularly the paparazzi – was awake. Yawning, Kate rolled herself up into a sitting position, untangling her legs from the crumpled Pratesi sheets, and began absent-mindedly checking for bites, a ritual which had been added to her usual cleanse-tone-moisturize morning routine. The mozzies loved her.

She checked all over but it appeared she'd got away lightly last night. Well, except for the huge lovebite Harry had left at the top of her left inner thigh. It was just as well she wasn't scheduled to see Alex Fallon for another ten days, she thought, as she kicked her legs through the mosquito nets. She pulled on a clean pair of knickers and the khaki linen shirt Harry'd pulled off last night and walked to the windows, throwing open the shutters.

The sky was deep blue, having long since cast off its dawn

robes, and the bay was already teeming as jetskis buzzed superyachts, the fishing boats put-putting over the horizon. There seemed to be more speedboats than usual clustered together, but then, on the stretch of beach immediately outside their grounds, Kate saw the clique of local supermodels already lying provocatively on their towels. Word had spread like wildfire around the island that Harry Hunter was resident again, and the glossy posse of girls in Brazilian microbikinis and gleaming tans grew by the day. Kate's hands automatically rubbed her belly.

She walked away from the window and went downstairs. Everything was quiet, although she knew that if she called, Mary would be in the room within seconds. Kate went over to the breakfast table and helped herself to a half of pink grapefruit, some natural yoghurt, granola and honey, and walked out on to the veranda.

'Would you like tea this morning, madam?' Mary inquired, as she set the bowls on the table.

'Yes please, Mary. Some Earl Grey would be lovely. Is Harry around?'

'No, madam.' Mary shook her head. 'He's still on his morning run.'

'Still?'

Mary said nothing.

Kate shrugged and tucked into her breakfast, picking up the papers, which had been left ironed and folded next to her chair. She clocked the date as she opened them up.

God, 30th of December! How bizarre. She was loving being here, but she'd never felt less Christmassy in her whole life. Harry had said they would ordinarily have gone skiing, but that what with her 'condition', it wasn't such a great idea this year.

She speared a segment of pink grapefruit and popped it into her mouth as she opened up the *Telegraph*. Sub-prime crisis, financial meltdown, teenage knife crime in London . . . Kate's eyes expertly scanned the first pages, looking for slurs, unfounded allegations, anything that yielded potential new clients, but her interest level was low and she had flicked through all the broadsheets before she was on to her yoghurt.

It was the *Sun* that particularly stuck the knife in. They'd been after her, lying in wait, ever since she'd threatened them when the *Tatler* story first came out. She was the new Neil Hamilton, Jeffrey Archer, Jonathan Aitken – she'd been caught lying and they wanted her blood.

'*It's a Girl!*' ran the bold black print. Kate choked on her breakfast, her spoon clattering to the floor. They'd used the photograph of her on Christmas Day, sitting by the pool, an arm just about over her breasts and her head thrown back in laughter, as Harry's muscular arms reached up to her.

She couldn't believe it! They couldn't print that. It was private. How on earth could they have known? Harry didn't even know! He couldn't find out like this.

Kate pushed her chair away and stood up, holding on to the table for support as she tried to clear her head.

She'd ring . . . she'd ring the office and get one of the other partners to slap it down. Get an injunction. Sue the malicious marrow out of the bastards. They wouldn't get away with this.

Who had done it? Who had betrayed her? Think, think. Think! She could imagine the size of the bribes being offered. £500,000? No, more. Easily. Harry's unborn child was already a celebrity and she wasn't even born yet. Already, there was a price on her head! It had to be someone at the clinic? A nurse? Fallon? Who else had access?

And then it came to her.

James!

She stood upright. It had to be. He'd do anything to hurt Harry. He'd been waging war against him for over twenty years – why stop now? This was his *coup de grâce*. Now that Kate was with Harry, it made her James's enemy too. Especially if Tor's pitiful voicemails were to be believed and she really had dumped him out of loyalty for her. Kate hadn't forgotten the way she'd found them together, or the way James had protected Tor. There'd been no doubt he was serious about her '. . . *It was never not going to happen . . .*' And now, because of Kate, he'd lost her.

It all made perfect sense. Harry was certain it was James who'd tipped off the press that they'd be coming out of the clinic. And now this.

Kate's mouth set. He wouldn't know what hit him. She'd get him struck off for this.

'Mary!' Kate shouted. 'Mary! Bring me the phone!'

Mary brought it over in an instant, seeing for the first time how very like the other women Kate was, after all.

Kate punched in the numbers for London automatically, hanging up as soon as the office voicemail came on.

Of course no one was in.

She ran upstairs and grabbed her mobile out of her bag. Nicholas Parker's number was in there somewhere.

She flicked through the address book and found it.

'Nicholas? It's Kate Marfleet.' Though she had taken to using her maiden name in most other matters, she continued to use her married name for work.

'Ah, Kate. Merry Christmas to you,' came Nicholas' flat voice.

'Yes, Merry Christmas to you too, Nicholas.' There was a

pause as she tried to remember her manners. 'Are you – uh – having a nice break?'

'Yes, very nice indeed.'

'Good. Well, I'm glad.'

'And you?' he inquired, reluctantly.

'Um, yes, very nice, thank you. We're, um, just by the beach for a few days.'

'Mmmhmm.' He already knew that. The pictures of her – practically topless – were everywhere.

There was another pause. She wasn't sure how to approach this – as client or partner. Her relationship with Harry was the elephant in the room between her and the firm. Having lied to them outright about the nature of their relationship when the *Tatler* article came out, she'd had to have a very difficult meeting with the other partners when the *Evening Standard* exposed her, and their coldness had left her in no doubt that if Harry ever went, so did she. In spite of all the years she had spent grafting, networking and building up her career, its destiny now rested entirely with him.

'Look, Nicholas. I'll just get to the point. Have you seen today's *Sun*?'

Nicholas sighed. 'No. I've been trying to have a day off.'

'I understand, but I'm afraid this matter is very pressing.'

'What've they done now?' He was becoming accustomed to his young partner gracing the news, rather than shaping it.

'They've revealed the sex of the baby.'

'What!'

'I know.'

'How could they possibly know that?'

'I have my suspicions about who may have leaked it.'

'And is the *Sun* correct in what it's printed?'

'Yes.'

'So you think they've definitely been informed? Not a lucky guess?'

'Well, let's face it, they always had a fifty per cent chance of being right if they did guess. But no, I would say they had information – they know how litigious we are. They wouldn't risk taking a chance on it.'

'What do you want to do?'

'I want to sue the *Sun* and the doctor involved for contravention of the Data Protection Act. And I want to go to the GMC to have the doctor involved struck off.'

'Who's the doctor?'

'James White.'

There was a pause. 'As in Lord White? The royal obstetrician?'

'That's right.'

There was an even longer pause. 'And you're quite sure it's him?'

'Positive.' Her tone left him in no doubt.

'OK, well, leave it with me, Kate. I'll make some calls and get back to you.'

Kate put down the phone, sank on to the bed and began to sob. It wasn't supposed to be like this. Nothing was sacred any more, nothing was hers. How could she live like this? What kind of mother was she, when she couldn't even protect her baby before she was born?

Her mobile rang and she picked it up immediately.

'Hello?' she sobbed, unable to keep the emotion out of her voice. Nicholas would take it as more evidence of her lack of professionalism.

'Kate, it's me.'

Kate was stunned into silence.

'Are you there? Don't hang up! I just wanted . . . I just wanted to check you were OK. And to wish you a Merry Christmas,' the voice added lamely.

'Monty,' she whispered, feeling the sobs gather pace again. 'How are you?'

'I've been better,' she blurted, trying to keep her composure but failing, as she heard the compassion in his voice.

'I can imagine,' he said, his chest tightening as he heard her struggle to control herself. 'Is there anything I can do?'

She shook her head and sniffed loudly down the line. 'No,' she gasped. 'No, it's my mess. I have to deal with it. I am dealing with it.'

'You know you can lean on me, Kate.'

'Mmmhmmm,' she said, unable to speak, as his kindness made the tears worse. She could almost feel his arms around her. She took a deep breath. 'Where are you?'

'In Norfolk.' There was a silence. 'With Tor and Cress and Mark,' he added quickly. 'Tor needs people around her at the moment. I'm not with . . . you know . . .'

'Have you seen Billy?'

'No, he's skiing. He hasn't come home since the summer,' he said quietly.

'I'm so sorry, Monty. I'm so . . . I'm so sorry . . . I'm so sorry about everything,' she cried, feeling all the guilt and regret pour out. 'I should have told you about the baby, but I didn't know how and then the papers found out and I didn't know that either and I've been such a bitch and . . .'

'Sssh,' he soothed. 'It's all OK. Don't worry about that. Just look after yourself. You've got a baby to think about now.'

'Uh-huh, OK, OK,' she gasped, looking down at her tummy, which was jumping up with her hiccups.

'Just give me a ring if you want to talk. Let me know you're all right.'

'All right, I will. Yes, I'll do that. Thanks, Monty. Thanks for being so nice. I don't deserve it.'

'Yes, you do,' he said quietly. 'You've had a hard time. You deserve to be happy. You deserve to be loved. You deserve to be a mother. I want it all for you. Kate.'

'Mmmmmmhmmmm,' she nodded, crying heavily again.

'Keep in touch, OK?'

She wailed as the line went dead, her head swimming with images of him, celebrating with their friends at their holiday house – enjoying a cold Christmas with blustery walks on the beach, the Atlantic churning up the seabed, the water brown and frothy as it bashed the sand; vats of soup and mulled wine simmering on the Aga she hadn't even cooked on yet, and their godchildren shrieking up and down the stairs as the grown-ups got pissed and played charades.

Tor, of course. This would be hard for her. Occasions like this must be the hardest to endure, and for all that had passed between them, Kate felt glad to think that she wasn't alone – and that neither was Monty. That they were all there together, looking after each other.

As for her? Well, Monty was right. She needed to cheer up. OK, so she couldn't cool down and she couldn't face Christmas food and it felt more like the middle of July than December, and there was an army of beach glamazons camping out in the hope of seducing her boyfriend. But! She was pregnant. She was going to be a mother. She was in love with a handsome, successful man who loved her back. And she was living in the lap of luxury. It was time to be grateful for what she had. Even paradise wasn't perfect.

Kate walked into the marble bathroom and washed her

face under cold water. She heard the phone ringing in the bedroom and she ran back in, just as Harry picked it up.

'Yes?' he said, as he winked at her, wearing just a pair of Vilbrequins. 'Hello, Nicholas. Happy Christmas and all of that.'

She held out her palms, indicating 'Where've you been?'

He held up a finger to silence her as Nicholas spoke down the line, a frown crossing his face.

'Uh-huh . . . They said what? . . . Christ, are you sure? . . . Well, is there any way we can stop them? . . . Should I come back? . . . Uh-huh . . . No, don't worry about it . . . Yes, I know exactly how to make this go away . . . I'll make a call and get back to you.'

He hung up and put the phone down, visibly paler and less pleased with himself than he had been when he'd picked it up.

'That was Nicholas Parker,' he said solemnly. 'He's just got off from talking to the *Sun*.'

'Yes, I know,' Kate said, watching him as he raked a hand through his hair. 'I spoke with him a short while ago.'

'So you know then?'

Kate nodded. 'What did he say?'

'He's trying to get an injunction against them, but he doesn't think it looks good.' He crossed the room and stood at the windows, staring at the beach goddesses dispassionately. 'He doesn't think we should go back till all this has been sorted. Thinks it's better if we stay away from the UK.'

He shrugged and turned back to her. 'But fine. We can just go straight up to LA from here. I've got masses to do there before the ceremony anyway.' He walked over to the desk and picked up his BlackBerry.

'What about the baby?' Kate asked.

'Oh, don't worry about that,' he said dismissively, scrolling through. 'Fallon's got contacts at Cedars-Sinai. We'll just transfer to them.'

Kate frowned. She couldn't believe he was so calm about it.

'No. I mean – how do you feel, now that you know it's a girl?'

'I know more than that. I already know which girl.'

Kate looked at him quizzically. What? 'Who are you calling?' she asked, frustrated and confused.

He held up a hand again as the line was picked up.

'It's me,' he said darkly. 'What the fuck do you think you're playing at? . . . Of course I know . . . Am I supposed to care? . . . No, never did. I was acting on the advice of my briefs . . . Yes, that's right, she is . . . The whole thing was a sting, babe. We read you like a book. Saw you coming a mile off . . .'

'Harry, what the hell are you doing? Who are you talking to?' Kate cried, rushing forwards and trying to grab the phone from his hands. 'Hang up!'

But he caught her by the elbow and held her back with a single outstretched arm.

'. . . Your claims won't wash when I show the evidence I've got that you were very, very willing . . . what evidence? . . . There's a tape in my possession which shows you in a few compromising, but rather athletic, positions . . . What? . . .'

He let go of Kate and marched across the room, banging keys on the laptop. He always left it on and carried it every-where with him – ready for when inspiration struck.

'You're bluffing . . .' he said, although Kate could see from the way he bit his lip that he was the one bluffing. 'You don't have the brains to do something as clever as that . . .'

But as the file programme came up, he could see with his own eyes that she did. He pressed the disconnect button and looked up at Kate, the blood drained from his face.

'Harry, tell me! Tell me what's going on!' Kate cried frantically.

'I don't believe it. She's wiped the tape,' he whispered. 'She's stolen the fucking evidence.' He paced the room, his hands in his hair. 'This can't be happening.' He wheeled round to face her.

'Emily's sold the story?' she whispered.

'The *News of the World* are running it tomorrow. Kate, it's going to destroy me. They're calling me a child abuser. They're running a campaign to have me put on the sex offenders register.'

Chapter Forty-four

Cress curled a cold hand around her glass of *vin chaud* and stared into the log fire, feeling the blood begin to flow again. It hadn't been the most successful Christmas ever, chez Pelling. Everyone – including Cress – had bitterly missed Greta, after Cress desiccated the turkey; and despite having thrown thousands at the children's presents this year, the day had lacked warmth somehow. So when Tor had phoned, inviting them up for New Year, Mark had actually packed within the hour, embarrassingly eager for the company of people other than his wife.

She watched Tor place the mince pies on the hearth to keep warm. She was needed here at least. For all Tor's public festive cheer, Cress had found her crying in the pantry, and when she came down for breakfast each morning she put her swollen eyes down to hay fever from the Christmas tree. No one was fooled.

Mark and Monty had retired to the local pub to watch the overly hyped Vegas fight on the big screens. It was downright perverse that Hugh wasn't with them, and Cress knew the boys felt their depleted number as much as the girls did.

'I wonder how Kate is,' Tor mused, watching the flames leap.

They all missed her, even Cress, though she'd never admit

it. There was no doubt Monty was lost without her. Tor had been stunned by his appearance when he'd arrived on Christmas Eve – 'We'll be each other's makeshift family,' she'd suggested – like the ghost of Christmas past. But to his credit, he'd been anything but a misery. He'd carved the Christmas roast and chased the children in the garden, and flown the stunt kites on the beach. He'd even been over to see Lily to try to discuss things rationally, but that had been a less successful endeavour. This was Billy's first Christmas away from home, and although her mother was staying with her, Lily couldn't be comforted. The revelations seemed to have dredged up all manner of trauma and she was more often than not plastered by lunchtime.

'I wonder if she's showing yet,' she went on.

'Humph! More than you know,' Cress muttered, grabbing a copy of *Grazia* magazine from her bag and tossing it to Tor.

Tor took in the cover, showing Kate, bikini-clad and pregnant, frolicking with Harry by the pool in Barbados.

Tor winced. 'She's really not coming back, is she?' Tor asked forlornly.

Cress shook her head. 'Doesn't look like it.'

They heard the front door slam.

'That's it. Wake the kids,' Cress muttered, rolling her eyes. 'You've had a few then?' she said sarcastically, as the boys trooped in, looking flushed and rather the worse for wear.

'It's New Year's Eve,' Mark retorted coldly, a supportive arm around Monty. 'We're supposed to get drunk. Anyway, Monty needed a few beers. He's had yet more shit news.'

Monty hiccupped and swayed a little, finding an armchair and collapsing into it. He dropped his head into his hands, looking utterly depleted.

'It's just one thing after another with this character,' Mark said contemptuously, handing over the newspaper they'd found in the pub.

Tor leant forward and looked at the headlines.

'Oh God,' she muttered.

'*Hunter Teen Sex Scandal*' ran the headline, alongside a picture of an old school photo with a pupil in uniform, ringed, and Harry, also ringed, standing with the teachers further along the line.

'Oh, he didn't!' Cress whispered. 'The stupid bastard.'

Tor stopped reading, midway through a paragraph, and gasped. 'She was fourteen!'

Cress stared at the schoolgirl in the picture. She was stunning, familiar.

She read the text: Emily Brookner . . . Cress frowned and tried to remember where she'd seen – no, met – her before. She'd definitely met her.

The girl at the Oxford Union? Yes – that was it. She had said she was with Harry.

Cress bit her lip and felt her blood cool as the events of that night rushed back. She may have come with him, but – thanks to Cress's ambush – she hadn't left with him.

No wonder she wanted revenge.

'Oh, poor Kate. This is the last thing she needs,' Tor said sympathetically. Despite Cress's straight-talking on the matter, she still didn't have her friend's savvy about Kate's role in the *Tatler* affair.

Cress rolled her eyes at her.

'No. I know you're cross with her, Cress, but look at things from her perspective: the poor girl's pregnant with his child, has had the sex of her unborn baby revealed to the world, been photographed in her bikini' – Tor's particularly forceful tone at this point revealed how completely beyond the pale that last point was – 'and now finds out he was having a fling with a girl he'd first seduced as a schoolgirl! It's not an auspicious start, let's face it.'

Monty slipped down further in his chair, his skin grey. 'How long am I supposed to put up with this for?' he mumbled. 'It's like torture. I can't even go to the pub without seeing a newspaper that has a picture of my wife cavorting with *him* on the front of it.'

Mark squeezed his shoulder hard, as if trying to aspirate his friend's anguish.

'Come on, mate. You'll get through this. Kate'll see sense. You're ten times the man Hunter is,' he said venomously, his eyes on Cress.

Tor looked at the clock. It was ten to twelve. They weren't on course for a happy New Year. She took a deep breath.

'Right, I think we should play a game, folks. The bells are about to ring and we can't see in the new year on a downer. Next year is going to be the year it comes right for *all* of us. So let's try to buck up and have a good night, OK?'

Monty watched her – she, who had lost more than anyone – feeling suddenly ashamed of his self-pity, noticing how her eyes were still puffy from this morning's furtive tears.

'We'll play Who Am I?' she continued, tearing up pieces of paper, and he sat forward to help her. They smiled at each other, knowingly; Cress and Mark groaned, but everybody wrote down some names and chucked them into an empty ice bucket.

Tor laughed as everyone stuck the pieces of paper to their foreheads. The boys had deliberately upped the ante – sportsmen and politicians were always killer. Cress had Idi

Amin taped to her head. She'd never guess it in a million years.

There was a knock at the door. Tor got up to answer it just as the bells started to chime.

She opened the door and looked into the darkness. She was still surprised by the absence of streetlights around here.

'Hello?' she called, unsure. Was it just kids larking about?

'Hi.'

A figure stepped forward. It was James. He was wearing a dark overcoat and carrying a lump of coal. No wonder he'd been hard to see.

'What are you doing here?' she gasped, too surprised to be angry and more worried that Mark or, worse, Monty might come out.

'First footing. I wanted to bring you luck for the New Year,' he said, proffering the coal.

'Oh, thank you,' she said uncertainly, reaching out to take it. But he grasped her hand in his and held it fast.

The minutes passed and they said nothing. All that had happened in Cornwall hung in the air, but for some reason her brain could only recall the good bits. Kate who? Amelia who?

There was a low cheer from the drawing room and the door began to open. '. . . And get some more booze while you're there . . .'

He squeezed her hand tightly.

'So good luck,' he said, stepping back into the darkness. His eyes moved up to the piece of paper still gummed to her forehead and an infectious smile broke out. 'You're going to need it.'

Tor's eyes widened in horror. She'd completely forgotten about that.

James laughed and winked at her, and then he was gone. She shut the door and pulled the piece of paper off, recognizing the distinctive hand.

She looked down and cringed.

'Miss Piggy'.

Cress!

Chapter Forty-five

Tor smoothed her skirt over her thighs nervously and looked around. She'd never been to an auction before, but it was exactly as she'd expected – well, fewer women in furs possibly, but certainly the patrician pinstripes and brooched cashmere coats were in abundance. And in contrast to Marney's school photo, which showed unfeasible numbers of golden-haired children, most of the heads here were grey – as though dipped in moonlight – and the air was as heavy with Elnett as with cologne. The atmosphere was clubby. People were stopping at each row, shaking hands and air kissing, exchanging pleasantries in French, Spanish, Russian, as well as the 'airhairlair' brigade, discussing their winter sun breaks and the poor shooting season – in fact, everything but the goodies they'd come to bag today.

Tor looked back down at her catalogue. The oil Harry wanted – a small Reynolds – was the sixty-third and final lot. He already had an impressive eighteenth-century art collection, and he'd been keen to come here and bid on this himself, but his lawyers had advised otherwise, at least until they had quelled the anti-Harry hysteria which was surging following the *News of the World*'s exposé. Tor had been calling his office all week, trying to get a figure for his highest bid, but hers clearly hadn't been priority calls and she had no fixed budget. Was the sky the limit?

She wished Cress had come with her, but a call from Richard and Judy had come in, and she had gone to the studios instead. *The Wrong Prince* had been number one for three weeks now, and to be honest, Cress was almost as much in demand as the mystery author anyway. Her profile during the *Tatler* hunt, Harry's latest (and worst) sex scandal and his impending Oscar nomination (which, although not formally announced for another two weeks, was the worst kept secret in Hollywood), and now as the gate-keeper of the identity of the author of *The Wrong Prince*, meant she titillated the viewers on numerous fronts – had she ever been Harry's lover? They worked so closely . . . What was he really like? Had she seen him with young girls before? What was she wearing to the Oscars? How did she feel when she first saw *The Wrong Prince*? Why was the writer hiding?

Tor looked back down and studied the catalogue.

'Heavens, Tor, is it really you?'

Tor looked up.

'Laetitia! Fancy! How are you?'

They kissed without making physical contact. Laetitia was looking 'appropriate', as ever, wearing a honey tweed suit with a nipped-in shooting jacket and wide-leg cuffed trousers. A pair of chocolate brown ballet pumps, a camel 2.55 Chanel bag and a violet pashmina accessorized perfectly, and Tor felt like an office worker by comparison, in her narrow catalogue-bought navy skirt and man's striped shirt.

'On your own?' Laetitia said, her head cocked to one side as she took in the empty seats on either side of Tor.

Tor nodded. 'Would you like to join me?' she offered, hoping desperately Laetitia wouldn't take her up on it.

Laetitia's eyes briefly widened in horror. 'That's sweet, but I'm with a group just at the front there. We always come to the fine art sales together, then go on to Fiorelli's for a spot of lunch afterwards.'

'Oh, that's nice,' Tor said weakly.

'But I can certainly stop for a moment. It's been so long, hasn't it? In fact, when was it last?'

Tor stopped to consider. 'Um, I guess it was Cornwall, in August.'

'Gosh, yes!' Laetitia exclaimed. 'An absolute lifetime. So much has happened since then!' She leaned in confidingly. 'I suppose you're just the person for asking after Kate Marfleet, aren't you? How's she bearing up?'

Tor shrugged lightly. 'Actually, I don't know. I've not seen her in a while.'

'Really? That does surprise me. You always seemed so – tight. Well, it's simply super news about the baby. Guy and I were so thrilled when we heard – well, read about it,' she said, correcting herself with a knowing smile.

Tor didn't say anything. She wasn't going to give Laetitia a single snippet of information. The woman was vile.

She felt Laetitia's eyes scrutinize her. 'Of course, you've been through the wringer too, what with the *Tatler* escapade. Poor you. I couldn't believe it when I read the things they wrote. I mean, I know the two of you were very touchy-feely at dinner, but it was clear that Harry had no real interest in you. I must say I just couldn't believe it when the papers wouldn't let it go that you were The One.' She tittered to herself, Tor so stunned by the stream of veiled insults that she didn't even know where to start responding.

'Besides, it was all in such poor taste given everything that had happened with Hugh. He was such a lovely man. So lovely.'

Tor nodded but didn't speak.

413

'And I expect you can imagine, Guy and I felt your loss more keenly than anyone. We felt so guilty.'

Tor's eyes narrowed. 'Guilty?'

'Yuh, it was such a shock when the policewoman answered his phone. I'll never forget it.' A steadying hand flew to her heart, as if the tragedy had been hers, and not Tor's.

Tor stared at her, hearing the din fade to silence. 'Sorry, you'll have to explain.' Her voice didn't sound like her own.

Laetitia stared at her. Tor looked odd. 'Well, because, when he didn't turn up, we began to worry and —'

'Turn up?'

'Yes. The night he . . . when he was coming over . . .'

'To you?'

Laetitia nodded. 'Didn't you know?'

Tor shook her head. 'He didn't say he was going to you.'

'Oh,' Laetitia said shortly, clearly miffed that her supporting role in the entire saga had been overlooked. 'Where did he say he was going?'

Tor ignored the question. 'Why did he say he was coming over?'

'I'm not sure. Guy took the call and said Hugh would be staying in the guest suite. Of course, if we'd known he'd been drinking, we never would have allowed it. But then, when he didn't arrive, we rang and . . .' she faltered, '. . . and the police answered.'

Tor tried to blink back the tears, but they fell anyway, and for the first time, she saw genuine concern cross Laetitia's face – not because she was sympathetic to Tor's plight, of course. Rather, it wouldn't do for other people to think she'd driven Tor to tears.

'Oh heavens, Tor,' she whispered. 'I really didn't mean to make things worse for you.'

Tor smiled and wiped the tears away, smudging her mascara. 'You haven't actually. You've made them better.'

Laetitia frowned as much as her fresh Botox top-up would allow. 'It doesn't look like it.'

'I know,' Tor laughed lightly, sniffing and wiping her eyes again. 'I know.'

They sat in silence for a minute, while Tor sniffed and intermittently giggled, and began to completely freak out Laetitia.

'Well,' she said finally, feeling an acceptable amount of time had passed since first making Tor cry. 'It's been simply lovely to see you but I'd better get back,' she said, waving breezily to the clique who had turned in their seats and were staring.

'Of course,' Tor said, enjoying Laetitia's discomfort, and watching her go. She realized how alone she looked in this big saleroom, where everyone seemed to move in packs or pairs, but she didn't care. Hugh hadn't left her for Julia after all. He'd lied. Tried to save face. There had been hope. He had still been hers.

The gavel banged down hard three times and the auctioneer took to the podium. The jet velvet curtains opened smoothly, revealing a small watercolour of Florence.

'Ladies and gentlemen, please refer to Lot 1 in your catalogues. We have for sale Signoria Square in Florence, by Bernardo Bellotto, student to Canaletto. In fine restored condition. Bidding will start at eighty thousand. Do I have eighty-five thousand? Yes, I have eighty-five. Ninety? Thank you, sir. A hundred thousand?'

And they were off.

Tor tried to pay attention but she felt an overwhelming urge to stand up and scream and dance and jump. She wanted to tell someone, but there was no one to tell. It had been her guilty secret, her burden. No one had known. Well, only James, and she couldn't ring him. What would he care about this little bit of small print? His life had moved on with Amelia. It was irrelevant to him whether Hugh had died going to stay with a friend, or with his mistress. That small twist simply preserved Tor's memories and reclaimed them as hers. It didn't change his role in the whole affair and the fact that Hugh would still be alive if James hadn't kissed her. In essence, nothing had changed except her emotional ownership over her marriage, but she felt heady with relief and as light as a leaf.

The sound of polite applause disturbed her thoughts and she looked back up. They were on to Lot 3 already. She checked the catalogue to see what was coming up, when there was a shuffle of people getting up from their seats to allow some latecomers into the sale.

She settled more comfortably into her chair and watched as the stream of top-tier paintings were paraded and bid for and won.

'Have I missed much?' whispered a silky voice.

Tor looked up to see Anna Brightling assuming her customary leg-wrapping pose, which showed off her ankles to their best advantage. As usual, she looked divine, in a pair of cream trousers, beige silk blouse and a baby blue sheepskin coat. Tor's shoulders slumped as she demoted herself from looking like an office worker to a polyester-clad bank clerk.

'How lovely to see you again,' Tor smiled. Anna had thawed considerably after their initial introduction at the cricket and Tor had come away liking her a lot. 'They're on Lot 36. Are you here to buy?'

'Not especially. I always come if I can, and I was in town today so I thought, why not?' She paused and lowered her voice. 'Anyway, there's a better than average chance of seeing James here.'

'Is there?' Tor quickly looked around.

'He never misses a fine art sale if he can help it. He's addicted to the thrill of the chase. He'll be ruined if he ever discovers eBay.'

Tor giggled.

'Are you buying?' Anna asked.

Tor rolled her eyes. 'Yuh, Harry wants the Reynolds.'

'Good lord. So does half the room. That's why everyone's here. What's your limit?'

'There isn't one. I am beyond nervous . . . I can't tell you. I've never done this before.'

Anna discreetly studied the room. She'd been coming here for years and she could see Tim Slatter from the Beaton Gallery and Gerald Monmouth from Duke's. There'd be no doubt they were interested. Their impassive stares and utter indifference to the preceding lots meant they were here for something specific, not to window shop.

'Well, I can see a couple of big dealers in here. I can tell you for a fact they'll be after it too.'

'Oh God,' Tor said, swallowing hard.

'Relax. Just enjoy it. It's not your money. Imagine how many women would kill to be in your position, to spend a couple of million of Harry Hunter's money.'

'A couple of million!' Tor spluttered. 'I can't spend that!'

'Oh yes you can – and the rest,' Anna muttered. 'Whatever Harry wants, Harry gets. Believe me.'

Tor shook her head. 'I need a drink.'

'Let's go get one then. We've got plenty of time.' And

before Tor could stop her, she was up and moving along the row.

They went out and immediately found a young waiter holding a tray of chilled champagne flutes. Dozens of people were milling about, a low buzz of conversation acting as tenor accompaniment to the alto action in the saleroom.

'Cheers! Here's to breaking the bank,' Anna smiled.

Tor took a gulp so deep that bubbles went up her nose and she tossed her head about like a horse.

Anna smiled. 'I used to get nervous too. But now – well, I've been coming here for years. James used to take me all the time. When we were doing up our first house together, we pretty much bought everything from here. His family are old patrons and get invited to lots of events. I've almost forgotten what it would be like to walk into the General Trading Company and just buy a table.'

Tor remembered how James had said he'd met Coralie here, buying her the painting to get her to have dinner with him. Tor realized she hadn't even warranted dinner, much less a painting. Twice, he had just pounced on her when she was half-cut at parties.

'So why are you trying to see James here?' Tor asked. 'Surely there are easier ways of getting hold of one's ex-husband?'

'Well, no one's been able to get hold of him since he was suspended. He's not answering his mobile and his secretary's fielding all his calls. I thought . . . ' She shrugged. 'I thought old habits die hard. He might turn up.'

Tor choked on her drink.

'Suspended?'

Anna looked at her. 'Haven't you heard? Surely you must have? It's been all over the papers.'

Tor shook her head.

'He's being hauled up in front of the General Medical Council. Harry Hunter's suing him, claiming James broke patient confidentiality and has been leaking information to the press.'

'James wouldn't do that!'

Anna was bemused by Tor's indignance. 'I don't think so either. Not really. But they do despise one another. And you can't keep taking the kind of hits Harry dishes out and not retaliate. Who knows – maybe he did seek revenge.'

Tor looked away. 'At the very least, he wouldn't do that to Kate,' she said. But even as she said it, she realized he would. Look what he'd done to Kate and Monty for his sister's sake. She'd been disposable once before. Why not again?

'I'm really worried about him, Tor,' Anna said, looking around, as if expecting him to walk in. 'This has really knocked him for six. It's put his relationship with the royals in jeopardy. Even so much as the suggestion that he's slip-shod with confidentiality could mean he's out.' She sighed. 'And if that happens, I don't know what he'll do. It's not just bread and butter to him. His entire career shadows his father's. Did you know his father was the royal obstetrician too?'

Tor shook her head. 'No, I didn't.'

'James went into medicine as a way of keeping close to his father. His parents' divorce hit him hard when he was young and there was a period when he didn't see him much at all. I think he chose medicine so it would be their shared world. That's why there was never any competition when it came to choosing between me and the job, you see.'

Tor nodded, wanting to know more, just as Lot 60 was called.

'You're nearly up. We'd better get back in there.'

They darted back into the saleroom, Tor colliding inelegantly with a terrific young blonde who was stalking out. Tor's bag dropped to the floor and she hurt her elbow against the door jamb, but the blonde didn't stop, nor apologize, nor miss a stride on her long lissom legs.

'God! Manners!' Tor cried after her, feeling horribly matronly as she did so.

She picked up her bag and dusted herself down, trying to gather her composure, looking for Anna in the crowd. Spotting her five rows from the back, she sat down, just as a mythological tableau was being lifted off the easel and carried away. Laetitia's glossy posse was still there, tossing their long manes about.

'Ugh, thank God we didn't have to sit looking at that! What a hideous thing,' Anna said unequivocally, making Tor giggle.

The champagne had definitely helped fuzz her brain, though her fingers still felt fizzy with adrenalin. She opened her catalogue at the correct page and looked up towards the podium, gasping with delight as a watercolour of three children playing in a stream was carried in.

It was just a watercolour, and quite small, but the two girls and small boy had been beautifully rendered and Tor couldn't help but clutch her hands to her chest. It could be her own babies. Oh, she wanted it, she wanted it so much!

She looked down quickly. There was no point letting her head go there.

'You like that?' Anna whispered. 'Go for it. It's a steal. Look, they're struggling to even make the reserve.'

But Tor shook her head briskly. 'I'd love to, but I just can't.'

Anna nodded, just as a new bidder came in and a small bunfight between two paddles ensued, driving the price up to an unexpected £18,000.

'Wow,' Anna whistled softly. 'Just as well, really.'

Tor rubbed her elbow distractedly . . . something about that blonde . . . but said nothing, picking up on the charge in the room as the big guns were wheeled in and the tension tightened. They were at Lot 61, and the bidding was becoming fast and furious, with lots of finger-pointing, chin-tipping, eyebrow-raising and zeros involved.

Finally though, it was her turn. The Reynolds was wheeled in and positioned against the jet velvet, and there was a long respectful silence as everybody took it in, like a pope lying in state.

'I'm sure this doesn't need much introduction, Ladies and Gentlemen. Lot 63, our final lot of the sale . . .' the auctioneer intoned before launching into his overture, pointing rhythmically around the room like a maestro to his orchestra, gathering up the crescendo of bids and sweeping Tor along until she finally, breathlessly, unbelievably, found herself the last note in the symphony and writing out a cheque for £5.7 million.

Chapter Forty-six

Cress started using her elbows as weapons as she pushed past the media scrum in the hallway. She'd had a nightmare getting here. The Euston Road had been closed off as word had got out that Harry Hunter was sequestered in the General Medical Council headquarters, and tourists, fans and stalkers had joined the ranks of journalists prepared to wait outside all day for a word, look or soundbite.

'For heaven's sake, move,' she hissed to yet another fully-paid-up member of the great unwashed who was barring her way to the door. She'd had enough of reporters for one lifetime.

The journalist turned, his eyes narrowing suspiciously as he clocked Cress's poison dwarf routine. Why was she familiar?

'It's you!' he cried suddenly. 'The publisher. What're you doing here? This is a medical hearing.'

'I'm supporting Harry, of course,' she lied, through gritted teeth. 'Now shift. I'm late.'

The journalist opened his mouth to ask her another question but Cress – stressed enough already – gave him a sharp jab just below his ribs (one of the advantages of being so short) and made it past the final frontier.

She fell into the room noisily, slamming the door behind her.

Everyone turned as she stood up and smoothed her hair. As long as the hair was in place . . .

There couldn't have been more than ten people in there. The hearing was confidential, and only legal representatives and witnesses were present. Cress had wanted to blag Tor as a potential character witness for James, just for the moral support. She still couldn't believe she was actually doing this.

Kate and Harry were standing off to the right, with their backs to the room.

Cress stared at her friend, so much the same – her usual bling cuffed around her wrists and fingers – and yet so different, with Harry Hunter's baby in her belly, and his hand on her bum.

Kate, sensing the scrutiny, turned around and stared straight at her. They hadn't seen each other since that night in Oxford, the night Cress had fought back and dumped her friend in it. Not that Kate knew that – yet.

Kate whispered something to Harry, who turned around and looked at her. Barely able to muster a smile, his face appeared to be set in a mask of cold, indignant anger. He had only one person in his sights today.

Kate walked over, her bump now prominent and taut in her black Diane von Furstenberg wrap dress.

'How are you?' she asked casually, stopping in front of Cress.

Cress shrugged. 'Good. You?'

Kate nodded. 'I will be, once this is sorted.' Her hands rested on her tummy.

'Look, there's something you should probably hear from me . . .' Cress began nervously.

A door at the far end of the room opened and a team of four men and two women trooped in.

'I'd better get back. But I appreciate your support,' Kate cut in, sounding like a politician on the campaign trail.

Cress watched her walk away. This was going to be so much harder than she'd thought. Although the proceedings in this room were closed to the press and entirely confidential, it didn't change the fact that she had to sit opposite Harry himself and tell the people in this room everything that had happened. And that was a big problem. She could tell the truth – but not the whole truth. She could admit that she and Harry were using the media as warfare against each other, but she couldn't reveal why – not without getting them both sent to prison.

The members of the General Medical Council sat in a line at the top table, facing Harry and Kate, and James. A single chair and table was set forwards of theirs, midway in the floor.

The man in the centre of the table, whose place name revealed him to be Mr Bracken, leant forward. 'We are here today to examine the complaint put before us that Lord White is in breach of his professional duties of care, revealing confidential information to members of the press regarding the pregnancy of Miss Kate Miller.'

Mr Bracken sat back a little and gestured to the empty desk. 'Lord White, would you come up, please.'

Cress looked over at James, who was wearing a sober grey wool suit and navy tie. She couldn't see his face but she could see he had lost weight. It made him appear even taller, and she could tell by the stiffness of his movements, and the way he formally buttoned his jacket as he walked, that he was stressed. It helped remind her why she was doing this.

'Lord White, do you accept the charges that have been levelled at you here?'

'I do not.'

'Could you start by recounting, in your own words, your encounters with Miss Miller and Mr Hunter?'

James cleared his throat.

'Miss Miller and Mr Hunter had booked an appointment to see Mr Fallon, a colleague of mine, at our Harley Street clinic on Tuesday November the 17th of last year. Mr Fallon was called into the Portland on an emergency to deal with an ectopic pregnancy. I agreed to take his clinic for him, that afternoon.'

'And did Mr Fallon brief you that you were going to be seeing Miss Miller and Mr Hunter?'

'No, I didn't have a clinic list until I got to the consulting rooms and I hadn't spoken to him directly. His secretary had contacted mine and I agreed purely on principle to help him out.'

'So you didn't know that he had put Miss Miller and Mr Hunter down as VIPs?'

'No. Not that it would have made any difference if he had. I have a great many high-profile patients. It doesn't alter the way I treat any of my patients.'

'So when was the first you knew that you were treating Mr Fallon's VIPs?'

'When I walked into the consulting room.'

'But I understand that you personally know both Miss Miller and Mr Hunter.'

'Yes.'

'So surely, then, you would have recognized their names?'

'No. I knew Miss Miller by her married name, Marfleet, so I didn't make a connection when I saw her name on the notes, and obviously, Mr Hunter's name was not on the cover of the notes. Up until I walked into the consulting room, I had no idea whatsoever that they were even in a relationship.'

'I see. Please continue, Lord White, with what happened next.'

'Well, Mr Hunter and Miss Miller were displeased to see that I was their acting consultant and asked to see someone else.'

'Why were they displeased to see you?'

'Miss Miller and I had had a disagreement – over a personal matter – a few months before.'

'And so did you refer them to another consultant?'

'No. I was the only consultant on duty.'

Mr Bracken smoothed his hair and adjusted his glasses.

'What was the purpose of their visit?'

'It was a booking-in appointment.'

'Why couldn't a registrar have taken the records and performed the scan?'

'Miss Miller had a complicated medical history and I felt she needed to be seen by a consultant.'

'Well, how did you know her medical history?'

'Because she had been coming to me for IVF treatment, prior to this pregnancy.'

'With Mr Hunter?'

'No. With her husband.'

'Oh. I see.' There was a terse silence. Cress saw Kate's head drop a little, and cringed for her. 'Go on.'

'I checked Miss Miller's blood pressure and took bloods and urine samples, checked and measured the fundus, and performed the scan.'

'Did you leave the consulting room at any time during the appointment?'

'No.'

'Not once?'

'Not once.'

'Did you speak to the receptionist or any other member of staff, during the appointment?'

'No. There was no need to.'

'I see. Then can you explain why Miss Miller and Mr Hunter believe that you tipped off a member of the press that they were at your clinic?'

'I can't.'

Mr Bracken looked down at his notes and took a sip of water. It was inconceivable that the royal obstetrician should be sitting before him here, up on these charges.

'Did you see Miss Miller and Mr Hunter on their subsequent follow-ups?'

'I did not. To my knowledge, Mr Fallon saw them for all their other appointments.'

'So you did not perform the mid-term scan which identified the sex of the foetus?'

'I did not, no.'

'Is there any way you could have got hold of the results of the scan?'

'Yes. All the films are held at the clinic. We don't permit doctors to take films or notes off the premises, even for VIPs.'

'And you didn't happen upon them, or look for them yourself?'

'No.'

'Thank you, Lord White. You may step back.'

James got up from the single desk and moved back towards his seat, his eyes catching Cress's as he did. He gave a small imperceptible nod.

The panel shuffled their papers, and Cress began swearing in a chant under her breath. She dropped her head in her hands, trying to massage away the headache she'd had almost permanently since volunteering to testify. Ever since Tor had rung her two weeks ago and told her Anna's news about James, she had known she'd have to step forward – even she, as unscrupulous as she was, couldn't let James take the fall. But that she'd have to sit there and tell it all directly in front of Harry and Kate was enough to bring her out in hives.

'The Council calls Mrs Cressida Pelling to step up, please.'

Kate turned sharply in her seat, realizing too late why Cress was here.

Cress kept her eyes dead ahead and walked to the desk in the middle of the floor.

'Mrs Pelling. Could you tell the council why you are here today?'

Cress gulped, keeping herself turned away slightly from Kate and Harry's table. 'Yes. Because I am the person who commissioned the photographs of Mr Hunter and Mrs Mar— I mean, Miss Miller going into the clinic.'

She heard a gasp from behind her.

'And why did you do that?'

'To prove to my husband that I was not having an affair with Mr Hunter.'

Mr Bracken – who clearly didn't read the tabloids – looked at her as if she was mad. 'Why did he think that you were?'

'Well, there was an article in *Tatler* magazine in November which wrongly claimed that I was one of three other women supposedly having an affair with Mr Hunter. The newspapers picked it up and sparked a debate on the whole issue. I'm afraid my husband believed it, so I had to resort to finding evidence that would show him he was really having the affair with someone else.'

'Mrs Pelling, what is your relationship with Mr Hunter?'

'We work together. I'm his publisher.'

'Well then, why would Mr Hunter go to such levels to try to destroy your marriage?'

'Mr Hunter is no ordinary man, Mr Bracken. He is a global icon, used to being trailed by packs of paparazzi and living life on his terms. Contrary to the emphasis that he's placing on privacy just now, Mr Hunter has a lot of fun manipulating the media for his amusement. The *Tatler* exposé was just one such example of that.'

'And you felt the logical way for you to convince your husband of your fidelity was by splashing pictures of Miss Miller and Mr Hunter across the national press?'

'My husband had stopped believing me. And when it came to choosing between protecting my marriage, or protecting the privacy of my publicity-hungry client, I was more than happy to play Mr Hunter – and Miss Miller – at their own game. The press weren't going to leave me alone until they too had definitive proof that I wasn't Harry's lover.'

'When you commissioned the photographer, did you know that Mr Hunter and Miss Miller were having a baby?'

Cress coughed.

'No. I didn't even know they were having an affair. I just wanted the evidence that he was having the affair with someone else. I didn't realize it was Kate.'

She looked quickly at Kate, whose eyes were shining with tears.

'The baby news was as much a surprise to me as it was to the rest of the nation.'

'And how exactly did the photographs get into the public sector?'

'I sold them to the *Evening Standard*, on the condition that they were put into the late edition on the 18th of November.'

'Why then?'

'Because Mr Hunter was leading a debate at the Oxford Union and as his publisher I had to attend. The press were going to go crazy seeing us both at the same event together since the *Tatler* story had broken. It was my opportunity to set the record straight once and for all.'

'I see. And do you know how the details of the sex of Miss Miller and Mr Hunter's baby came to be released?'

Cress shook her head. 'No. I've got no idea about that.'

'No one approached you? You didn't commission someone else to do some investigating?' There was a note of sarcasm in his voice.

'No. I had got what I needed with the photographs. My husband finally believed I wasn't sleeping with Harry.' For all the precious good it's done me, she thought to herself. It wasn't guilt that was breaking up their marriage. It was anger. They were still sleeping in separate bedrooms.

'Do you know Lord White?'

Cress looked at him and smiled. 'Yes. He was my obstetrician.'

'How many children do you have, Mrs Pelling?'

'Four.'

'All under Lord White?'

Cress couldn't help crack a smile. Oh, for a little light relief. 'After a manner of speaking, yes.'

Mr Bracken frowned slightly as he realized his slip. 'What age is your youngest child?'

'My youngest is three now.'

'But you're still in contact with Lord White?'

'Yes. We bump into each other quite regularly at various social events.'

Mr Bracken stared at her, baffled by her complex personal life but impressed nonetheless by her courage.

'Coming here today must put you in an awkward position with Mr Hunter.'

That's the understatement of the bloody century, Cress thought to herself.

'Yes, it does. But I had to defend James. The claims by Harry and Kate are utter hogwash. James had nothing to do with the photographs – they were mine and I've got the photographer's invoice and *Evening Standard* payment to prove it.'

There was a pause. 'Well, thank you, Mrs Pelling.' He looked at his fellow board members. 'Unless any of the members of the council have any questions for you . . . ?' He looked up and down the table at the stern faces. They all shook their heads.

'No, no. Then you may step down. Thank you for your time, Mrs Pelling.'

Cress got down and walked back to the gallery, keeping her eyes well away from Harry and Kate, throwing a wink instead at James, who nodded in appreciation as she passed.

She walked to the back of the room and opened the door. The press had been chucked outside by the security guards, and the hallway was now hospital-quiet. She looked quickly back at Kate and Harry. Their backs were ramrod straight. She could only imagine the looks on their faces.

She didn't want to hang around to find out. Quickly fishing her shades out of her bag, Cress left the building by a back door and strode out into the winter sunshine, marvelling at how good it felt to have done the right thing for once.

Chapter Forty-seven

'How did it go?' Tor called down as she heard Cress get in. Mark was in New York until tomorrow, and she was sitting in a bubble bath in their en-suite, nursing a gigantic glass of red and not caring that she was getting black teeth. She'd been on tenterhooks waiting to hear from Cress.

Cress came in and leant against the door frame. 'You're in love with him,' she said, slowly.

The water in the bath felt instantly chilly.

'What?' Tor managed.

'When are you going to just admit it? When are you actually going to instigate a proper heart-to-heart conversation with me about it?'

'I don't know what on earth you're . . .'

'Let me see,' Cress interrupted, kicking off her heels and perching on the edge of the loo. She poured herself an equally generous measure. Today's virtue had earnt it. 'I saw the way he looked when he found out Hugh had died and how he looked at you at the cricket, and I saw the way you looked when you saw him at my party and at the tennis and at the cricket. And you are lying in my bathtub looking like Long John Silver, completely wasted with nerves about the future of his illustrious career when you could have rung me and asked how it went, *tomorrow*, like any other concerned but detached friend.'

Tor gawped like a guppy fish.

'It's clear as day that you're potty about each other. I just can't quite believe it took me so bloody long to realize it.'

'You're an absolute fantasist, is what you are,' Tor huffed finally.

'Don't be coy with me, Victoria.'

Tor fell silent again and pouted.

'Have you kissed him?'

Tor stayed silent and pouty.

'Had a fumble?'

Tor pouted harder.

'Oh my God, you've bonked him!'

Tor disappeared under the bubbles, only her glass of red still visible.

'I can't believe it,' Cress shouted, so that Tor could hear her underwater, although frankly, Tor could have heard her in space, she was so loud. 'You've slept with my official crush! Uuuuugh! It's so not fair!'

Her voice dropped, and after a couple of moments of silence (and because she couldn't hold her breath any longer) Tor tentatively surfaced.

'So was it fabulous?' Cress giggled.

Tor looked away. 'Yes,' she said sullenly, like a teenager.

'So what happened? Why aren't you together? And why am I having to drag it out of you?'

'Oh, I wanted to tell you, Cress. I really did, but everything's just been so complicated. I've felt so . . . guilty.'

'You mean because of Hugh?'

'More than you know,' Tor said quietly, not able to meet her eyes.

'Tor?' Cress asked slowly.

Tor swallowed hard. 'The night of your party . . . we kissed . . .'

'What – you and James . . . ?'

Tor nodded. 'Hugh saw us and stormed out. I got home and he was packing up.' She stopped briefly. 'He said he was going to move in with his mistress.'

Cress dropped her glass on to the bath mat.

'What?' she screeched.

'Yes, I know. It was a shock to me too.'

'Do you know who she was?'

'Her name's Julia McIntyre.'

'Shit – I know her! The rich divorcee, great boobs.'

'Yeah, that's the one,' Tor said lightly, wishing that wasn't everyone's first and abiding memory of her. 'I've since found out he wasn't actually going to her. He was going to the Lathams. He just said that to hurt me.'

'But he was definitely having an affair?'

Tor nodded.

Cress tried to keep up. 'I can't believe you've kept this all to yourself,' she said finally.

'I'm sorry. I wasn't trying to keep you out. I just felt completely ashamed. It made me feel like it wasn't my *right* to grieve. He was someone else's when he died. And I can't get past the fact that he died because of my actions. Mine and James's.' She paused. 'Well, James's mainly. He was the one who kissed me.'

Cress fell into silence. 'But you kissed him back, right?'

'Whose side are you on?'

'Yours, of course. I'm just trying to establish the . . . God, I cannot believe Hugh was having an affair. I can't believe he was capable of it. He always seemed so devoted . . . It

435

just goes to show, doesn't it? All men are capable of cheating. *All* of them.'

Cress bit her lip. She knew she was driving Mark steadily towards Greta but she didn't have a clue how to stop it. Years of anger and resentment and frustration at playing second fiddle in her life had finally bubbled over in Mark, and as much as she had been trying to convince him now of her new priorities, she was increasingly scared he had drifted too far out of reach. The Harry scandal had breached the trust between them, and her response to it – commissioning the photographs – had eroded his respect for her. Now more than ever he could never find out about the truth of her hold over Harry. She had realized, too late, how far she had fallen from being the woman he'd married.

Tor drank some more wine, an eyebrow cocked. 'Anything you want to talk about?' she inquired.

Cress froze. Tonight was about Tor's secrets. 'No.' She paused, trying to regain her train of thought. 'So all you guys did was kiss?'

Tor nodded.

'But Hugh was actually having a full-blown affair?'

Tor nodded again, trying not to remember Hugh's pornographic account of it all.

'Well, then it seems to me you're entitled to get your happiness where you can find it.'

Tor looked at her, puzzled.

'No, babe, sorry,' Cress said crossly. 'You know I adored Hugh, but if he was the one playing away, he was the one who jeopardized your marriage, not you. And what happened is totally fucking tragic, but you can't shoulder the blame for it. You've more than paid your dues. It was a kiss, end of.'

'Yes, but Cress, if James and I hadn't kissed, Hugh wouldn't have packed up and gone out again.'

'And why did he have to do that, huh? He could have gone into the spare room – like most people do after a fight. He didn't need to be so bloody dramatic and flounce off, saying he was going off to his mistress's, and get behind the wheel of a car when he was completely pissed after a party. Did he? He didn't need to do that!'

Tor considered her friend's words. She'd never thought about it like that before. Cress had a wise head on those tiny polished shoulders.

'You're just saying what I want to hear,' Tor said, uncertainly.

'No. I'm saying what you need to hear. You didn't chuck him out, did you?'

Tor shook her head vehemently. 'No! I was desperate for him to stay.'

'Precisely,' Cress said, draining her glass. 'So tell me what happened with James after the kiss?'

'Well, then the next time I saw him was at the tennis when . . .'

'When you knocked ten bells out of him. Fair do's. Then what?'

'Then the rest happened in Cornwall – after you left.'

'Bugger! I knew I should have stayed.'

'Why did you go? You never explained.'

Cress waved a hand dismissively. 'Harry driving me demented. Same old. Go on.'

'Well, Kate found us in bed together. Unfortunately, just after she'd found out about Billy. She was livid with James but she really took it out on me too.'

'Sleeping with the enemy?'

Tor shrugged. 'Something like that.'

'Well, that certainly explains a few things. I couldn't work out why she was so hostile to all of us.'

Tor sighed. 'I think she thinks we've sided against her.'

'So this afternoon won't have helped.'

Tor shook her head. 'No. Worst fears confirmed, I'd think.' She stared into her wine glass like it was a crystal ball. 'I simply can't believe that we're so isolated from her.'

'I can,' Cress said quietly. 'I reckon it's exactly what Harry wants. To divide and conquer.'

Tor frowned. 'Why would he want to do that?'

'To get at me.'

Tor stared at Cress. 'Cress, what exactly is going on with you two? It's like you're out to destroy each other. I don't get it.'

'Just as well, babe. It's complicated – and confidential. I can't go into it.'

Tor stared at her. She could tell from Cress's face this was no mere jape.

'You look pale.'

Cress automatically massaged her brow. 'Mmm, headache.'

'Why aren't I surprised?'

'It's just stress.' Tor shook her head as Cress poured them each another glass. 'This'll help, though.'

'So has he been exonerated?'

'Not entirely. My evidence proves beyond doubt that he didn't sell the photos, but while Harry has no proof that James leaked the scan information, James equally doesn't have any proof that he didn't. It's such a high-profile case, they can't risk getting it wrong. They've adjourned for two weeks while the committee makes its decision.'

Tor nodded, still anxious.

'Why don't you ring him, offer him your support?'

'Because I don't think his pregnant girlfriend would be too impressed.'

'Pregnant girlfriend?'

'Amelia Abingdon?'

'No way!'

'Yes, way! I told you that at the cricket.'

'Did you?'

Tor nodded.

'Really?'

'Yes.'

'Oh.' Silence. 'That's a fly in the ointment then.'

'Yes. It is rather, but there you go.' Tor smiled sadly and they sat in silence for a few moments more.

'Amelia Abingdon – *really*?'

'Yes, really.'

'Well, it'll never last. I bet he's only with her because of the baby.'

'You don't know that.'

'And she's only with him for the title.'

'You don't know that either.'

'Well, there's one thing I do know.'

'And what's that?'

'That in spite of Hugh, and Kate and Monty, and Amelia and the baby, you both want to be with each other.'

'Listen, I lost my husband and a best friend *because* of him. I'm not going to betray either of them or compromise my moral integrity just to have great sex and financial security for the rest of my life.'

Cress stared at her. 'No. That would be crazy,' she said sardonically. 'What does he take you for?'

Tor fell silent.

Cress took a deep breath. 'Well, it just seems curious to me that in the face of such enormous tragedy, your story with James hasn't yet played itself out. Usually an event of that magnitude is an absolute end point for a relationship.'

Tor sighed, defeatedly. 'Oh, I don't know why it keeps dragging on. It shouldn't be so hard – in a population of 60 million – to keep away from one man. Should it?'

'No. It shouldn't,' Cress agreed. 'You shouldn't have to feel like you're swimming against the tide just to keep someone *out* of your life.'

Tor nodded, pleased that Cress had seen she was right. 'Precisely. Thank you.'

'Which suggests to me that perhaps he's supposed to be in it,' Cress went on, nailing her point with a satisfied smile.

Tor narrowed her eyes crossly. 'Oh Cress, let's be realistic. This is not Mills and Boon, it's Battersea, and a happy ending here is getting your child into the nursery of your choice, not . . . not love conquering all!'

Chapter Forty-eight

You've come a long way, baby, Kate thought to herself as she watched Keira Knightley being powdered and Dame Judi Dench being primped. Mobiles were going off like fireworks on November the Fifth, and there was so much egoism in the air, you could practically chew on it.

The year's Hollywood elite had gathered here for the Academy Awards nominees' photograph, just before the annual nominees' lunch, and Kate was intrigued by the tense atmosphere and frosty body language. Even the entourages were jockeying for position, with one of the Best Actor PAs complaining about the lighting and a Best Director's right-hand man demanding body-temperature triple-purified oxygenated water for his boss.

Kate blew out her cheeks and stepped back from the set. Even with the air-conditioning on full blast, the heat from the lights was intense. She shrugged off her wispy pistachio cashmere shrug and smoothed her pink silk dress over her bump, feeling conspicuously like a hippo.

Harry hadn't been near her for weeks. The combination of his new book deadline for Cress (which he had missed two weeks ago), the forthcoming Oscars, the stress of the *News of the World* case and his action against James was really getting to him. And by his own admission, when he'd turned her down the other night in bed, he wasn't one of those men who found pregnancy sexy. He hated the way her nipples had darkened, and had started finding fault with her, saying she had begun to 'waddle', and that her ankles had thickened.

She looked down at her tummy, which was satisfyingly prominent now, entering rooms a couple of seconds before her and demanding to be acknowledged in conversations. She was carrying well, she thought. High and in front. She still had her waist (from behind), and none of it had gone on to her bum yet. Still, that appeared to count for nothing. It seemed to be the tummy Harry had a problem with, and she was growing more anxious by the day at his increasingly distant attitude towards the baby.

Her mobile buzzed and she picked it up. It was Monty. She'd taken a couple of photos of her bump in the mirror and sent them on to him – at his insistence. Ever since the newspaper coups at Christmas, he'd started calling regularly, just to 'check up' on her. She hadn't told Harry of course. There was no need to. But it was comforting to have him back in her life, even if it was just a 'How's it going?' every week. He'd wrong-footed her with his forgiveness for her behaviour following the fall-out of their marriage.

'It's a boy!' said his text. Kate smiled at the irony. Thanks to the *Sun*, everyone in the western world now knew she and Harry were having a girl.

Hearing a 'hurrah!' and a small round of applause, Kate looked up and saw Harry clapping, his eyes dancing, as Amelia Abingdon, looking utterly radiant in a lemon chiffon babydoll, picked her way daintily to the centre front gilt chair, which was awaiting her pert little bottom.

'Sorry I'm late, everyone,' she said sweetly in her plum

voice, one hand resting on her bump by way of explanation.

'You're worth the wait, Amelia,' Harry said from his spot immediately behind her. Although he was 'only' up for Best Adapted Screenplay, and would usually be positioned some-where in the shadows at the back, he was every bit as much a leading man as the Best Actors and had been given a suit-ably prime spot. From the look on his face as Amelia settled herself, allowing him to peer down at her ample décolletage, her pregnancy didn't seem quite as unattractive as Kate's.

'Right, everybody,' the photographer called. 'We're good to go. Mike, just test the light-stop behind E6 for me, please.'

Kate waved at Harry, but he was too engrossed in conver-sation with Keira to notice. Kate sighed and, grabbing a bottle of water from the catering table, walked out of the studio.

'I'm just getting some air,' she said to a black-suited security guy. The Academy took the security of their Finest incredibly seriously, and there were people with buzz-cuts and walkie-talkies all over the place.

She pushed open the doors and went and sat on the steps, overlooking Hollywood Boulevard. Her bump was too big to sit forward now, and she leant back against the wall, feeling as if she was in a Coke advert as the sun beat down and kids on skateboards raced past.

Even in February it felt like summer and Kate placed a protective arm over her bump. Across the street, she could see a woman coming out of her condo with three little girls. She watched the woman bend down and speak to the biggest child for a moment, then go back into the building. The eldest two sat on the stone steps, waiting, playing on their Nintendos, calling out something to the younger girl, who was untangling a skipping rope and singing to herself. Kate watched the three sisters, and thought about all the things she'd teach her own little girl – French knitting, clapping games, playground rhymes and cat's cradle. Would this baby be an only child? Harry didn't seem overly enthusiastic about having more.

She could feel something pushing forward into her consciousness. What was it? She squinted through the sunlight, and shaded her eyes, just as the sun goddess herself came and sat down next to her, a vision in primrose.

'It's Kate, isn't it?'

Kate looked into Amelia's smiling eyes. 'Yes.'

'Mind if I join you? I was suffocating in there. They're still fannying about with the lights. I just need a couple of minutes of fresh –' she took in the slow crawl of traffic – 'well, freshish air.'

She took a swig of water. 'It's been bothering me where we've met before. Was it at Rick Stein's last summer?'

'Yes. I'm impressed.' The memory that had seemed momentarily to be of importance sank back unasserted into the ether.

'Well, I remember a rather memorable conversation we had.'

'Oh?'

'About a certain man-whore.'

Kate laughed. 'Quite! You said we'd all have tales to tell about him.'

Amelia smiled. 'And now you do. Have you been together long?'

Kate rubbed her tummy and smiled. 'Since the summer.'

'Ah, so it was that imminent. It did sound like something was brewing,' Amelia smiled. 'Well, congratulations.'

'And you,' Kate said, nodding towards Amelia's bump. 'You're disgustingly neat.'

Amelia shrugged and rolled her eyes. 'James has got me on a macrobiotic diet.'

Kate tensed, her antenna up. She'd clean forgotten about their relationship. Obviously, she was too late in her pregnancy to fly now – that was why she hadn't been with him at the GMC hearings – and Kate hadn't seen them together since the launch in Norfolk, so she didn't automatically think of them as a couple. She kept thinking about him in connection with Tor . . .

She must want something.

As if reading her mind, Amelia cleared her throat. 'Actually, it's funny to have run into you today. There was something I was hoping to speak to you about.'

'Oh yes?' Kate said levelly, ready to put her work hat on and drop the temperature several degrees.

'It's about James. He's terribly unhappy, you see.' She heard Kate snort, but went on. 'That GMC hearing really shook him. He always saw it as the one thing in his life that was untouchable. I wondered whether you and I could intervene and try to get the boys to sort things out once and for all.'

'I sincerely doubt that, Amelia. Things have gone too far.'

Amelia paused for a moment. 'But why does Harry hate James so much?'

'Why does Harry hate James?' Kate snorted. 'You mean why does James hate Harry so much, surely? His breach of confidentiality is just the latest in a series of persecutions.'

'Persecutions? What has Harry been telling you?'

'Enough. Everything. Don't forget I'm his lawyer too. He's told me about events that go way back to their school days. I know what I'm talking about, Amelia.'

'You have known James for a long time, Kate, and we

both know how important his career is to him. Even putting aside the man's sense of honour, you can't ignore his ambition. Do you really think he'd engage in a tit-for-tat that could ruin everything he's worked for? His relationship with the palace – his family's connection with the royals? Even though he's been cleared, things may already be beyond repair.'

'He broke his Hippocratic oath to try to hurt Harry, Amelia. Harry said he would. Months ago, he told me James wouldn't stop until he had broken him. And he was right.'

'Wouldn't stop what?'

Kate looked at her. 'James is blackmailing Harry,' she said curtly.

Amelia laughed out loud. 'I don't think you believe for one minute that James is actually capable of that.'

Kate spun round. 'On the contrary, I think he's perfectly capable of it. He has proved to me time and again that he is a skilled liar, only out to protect his own interests.'

Amelia stopped laughing and swallowed. She knew exactly what Kate was referring to. James had told her everything.

'Well, with what would James blackmail him? They're scarcely in each other's lives. How could they hold any incriminating information about each other?'

'It's something from the past. Something that happened at school.'

Amelia stared at her, her voice rising. 'At Eton?'

'Yes. There was a boy there – Hillier – who died. He fell off the roof one night. Harry was up there with him but no one except James ever knew that he had been there when he fell. Then when Harry's contract came up for renewal, Hillier's name was suddenly mentioned and the threat was made to go public about his involvement, unless he signed with a much smaller firm – a firm far too small for someone of his calibre. It was humiliating for him. James was the only person who could have supplied Hillier's name. He's behind it all. He's the one trying to ruin Harry. Not the other way round.'

A couple of tourists up the street spotted Amelia and were pointing, beginning to take pictures of her on their phones. Amelia stood up slowly, choosing her words carefully.

'Harry's lying to you, Kate.'

Kate shook her head. 'I don't think so.'

Amelia looked down nervously to the ground, aware that the gathering crowd had broken into a trot.

'He is. And I can tell you why I know he is: because one vital piece of information in that story is wrong.'

Kate frowned. What could Amelia possibly know about all of this?

'Which is?'

'The boy who fell was not called Hillier. His name was Julian Abingdon.'

Kate looked up at the mention of his name.

'Abingd— '

Amelia's voice was tight but she was looking straight at Kate. 'He was my cousin. Check the records. It's all there.'

Kate swallowed, horrified and confused.

Amelia's hand had started inching towards the door as the crowds ran towards her.

'If I was you, Kate, I'd ask myself why Harry deliberately gave you the wrong name. He knows full well it was my cousin that fell. And he also knows James would never use my cousin's death as leverage against him. If what you're saying is true and he is being blackmailed by someone – and I can well believe he's a man with enemies – that story is

447

not the reason why. But – I don't know – maybe that boy is.'

Kate couldn't find the words to respond, but she heard the door swoosh shut, just as the fans descended upon the steps, calling for Amelia and holding out Hollywood maps and tour books for autographs. The security guard immediately stood in front of the doors, and Kate wondered how she too would be able to get back in again. Would she have to call Harry to come and get her?

She flinched at the thought, and shook her head in bitterness at how much she had come to rely upon him. Six months previously, she wouldn't have recognized herself. She'd lost her independence in every way. Her career now existed in name only, and was dependent upon Harry's patronage; she had lost her friends, her family and left her home and country. Their entire life was lived on his terms, with his money, and seemingly, through his lies.

To hell with the nominees' lunch, she thought suddenly, anger beginning to pulse through her. She had to get her head straight, had to get the facts straight. She got up from the baking pavement and skipped down the steps to the waiting stretch.

'Take me to the library, Christophe,' she said into the speaker, as she slid along the gleaming back seat.

Ignoring the grand cuvée on ice, she poured herself a glass of mineral water and stared out of the window. She dealt with cover-ups and alibis and full-blown fabrications on a daily basis, and her gut told her Amelia wasn't lying. Which meant Harry was.

But why? And how much? Was he lying outright, or merely playing games with the truth? She hadn't forgotten Cress's text the night of the Oxford debate. She had clearly seen

Hillier's name. Amelia was right – somehow this Hillier chap had to be involved in this. And somehow, so did Cress.

Eight hours later, as Cress picked up her mail from the hall console, ready to leave for the airport, she was excited to see a hand-written stiffy in the pile of typed bills and automated junk mail. She took the letter opener from the study and opened it carefully, enjoying the crisp slice through the tissue-lined envelope. Such a rare treat, she mused, pulling out the red-edged card.

The message, in an elegant black italic hand, was stark, plain, succinct.

And terrifying.

> **Bring the manuscript to Los Angeles.**
> **His time is up.**

Chapter Forty-nine

'Just press one of these buttons and I'm at your service, madam,' said the butler, after he'd shown Cress around the suite. 'Should I unpack for you?'

'No, no, that's quite all right, Robert,' Cress said quickly. She didn't want anyone else – not even Mark – rifling through their belongings. And Greta could do the children's. She certainly wasn't being paid just to look pretty. 'Just tell me, which one's the front door again?'

They were standing in a large travertine hallway, with five burr walnut doors fanning out, pentagonally, around them. It was like being Alice in Wonderland. She felt completely disoriented.

Robert smiled and stepped forward. 'This one, ma'am.'

'Right, got it,' Cress said, although she didn't.

'Shall I bring through some tea?'

'Smashing. I'm gasping.'

As Robert left through the correct door, Cress tried two more before finding the one that led to the master suite. It was vast. She and Mark each had a separate bathroom, and the bed was so big, she was sure they could go days in here without ever bumping into each other – much to his delight, no doubt, she thought dryly.

The whole suite had been done up in Ralph Lauren blues

and whites, with huge shells and corals on minimal black consoles, and pristine white sofas in every corner, making Cress wince at the very thought of the muck and grime that accompanied the children like shadows.

Walking across the carpet, which was so soft she could have sworn it was a cashmere blend – hmmph, Tor had been wrong about that after all – she grabbed the white linen hanging bag that had Valentino emblazoned across the front in strict black letters.

She unzipped it and took the dress out, shaking out the creases so that leaves of tissue escaped silently from the crimson folds and floated to the floor. Suspended on just its padded silk hanger, it still hung ghost-like, in a womanly silhouette, the embonpoint expertly crafted to lift and shape, the waist to whittle, the hips to smooth. It was classic and dramatic and Mark would love it. God knows, Valentino would have to do for her marriage what Relate did for others.

She adjusted her watch to local time and turned her laptop on, jumping into the steam shower while it booted up. She could literally feel the aeroplane's grime dislodge from her pores, trying to cleanse, to purify, to atone. Grubbiness was a feeling that dogged her now – as though all the mud-slinging with Harry had begun to stick on her and stain her. She felt toxic, the almost constant headaches symptomatic of the drug that was really poisoning her: her own ambition.

This was the price she had to pay for her greed, her lust for power. With this new note . . . his time is up . . . his time is up . . . It provoked the unspoken question. Was hers, too?

She emerged fifteen minutes later, her skin glowing and her hair slicked back as neat as a pin – she looked polished but she still felt grimy.

Robert had set out the tea as if she was the Queen. Stiff pyramid-shaped tea-bags from Fortnum's were set out on their own tiny individual ceramic trays, with protractor-cut cucumber sandwiches and fondant-coloured madeleines arranged on a cake-stand.

She muttered to herself, grabbing one, as she scanned her emails. 'And to think I would have been happy with PG Tips and a packet of hobnobs.'

She clicked on a new message from Rosie.

Located a Bridget Hillier on electoral register in Bern. Still looking for Amelie. Will put searches on birth, marriage and death records there.

Cress sipped her tea and looked at the information thoughtfully. So she lived in Switzerland? Well, that explained why she was never at the Felden Street flat. But then why use a British PO box number? Was the daughter using it? She had to find Amelie.

She crossed the room, deciding she'd better unpack before Robert, in all his efficiency, disobeyed orders and did it for her. The children were down at the pool with Greta, and wouldn't be back for at least another hour, and Mark was catching the late flight over from New York this evening so there wasn't any danger of him walking in.

She picked up her butterscotch leather Coach file and pulled out the reams of paperwork. Contracts, drafts, proposals. She held the wedge, scanning for the glossy cover, but even before her brain processed what her eyes could see, she knew it wasn't there. Frowning, she put her hand back in.

Where was it? Jesus! She searched again, more frantically,

but as she felt the soft hide brush her hands on both sides, there was no disguising the fact that the bag was empty.

Dropping it, she stood up and walked around the room blindly, her hands raked in her hair, her breath rapid. She couldn't have left it! She'd gone there specifically to get it. How could it not be in her bag . . . ?

And then she remembered. She'd dropped her phone, getting it out of her handbag. It had rolled under one of Tor's dining room chairs. She'd put the envelope down on a box as she got on her hands and knees to reach it. And then – then what happened? She closed her eyes and tried to concentrate. Tried to be calm.

Rosie. It had been Rosie on the phone. They'd talked about the artwork for Harry's new cover, and she'd locked up while Rosie had gone through the strapline options. Shit! Shit, shit, shit, shit, shit! The manuscript – it must still be on the box.

It was safe enough where it was. The only other person with keys was Tor, but she needed it here. Now! Whatever was going to happen out here clearly couldn't happen without it and she couldn't afford to keep it in her possession. If she didn't give it up – extricate herself now, while she still could – she would be implicated too.

Think, Cress! Think!

She paced the floor, her mind racing, her eyes wide. Then she ran to her handbag and grabbed the offending phone. Frantically she punched in the numbers for Monty's apartment, where Tor and the kids had stayed last night, before going on to the airport.

Monty – who was driving the Summershills to the airport – picked up.

'Monty, I need to speak to Tor!' she yelled.

'Cress, is everything alr—'

'Yes, yes. I just need to speak to her now!'

'Tor, it's for you,' Monty said, handing over the phone. 'She's in one of her frenzies,' he said quietly.

Tor rolled her eyes.

'Hi, Cress,' she said distractedly, as she flipped through the passports. 'What's wrong? Monty says you're frantic.'

'I am. I am.' Cress paused as she tried to think about how to phrase it. 'I need your help.'

'You're not sure about the wall colour?'

'Huh? No, no, it's not that. I haven't been over to the apartment yet. Tor, I really need you to go to Big Yellow Storage.'

'What, now?'

'Yes.'

'But we're just about to leave.'

'I know, but this is really important.'

She heard Tor sigh with frustration. 'Cress! What can be so important in the lock-up that you need me to risk missing our flight?'

'There's some paperwork I need. I *really* need it. It's on a box on the left as you go in. You can't miss it. It's a Littlington Hall brochure.'

'A Littling— Cress, you can't be serious! What do you need that for in LA?'

'I just do, Tor! I can't explain. I'm in a horrid rush. I'm late for a meeting,' she lied. 'Please. If you go now, you'll make it.'

'But it's in the opposite direction to the airport.'

'Thanks, babe, you're such a star! I massively appreciate it. I'll tell you everything when I see you. OK, bye!'

'Wait, I — ' But she had gone.

Tor looked at the phone and shouted at it crossly. 'Oh, for God's sake! Kids, in the car now please. We've got to go. Now!'

Tor sat back in her seat and gave a huge sigh of exhaustion. Since Cress's phone call, it had been pedal-to-the-metal trying to get everything done in time. Traffic around the storage centre had been shocking, and the fact that Monty drove her car like a sofa didn't help. Meanwhile Marney had cried the whole way because she'd left behind her favourite comfort blanket in the rush, and Oscar had tripped and got a nosebleed because his shoes were on the wrong feet.

Tor looked up and down the row of seats at the children, who were now settled with comics, colouring pencils, sweets and round-the-clock films. She took a sip of her gin and tonic and closed her eyes. She could relax at last.

Tor wondered how Harry's apartment looked. She had to admit she was excited to actually be getting to see it. She couldn't wait to see the Reynolds in it. The red tape for exporting the painting had been shocking, and she had initially only been coming out to take possession of it at Harry's address. But once Cress had got wind that she had to go to LA, the whole trip had snowballed and now here she was, with the whole family in tow, attending the Oscars too, as part of Harry and Cress's party, before they all went to Disneyland together.

Even Hen was coming. The Museum of Contemporary Art in Los Angeles was putting on a major exhibition of Christian Dior, and, as one of his favoured models, they had asked her along as a guest of honour. She'd packed up twelve museum-quality pieces of vintage couture and they were flying with her at the front of the plane.

Tor took another sip of her drink and looked out of the window. Cress had some serious explaining to do. It was just as well the flipping brochure had been exactly where she'd said it would be, else they wouldn't have made it. They'd only just got there with a few minutes to spare before the check-in desk closed. She'd even had the nerve to text her – she didn't dare ring again – and instruct her to put the brochure in her bag, not in the hold. I mean, really? What could possibly be so important?

Tor fished around in her bag and took out the prospectus. She had to make a decision about whether to take up Marney's place in Year One by Easter, six weeks away. The school had agreed to hold a place over for her, for compassionate reasons, for this year, but they were heavily oversubscribed and if she wasn't going to take them up they needed to offer it to someone else.

She looked at the cover, as glossy as *Vogue*, with photogenic children playing in the strategically planted daffodils and swinging from monkey bars, their straw boaters seemingly surgically attached.

Tor took another sip of her drink. Now that the money had come through from Planed Spaces, she could afford – in principle – to send Marney there, to pick up life in London again. She had just renewed the tenants' contract for another six months, but it was up at the beginning of September and she knew she had to make a decision about where their lives were going to be based.

She thumbed idly through the pages, blankly acknowledging the techno white boards and IT suites, flashy recording studio and pool. She liked the uniform too, which she knew shouldn't count, but actually did.

She flipped through to the back cover, and was checking the termly fees and additional extras (of which there were many) when Millie scrambled up to sit on her knees and knocked Tor's arm, sending the gin everywhere.

'Millie! Be careful! Look what you've done,' she tutted. Luckily, the pages were so highly glossed that the drink collected in mercurial clumps and skittered off them without soaking through. But the old brown envelope tucked into the back cover was so old and crinkly, it absorbed it like blotting paper.

Tor quickly put the remains of her drink down on Millie's table, and pulled out the paperwork, wiping it with the sleeve of her jumper.

She wiped away the excess liquid from the worst affected sheets at the top of the pile and began blowing on them. It looked like they'd be OK. Did it matter? What was it anyway? She eyed the papers. A manuscript?

A piece of thick parchment was paper-clipped to the top, and typed with the words:

'Bright with names that men remember; loud with names that men forget.'
Don't let him be forgotten. Do the right thing.

Tor frowned. What did that mean? She thought . . . she thought she'd heard that somewhere before.

She turned the note over but the other side was blank.

She looked at the next sheet. It was a title page.

Scion

by Brendan Hillier

Beneath that was written, in faded red ink:

July 17th 1989
  I'd be grateful to get your feedback on this. It's taken two years but I hope you agree that it's got something.
  Kind regards,
  B. Hillier

Tor gawped at the pages and read them again. It couldn't really be saying what it was saying, could it? I mean, it couldn't be real. Surely, it was a joke. *Scion* was Harry's book. It was what had made him. He owed everything to that story – his fortune, his reputation. Hell, he was about to get an Oscar for it.

But this – this clearly suggested the book had been written by another man.

She looked back at the cover note . . . do the right thing . . . and closed her eyes in quiet despair as the true scale of her friend's ambition dawned upon her. The stress headaches, the war with Harry . . .

It had been too much to resist. Cress clearly wasn't anywhere close to doing the right thing.

Cress took out her earplugs, pushed the mask off her eyes and was deliberating on what to do next to kill time without actually doing anything that involved moving her head, when she saw the red light flashing by the phone. She picked it up. The connection from the in-flight phone was crackly.

'Cress, it's Tor. I've got the paperwork you wanted.'
Pause.
'We need to talk.'

Chapter Fifty

Tor found Cress sitting by the pool, sucking in her tummy and ignoring the children, who were doing handstands with Greta underwater – not because she didn't want to see their latest accomplishment, but because the sight of Greta in a bandeau bikini was more than she could bear.

'What have you got yourself into?' Tor said quietly as she sat down, still in her jeans.

Cress didn't say anything, just quivered silently behind her magazine – not with fear, but with relief. Someone knew. Thank God someone knew! Ever since she'd picked up Tor's message, the minutes had shuffled reluctantly round the clock as she'd waited and waited for Tor to cross the Atlantic and then the whole of the United States, so that they could have this quiet, aghast conversation.

'Who is he? Who is Brendan Hillier?'

Cress dropped her magazine and Tor could see, even behind her giant shades, how exhausted she was. How long had she been carrying this secret?

'Well, he's dead,' Cress said baldly. 'A dead writer who wrote *Scion*. That's about all I know.'

'That's all?'

Cress shrugged. 'Believe me, I've been trying to find out

459

more about him. The death certificate says he died in August 1989. Diabetic coma.'

'August '89? The date on his covering note says he sent it in July.'

'I know.'

'Who was he sending the book to in 1989?'

Cress shrugged. 'I assume to the person who sent it to me. But I don't know who that is.'

'You don't know?'

Cress shook her head.

'Someone served up Harry Hunter on a plate to you and you have no idea who that person could be? Don't you think that's rather dangerous? How do you know they don't want a pound of flesh from you too?'

Cress bit her lip. 'Well, I think they do, now.'

Tor frowned at her.

Cress's face collapsed. 'All they asked me to do was "*the right thing*". I was supposed to expose him. Blow the whistle. But I didn't! Why didn't I?' She clenched her fists into a ball and punched her thighs. 'I creamed the profits from Harry's lies for myself and to consolidate Sapphire's position in the market.'

Tor shook her head, despairing and disappointed.

Cress sighed. 'And now there's a new demand. That's why you had to bring out the *Scion* manuscript. He wants it back – whoever he is. He said Harry's time is up. I was supposed to expose him, but I didn't. So I guess now he's going to do it himself.'

'So then you're out of the loop?' Tor said, brightening a little.

'Or in the frame,' Cress replied miserably. 'What if he chooses to implicate me with Harry's lies? I didn't do what he asked in the first place. Quite frankly, he *should* drop me in it. I'm no better than Harry.'

A waiter came up.

'Oh, um, a Perrier please. Cress?'

Cress shook her head, and then, after a moment, changed her mind and called the waiter back. 'Actually, I'll have an iced towel.'

'Well, at least all this explains why the two of you have been at each other's throats.' She paused, thinking. 'In fact, under the circumstances, you both appear to have behaved reasonably well. At least he's only been trying to discredit you through the media.'

'Tor, he's damn near broken up my marriage and my family.'

'Yes. But he could have done a lot worse than that. Your house could have been ransacked, the children . . .'

'Tor, don't!' Cress cried, sitting bolt upright.

But Tor shook her head. 'Think about it, Cress! You're blackmailing the most famous man in the world. You can't honestly think he'd let you get away with it? You'd have given up that manuscript in an instant if he'd gone directly for your family, and he'd have been in the clear. You've been unbelievably lucky that he's not entirely without scruples.'

Tor's Perrier and the iced towel arrived, and Cress immediately covered her face with it, her hands up to her head, letting her tears soak into the chill as she realized how much she'd put her family in jeopardy.

Tor leant forward and squeezed her leg. 'Cress, I'm not trying to frighten you. I'm just saying you've been very lucky. But we need to get rid of that manuscript – give it back to whoever wants it – and then let Harry know it's gone too. You need to remove yourself from this equation completely. Let whoever's after him deal with him themselves. It sounds like they're going to anyway, now.'

'But I don't know who that is, Tor – I've got no idea who wants it back.'

'Well, they'll be in touch if they made you bring it out here,' Tor said.

Cress stared at her friend who was trying so hard to make this all go away.

'Where is the manuscript anyway?' Cress asked suddenly.

'I just left it in your suite.'

Cress gasped. 'You did what?'

'Don't worry,' Tor reassured. 'I hid it under the mattress. Even I knew better than to leave something like that lying around.'

Cress stood up and pushed her feet into her flip-flops. 'Well, we'd better put it in the safe.'

They went over to the lifts and got in, Tor pressing the button for the sixth floor.

They sped up.

'You're panicking over nothing,' Tor muttered, as Cress put the key in the door. 'I'm not a complete . . .'

The scene that greeted them left them both speechless. Clothes were everywhere, cakes trodden into the carpet, tea spilled over the bed, the red Valentino dress torn, the mattress half on the floor.

'No!' Cress cried, as her brain processed what her eyes were seeing. She ran over to the bed, trying to lift the mattress, but it was no good.

She knew even before she got there that the manuscript had gone.

*

462

The hotel staff had no record of a Robert ever having been employed by the hotel. In fact, to Cress's mortification and fury, her suite didn't come with butler service at all, and nothing they did – replacing her Valentino dress with an identical replacement, upgrading her to the presidential floor – could comfort her.

'It's Harry!' she wailed. 'He's set me up, don't you see? He got me to take the *Scion* manuscript – my leverage against him – out of hiding and to bloody bring it to him! The bastard! The bastard! There never was a plan to expose him. He's tricked me. He's stolen it back!'

Chapter Fifty-one

Tor stopped and blinked as she stepped out into the blinding sunlight, raising her arm to shield her eyes. It was eight o'clock, and she was surprised to see that the terrace was already full. She had assumed everybody would choose room service, today of all days, but there was a carnival atmosphere about already and the excitement at the day's forthcoming activities was palpable. As she looked around, Tor realized she recognized at least one person at every table, and she put her arms around the children's shoulders, less as a protective measure than as a way of guaranteeing they didn't break away and cause chaos and destruction.

Yellow parasols were opened above teak tables, casting not shadows but pools of sunny light on to the limestone floor and bathing the A-list diners in gold. Le monde dorée, she thought to herself.

'Look, Mummy, there's Aunty Cress and Uncle Mark,' Marney said happily, pointing towards the Pellings, who were eating breakfast in uncharacteristic silence. Cress had her giant shades on already, and even beneath the yellow parasol she looked bleached in the morning sun.

They made their way over. 'Quietly, please, Marney. People want to eat their breakfast in peace. And don't run,' she hissed, as Marney broke into a gallop.

'Hi, Tor,' Mark said, getting up and kissing her on both cheeks. He waved over a waiter. 'Could you put another table next to this one please?'

Tor stood back a little while the waiters moved tables and chairs to accommodate them. 'How are you, Mark? When'd you get in?'

'Half ten last night. Got the red eye from New York. D'you sleep well?'

She shook her head. 'Jetlag. I'd forgotten it's such a killer.'

She sat the children at the far end of the table with Cress's lot, who were sitting with Greta.

Mark poured her a juice. 'What time were you awake?'

'Four.'

'Ouch.'

'Yuh! How are you, Cress?' Tor asked, as she took her seat. 'Still got that headache? You know she's been getting these headaches?' she directed to Mark.

'No,' Mark said, mildly irritated. 'Since when? You didn't say anything,' he said accusingly to Cress.

Cress just winced and waved his questions away. The pressure in her head had intensified to the degree that she kept seeing black screens after she blinked, and it hurt her to move or turn.

'I think you need to see a doctor, Cress,' Tor said, putting her hand on her friend's. She knew she wouldn't have slept a wink last night, worrying what Harry's next move would be. 'It's clear you're in pain.'

'It's just jetlag, I'm fine,' Cress dismissed, pulling herself up a little so as not to look quite so feeble, but the scrape of a nearby chair against the floor made her drop her head again in agony. They all looked over, and saw James holding Amelia Abingdon's chair for her as she sat down.

Tor immediately looked away. Cress's head was back in her hands.

'Right, that's enough. You're going to lie down. You're in no fit state to be up. Come on.'

She looked at Mark, feeling inexplicably cross that he wasn't doing more to look after his wife. 'Mark, is it OK if I leave the kids here with you for a second? They'll be fine with croissants and juice.'

'Yes, no problem. We'll be OK, won't we, Greta?'

'Sure,' Greta smiled, giving Mark a satisfied look. He held her gaze openly. 'The more children, the better.' She had long since learnt that to win out over Cress she had to compete not as a woman, but as a mother.

Cress winced again.

'Come on.' Tor took Cress by the arm and led her towards the lobby.

'Heard from Harry?' Tor whispered, trying to find a route that would subtly lead them away from James's table.

'No. Doubt I will either.'

'Why?'

'Well, the manuscript may be back in his possession but what's he going to do to me? If he reveals my lies, he has to reveal his own, and he certainly can't afford to take that chance. If anyone ever found out he didn't write *Scion*, he'd be destroyed. All yesterday means is that he's broken free. Stolen back his freedom. He'll terminate his contract with Sapphire and move on to bigger and better, and I won't be able to stop him. Not now that I don't have any proof.'

'What will happen to Sapphire when he goes?' Tor asked, realizing there was no way around the tables without doubling back on themselves. They would have to go straight past James.

466

'Well, we've still got one lifeline. *The Wrong Prince* is well on course to become a global best-seller and the film rights have just been negotiated. That deal alone is worth about eight million dollars to us, so we won't be left completely high and dry.'

Tor steeled herself to give a cursory nod as they passed, but James stood up.

'What's the matter?' he asked, concerned, as he saw Cress's evident pain.

'I'm fine. It's just a hangover,' Cress dismissed.

'Must be pretty bad,' he said, unconvinced. His eyes slid over to Tor and she looked away. Amelia was watching.

'It's my advanced age,' Cress said caustically.

'Tor, I'm so pleased to see you,' Amelia said, awkwardly getting to her feet too. 'I've been so keen to meet up with you. I sent you a postcard but . . . it must have got lost in the post.'

Tor felt her smile freeze. 'Yes, it must have,' she said weakly.

Amelia looked down at her bump and shrugged. 'I need a nursery,' she said almost apologetically. 'Quite urgently.'

'I can see that! When are you due?'

'The day before yesterday.'

'Oh!' Tor paused, thinking back. 'But didn't you say you wanted to do up the place in Pimlico?' she asked.

'I do! I know it's crazy me being out here this late in the pregnancy, but – it's the Best Actress award! I may never be nominated again.' She shrugged. 'And anyway, I've got James on tap, so I'm in safe hands.'

'That you are,' Tor said casually, not daring to look at him. His hair was still wet from the shower, a droplet of water trickling down his cheek towards his lip.

Lucky droplet, she thought, before she could catch herself.

She steeled herself to stay in NCT mummy mode. 'How are you feeling? Any aches yet?'

'Not yet, thank heavens. I just need a couple extra hours . . .' She crossed her fingers. 'And then this baby can come.'

'The organizers must be having kittens you'll go into labour.'

Amelia shrugged. 'They're quite used to it, actually. Rachel Weisz, Catherine Zeta Jones, Annette Bening – they all attended ready to drop.'

'Oh yes. So they did.'

Amelia paused. 'I don't suppose – I don't suppose you've got a minute to come to my room and just look at some swatches I've got.'

Tor shrugged apologetically. 'I've really got to get Cress back to bed. She's dead on her feet.'

'I'll take you,' James offered, smiling at Cress. 'I owe you.'

'No you don't,' she said, but he took her arm anyway and led her to the lifts.

'You really should stay and have your breakfast,' Tor said to Amelia, aware she sounded like a midwife.

'I'll have them send it up,' she said casually. 'It's more important I get your expert eye on my curtain fabrics. I'm a total disaster when it comes to colours and things.'

'I don't believe that,' Tor said generously. As much as she didn't want to like Amelia, she did. It was damned annoying.

They rode up in the lifts, stopping on the eighth floor, where they all got out. There were only four suites on the floor. James took Cress to her room, while Tor and Amelia carried on to hers, the Emperor Suite.

The door was opened for them by the – legitimate – butler as they approached.

'Oh, Stephen, would you mind awfully arranging for my

breakfast to be sent up here after all?' Amelia said smilingly, without stopping.

The door closed behind them and Tor tried not to gawp as she took in the unrestrained opulence. She'd never seen such lavishness. It was like a mini Versailles. An eight-foot crystal chandelier hung from the domed ceiling in the hall, with arched double doors leading off from all sides, the floor hewn from tumbled marble.

A ten-foot mirror hung on one wall, and Tor saw her hair had dried into natural waves. She put a hand to her face, feeling conspicuously bare of make-up and out of place.

'Come through,' Amelia called from the drawing room. Tor walked in and her gasps finally escaped her. Bouquets and sprays of flowers were absolutely everywhere. It was as though the walls were hung with petals, with Lalique vases of yellow, cream, white and red roses standing proud against the more eclectic irises, camellias, orchids and tuberose. The air was heady with their scent.

Stephen came in.

'A call for you, Miss Abingdon. It's Mr Howard.'

Amelia's shoulders slumped. 'Sorry. Do you mind if I take this? I'll only be a few minutes.'

Tor raised her hands. 'No, of course not.'

Tor stood in the middle of the flowers, wondering how on earth she found herself in this position – standing in the middle of Amelia Abingdon's suite on the day of the Oscars, discovering Cress had been blackmailing Harry Hunter, that Harry was an absolute fraud, that he'd robbed Cress . . . She shook her head and checked her watch.

Oh God! It was nearly nine. She had to be at Harry's apartment by ten. The Reynolds was arriving today, and as his representative to sign on the dotted line at Bonham's, she was the only one authorized to receive it. The last thing she wanted now was to help out Harry – to work for him – but the security for flying it over from London had been shocking and she knew there'd be so much more hassle if she didn't just receive the damned thing.

'Psst.'

Tor spun around.

James was leaning against a doorway, one ankle crossed over the other. His hair had dried and he was staring at her with an intensity that just about made her clothes fall off.

'James!' she cried. 'Is Cress OK?' she managed.

'No. But she won't let me examine her. She's still maintaining it's a hangover.'

He stared at her but said nothing. Cress would have to wait.

'Come over here. I've got something for you,' he said instead.

Tor didn't move.

'Come on. I won't bite,' he smiled, and she hated the teensy little voice in her head that rather wished he would, that it could be fun . . .

He moved into the bedroom behind him and Tor tentatively followed, telling herself, 'He's a lying bastard, he's a lying bastard, he's a . . .'

His dinner suit – that one he always looked so damned good in – was hanging on the wardrobe door. She looked around to see if she could see Amelia's dress, or, even better, her jewels – they were bound to be priceless – but they were nowhere to be seen. In fact, there was no evidence of Amelia anywhere in the room at all. She has a separate dressing room, Tor thought, peeved.

He held out a large flat parcel wrapped in brown paper and tied with string. 'This is for you,' he said quietly.

Tor looked at him, steeling herself to say what she had to say. 'I don't want anything from you, James. I thought I made that clear.'

He winced. 'Please, Tor. Just look at it, at least,' he said finally.

She moved forward and took the package. James sat down on the bed and looked up at her, watching the confusion and conflict cross her face.

She bit her lip and slowly removed the string. She peeled back the paper and gasped with surprise as she saw the oil of the three children playing on the beach.

'I can't accept this!' she cried.

'Please, Tor,' he urged.

'But – but how did you even know?'

He paused for a moment, leaning back on his elbows. 'I was there,' he said simply. 'I saw you sitting with Anna. And when I saw your face light up at this, I knew I had to get it for you.'

'I don't know what to say,' she murmured. No one had ever done anything like this for her before. She just wasn't that sort of woman.

'Don't say anything,' James said, encouraged by her fluster. He couldn't believe she was here, so close. He got up and stood in front of her, pushing a tendril of hair back behind her ear, cupping her face, forcing her to look at him. He was just inches away and she gave a little shiver as she tried to focus and resist and remember why it was that this shouldn't be happening. But she was just so tired. And he made it impossible for her to think when he insisted upon looking at her like that with those dark, dark eyes. And his hands, which

471

were sliding slowly down her arms – she didn't remember them being so big, or so warm, or so very dextrous . . .

There was a sudden knock at the door and Tor leapt away.

'Sorry to interrupt, Mr White, but I'm afraid Miss Abingdon needs you.'

Tor saw James's jaw clench with frustration.

'She thinks her waters may just have broken,' he added with impressive understatement, as James failed to move.

James put his hands on his hips and dropped his head. 'Christ! Timing.'

The momentary interruption was all Tor needed to gather her wits about her.

'I was just leaving,' Tor said primly to Stephen. She walked past James but he grabbed her arm and held her fast.

'Please, Tor! Stay here,' he said urgently. 'We need to talk. We have got to clear things up. Just give me a couple of minutes.'

'I'll hand it to you, James, you're very good,' Tor said calmly, tossing the painting on to the bed. 'The expensive painting, the flash suite. Pregnant girlfriend in the other room! Oops, how easy it is to forget,' she said sarcastically. 'Just what is it you think you're doing with me, James? Why do you keep chasing me? You've already had me. Wasn't that the point? Or did the fact that I threw you out mean I was a new challenge all over again?'

'Pregnant girlfriend? But Tor, she's not my girlfri—'

He was cut short by Amelia giving out a cry that even James, in all his desperation, couldn't ignore. He stood there staring at Tor for a couple of seconds, then marched across the room and picked up his doctor's bag.

'We need to talk about this properly. You've got it all wrong,' he tried, as Amelia's whimpers carried across the hall.

'I'm really not interested in hearing more excuses from you, James,' she said bleakly, heading towards the door. 'It's never going to happen. There's too much that's wrong.'

'But we're not together,' he called after her.

But she kept on walking.

'Damn it, Tor!' he shouted angrily, punching the door in frustration. He dropped his head back against the door frame and tried to get it together. But the sight of her walking away from him again . . .

With a shaking hand, Tor pressed the down button. The lift doors pinged open almost immediately and she practically fell in, relieved and devastated to have escaped.

Chapter Fifty-two

'Come on baby,' Kate said huskily, straddling Harry as he sat at the desk, and pushing her luscious breasts in his face. 'It's been nearly a week. You're driving me crazy,' she pouted, raking her hands through his hair, nibbling on his ear, her hands wandering all over his chest and down, trying to wake him up and get him going.

God, it was hard work these days. How the tables had turned! With the pregnancy well established, her hormones were rampaging through her and Harry couldn't be less enthused.

'Kate, look . . .' He tried to look around her at his notes. He'd been working on it for hours, but he still couldn't get his acceptance speech quite right. 'Not now, OK?'

'But I can't wait any longer. You've got me too wet for you,' she said, taking him in her hand and whispering filth in his ear to turn him on. He loved that. She felt him harden but it was still against his will.

'S'not the time, Kate, OK? . . . Later . . . I promise.' But his breathing was becoming ragged as her hands became more insistent.

'That's what you always say,' she said, pushing a magnificent breast towards his mouth. 'Come on, baby, let's go,' she said, her breath getting quicker with her hands. She lowered herself down on him and threw her head back, her feet resting on the sides of the chair. She wasn't going to let him get away this time.

She wound her fingers in his hair and felt his hands pulling down on her shoulders, forcing her down on him, harder, faster, faster, faster.

He groaned just as she couldn't keep her own eyes open any longer and she buried her face in his neck, relieved, relaxed, sated.

'Well now, isn't that better?' she said finally, a wicked grin on her face. She leaned back on the desk triumphantly, her elbow knocking some papers on to the floor.

'Look what you've done!' he said angrily, grabbing her around the waist and hoisting her off him.

'Oh, lighten up, Harry!' Kate retorted, stung by how little effect their lovemaking had had on his mood. 'I'll deal with it for you. Look! I'm picking them up. It's no big deal.' She scooped a handful of the papers into a messy pile.

'They weren't like that – I had them . . . Oh, just give them to me!' Harry fumed.

'Uh-uh-uh. Not until you chill out.' Kate held the papers above her head, a coquettish smile on her face.

'I'm not in the mood for this, Kate. I just want to get this speech written. Just give me the bloody papers.'

Kate waggled the papers but didn't hand them back.

Harry got up from the desk but she scampered behind the armchair cheekily. 'Come and get them,' she smiled, ducking and weaving as Harry snatched at her.

'Now, Kate! I mean it.'

Kate made a dash for the door, but Harry was too quick for her and he grabbed her elbow, jerking her backwards roughly and causing the papers to scatter wildly around the room again.

'Jesus, Harry!' Kate cried, rubbing her wrenched arm, shocked by his roughness. 'What's the matter with you? You could have hurt the baby.'

'The baby, the sodding baby! That's all you bloody think about,' he said sharply. He sat back down at the desk with his back to her.

Kate tied her dressing-gown tightly around her and sat quietly on the edge of the armchair for a moment. She knew he was under the most enormous stress.

There was no doubt Emily had scored a knockout. Kate had completely underestimated her. She'd been so immersed in her own personal life, she'd taken her eye off the ball.

But it wasn't the many sordid and lascivious details of the statutory rape allegations being spelled out that were such a problem. It was that they had collectively forced a sea-change and turned the public mood. Harry had morphed from fallen angel – flawed but gilded – to national disgrace, and the dramas that had once titillated the public now appalled them.

The broadsheets' reporting of his civil action against James – who was defended mightily as the esteemed royal physician – painted Harry as pernicious and vindictive, and set the new moral tone, adding momentum to the campaign to make an example out of him and have him prosecuted, if not by Emily, then by the CPS.

Usually Kate would have been on the phone, calmly threatening to hang an editor by his balls, all the while munching on a croissant. But stuck here in LA, she was eight hours behind everyone else. The day's news was chip wrappings by the time she found out about it, and Moreton's were pushing her ever more out of the loop. She was barely consulted on anything now, and when they did contact her, it was as the client, not the brief.

'Actually, Harry, there's something I need to talk to you about.'

Harry angrily dragged red weals across his speech and spun around to face her.

'Jesus, Kate, can you not see that I'm racing against the clock here, trying to get this wrapped up? We've got to leave in three hours.'

'It's important.'

Harry looked at her, his eyes flashing. 'It always is, with you.'

'You have to drop the case against James. You're not going to win it.'

'Says who?'

'The papers are painting this action as capricious. It's doing serious damage to your reputation pursuing it. You're being portrayed as a spoiled, self-indulgent bully. You've lost the public's sympathy, Harry. They don't care whether James did or didn't sell that information to the papers. They just don't want you to win.'

'I care! It's got nothing to do with anyone else but us. I want the truth!'

Kate paused. She sincerely doubted that. 'Well, if that's the case, then I think I can give it to you.'

Harry stared at her. 'What do you mean?'

'I think I've worked out how the information was obtained.' Kate swallowed hard. 'And it wasn't from James.'

'What?' He was furious. 'How do you know?'

Kate walked across the room and stood in front of the stone fireplace.

'On Christmas Day, when you – when you went diving, I just wanted to get away from all the photographers. They were everywhere. I couldn't sit by the pool, and all those stupid girls were out on the beach, so I couldn't go there . . .'

Just as well, Harry thought to himself, as he remembered his Christmas present to himself.

'. . . So I drove into town, and I saw a little girl as I parked the car. Her family were in church and she was outside on her own. I was a bit worried about her.' Kate shrugged. 'We started talking and she was curious about the baby . . .'

Harry's eyes narrowed.

'. . . I told her we were having a baby girl.' She paused, trying not to be intimidated by the look on his face. 'I even told her the names we liked.'

'You did what?' He jumped up.

'She could only have been six or so, Harry. It didn't cross my mind that . . .'

'You stupid cow!' he hollered. 'If any of the reporters saw you together, they probably only had to buy her a lollipop to find out what you were talking about.' He ran his hands through his hair and started pacing the room. 'Jesus! I cannot believe you were so bloody stupid. How could you trust her? You can't trust anyone! Haven't you realized that yet?'

Kate hung her head. 'I'm sorry. I . . . I've just been in such a state. There's been so much going on, what with Emily and James; and I was just so excited about the baby and I couldn't really share it with . . . with you . . .' She flopped her hands to her sides. 'My head was elsewhere. It was a lapse of judgement. I'm sorry.'

Harry stared at her, his eyes like slits.

'Who else knows about this?'

Kate shrugged. 'No one. I only put two and two together this morning in the shower. I'd forgotten all about her. She only popped back into my head because I was going over baby names again and I remembered how she couldn't pronounce . . .'

'No one must find out about this,' he interrupted. 'It changes nothing. We're carrying on as before. White's going to carry the can for this.'

'But Harry! He's done nothing wrong.'

'I want him ruined, Kate.'

'You said you wanted the truth.'

Harry flashed his eyes at her. 'Bollocks to that! I'll be damned if I'm going to play at being gentlemen now. He's on the ropes. This is my chance.'

Kate slapped her hands against her thighs in frustration. 'This has got nothing to do with the baby at all, has it? You couldn't give a damn whether he is or isn't speaking to the press. This is just a vehicle for you, an opportunity to hit back at him.'

'So what if it is? Why the hell shouldn't I? Look what he's been doing to me!'

Kate crossed her arms. 'You mean the blackmail? Being in cahoots with Cress?'

'That's right!'

'Because of that story you told me – the boy who fell?'

'Yes.'

'Hillier?'

'Yes!'

'Yes what?'

Harry paused, confused. 'What do you mean?'

'Well, which one are you being blackmailed over? The story about the boy who fell? Or the story about Hillier?'

479

Harry stared at her, frozen.

Kate dropped her voice. 'Because they're not one and the same, Harry. They're two entirely different stories. You know full well that the boy who fell was Julian Abingdon.'

Harry still said nothing.

'So why did you tell me it was someone called Hillier? Why have you put him into an entirely different story? Why are you trying to throw me off the scent with half-truths? What is it you don't want me to know about him?'

Harry shifted weight. 'Hillier. Abingdon. Whatever. So I got the name wrong. It was a long time ago.'

He shrugged.

'I don't think so.' Kate shook her head. She wasn't going to be deterred. 'Something is going on with Hillier. And Cress *is* involved. I saw his name on her texts.'

She watched the high colour drain from his cheeks. 'You're lying to me. You lied to me to peel me away from my friends and family so that you'd be the only person I had left. And it's worked, hasn't it? I mean, just look at me!' She threw her arms up in the air, indicating their lavish home. 'Following you around the world – dashing across borders before your latest sex scandal sees your visa denied, carrying your baby, living your lies, hating your enemies, dovetailing my career to pursue your feuds.'

He watched her, so sure, so right, the synapses of her brilliant brain skipping from one truth to another, untangling his web, dismantling his defence.

'But I'm not the enemy, you know,' she said more quietly, taking his silence for acquiescence. She moved over to him and placed her hands on his chest. 'Yes, you've lied to me. But I still love you. I'm on your side. But you have to trust me. I can't help you if you don't trust me. I'm your brief. I . . .'

'No, you're not.'

She paused for a beat. 'I know. I know I'm your girlfriend and the mother of your unborn child, but I'm also still your legal counsel . . .'

'No. You're missing the point.' His voice was flat.

Kate stared at him.

'I took a call from Nicholas Parker yesterday,' he said levelly, though she could see a spark flicker in his eyes.

'And?'

'They're stepping down as my legal representatives.'

'They're what?'

'They think I'd benefit from a new team, a fresh campaign.' Harry paused. 'Makes me sound like a fucking politician, don't you think?'

Kate's hands flew to her cheeks. 'I can't believe they've let you go. You're their biggest asset.'

'And their biggest liability it would seem. The mauling I've been taking in the press hasn't done their reputation any good either.'

'Even so . . . I'll speak to Parker, Harry. I'll sort it out. '

'No you won't.' Harry regarded her coolly. 'He asked me to pass on a message to you too.'

Kate swallowed hard. 'Which was?'

She saw his eyes dance. 'You're fired.'

Going against James's direct orders, Cress refused to stay in bed and hopped into the car that she had arranged to take her and Tor over to Harry's apartment. The party to cele-brate Harry's screenplay deal with Dreamworks was being hosted there tomorrow night, and she hadn't even had time to check out the décor yet. This was no time for lying about in bed. A couple of painkillers would have to do now what a lie-down could do later. The show had to go on – now more than ever.

Tor was sitting opposite her, tapping her thigh impatiently and transferring all her agitation at James to the deplorable state of LA's traffic.

'You seem hot and bothered,' Cress observed laconically. It was clear Tor was the one who needed support this morning.

Tor looked annoyed. 'Well, of course I am. The Bonham's couriers will be waiting. I specifically said I'd meet them there at 10 a.m. You can't very well keep a five million pound masterpiece hanging around on the pavement.'

Cress said nothing, but the smile hovering at her lips showed she didn't believe that excuse for one second.

'Besides,' Tor continued, trying to prove her friend wrong; she knew exactly what she was thinking: 'This is going to be the first time I've seen the apartment. What if it hasn't worked? It'll be a disaster. I'll be devastated.' She threw her hands into the air, dramatically. Cress was still staring. 'So I'm nervous.'

Just then her tummy rumbled and she clapped her hand over it, realizing she still hadn't had a chance to eat yet. Cress's headache had deferred breakfast and then with James . . . well, her mind hadn't been on food.

She shook her head with disgust at herself. She couldn't believe he'd done it again. Snared her, fooled her. What kind of an idiot was she to keep falling for his sexy smile and thoughtful paintings?

Traffic started moving and they pulled on to a freeway that appeared to be every bit as wide as Wales. Tor closed her eyes, trying not to freak out at all the overtaking on both sides and at Cress's scrutinizing stare.

'Just tell me what he did this time,' Cress said quietly.

Tor opened one eye. It was useless trying to lie to Cress. She was the master liar, after all. She'd blackmailed Harry Hunter, for heaven's sake.

'He gave me a painting I'd wanted. One I saw at the auction.'

'Did you accept it? Please say you didn't do anything stupid – like decline it?'

'Of course I declined!' Tor screeched, making Cress wince – the painkillers could only do so much.

They sat in silence the rest of the way, Cress massaging her temples while Tor dozed off some jetlag. She'd had a dreadful night.

They pulled up outside the apartment block fifteen minutes later, and the Bonham's couriers were only just pulling up ahead of them, having been caught in the same traffic quagmire.

'Oh, thank God,' Tor exclaimed, bounding out of the car, relieved to have some distance from Cress and her penetrating questions. Sympathy wasn't helpful right now.

The Bonham's boys smiled, as Tor handed over her passport and they verified her ID. She looked at the cargo. It was huge. The painting was triple-wrapped in linen and boxed in a double-framed crate that made it almost twice its actual size.

Cress went ahead, entering the nine-digit security code and unlocking the doors, but she stood back to let in Tor, who was practically frothing at the mouth to see it all. She ran past and felt a rush of adrenalin as she walked in. Throughout the project, she'd been working off photographs and architect's drawings, creating mood boards that looked great as a presentation but gave her no real idea as to whether it would actually come together in the space.

But immediately she walked in to the vast open-plan space, she knew she'd pulled it off. Ever since Harry had first mentioned getting the Reynolds at the dinner in Cornwall, she'd had a hunch to put a severe gunmetal grey on the walls; and looking around now, she knew she'd been spot on. The triple-aspect arched French doors meant there was more than enough light flooding in, and the scheme looked brooding, clean, dynamic and masculine. A white Barcelona chair and footstool – apparently he had one in his London flat – also helped to refract the light, and white leather shutters were folded back against the walls.

She walked over and sat down at the black crocodile-skin desk, running her hands over the gleaming hide. If you didn't have someone to love, this was surely the next best thing.

Tor flitted around the space, appraising the 300-year-old sculpture of Artemis she'd had shipped over from the Sotheby's Garden Sale in Sussex and fine-tuning the position of the status photographs and publishing industry awards Harry had sent over.

It worked. It really worked. And her heart gave a little soar as she heard Cress's gasp as she followed her in.

'Holy cow, Tor!'

The couriers whistled as they walked in with the boxes too.

'Nice. Whose place is this?' one of them asked.

'Harry Hunter's.'

The courier grinned and shook his head. 'Of course, the golden boy's. He's got it all, hasn't he?'

He's certainly got something, Tor thought to herself, as it struck her again what fool's gold it was.

'Right. Where's this baby going?' asked the other courier.

'Over there, please,' Tor said, indicating the wall behind

the desk. Everything was ready for it. The space had been measured and the lights positioned accordingly. Tor stood with her hands clasped beneath her chin as the men skilfully opened the crate and lifted out the painting. Once again, it knocked the stuffing out of her. It had a handsome pathos that was intriguing and absorbing. It was impossible to walk past it. It positively shone.

The two women watched it lifted into position and straightened. Cress smiled at her and patted her on the shoulder.

'A job well done, girl,' Cress praised her. 'Summershill Interiors is well and truly flying now.'

Her mobile rang and she turned away to speak to Mark, who was down at the pool with the children. Tor quickly got on the line to speak to hers and check they were wearing sunscreen and not splashing any celebrities, before handing the phone back.

When she turned around, the men were waiting for her attention.

'And where would you like this one?'

'This what?'

'This painting. The . . .' The courier checked his paperwork. '*The Death of Orion*.'

Tor frowned at him. 'I'm sorry. I don't know what you're talking about. We haven't bought another painting.'

The man checked his paperwork and shrugged. 'It says here it's to be delivered to this address, today. Look, it's addressed to Harry Hunter.'

Tor looked at the clipboard. It did indeed say the painting was to go to Harry. 'But we didn't buy this.'

'Well, someone did. Maybe it's a gift.'

'Shall I get it out for you to look at?' the other courier asked. 'Maybe that will remind you.' And before she could reply, the two men levered open the crate. They were super-keen to complete the delivery and knock off before the roads became completely impassable.

They lifted out the painting and Tor was stunned to find herself staring at an epic depiction of a white-robed goddess standing proud on a cliff, her bow raised, the shot arrow sailing through the flaming sky towards a man swimming far out in the ocean. It was the mythological painting she and Anna had derided at the auction. What on earth was it doing here?

'So you do know it then?' the courier asked, seeing the recognition flit across her face.

'Yes, I uh . . . Yes.' She couldn't help but frown at it.

'Yeah, it's not my taste either. Still, it's a famous one this, the hunter hunted. It's showing Artemis, the goddess of the chase, mistakenly killing her lover, Orion the hunter. She was tricked into it by her jealous brother Apollo, you know.'

'I . . . uh, I didn't know actually. You're very knowledge-able.'

The courier's chest swelled with importance. 'I take an interest in what I'm carrying. I don't just deliver sacks of potatoes.' He looked at Tor. 'So where would you like it?'

Tor looked at them, dazed, trying to make the pieces of the puzzle fit.

'Um, put it on the desk please. '

They put it carefully down and he handed her the clip-board.

'OK, if you could just sign here, here, here and here.' She signed for the painting as he made a feeble attempt to chat Tor up. 'You going to watch the awards?'

'Yes, I'm going to them, actually.'

Their eyebrows shot up.

She shrugged. 'Part of Harry's team. Cress here is his publisher.'

The courier whistled. 'Well, we'll look out for you on the red carpet. Make sure you don't wear too much,' he added with a wink.

They shut the door behind them, and Tor and Cress stared down at the Victorian monstrosity.

'What's going on, Tor?' Cress asked, perplexed.

'I don't know,' Tor replied, equally baffled. 'But it must be a gift for Harry.'

'From Kate? The studio?'

Tor shrugged.

'Nah, it must be an admin error. It's pretty hideous,' Cress said dismissively, beginning to walk around the room again. 'I doubt you could even flog it on eBay.'

'Mmmmmm.'

'Just put it down over there. He can look at it himself. He'll be by later to check this place out.'

Tor propped it up, facing the wall.

'What's that?' Cress asked, moving towards it.

Tucked into the back of the frame was an envelope. Tor bent down and pulled it out. 'It must be a note saying who it's from.' She chuckled. 'You wouldn't think you'd want to put your name to something in as poor taste as this.'

Cress took the envelope from her and looked at it. She could feel the tissue inside as she pressed her fingertips together.

Quickly, she began to open it.

'Cress. That's private. I don't think you should . . .'

Cress pulled out the red-edged card and read the elegant italics she knew would be written there:

*Freedom is but the distance between the hunter
and the hunted.*

Tor, who was peering over her shoulder, gasped and clapped her hand over her mouth.

'It's not a gift at all,' Tor said finally. 'It's a threat.'

Cress stared at the writing. 'This is from the same person who sent me the note in London – telling me to bring out the manuscript.' She looked up at Tor. 'You know what this means, don't you?'

'No,' Tor said, frightened to death by yet another development. She wasn't cut out for this kind of cloak and dagger thing.

'It means it wasn't Harry who stole the manuscript from me,' Cress managed. 'It means it's not over yet.'

Tor's heart galloped and she perched on one of the crates for support.

'You've seen this painting before?' Cress asked. *'The Death of Orion?'*

'Yes, at the auction. At Bonham's.'

Cress's eyes narrowed. 'So who else was there?'

'I . . . uh . . .' Tor stalled.

'You've got to think, Tor. Whoever's sent this to threaten Harry is the same person who sent me the note last week.'

'OK. Well, there was Anna Brightling, and um, Laetitia Latham . . .'

'Who else?'

Tor had suddenly paled. She looked away from Cress.

Cress watched her closely, her own mind racing. 'What is it?'

'Uh, nothing. I . . . uh . . .' Tor tried to gather her wits. She didn't want to say it.

Cress studied her friend through narrowed eyes, then marched over to the laptop on the desk, punching the keys. She knew her too well.

'What are you doing?' Tor asked, quickly, full-blown panic written all over her face. 'What are you typing?'

'There was a quotation on the cover note that came with the *Scion* manuscript. The one that told me to make sure Hillier wasn't forgotten.'

Tor shook her head, trying to remember it. 'Uh . . . I don't know which . . .'

'"*Bright with names that men remember; loud with names that men forget . . .*" D'you remember?'

Tor nodded. She'd read it only yesterday.

Cress read the screen, then sat back. 'It's Swinburne.' She looked at Tor meaningfully. 'From the poem, 'Eton: An Ode'.

'Eton?' Tor repeated dumbly.

'That night at the Roof Gardens, he said it, Tor. He said it when we asked how he and Harry knew each other. Hunter thought he was being clever, trying to show off. But I don't think he was. I think he was trying to let me know *who* he was.'

'I don't know who you're talking about,' Tor lied, her heart hammering her chest, trying to get out. She didn't want to hear this. He couldn't be part of it. He couldn't!

'You told me just an hour ago he bought you a painting from the same auction.' Cress tipped her head sympathetically. 'You know full well that it's James, Tor.'

Chapter Fifty-three

. . . Ninety-seven, ninety-eight, ninety-nine, one hundred.

Mark collapsed down on to his chest and rolled over, grateful for the ordeal to be at an end. He stared up at the heavily corniced ceiling, exhausted.

So this was ageing. Not so long ago he could have done those press-ups, well, not quite single-handedly, but certainly with rather more bounce, and maybe a hand-spring at the end for flourish.

He put his hands behind his head and willed himself into the stomach crunches, scrutinizing it each time he curled up – it was still flat, just with a slight covering now, and a lot more chest hair. OK, so he wouldn't be asked to do a shoot for Abercrombie & Fitch any time soon, but he could live with that. He was thirty-nine. Not nineteen.

Nineteen. Nineteen. His mind began to wander back to that far distant land. Back when beer cost 'a pound a pint' at the student bar and the day didn't start till 2 p.m. and the girls had tits under their armpits.

The image of Greta in his shirt flashed before him again. Like it always did. Cress had been sleeping in the spare room for nearly six months now, and Mark had developed a time-sensitive fantasy that brought him off quickly and efficiently in the shower each morning – it was always of Greta in those daisy pants and his shirt.

Of course, he threw in some variety by changing it around occasionally – sometimes she was in just the pants; others, just the shirt. But increasingly, he was finding that wasn't enough. He wanted more. He wanted to touch her, taste her, make her laugh, make her come.

She was different to Cress in every way. Kind, sweet, funny (OK, scratch that, Cress was funny too); from what he'd seen of her in her bikini this week, her stomach was firm but not rock hard, with a better six-pack than his. Best of all though, she wanted him, and him alone.

She laughed at his jokes, cooked his favourite suppers, mothered his children; wore his shirts to bed, for Chrissakes. She was more of a wife to him than Cress. Especially when you considered that he wasn't sleeping with her either.

Abandoning the crunches, he stood up, his groin aching more than his abs. He couldn't believe that he was here, in this mess, lusting after the nanny like a teenager. A tiny voice somewhere in the back of his brain warned him that he was becoming everything he'd said he never would – middle-aged, sex starved, desperate – but it wasn't anywhere near as loud as the voice in his head advising him to get Greta out of her bikini.

Was it his fault his wife had completely withdrawn from him? That she found greater satisfaction hunting down authors who wanted to remain lost and studying her account-ants' spreadsheets than she did in bed with him? It was clear she couldn't bear him to touch her. He'd seen her flinch the last time he'd taken off her bra. Actually flinch, like he was molesting her.

He couldn't live in this emotional and physical vacuum any longer. Something had to give.

He turned as the key slotted into the lock and the door opened. The children bundled through, heading straight for the kitchen and the freezer filled with lollipops.

Greta followed through the door a second later, staggering beneath the weight of the wet towels and beach bags. She stopped as she saw him standing there and instinctively recognized the sea-change in him.

She had known this moment was coming. Day by day, inch by inch, they had been drawing closer to each other. Right in front of Cress, right under her nose, and she hadn't noticed a thing.

Dropping the bags, she slowly moved towards him, her eyes never leaving his. She pulled her hair out of the pony-tail and it tumbled on to her shoulders; those tiny shoulders that could barely keep his shirt on.

She was so close now. His heart was pounding faster than it had during one hundred press-ups.

'Oh, for God's sake, Greta,' Cress barked, barging in. 'Why have you come up here with the kids? I told you to keep them out of the way today. I need to get ready,' she scowled.

She stopped and looked at Mark, who looked flushed and slightly wild.

'You look hot and bothered. Have you been exercising? Well, jump in the shower then. We've got to leave in an hour and I don't want you making me late. This is a big day for me.'

Tor climbed out of the bath and tried the Emperor Suite again, but the call was just diverted back to the operator.

'I'm sorry, Mrs Summershill. No calls are being put through to Miss Abingdon's suite today.'

She tapped her nails on the desk, lost in thought. There

was just over an hour to go till the car arrived. Even if she could get herself ready in that time, she knew she wouldn't get anywhere close to getting into the suite. Amelia was either in full-blown labour or – on the off-chance that it hadn't kicked off yet – getting ready for the biggest night of her life. Best Actress nominees didn't just appear; they had to be made.

She would have to wait to see James.

She wrapped the bath towel around herself and started doing her hair, combing it, sectioning it, curling it, her freshly manicured red nails moving rhythmically and expertly.

There was a knock at the door and Hen came in, fresh from a preview meeting at the museum, a glass of champagne in each hand.

'Santé,' she smiled, handing one to Tor. 'I thought we could have a little tipple now, just to set you on your way.'

Tor giggled. 'Lovely.'

'Cheers!'

They clinked glasses and took a sip each.

'Did it go well?' Tor asked, finishing off the last sections.

'How could it not? The curator has done an incredible job. It's brought so many wonderful memories flooding back. I feel so privileged to have shared in it.'

'It's an amazing history,' Tor exclaimed. 'You're so lucky to have worked with him, first-hand. All those incredible dresses.'

'Talking of which – let me see what you're wearing,' Hen said excitedly.

'Ooooh, wait till you see it, Hen. It's just divine. Cress treated me,' Tor said, jumping up off the bed and walking across the room. 'But honestly, it cost the same as a small car and I don't know when I'll ever wear it again . . .'

Her voice trailed away and she spun round.

'Oh my God!' she whispered.

'What? What's wrong?' Hen said, looking concerned.

'The dress! It's not here.'

'Of course it is! Check the wardrobe. The maids will have hung it up for you.'

Tor shook her head but opened the wardrobe doors anyway.

'No, no. I know it's not!' She turned around and looked at Hen, wan with shock. 'It's hanging on the banisters at home. I didn't want to crease it so I put it in a separate dress bag. But then Cress rang, ordering me across town, and I panicked because I thought we were going to miss the flight and . . . since getting here it's all been so crazy I didn't even notice . . .' Tor looked at Hen and wanted to cry. 'What am I going to do? The car's coming in twenty minutes. There's no way I can get anything now!' Her voice rose with hysteria.

Hen thought fast. She stood up and put her glass down on the dressing-table. 'Right, now don't cry, Tor, we can fix this. No, don't cry – you'll mess up your make-up. Just stay here. Stay calm, OK? I'll be right back.'

Tor stared as she shut the door behind her. This was all Cress's bloody fault. If she hadn't been so busy bloody black-mailing Harry and sending her off to lock-ups at the last minute, she'd have her lovely Valentino and the party would have begun.

She sank down on to the bed and tried not to cry, but it was becoming increasingly difficult to block out all the stresses she'd had since getting here: bolstering Cress, walking away from James, taking delivery of Harry's paintings, all the subterfuge and threats. And now, her lovely bit of frip-pery, the wisp of petal pink silk that was going to take her

494

to the party of her life, was stuck hanging from a stair banister in Battersea.

She drained her glass – and then Hen's – in desolation, staring absently at her red-painted toenails, which always so delighted Oscar. The door opened and Hen staggered in, hidden behind a tower of polythene-covered dresses.

'Oh my godfathers, Hen!' Tor exclaimed. 'Where on earth did you . . . Oh no, Hen, you can't!' she exclaimed. 'I can't wear one of these. They're for the museum. They're priceless. What if I mark one of them? Or spill wine?'

Hen tutted. 'They are dresses, made to be worn, Tor. And they are mine. I decide what happens to them. Now choose one quickly. We haven't much time left.'

She dropped the dresses in a heap on the bed, sliding out like a rainbow in their clear hanging bags – mauve, tangerine, lime, blossom pink, ivory – showing off 1950s pleated chiffons and paste jewels.

Tor clapped her hands together and gave Hen a big hug. She moved over to the bed, dipping through the collection, led almost as much by feel as by sight, letting her fingers trip over the different weights. Every single piece was couture and gossamer-light, lined with charmeuse silk and organdie.

She immediately stopped at a crisp organza dress bedecked with an ivy print. With tiny puff sleeves, the blouse of the dress wrapped over and cinched into a tiny waist before kicking out into a full-circled skirt which actually had – oh heaven! – a net underskirt. Tor had always dreamed of dresses like this as a child.

'I thought you'd like that,' Hen smiled. 'I wore that to my twenty-first birthday party, the night I met my first husband.'

'Oh, Hen. I can't wear it then.' Tor put the dress back on the pile. 'It's far too precious.'

'Nonsense,' Hen stopped her. 'I wouldn't have brought it over if I didn't want you to wear it.' She held the dress out for Tor.

'Try it on. Try them all on. Have some fun. I'll give you some space to finish getting changed. Come and knock on my door before you go, if you get a minute.'

Tor held the dress up to the light, swaying it from side to side to make the skirts swish, like Julie Andrews with the Von Trapp curtains, then put it back down on the bed. She let her towel drop and stepped into an ice-blue satin full-length gown. It was formal but it puffed out over her tummy – there were too many photographers around for taking a chance on that, she decided. A black wool crêpe dress was sensational and would have made Roland Mouret weep at the artistry, but it was black. A bit . . . blah. She could do better. She picked her way through everything, knowing that it was the dress with the meringue-peaks and sophisticated ivy print that was going to work.

If destiny was a dress, she knew she'd found hers. She stepped into the skirt, breathing in as she did up the zip. There was a small corset inside that whittled her waist away to little more than a handspan, and she looked into the mirror, already knowing what she'd see. It fitted her perfectly – the short sleeves flattering her arms, the bodice shaping her into a siren, her legs looking gloriously slender peeking out from under the full skirt. The colour was just a dream against her hair and she pirouetted across the carpet with delight.

She went into the bathroom and adjusted her make-up. The dress demanded a more elegant face. Rummaging around her make-up bag, she went heavier on the kohl and mascara, and finished with a rare sweep of red lipstick. Thankfully, she had packed some red peep-toes – just in case – and as she moved across the carpet, she felt like a young Grace Kelly.

She stood in front of the mirror for a moment, seeing both her loveliness and loneliness reflected back at her. If only Hugh was with her now . . .

Her phone rang and as she checked her watch – 2 p.m. – she knew the car was waiting for her downstairs. Phew! Chic snatched from the jaws of defeat. It was time to go.

Cress and Mark were already waiting for her in the stretch limo when she got in.

'Oh Cress, you're a vision! Isn't she, Mark?' Tor asked, as she slid along the seat.

Mark nodded. 'She certainly is,' he said, without looking at her.

Cress smiled. She'd twisted her hair back into a chignon and her make-up artist had done a good job of disguising the exhaustion she was carrying. The dress was a great colour on her, though there was no disguising the fact that she'd lost a ton of weight since buying it. Her shoulders were bony and shiny, her collarbone prominent.

'I completely love your dress,' Cress gasped, as Tor fussed with her skirt, trying to prevent it from creasing. 'But – what happened to the Valentino?'

Tor rolled her eyes. 'Forgotten in the rush following a certain last-minute phone call.'

'Eeek,' Cress said quietly. 'Sorry.'

'What's that? What happened?' Mark asked, trying to tune in to the women's girly conversation.

'Doesn't matter,' Tor dismissed. 'It's all turned out well.'

'Did you manage to get through to Amelia's room?' Cress

asked lightly, casting a glance at Mark, who'd taken out his BlackBerry and was checking emails.

'No,' Tor shook her head. 'She's in labour. Sucky timing.'

Cress shrugged. 'Maybe that's a good thing. It'll keep some people otherwise engaged. I'll feel a lot more relaxed once the eyes of the world are upon something else.'

'Mmmm.' She still couldn't believe that James was behind this – that he would somehow sabotage Harry and Cress at the ceremony this afternoon.

Cress brought her shades down and settled back for a doze. Tor looked out of the window and wished she'd brought a book. Everyone at the hotel had said the traffic into the theatre was a nightmare, even though it was so close.

And they were right. Forty minutes later they were still snaking along Sunset Boulevard.

Cress stirred.

'D'you know when Harry's arriving?' Tor asked casually, peering over Mark's shoulder and doing his Sudoku for him.

'Um, after us. His car's picking him up at half past. They let the non-nominees go through first, nice and quickly, so that we don't crowd the carpet and make it look messy.'

The car had stopped moving, and although Tor couldn't see out of the front windscreen – it was about thirty feet away and hidden behind a blackout screen – she knew they were close. The pedestrians and shoppers on the pavements had thickened into crowds and onlookers, and already, still several blocks away from the Kodak theatre, the noise was thunderous.

The pop-glare of the cameras was bright even behind the tinted windows and Cress readjusted her shades.

The screen dividing the passengers from the driver slid down.

'We should be there in four minutes, Mrs Pelling.'

'Mark, it's nearly time to get out,' Cress said. 'You'd better put that away.'

Reluctantly he put away his beloved gadget and loosened his collar with a finger, trying to keep cool. What he'd do to be sitting in front of a Reuter's screen right now. This was not his definition of fun.

'Which beach has Greta taken the children to this afternoon?' Tor asked, distractedly.

Cress shifted uneasily. 'Actually, she hasn't. They're with a nanny from the hotel.'

Tor's eyebrows shot up, her jaw dropped.

'It's OK! It's all under control!' Cress said, putting her hands up. 'There was a discrepancy with some of the names on our list. I had to ask Greta to go ahead and sort it out.' She shrugged. 'I had no choice, Tor. But don't worry, they'll be fine.'

'Oh my God, Cress!' Tor said, trying not to come out in a cold sweat on the dress. 'A complete stranger is looking after my kids? Are you kidding? Quick! Give me your mobile. I've got to call Hen. Hurry. Give it to me!'

Tor looked away, tense, as she made the call.

The car came to a stop and the driver got out, opening their door and letting the noise and lights stream in.

Cress and Mark got out first, while Tor finished talking to Hen.

Hurriedly she slid along the seat on her bottom and swung her ankles out first, and a cheer went up as her red shoes and blonde hair were glimpsed by the crowds. She emerged sleekly, but blinking, into the mid-afternoon sun, like a bear coming out of his cave after the long winter sleep. The applause swept all around her and she could see microphones waving for attention, sheets of paper flapping for her autograph.

She huddled in to Cress and Mark, and they all laughed nervously at the madness engulfing them, as absolute strangers lauded them like stars even though they clearly could have no idea who they were.

A stressed-looking ponytailed woman in a floor-length sequin dress that looked like something Goldie Hawn would have worn ten years ago came up to them, brandishing her clipboard with one hand and holding the tiny mike which was wired round her ear with the other.

'Names, please.'

'Cressida and Mark Pelling; Victoria Summershill. We're with Harry Hunter's party.'

The woman scanned her lists.

'I'm sorry. Could you repeat those names to me?'

'Cressida Pelling; Mark Pelling; Victoria Summershill.'

She looked again, and then shook her head. 'I'm sorry. I don't have you down here. You'll have to step over there, please,' she said, indicating to the crowds.

'What?' Cress said quietly.

'If you could step over there, please.'

'No, no, I couldn't step over there,' Cress said, more loudly. 'Check your list again, please.'

'Your names aren't on the list, ma'am. Please, clear the carpet for the next guests.'

'I am telling you to look again! I am Harry Hunter's publisher. I own Sapphire Books. I own Harry, godammit! If we're not coming in, nor is he.'

'Mr Hunter is already here,' the woman said, standing her ground. She was used to this game. Gatecrashers, getting more sophisticated, more ballsy every year.

'What? But his car's not booked for another twenty minutes!'

The woman said nothing but merely raised her eyebrows, and Tor became aware that two black-suited brick walls had come to stand behind them, just as the crowd let out a huge roar.

Tor swallowed hard and tried, for her children's sake, not to die. It was one thing not to get into the VIP area at Mahiki, or to have your card refused at the service station, or to be kicked off the courts at the Harbour Club because they'd finally realized you weren't a member, but to be turned away from the Oscars in front of all these people, in front of all these cameras, in this lovely dress . . .

'Is there a problem?' inquired a clipped English voice.

Tor, Cress and Mark turned in unison.

'Amelia!' Tor cried. 'But – but I thought you'd gone into labour.'

Amelia stepped forward on the pretext of giving her a kiss. 'Officially speaking I have,' she whispered in Tor's ear. 'But my contractions have worn off and I've reminded James I've technically got another nineteen hours to go before they have to get the baby out. So I'm taking my chances.'

Tor couldn't help but giggle at her nerve. 'Good on you!'

'What's going on here?' James asked, stepping forward.

'Harry bloody Hunter! He's struck us off the guest list,' Cress fumed.

'But you're his publisher!' Amelia exclaimed.

'I am!' Cress shot a stony look at the official. 'I told you I was.'

James' mouth set. 'His latest game?'

'You should know,' Tor thought to herself, as she watched him.

The woman was unmoved. She looked at Amelia. 'I'm sorry, Miss Abingdon, but we have to move these people off the carpet now. NBC are waiting to speak to you.'

Tor caught sight of an emaciated brunette practically going purple trying to get Amelia's attention.

'I want Mrs Pelling's group added to my guest list,' Amelia said firmly.

'I'm sorry, Miss Abingdon, that won't . . .'

'Or I'm turning around and going back to my hotel now. I'm in the middle of having my baby anyhow.'

The official swallowed nervously. Amelia Abingdon was up for Best Actress. There was no way she could walk out now. The producers were expecting her. If she did win, there'd be no one lined up to accept on her behalf.

She turned away and spoke into her mike, her glossy ponytail bouncing around as she barked orders further up the receiving line.

'OK, if you'd like to proceed up the carpet, the officials will show you where to go,' she said finally, a rictus grin stretched across her face.

Cress and Tor breathed the biggest sighs of relief their corsets would possibly allow, while Mark and James shook hands, mutually glad that the prospect of the women going into histrionics had been averted.

'I don't know how to thank you,' Cress said to Amelia, as they started shuffling up the carpet, leaving Tor free to plead with James.

'Just get Tor to design me a nursery and we'll call it quits,' Amelia smiled.

Tor bit her lip as James advanced towards her. He paused for a moment and then bent down to kiss her on each cheek.

'You and I are going to talk. Today,' he said into her ear.

Tor nodded and looked at him. 'Yes. I know.'

James smiled. That had gone better than he'd expected, for once. 'Good,' he said, resting a heavy hand on her waist, just as the party turned on to the main stretch and the crowd went wild, chanting Amelia's name.

Amelia came over and linked her arm through James's. 'Do you mind if I borrow him for a bit?' she smiled, without any trace of sarcasm. 'The photographers want him.'

'Uh . . . yes, yes, of course,' Tor said backing off, her eyes unable to leave James's.

'I'll find you inside,' James said emphatically. 'Don't go anywhere.' He leaned in to her and dropped his voice. 'I can't believe how good you look in that dress. You know, my mother wore that the night she met my father.'

As soon as he said it, she saw that he realized his mistake, but Amelia was already leading him off.

Tor looked on, as Amelia led him away, the realizations rushing forward. That first morning at the market, Hen had said, 'James said it was you.' She couldn't understand it at the time; she'd never met a James Colesbrook. But of course, George Colesbrook was his *step*-father. Tor had assumed Hen had been sent around to her by Kate, but she'd been sent by James. He'd been spying on her all this time.

'Did he say anything?' Cress hissed, coming to her side.

Tor looked at her. 'Hen's his mother,' she said, stunned.

'What?'

But there was no time to extrapolate any further. A couple of minders, picking up on the cheers from the crowd as the two unknowns walked past, hustled them over to the press pits, and the women found themselves giving interviews to E! and Fox, and MTV, talking about their outfits.

Tor had never known anything like it, and yet it was exactly as she'd imagined it would be. As they walked into the lobby of the theatre they paused, adjusting to the steady light (the constant popping of the flashes outside had exacerbated Cress's headache further), and busied themselves with tracking down some flutes of fizzing pink champagne.

Tor tried not to gawp as they walked around the room, circumventing the Who's Who of Hollywood: Quentin Tarantino, Orlando Bloom, Ron Howard, Kate Hudson, Catherine Zeta Jones, Clint Eastwood. She kept her eye on the door, waiting for James to walk through with Amelia. She had to speak to him. Not just about Harry now. About Hen too.

'Christ, this is crazy,' she said, as Cress came and stood next to her, looking into the theatre. The rows of seats were drenched in darkness, serving to amplify the dazzling wattage of light focused on the stage. A dramatic curved staircase was built in the centre of the stage, with huge screens set up on either side; giant, rather gawdy, Oscar statuettes were positioned at each entrance and exit point, pink and gold banners swagged across the ceiling and a small rainforest of flowers festooned from epic planters.

'It's like Centre Court, isn't it?' Tor said to Cress. 'Much smaller than you think it's going to be.'

'Over there!' Cress suddenly hissed, pointing rudely towards a sleek blonde head that was bobbing through the crowd at the far end of the room.

'Who is?' Tor asked quickly, wondering who – in such esteemed company – merited singling out.

'Greta!' And she pushed past Penelope Cruz, after her. She wasn't letting her get away with such shoddy incompetence. Mark could shove his contract where the sun didn't shine. That girl was going – today!

Tor and Mark – for want of anything else to do and feeling rather like lemons anyway – followed, apologizing for all the elbows Cress was jogging as she barged past.

They finally caught up with her by the back stairwell at a fire exit.

'Where's she gone?' Tor gasped, looking around. There was nobody back here, save a few waitresses dashing in and out with trays.

Cress shrugged. 'She definitely came this way. I saw her. Just wait till I get hold of her . . . Correcting that guest-list was precisely why I sent her ahead. The silly cow was supposed to have averted that crisis out there. I mean, supposing Amelia hadn't come along? We'd be sitting on the pavement in our finery, right now.'

'Leave her alone, Cress,' Mark said brusquely. 'It wasn't her fault.'

'Oh, do shut up, Mark,' Cress snapped. 'I'm so not in the mood to indulge your adolescent crush today. Really!'

Mark's jaw clenched and he blushed like a schoolboy, but he said nothing.

Tor looked at Cress, not wanting to get caught in the middle of a domestic. 'Cress, I um . . . I really need to go and find James. I'll just . . .'

She tipped her head towards the corner, just as Kate came around it, one hand on her bump, and looking frantic. Kate carried on a few paces before she saw the group. She stopped abruptly, but unless she turned on her heel, there was nowhere else to go.

Slowly she walked up to them, the silk jersey of her strapless jade Versace dress beautifully encasing her tight tummy, a high slit making a feature of her legs. She had let her hair grow long again, and was wearing a stunning emerald collar.

Though her jewellery collection had always been impressive, it had moved into another bracket altogether since she had hooked up with Harry.

'Hello,' she said cautiously, feeling conspicuously outnumbered.

Mark looked distinctly uncomfortable as he sensed the electric tension between the women.

'Kate,' Cress said evenly.

'Hi, Kate,' Tor said, hoping to neutralize Cress's combative tone. 'You look amazing.'

'No Harry?' Cress asked.

'No, I was just looking for him. I can't find him. I've looked everywhere.'

'Have you checked under all the rocks?'

Kate's eyes narrowed as she squared up. If Cress thought pregnancy had made her go soft, she could think again.

'Was getting us knocked off the guest list your idea or his?' Cress continued. 'What was it – payback for the photographs?'

Kate bit her lip – she had no idea what Harry was up to now; another of his secrets – and looked around the room again. She saw Amelia Abingdon walking in, looking flushed and luscious, draped in whimsical white silk tulle with a red velvet ribbon beneath her bust, ruby and diamond pendant earrings dangling daintily from her ears. She did a double-take when she saw James follow her in, looking distracted as he scanned the crowd. Was he looking for Harry?

There was a sudden kerfuffle inside one of the storecupboards, and two Gucci-clad security men leapt forward.

'Oooh, she might know,' Cress said, spotting a waitress coming out of a door.

'Excuse me,' she said accosting the woman. 'Have you seen a young blonde girl back here, pretty, skinny?'

The waitress's eyes skimmed the room in recognition. 'Um, ma'am, could you be more specific? Most of the women here, uh – look like that. Do you know what she was wearing?'

'No, no, I – I could only see her head. Oh, hang on – Mark!' she called, motioning for him to come over. 'Mark, do you remember what Greta was wearing when she left to come here?'

'Yes,' he said, without pause. 'A mid-length cobalt blue dress with sleeves.'

Cress looked at him. 'But – that's my new dress. For the party tomorrow night.'

'Well, I told her to quickly choose something of yours to put on . . . What?' he said, hands up. 'She couldn't very well turn up here, trying to get us back on the guest list, in jeans, could she?'

One of the security guards burst open the door to the cupboard violently, the other one's gun trained on . . .

'I'm sorry, ma'am, I must get back,' the waitress said to Cress, indicating her tray. 'These will be getting cold. But I haven't seen anyone in a blue dress like that today. I'm sorry.'

Cress spun round to face Mark.

'Mid-length? Cobalt blue? What are you, a bloody fashion editor? Since when did you ever know that cobalt is even a colour?' Cress demanded.

But Mark wasn't listening. He was staring into the cupboard, his mouth open.

For there, inside, was Harry enfolded in Greta's long legs, his trousers down around his ankles, Cress's new dress crumpled up around Greta's waist.

Chapter Fifty-four

'Oh my God,' Cress whispered, hardly able to believe what she was seeing.

She looked over at Kate, whose view of the couple was obscured only by the door. Two paces and she'd see them. The security guards made a swift and silent exit, once they realized that etiquette, and not security, had been breached. Mark – who looked as if he'd just had a stroke – didn't move, so Cress ran to the door.

'You're fired!' she hissed, and slammed it shut.

'Ladies and gentlemen, please take your seats. The ceremony for the Academy Awards will begin in three minutes,' intoned a smooth voice through the loudspeakers.

Cress quickly opened the cupboard again. 'Not you,' she hissed hatefully at Harry ... 'You!' Greta quivered under her glare. 'And I want that bloody dress back dry-cleaned.'

'Shit, where is he?' Kate muttered, looking around the room. 'This isn't funny.'

'You'd better take your seat, Kate,' Cress said, all animosity suddenly forgotten. Whatever professional rivalry had passed between them, Kate didn't deserve to find Harry like that. 'He's probably in the loos or something. He's probably even sitting down wondering where you are. Let's face it, the vain pig's not going to miss an opportunity to put his face on global telly, is he?'

She tried to guide Kate away from the hallway, but Kate just stared at her suspiciously. What was with the volte-face?

Cress tried the distraction method Tor was so good at. 'Oh look, is that Julia Roberts?'

Kate followed her point to Julianne Moore, and burst out laughing. 'God, your star-spotting is even worse than your cooking, Cress,' Kate said without thinking.

Tor smiled hopefully as she felt the women's chemistry momentarily reassert itself.

Cress stuck her chin in the air. 'Yuh, well actually, I do a pretty mean boeuf en croûte these days. You've been missing out. You're not the only one who's had things going on, you know.'

Kate smiled in spite of herself. God, she'd missed their sparring.

'Ladies and gentlemen, this is the two-minute call. Kindly take your seats.'

'Come on, Cress, we'd better go,' Mark said. 'We've got no idea where we're sitting.'

'Actually, you're next to us,' Kate said, shrugging. 'I saw your names on the chairs.'

Kate turned to lead them all to their seats, just as a flash of dishevelled cobalt streaked out of the storecupboard, to be followed by an unruly mop of blond curls beginning to emerge from behind the door.

Her heart stopped, her breath caught and the baby kicked, but her feet carried on where her courage failed and she found herself turning on her heel.

*

They were all seated towards the front in the centre aisle, with Harry – as a nominee – given the aisle seat. The card lollipop with a picture of Harry was still on his chair.

'Here you are,' Kate said numbly, nodding for the people who were 'filling' the gaps in the crowd to leave. Cress and Tor and Mark waited for them to come out of the aisle, and Tor, although acutely aware that she was blocking Charlize Theron's view, scanned the crowd desperately for James.

'You first, Tor,' Cress said. She wanted to be sure she was near to Harry. She didn't trust him. There was no way she was letting him up on that stage without her, although she realized she'd have to navigate her way past Kate and that rather big bump first.

They took their seats, fidgeting about a bit. 'How long does this go on for, by the way?' Tor whispered to Cress.

'Four hours.'

Tor paused. 'You're kidding! Are there any breaks?' she asked, loading the question with significance.

'It's OK. They stop for commercial breaks. You can escape to the loo then,' Cress said, missing the point. She was still fired up about Greta. The lights along the aisles dimmed suddenly and Harry dashed into his seat, smoothing down his jacket.

He joined in with the clapping as Chris Rock, this year's host, ran out on to the stage, arms aloft. Running an insouciant hand through his floppy hair, he leaned over and kissed Kate on the cheek.

'Sorry, baby.'

'You bastard!' she hissed, feeling the tears run down her cheeks. 'How could you?'

'Hey, relax. I just got stuck in the men's loos. I ran into Steven and we went over a couple of details about the financing for the next film. It's no big de— Shit, smile, you're on camera!' he said, clapping and fixing a beaming grin across his face, just as the cameras found him and Kate and their image was beamed around the world.

Fifteen hundred miles away in Chicago, Monty swallowed hard. He had rescheduled all his meetings so that he could watch the ceremony in the hope of catching glimpses of Kate. He gazed at her glittering eyes, her trembling mouth and thought he'd never seen her look so beautiful. Or so unhappy.

The next twenty-five minutes were the longest of Kate's life as she tried to dam down the pain and stem her rising panic. This couldn't be what she thought it was. It couldn't be. She was only six months.

Another wave hit her, and she took a deep breath as she felt the heat soar and the squeeze grip and twist. Her tummy felt like rock. Had she been standing, she was sure her knees would have buckled under her.

As the lights finally went up for the commercial break, Kate staggered to her feet and pushed past Harry, rushing towards the lobby, holding on to the chairs, oblivious to the concerned stares of the illustrious crowd.

'Kate! Come back! Where're you going?' Harry called after her, just as Will Smith stopped by to say hello. 'Oh, hi mate, how's it going?'

She got into the lobby and looked around frantically, fat, noisy sobs finally escaping her. She had to get some air. See some daylight. She . . .

'It's OK, Kate, come with me,' a calm voice said. 'You need to stay sitting down.'

Kate spun round and looked at James.

'I was watching you in the theatre . . . Here,' he said, checking her pulse. 'Let me check you over. Just try to calm down for me.'

Tor rushed up, skirts rustling, her cheeks flushed with panic.

'James!' She took in Kate's slumped form. 'What's going on?'

'Tor, I need you to get Kate some water.'

Tor flagged down a passing waiter, demanding a 'still water for the pregnant lady!' as though it were a life-or-death situation. She turned back and saw the pain cross Kate's face as another contraction took hold. Her mascara had streaked and she'd got hiccups from all the crying. She looked a mess. What the hell had happened in there? She'd been fine before they went in.

'Oh my God, is she going into labour?' Tor asked, rummaging in her clutch for a travel pack of tissues. She took one out and carefully bent over Kate, gently cleaning away the black tracks.

James shook his head, his hand laid across the top of her tight tummy. The last thing he needed was two women in labour – he'd be pulling a baby out with one hand and holding a baby in with the other. 'No, but she's having some pretty severe Braxton Hicks. Kate, I really need you to calm down for me, OK? Can you tell me what's happened? What's upset you?'

Kate shook her head, crying harder again. 'I can't . . .'

'She needs to lie down,' James said, looking around for one of the multitude of officials. He found an Armani-suited clipboard carrier. 'Excuse me, I'm a doctor. I need to find somewhere for this lady to lie down. Do you have a private room we can use?'

The official took in Kate's pregnancy, hysterics and tepid pallor, but still hesitated. 'There is, but . . . I'll need to get security approval on this first, sir.'

'Oh, for heaven's sake,' James muttered, mortified that of all the names he was going to have to drop . . . 'She's Harry Hunter's girlfriend. Would you like to explain to him your-self that you left his girlfriend labouring in the lobby?'

That decided it.

'Please come this way, sir,' and he led the trio up the back stairs to a small manager's office.

Tor took in the room, her nose wrinkling in disgust at the highly flammable-looking sofa and grey nylon carpet tiles. Her hair felt static just at the thought of it all. The whole space was windowless, airless, tasteless. She watched James as he authoritatively moved across the room, switching on the electric fan on the desk and positioning it towards Kate.

Kate felt the breeze cool her skin and she instantly felt her body relax a little, the contractions begin to ebb. She closed her eyes and tried not to see Harry emerge from the broom cupboard with Greta again.

James came back to her and sat on the edge of the sofa. He opened his doctor's bag and took her temperature and pulse again.

'Good. That's good, Kate,' he soothed. 'Just stay still.'

Kate opened her eyes and looked at him. 'Why is it that every time I cast you in my mind as the villain, you go and do something heroic?' she said furiously.

James gave a wry smile. 'You know I'm neither.'

'I don't, actually,' she said contrarily – she hadn't forgotten his lies to her and Monty – and then paused. 'Although I do know you didn't shop us to the papers.'

James, who was reaching into his bag, hesitated, then sat back up and looked at her sombrely.

'How do you know?'

She shrugged lightly. 'I remembered telling a little girl in Barbados on Christmas Day. How sad is that? Shopped by a six-year-old!' She shook her head sadly. 'I told Harry, but he doesn't care, James. He wants you to take the fall for it anyway. He's determined to destroy your career.'

James dropped his eyes, his mouth set in a grim line.

'I see.' He looked back at her. 'Why are you telling me this?'

Kate took a deep breath. 'Because it's over. He's been lying to me, cheating on me.' Her eyes filled with tears again, and Tor automatically reached for a clean tissue. 'I lost my job and he absolutely loved telling me that.' She began to sob. 'He's just been using me all along.'

'Using you for what?' James asked quietly.

Kate looked up at him. 'To undermine Cress; to break up what he saw as her power base, to make her weak.'

James frowned. 'Why would he do that? She's his publisher.' He began rummaging in his bag for the sphyg-momanometer.

Tor stepped forward, taking his distraction as proof of guilt. 'I think you know why, James.'

James stopped and looked at her. Tor? Why was she getting involved with Harry's dramas?

'You sent the manuscript to Cress, James. I know you did. It must have been sent originally to George, yes?' Learning that Hen was James's mother had made all the other connections fall into place. 'He was the top literary agent at the time, right?'

'What manuscript is this?' Kate cut in, flummoxed that Tor was involved. So Harry had been right about that – it wasn't just James and Cress. It had been the lot of them, against him. Maybe she'd been wrong about him. Maybe there was still hope.

'Brendan Hillier's.'

'Hillier?' That name again.

Tor nodded. 'He wrote *Scion*. You didn't know?'

All hope was dashed. Kate shook her head, numbly. 'I knew that Harry was being blackmailed by James and Cress about something. And I knew a Hillier person was involved. But I didn't know how.'

Tor shrugged. 'Because Harry didn't want you to find out he's a thief and a fraud. That his entire fortune and reputation has been built on lies.'

Kate sank back into the sofa, feeling another contraction build. This was all too much to handle. Harry's infidelity, his lies, right from the very beginning . . .

Tor looked back at James. 'But why are you involved in this, James? Why do you hate him so much? And what on earth were you thinking getting Cress involved?' she asked, her voice quiet. 'Surely you would have known she'd never do the right thing? She's not like the other yummy mummies in your waiting-room.'

James stared at her, his jaw clenched, furious she was involved; furious she was judging him.

He got up and walked across the room, staring at the plastic wall panels, battling the urge to talk with the lifelong habit of bearing the secret.

Slowly, he turned around and met her eyes.

'I gave it to Cress, because I couldn't do it myself,' he said finally. 'I couldn't risk putting myself in the middle of a scandal like that. It would have been too high-profile. It would have jeopardized my position.'

Tor shrugged, not following him.

'With the royal family? My family's connection with them is long and valued. I had to be utterly discreet. As for Cress, she was far from my first choice with all this, believe me. When *Scion* was published, I went straight to Hillier's estate, telling them everything I knew. But I heard nothing back. The years were passing and Hunter was signing film deals, amassing a fortune, a reputation, on another man's talent.'

'Then I remembered Cress was a publisher. I thought she'd know what to do – that she'd do the right thing.' He snorted. 'I should have known the temptation would have been too much.'

There was a sudden bundle of red as Cress burst in through the door.

'Speak of the devil,' James said, raking a hand through his hair and turning away again.

'There you are! I've been looking all over. One of the officials said the baby's coming – is it?' she asked Kate.

Kate shook her head.

Cress took in the stony silence.

'What's – what's going on?' she asked nervously, looking at James's back.

'Where've you been?' Tor exclaimed, agitated. 'I've been trying to negotiate on your behalf.'

'Negotiate? You make me sound like a bloody terrorist,' James said, whirling around and losing his temper.

But he was drowned out by even louder shouting down the hall.

'Where is she? Tell me where she is or I'll have your bloody job!'

Kate instantly recoiled into a ball, her blood pressure rocketing again as she heard Harry bullying the staff.

'Don't let him in,' she whispered, urgently.

James sprang across the room to shut the door, but Harry was already there.

He paused for a long moment when he saw the assembled group.

'White! I should have known. And what's your bloody excuse this time?' he thundered as he saw Kate cowering on the sofa. 'Come to get your latest press release?'

James – forced to walk back – came to an abrupt halt. The two men stood square on, their faces inches away from each other. 'You know damn well those stories never came from me . . .'

'Don't, Harry!' Kate said, trying to get up, but another rising contraction stopped her. Tor ran over to her friend.

Harry ignored her.

' . . . Do I, White? I don't think I know anything of the sort,' he lied badly, deliberately. 'I think you've been the snitch all along and I intend to make sure you pay for it.'

A snarl curled his upper lip and he dropped his voice. 'Your reputation, your career – they're mine now, and I'm going to savage them – just like you've been trying to do with mine.'

James regarded him with contempt. 'You don't have a career of your own, Hunter. You've had to steal someone else's. Ride piggyback on another man's talent. Tell me, just how small do you really feel inside when you go to bed at night – knowing that none of it's rightfully yours?'

Harry gave a short laugh. 'The only thing I'm feeling inside when I go to bed at night is your women. The French bird . . . Anna . . .' He whistled. 'Christ, she's a real wildcat, isn't she?'

Tor gasped and looked at James. He saw her hand fly

to her mouth and looked over at her. Their eyes met, and she could see instantly the betrayal written all over his face.

'. . . The delectable Amelia,' he sneered. 'Well, not yet, but she's on my list . . .' Kate closed her eyes, feeling revulsed as she realized that Greta couldn't possibly have been the first, or only, betrayal.

'. . . And of course, sweet Lily . . .'

James looked back at Harry and threw a right hook that caught him by surprise and sent him sprawling across the room, just missing Kate by inches. She screamed, and Tor and Cress bundled her up from the sofa, dragging her to relative safety behind the desk.

Harry smiled. 'I guess I deserved that.' He got a hand-kerchief out of his pocket and shook it open, pressing it against the open cut on his lip.

He looked back at James, sarcasm dripping all over him.

'But you're on the mat and I'm counting you out, your lordship. Your days of looking at pussy for a living are over.'

The tannoys crackled into life.

'Ladies and gentlemen, please return to your seats. The ceremony will continue in four minutes.'

Harry turned towards Kate and pulled her away from the girls by her elbow.

'Come on, babe. Let's get back to the real action. I've got an Oscar to collect. Can't be standing in a broom cupboard, chatting.'

'Get off me, Harry . . .' Kate protested, the image of him in the storecupboard, shagging, filling her head again. After everything he'd just said, how could he possibly think she'd . . . ? But he ignored her, pulling her away, triumphant and invincible.

He was at the door when James spoke.

'He's not the father.'

There was a stunned silence, as all eyes fell to Kate's bump, and then swivelled back to James.

'What did you say?' Kate whispered.

'I said he's not the father of your baby,' James replied coolly, his eyes steady. 'He can't have children.'

Harry laughed. 'Oh! And where did you get that little medical nugget from, White? Tell me, are you intending to sell that to the papers too?'

'Shut up, Hunter,' Kate hissed viciously. She wanted to hear what James had to say.

'He's sterile.' James was stock still, his hands thrust into his pockets.

Harry stopped laughing. Kate was lost in her thoughts, her own words flooding her memory from that day in Harley Street: '. . . *it is strange though, that there haven't been any paternity claims against you. God knows, there's been enough opportunity. You've hardly been discriminating . . .*' His lack of interest in the baby, how little he'd cared about the *Sun* revealing its sex, his revulsion at her pregnant body . . . it all made sense.

'You knew all along the baby wasn't yours,' she said, turning towards him, her voice low. Her emeralds glittered underneath the strip lights and she looked strong and powerful, like Cleopatra.

Harry looked at her, momentarily taken aback by the change in her demeanour. She was the old Kate again – challenging, prickly, superior – the Kate who had excited him so much, back before he'd broken and domesticated her.

He shrugged. The game was up. 'Vasectomy.'

Kate swallowed. 'And you were going to bring her up as yours?'

'No. I was never going to do that. I knew I wouldn't need you by then.'

Her eyes widened. 'You wouldn't *need* me by then?'

'Conflict of interest, Kate. I knew if I secured you, she couldn't.' He nodded towards Cress. 'It was that simple. Besides, I wondered whether you knew what she was up to, and who was pulling her strings. You girls were a tight unit. I thought some pillow talk and jewels might loosen your tongue, but I'd overestimated your friendship. It folded pretty quickly, let's face it.'

Kate's cheeks burned with shame. He was right. She knew she'd abandoned her friends almost overnight, bundling them together with Monty's faithlessness.

'And – and us?'

He winked and flashed her a dazzling smile. 'Consider it a bonus.'

'You sonofabitch!' she cried, slapping him so hard around the face she left a handprint like a port wine stain on his cheek.

He grabbed her wrist, holding it in a vice grip, his jaw tight, his eyes flashing dangerously. She saw his instinct to smack her back cross his face and she recoiled, terrified. But her fear seemed to satisfy him and he threw her wrist down.

'Don't do that, sweetheart,' he said, rubbing the sting. 'I need to look pretty up on that stage tonight.' He stared at her for a moment, unmoved by the tears in her eyes. 'We'll dispense with the emotional goodbyes, shall we?'

He walked back towards the door.

'It wasn't a vasectomy,' he heard James say to Kate. 'The medical term for it is epididymo-orchitis, a form of secondary infertility. In Harry's case, caused as a result of a devastating blow to the groin.'

Harry turned back and the two men looked at each other, both recognizing the killer blow that was about to be thrown.

'In his instance, delivered by my sister,' James said. 'Right after he raped her.'

Chapter Fifty-five

No one in the room spoke. They hardly dared blink.

'. . . Would all nominees please return to their seats. The ceremony will continue in two minutes . . .'

James looked at Harry. 'Feel free to go, Harry. I can carry on for you here.'

Harry looked at him, the cocky grin no longer decorating his face, his eyes hooded and simmering.

There was a pause. 'No. I'm more entertained by what you've got to say, White,' he said flatly. 'I haven't had so much fun in years.'

There was a tap at the door, and a minion with clipboard and headpiece coughed uncomfortably.

'Excuse me, Mr Hunter, but you are requested to take your seat, sir. The ceremony is about to begin again.' He peered around nervously at the assembled group.

'Fuck off,' Harry sneered. 'I'm busy.'

'I'm sorry, sir, but you can't stay up here. Your category will be announced soon and we need all nominees to be back in their seats.'

Harry glared at the meek messenger. 'Fine!' he said finally. 'I'll be down in a minute.'

Harry waited for the sound of the messenger's footsteps to disappear down the hall, before he looked back at James.

'She was up for it. You can't prove otherwise,' Harry said menacingly.

'Not sixteen years later, no,' James said flatly. 'But she was fifteen, you were nineteen. At the very least it's another statutory rape charge against you. The British public is already finding your predilection for underage girls unsavoury, to say the least.'

'She was a little tease.'

'No,' James countered, his voice rising slightly. 'She was a little girl, interested in ponies and gymnastics. She thought of you as a brother.'

Harry began to pace. 'You're just bluffing, clutching at straws. You expect me to believe you've had access to my medical records? That's another sackable offence, White.'

'No. I've never had access to your records. But I did have lunch at the club with George, just before he died. He gave me an old manuscript he'd been holding on to for fifteen years.'

Harry shrugged, incredulous. 'And? So what? What's that got to do with anything?'

'He told me everything. How you stole Brendan Hillier from him. Even though you'd been there when he came out of the study with the manuscript. Even though you went down to the cellar yourself to get the Château Lafite for him, knowing full well he had vowed never to open it until he had just cause to celebrate. You lived with us long enough, Hunter – it was no secret how badly he was affected by Lloyds. He lost everything. And *Scion* was going to restore it all again.

'And why shouldn't it have? It was his right to prosper from it. He'd discovered Canterman, Faulkner. He was the best there was. Of course Hillier would have gone straight to him.

'But you? A cocky little upstart with a chip on your shoulder about your free passage through school? You thought you'd take him on yourself. Why not? It couldn't be that hard surely. If George Colesbrook thought he was a sure thing . . .'

Harry shook his head, tutting.

'Your story's flawed, White. Tu casa, mi casa. Why would I bite the hand that fed me?'

James stared straight at him, seeming to grow four inches taller.

'Because Anna chose me. And you couldn't bear it.' He laughed humourlessly, his hands on his hips. He looked at Kate. 'Can you believe it? That was what it all came down to.' He looked back at Harry. 'The dreadful – cataclysmic – event that compelled you to turn on the family that had treated you as one of their own. You took Lily to the tree-house that night – the night of my first date with Anna – because you couldn't stand that she had chosen me over you.'

He looked at his feet. 'You grabbed her childhood and crushed it, and then you terrorized her – threatening to hurt her if she told anyone.' James's voice broke, and when he looked up, Tor could see that the rims of his eyes were red and shining. 'What kind of animal are you?' he asked disgustedly.

Kate felt a wave of nausea rise up and clamped a hand to her mouth, scanning around for a bin. She couldn't believe she'd got so close to this man, actually loved him. How could she have got it so wrong?

She felt a hand on her shoulder. It was Tor, tears streaming down her cheeks. 'Are you OK?' she whispered.

Kate nodded, ashamed.

'I'm sorry, Kate,' James said, looking at her. 'I realize this must be hard for you to hear.'

Kate shook her head. 'I want to hear it. Every last bit of it. Because then I will do whatever I can to make sure he pays for it.'

James said nothing but looked back at Harry, one eyebrow cocked.

'It took my parents all night to get her to tell them who had done this to her. It didn't cross their minds that it could have been you. She was traumatized, wouldn't let them call the police. She threatened to run away if they involved them.'

He took a deep breath, as if trying to draw on some inner strength, inner control. He looked back at Kate.

'Anyway, the next morning, Harry rolled back in, thinking she'd kept his secret. He actually pretended to be falling back in from a night on the tiles. Can you imagine? He raped my sister and then came back for breakfast? George confronted him and told him to leave. But Harry guessed Lily's fear and called his bluff, threatening to tell everyone they'd been carrying on unless George let him represent Hillier himself. George just let him – he'd have done anything to be rid of him.'

'All this is an interesting idea for a novel,' Harry said carelessly. 'But it actually doesn't go any way into explaining your supposed access to my medical records.'

James stared at him for a moment, contempt written all over his face.

'Lily was covered in bruises when she came home. She'd clearly fought you tooth and nail. So George went to the hospital that night. He knew from the severity of Lily's injuries that you must have been hurt to some degree, and he wanted

525

to see if anything was incriminating. He was still hoping he could persuade Lily to report you to the police. You were sleeping when the nurses brought him to you, so you never knew.'

'Now I know you're lying,' Harry sneered. 'They would never have given him access like that. He wasn't my next of kin, there's no way they . . .'

The look on James's face stopped him.

'Did you never stop to wonder why you came to stay with us so regularly, Harry? You didn't find my family's kindness and generosity towards you – undeserved?'

Harry visibly paled as he slowly absorbed the insinuation.

'That's right,' James said slowly. 'Freud would have had a field day with you.'

He watched a muscle in Harry's face twitch.

'I can see this is all news to you. That's interesting. We sometimes wondered whether you had guessed – you attached yourself to us so readily, like a limpet.'

'We – we're not brothers, White.' But Harry was pale and waxy.

'Only through marriage. But trust me, the idea's more diabolical from where I'm standing,' James sneered. 'Your mother, Vivian, was George's first wife. She had multiple sclerosis, which worsened dramatically following your birth. She and George were unable to cope so they gave you up to the Hunters, old friends of theirs who were unable to have children.'

Harry started pacing the floor, his hands clenching and unclenching into fists.

'Vivian died when you were three, but George stayed in regular contact with the Hunters, keeping up with what you were up to. When Janet Hunter died in that car accident when you were – what? fourteen? – it was agreed that you would stay with us during the holidays and start to be brought into the fold. They thought it would soften the blow if you had already made emotional attachments with us. George had planned to tell you that summer . . .'

There was a long silence as Harry grappled with the enormity of James's words.

His hands flew up to his temples, grabbing his hair, disappearing in the curls.

'No!' he suddenly burst out angrily, slamming a fist against the wall. 'I don't believe any of this. You're fucking with the truth because I got it on with Lily.'

'I know why you raped Lily; I know why you stole from your father; and I know – why – you're – sterile,' James said contemptuously, letting the insult to his virility hang between them.

James shook his head.

'I'll hand it to you, though. You made the last five minutes of fertility count. It was another five months before we realized Lily was pregnant.'

'Bullshit!' Harry exploded, rushing forward and grabbing James by the collar, but James, quicker than him – stronger, angrier – threw him up against the wall, knocking him off his feet with a solid punch to the nose.

'Jesus!' Harry cried, unsteady on his feet, as blood poured down his nose and on to his shirt. 'You've broken my nose!'

James stared down at him, his face flushed, his eyes wild. Finally, after all the years of containment, he'd struck back.

His voice was flinty when he finally spoke.

'Would you like to know your son's name, Harry?'

Kate gasped, her hands flying to her mouth.

'Billy,' she whispered.

James pulled his eyes away from Harry and faced Kate. She deserved a fuller explanation after all the damage this had done to her. 'Yes. I'm sorry, Kate, that you and Monty have been caught in the crossfire of all this. Monty and Lily did have a brief relationship immediately afterwards, but Lily was – well, they would diagnose it as post-traumatic stress disorder nowadays. Poor Monty didn't know what had hit him. Lily was on a mission to cover Hunter's tracks and she saw Monty as her decoy.

'Please understand, when she asked the family to name Monty as the father, we couldn't refuse her. She was trying to overwrite the pregnancy with a better reality. She's never really recovered from what happened. She was convinced she'd brought it upon herself, and nothing we ever said could convince her otherwise.'

'Poor, poor Lily,' Kate whispered, her eyes bright with tears. No wonder she wouldn't see Monty or discuss it rationally with him.

'There's something I don't get, though,' Cress said, rousing herself from her uncharacteristic silence. 'If Hunter took the book from George saying he was going to represent him himself, why has the book been published in Harry's name and not Hillier's?'

James's eyes narrowed as he watched Harry.

'I can only guess at that. George died a couple of weeks after telling me all this and *Scion* was published a few months later. When I saw Hunter's name on the cover, I looked into tracking down Hillier myself. It turned out he'd died the same week you went to sign him, Hunter . . .'

'What? You're accusing me of having a hand in his death now? Rape and theft's not enough? You want to add murder to the list? My lawyers are going to have a field day with you . . .'

'You don't have any, remember?' Kate muttered.

Harry shot her a dark look, but carried on. 'Is there anything you won't accuse me of?'

'Is there anything you won't do?' James shot back.

He had no answer to that.

'Whatever the circumstances of Hillier's death, I can only assume Harry saw an opportunity to take all the glory and not just a fifteen per cent cut.'

He looked back at Harry.

'My guess is you became a teacher simply as a cover for passing the time while you waited for George – your witness – to die, knowing you'd shoot to fame and fortune the second he was gone. When the book did indeed come out – under your name – I wrote a letter to Hillier's solicitors, asking them to forward it to Hillier's heir. It detailed everything you'd done, Hunter. Stealing from George. Stealing from Hillier himself.'

'So what happened?' Cress asked.

James shrugged.

'I didn't hear anything. I found out later the family were living abroad. So I decided to send George's copy of the manuscript to you. I thought you'd do the right thing.'

Cress hung her head in abject sorrow.

'I am so, so, so, so sorry James. I – I don't know what to say. If I'd had any idea . . .'

James looked at her.

'If I'd had any idea your morality needed conditions attached, I wouldn't have bothered,' James said, tersely.

Cress looked back down. She deserved that. She deserved everything that was coming to her.

There was another knock at the door. This time, a whole team of officials moved into the room.

'We really need you in your seat now, Mr Hunter. The awards have recommenced.' In the background, they could hear the orchestra in full flow. 'And if your wife's not having the baby after all, we need this room back, sir.'

Harry saw his chance. He had to get the hell out of there.

'Well, I need a new fucking shirt!' he hollered at a pretty clipboarder and marched towards the door, before spinning around and pointing a finger at James. 'I'm not through with you, White,' he threatened. 'You'd better come up with some evidence to prove any of that bullshit, because after this, being struck off will be the last of your worries. Do you hear me?'

And he whirled out of the room, buttons popping as he ripped off his bloodied shirt, like Rambo in black tie.

There was a stunned silence at his enduring arrogance and audacity. How could he still shout them down in the face of his own appalling ruthlessness?

Only one person could find their voice.

'So what now?' Tor asked.

'What do you mean?' James turned to look at her. He was shattered, physically drained by the showdown, sixteen years of seething contempt expelled in a tacky backroom in Los Angeles.

'What are you going to do with the *Scion* manuscript, now that you've got it back? Are you going to implicate Cress too?'

James frowned.

'I don't have the manuscript back.'

'But – Cress's room. It was trashed.'

There was a pause. James stiffened. 'And you think I did that?'

'Well . . . yes. Of course.'

'Why of course?'

'Because everything points to it.'

'Everything?'

'Yes – the hideous painting from the auction . . .'

'You loved that painting!' he cut in, hurt written all over his face.

'No, not that one,' she said quickly. 'The Orion picture, you know, with the threat attached – "Freedom is but the distance between . . . the . . . hunter . . . and the hunted",' she said, faltering, her voice tailing off.

'The threat?' James said quietly, his eyes dark and intent. 'I see.'

Tor swallowed hard beneath his scrutiny. 'Are you saying . . . ?'

'That it's nothing to do with me? Yes. I am,' he said. His voice was cold and hard now. 'Much to your bitter disappointment, I'm sure. I'm sorry not to live down to your low expectations of me.'

'That's not true,' Tor protested, taken aback by his sarcasm.

'Admit it, Tor! You're always so ready to cast me as the villain, as some evil bastard who's out to destroy your life and your friends. You're on the constant lookout for ammunition to hate me further. The simple truth is you don't want to think well of me because you're never going to forgive me for what I did that night. For the one time in my life, I went with my instinct. I wanted you and no! I didn't care if it meant I came between you and your husband. And as a direct result, he's dead. And I have to live with that.'

He sighed. 'But you're not interested that I'm as devastated as you about the role I've played. I have tried to make it up to you. I've wanted to look after you, start a new life

531

with you. But how can I when you can't bear the sight of me?'

And without another word, he strode out of the room, sending the minions out on the hallway scattering like skittles in his wake.

Chapter Fifty-six

Tor stood in his backdraught, shaking like a leaf. Furious and wretched all at once.

'Did you hear that?' she cried, half-laughing, as hysteria began to take a hold. 'He wanted to start a new life with me. He's responsible for destroying my old life and he's standing there talking about setting up home with me. Oh my God!' she cackled, the laughs turning into sobs as Kate and Cress ran over to her and put their arms around her.

'He's gone, he's really gone,' she sobbed.

A rush of static interrupted them as the posse of officials collected themselves off the floor and gathered at the doorway.

'We need to clear this room now, ladies.'

'Of course,' Cress stammered, shepherding Tor and Kate – who was still clutching her belly – out of the room.

They were just at the stairs when one of the officials called them back.

'Uh, ladies, you forgot your bags.' He was holding up Tor's clutch, and James's gladstone.

'Oh, thanks,' Cress said, running back down the hall to get them, her fingers fumbling as he handed them over. The two bags dropped to the floor. Tor's was clasped shut but James's stethoscope, sphygmomanometer and medical notes went everywhere.

'Shit! Shit! My fault,' Cress said, stooping down to pick everything up. She grabbed the notes into a rough pile and slid them back in, her eyes falling on a stray envelope that had wafted down the corridor.

'Tor, can you just grab that,' she called, while grappling with the stethoscope like an unlucky snake charmer.

Tor walked along the corridor, sniffing and hiccupping, and picked it up.

'There you go,' she said.

'Thanks,' Cress said, going to put it in the bag.

She stopped.

'Uh . . . Tor?'

'Mmmmm?' Tor hiccupped.

'Have a look at this.' Cress turned the envelope over and handed it back to Tor. Tor stared at the company logo printed on the front.

'Can you think of any reason at all why James White should be receiving letters from Planed Spaces?'

The ceremony was in full swing again and Chris Rock was back on stage, introducing Clint Eastwood to present the Best Director award.

'I'm afraid there's no admittance when we're taping, ladies. You'll have to wait for the next break,' said the official at the door.

Cress rolled her eyes. 'God, Mark'll be going spare. I told him I was only popping to the loo. He's got Scarlett Johansson on his other side. I swear he kept forgetting how to breathe.'

'It's OK. He knows you'll be back in the next break,' Kate said easily. She dropped her voice a bit. 'Why don't you go and get Tor a drink? She needs one.'

'I'd have thought you would too, Kate,' Cress countered. She was taking the break-up remarkably well.

Kate smiled, rather surprised herself. 'Actually, I've never felt better. And I will have one. I'll join you in a minute. I've just got to make a phone call.'

Cress nodded knowingly and moved Tor towards the bar. Kate walked over towards the main doors. She pulled her mobile out of her bag and dialled.

She waited and redialled but there was still no reply. Bugger.

She went back and joined the girls. They'd ordered champagne spritzers and were watching the event relayed on huge plasmas.

'Quite odd, really,' Kate mused, picking up her glass. 'To be at the Oscars, but still watching them on telly.'

'Don't let the folks back home know. We'll never hear the end of it,' Cress muttered distractedly. She was biting her nails, agitated that Harry was in there and she was out here.

After the revelations upstairs she was still no nearer to knowing who'd stolen back the *Scion* manuscript. If not Harry himself, and not James – despite having sent it to her in the first place – then who? And why had they stolen it now? Why had she been made to bring it out here? She bit her cheek anxiously. It had to be something to do with tonight. The timing couldn't be coincidence. The eyes of the world were on them. Harry was going to be exposed, here, at the Oscars. And quite probably Cress along with him.

'So – give me the scoop, Cress,' Kate asked, oblivious to her friend's ongoing drama. 'Tell me all about your new super-author. I've been dying to ask. *The Wrong Prince* has been strictly *verboten* in our household. I had to smuggle in a copy and keep it in my knicker drawer! Even just the mention of it drove Harry into a howling rage. He's been driven demented seeing you on telly everywhere, talking it up. He's convinced the whole anonymity issue is just a media ploy to fan up the hype.'

Cress snorted.

'Huh, I wish! I'm afraid I've got absolutely no idea who the guy is. He's refused all personal contact and I'm taking it personally.' She shrugged. 'He'll only liaise via email which – before you ask – is a floating hotmail account used at various internet cafés. I had my techies checking out the URLs.'

Tor hiccupped and sniffed, the tears still plopping quietly from her eyes.

Kate covered a hand with hers, but carried on. She loved a mystery.

'Really?' she drawled. 'But what about signing the contract? Surely he had to give you a name then?'

Cress shook her head. 'He's signed over power of attorney to his solicitor and that's the name on the contract. There's a separate affidavit that declares his identity but my senior brief has to keep the information confidential. His name is only to be released in the event of his death. How frigid is that! Brendan bloody Hillier. He's the bane of my life.'

'Hillier again? What's he got to do with this?'

Cress raised her eyebrows. 'Didn't you notice, on the dedication page?'

Kate shrugged and shook her head. 'Was I supposed to?'

'Whoever wrote *The Wrong Prince* has dedicated it to Brendan Hillier.'

'No!' Kate gasped. 'That can't be a coincidence.'

'Of course it can't.'

Kate fell silent, her brain trying to play catch-up – Brendan

Hillier the true author of *Scion*; *The Wrong Prince* dedicated to him . . .

'Well, have you discovered anything about the author?'

Cress shook her head. 'We had a PO box address which was registered to an address in Fulham which – wait for it – belonged to a Bridget Hillier. I think that's his sister. She's about the same age as him, but she's living in Switzerland. Supposedly her daughter Amelie uses the flat occasionally but it seems she's rarely there, and we can't find any trace of her at all – either here or abroad.'

Tor butted in, nodding towards the screen. It had come to rest upon yet another gorgeous young blonde.

'Who's that? She's familiar,' she said, miserably.

'Yuh, most people here are, Tor. They're actors – that's the nature of their jobs!' Kate said, talking down to her tummy. 'Ooh, the baby kicked – d'you want to feel?'

Two sets of hands reached out and felt the rhythmic drumming of baby heels.

'Wow, she's a feisty little thing,' Cress smiled.

'Yes, I think I've put her through the wringer today,' Kate said, rubbing her tummy soothingly and apologetically.

'No, I really recognize her. What's her name?' Tor was looking at the screen with renewed focus. 'I've seen her somewhere. Where was it?'

Kate and Cress looked up at the screen.

'That's Emily!' Kate exclaimed. 'What the hell's she doing here? She's a PR, not an actress.'

'And to think I thought this was an exclusive shindig,' Cress muttered. 'Half of bloody London's here. It's like going to Chamonix.'

'You recognize her from the Oxford fiasco, Tor – thanks for that, by the way, Cress,' Kate said sarcastically.

'Apology accepted,' Cress retorted deadpan, and the two women burst out laughing at the ridiculousness of the fixes they'd put each other in.

'Do I?' Tor frowned.

'Yup. She was living with Harry at the time that the news of my pregnancy quietly rippled into the public consciousness.'

'And then she kissed and told about their underage affair at Christmas,' Cress added. 'Don't you remember Monty brought the paper back from the pub?'

'Oh God, did he?' Kate winced. The thought of it made her heart hurt.

'I guess that's it,' Tor said slowly. But still she frowned.

'So, have you chosen a name yet?' Cress asked, one eye on the screen. The nominations were being read for Best Actress. Harry's award was up next. She felt sick.

'Hmmmm?' Kate murmured, hands on tummy.

'Name?'

'Oh yes, Ottilie.'

'Oooh, I love it!' Cress squealed. 'I wish I'd thought of it.'

Kate giggled, pleased that someone approved of it, at last.

Tor gasped. 'No! I know where it was. I've got it. It was at Bonham's.'

'Come again?' Cress asked.

'That girl – Emily . . . ?'

'Brookner,' Kate supplied.

'Yuh, yuh, whatever. She ran into me as I was going back into the saleroom. Anna and I had popped out for a drink because I was so nervous and she just about knocked me over. She didn't even stop to apologize. I remember it because that horrid picture, the Orion one, had just been sold, and Anna and I were laughing at it.'

Cress looked at her, eyes narrowed. 'The Orion picture?' Her mobile buzzed.

'Well, I can tell you something else, she's not just rude, she's also bloody odd,' Kate said, leaning forward. 'She lived with Harry for what – five months? She refused point-blank to leave the house with him. Not once, until Oxford.'

Tor gawped. 'Really? How strange. That doesn't sound right. From the looks of that dress, she's not shy.'

Cress got her mobile out of her clutch. It was a text from Rosie. She stared hard at it.

Got a strike on marriage cert in Bern: Bri. Hill. marr'd R. Brookner, 1986.

'. . .Yuh, I know! I was beginning to think she was agoraphobic. I thought we'd never get a picture of them together . . .' Kate was saying.

'Why did you want a picture of them together?' Tor asked.

'So that there was evidence of a continuing and consensual relationship. Would have made it harder for her to argue emotional distress from the earlier affair at school.' She shrugged casually.

'Ooh,' Tor said quietly. She paused for a moment. 'You're quite frightening, you know that, right?'

Kate winked. 'I bloody well hope so.'

Cress looked up at the blonde on the screen and back to her mobile.

'Kate, what did you just say Emily's surname is?'
'Brookner.'

'Brookner,' she repeated under her breath, looking back down at her mobile. 'Oh my God. We were looking under the wrong name. It wasn't Amelie Hillier; it was Amelie Brookner,' Cress whispered.

'No, it's Emily,' Kate corrected.

Cress looked at her. 'Yes. But the old lady – she was foreign. Her accent . . . she pronounced it Amelie – but she was saying Emily.'

'Are you – are you saying Emily Brookner is Brendan Hillier's heir?' Kate asked in disbelief.

Cress nodded. 'I think I am.'

'James said he wrote a letter to Hillier's heir, explaining everything that had happened,' Tor murmured.

Cress bit her lip. 'And you just said you saw her at Bonham's, Tor, leaving right after that picture was sold – *she* bought the painting! And the writing on the note that accompanied the painting was the same writing as on the note telling me to bring the manuscript out here. It must have been Emily who stole the manuscript from my hotel room.'

'But how would she know you had the manuscript, Cress? James sent the manuscript to you only after he didn't hear anything from her. She doesn't know he then sent it on to you. She only knows Harry stole the book from her uncle, surely?'

'Let's face it, Tor, once she found out Harry hadn't written *Scion*, and she saw he'd signed to a tiny company like mine, it would be a fair assumption to make that I was involved too – I would only ever have been able to secure him because I held a trump card – the *Scion* manuscript.'

'But that doesn't explain why she deliberately inveigled her way back into the middle of his life though,' Kate thought out loud. 'If she only needed to get the manuscript back off *you*, why go to the bother of blackmailing *him* about the earlier affair?' Kate shook her head. 'It doesn't quite add up. There's something else we're missing.'

Tor thought for a moment, frowning, her hiccups abating with the concentration. 'The manuscript was originally sent in 1989, wasn't it?'

Cress nodded.

'And the message Brendan had written on it said he'd been working on it for two years.'

'Right,' Cress said. 'So?'

'So, in 1987, no one worked on PCs. They were still using typewriters. Don't you remember? They had only just got the PCs in the library when we were doing our final year dissertations?'

'So?' Cress said, blankly.

'So if Brendan wrote *Scion* on a typewriter, then there wasn't a back-up copy on a computer somewhere. Which means that when he sent *Scion* off to George Colesbrook for representation, he must have made a copy. He wouldn't have sent his original and only draft, would he?'

Cress's eyes danced. 'You're damn right he wouldn't have.'

'Which means that out there somewhere, there must have been another manuscript,' Tor finished breathlessly. 'And Harry had it.'

There was a pause as everyone's brains raced.

'So then, Harry played entirely into her hands,' Kate said, impressed. 'Harry must have taken the original manuscript from Hillier when he went to sign him, and *that's* why she blackmailed him. She needed a way back in to his life and she knew he'd try to neutralize her threats by seducing her all over again. He did what she knew he would – moved her in and gave her access all areas. *She* played him.' Kate nodded, delighted. 'You know, this girl's growing on me.'

Another message beeped on Cress's phone.

'God, what's going on?' Cress said agitated. 'I've only been uncontactable for a couple of hours. The whole operation grinds to a halt if I'm not there to – '

'. . . What are you going to do, Emily?' Kate said to the beautiful image on the plasma.

'Holy cow!' Cress held up the BlackBerry, and Tor and Kate took in the headline Rosie had downloaded from Reuters. 'I think she's already done it.'

Tor looked at Kate, dumbstruck.

'Oh my God,' Cress whispered as the cameras swung over the glittering audience and found the most golden smile of all. 'Why do I have the feeling Harry's the last to know about this?'

Chapter Fifty-seven

Harry sat in the dark, not listening to a word of Chris Rock's banter, his mind racing as he tried to absorb the facts that had been bombarded at him like machine-gun fire. George Colesbrook his father? Billy his son? White his step-brother?

His chest felt tight and he loosened his tie, undid his top button, trying to cool down, stay calm. All that was in the past. Behind him. His category was next up. He was the sure thing. He had to get it together. Deal with now.

Harry breathed deeply. He shifted in his seat and looked round the theatre, the red flashing lights of the cameras trained on him like snipers. He saw Cress's husband three seats away, slightly hypoxic and sitting in a ridiculous position, clearly trying desperately not to touch legs with Scarlett Johannson, who was on his other side.

He swallowed hard again and tried to think about his speech. He reached inside his jacket but the notes weren't there.

Of course they weren't! He closed his eyes in despair. If only Kate had left him alone earlier, he could have prepared properly. Stupid bloody woman. He'd have to wing it.

He took a deep breath and tried to focus on the ceremony. Ordinarily, it would be a breeze. Amelia was on stage,

accepting her award, her stupendous cleavage drawing attention away from her big belly.

Her cheeks were flushed, like she'd just been shagging
White in the aisles, and her speech went on far too long, all
breathy and full of sincerity. But eventually, she tottered off
stage – managing to avoid the duck waddle that afflicted so
many women in the last stage of pregnancy.

The applause died down, and Harry breathed a sigh of
relief as the cameras panned back to Chris Rock. He was a
lot less pretty than Amelia, but he was the segue to Harry
Hunter.

Everyone knew this was his moment. There had never
been any doubt that it wouldn't be.

He could feel the cameras circling him like a panther,
taking full advantage of their opportunity to get gratuitous
shots. He gave a faint smile, bringing some twinkle into his
eyes. An arched eyebrow, a floppy forelock. He knew what
the public wanted.

He didn't see the stunning blonde sashay across the top
of the sweeping staircase.

'And now, to present our next award for Best Adapted
Screenplay, we have a world exclusive!' Rock shouted,
striding across the stage like a ringmaster. 'Yes, that's right!
You heard me. It's the book that's at the top of every best-
seller list, it's already been translated into thirty-three different
languages – and counting; and it's been bought by
Dreamworks so that they can bring it to a silver screen near
you. Her identity has been one of the most closely guarded
secrets since Suri Cruise was born. But tonight – at the 69th
Annual Academy Awards – it is my deep honour to present
to you the author of *The Wrong Prince* . . .'

Rock paused dramatically, enjoying the suspense.

'Emily Brookner!'

Even with the pressure of six billion viewers watching him, Harry couldn't keep his jaw up.

Emily? The author of *The Wrong Prince*? It couldn't be! But the thunderous applause that erupted at her worldwide unveiling told him it could.

Clapping mechanically, he watched her sweep down the stairs like an angel, aware that much of the crowd's appreciation was for the cornflower blue silk mini-dress that was rippling over her body like lover's laughter. The poor cameramen didn't know whether to go in tight for a face shot, or to pull out and pan up and down lingeringly over her killer body. A sapphire-studded gold-dipped key hung down from her neck, winking at the audience as it swayed happily from breast to breast.

'Thank you, Chris. Thank you. Thank you,' she laughed as she got to the podium. 'Wow! Thank you. You're so kind.' She looked out across the sea of fame, looking for all the world like one of its mermaids, and waited and waited and waited for the applause to die down and people to return to their seats.

The minutes passed and she giggled beguilingly, tossing her hair back, letting the world put that beatific face to the words that had enthralled so many of them already.

'Gosh! Is there going to be any time left for the award now?' she giggled to Chris, aware of the strict timings for the show; and the audience laughed with her, charmed.

Taking her cue, the clapping faded away and everyone finally sat back down again.

'Ladies and gentlemen,' she said in her particular blend of posh and London accents. 'It gives me great pleasure to announce that the nominees for the category of Best Adapted

Screenplay are: Robert Bush for *Blind Man's Gold*; Dan Frinton for *Broken Angels*; Harry Hunter for *Scion*; Joseph Rathburne for *The Pale Mountain*.'

She stepped back as edited clips from the films flashed up on the screens behind her, though Harry was sure no one in the room was watching them. She looked tantalizing, entrancing. He'd had her at two different points in her life, and now that she so clearly belonged to the public, he wanted her back all over again. He'd been a damned fool.

Even her ruinous revelations, which had done so much damage to his reputation at home, didn't deter his new ambition. In fact, they fuelled it. Few of the audience here tonight would be aware or care that she was his schoolgirl kiss and tell; Errol Flynn, Roman Polanski – they'd paved the way before him. Besides, British tabloid sleaze barely made a ripple in the American market.

And he knew exactly what to do to make all that go away, put a different spin on it all. Harry knew that the pairing of their talents and looks would be irresistible. He hadn't been off the mark when he'd argued in Oxford that celebrity was the new religion. Their combined wattage would dazzle the world.

'And the winner is . . .'

He ran a hand through his hair, feeling his star rise again.

'Harry Hunter for *Scion*!'

She read the words as though they made her the happiest woman on earth, and he couldn't wait to get up there and whisper something filthy in her ear. He'd have her back-stage, he decided.

The applause was astounding and he strode towards the stage, a man on a mission. His whole life had built up to this moment and he was going to give them all something they'd never forget. He could trounce that world exclusive in a heartbeat.

He bounded athletically up the steps and, grabbing a microphone from the podium, fell into a dramatic, deep bow at her feet.

'Emily Brookner,' he said in his deepest, most Etonian voice, looking up at her with sparkling eyes. 'We go back a long way. We have loved and fought, made up and broken up. And the truth of the matter is, I'm hideously miserable without you. Please, darling: will you marry me?'

A collective gasp sucked through the room and around the world. The theatre fell silent, Emily blindsided by his Byronesque pose.

In the control room, the directors were going berserk. A commercial break was scheduled in seventy seconds, and there was no way they could go to it. Harry Hunter proposing to the new darling on the block was a ratings winner. 'Please! Say yes! Say yes, baby!' they were screaming into their mikes.

Composing herself, and willing herself to stay focused, Emily ignored the kerfuffle in her ear and looked out to the audience, smiling and bemused.

'Oh, Harry!' she smiled dazzlingly, finally. 'You know perfectly well I'm already married, you naughty boy!' She looked out to the audience. 'He's such a card.'

Harry's face froze, the smile wiped clean off, as the audience fell about laughing at this British skit. He tried to get up off his knees, but Rock – wanting to prolong the sideshow – stepped in.

'You're kidding, right? You only twelve, girl! What you doin' married?'

Emily laughed. 'No, no. It's true. Last month, in the Maldives. We've just come back from honeymoon.'

'Is he here?' Rock couldn't believe his luck.

She nodded. 'Just over there.' And she indicated towards the wings, where Chandos was standing.

'Well! Come out here then, Mr Lucky!' Chris called to Chandos. 'You're in the right place. Nowhere loves a happy ending more than Hollywood, right?'

At that, the audience were on their feet, as Chandos strode across the stage looking like a cavalry officer. He picked Emily up and kissed her deeply, forcing the producers to go to a commercial break after all. It was a family show, for Chrissakes!

Harry came back up to standing, humiliated and redundant, clapping feebly as his crowning moment was stolen by the girl who had already taken everything from him – his reputation in his home country and his No.1 slot on the international best-seller lists.

It was three minutes before Chandos put her down, as the crowd whooped and cheered and prolonged Harry's agony. Just hand over the fucking statue and let me off this stage, he fumed to himself, while he clapped and laughed and looked for all the world like he'd just been joshing them all along. 'You can't blame a poor fellow for trying, right?'

With everyone back in their seats, Emily finally picked up the Oscar and handed it to Harry. She placed a hand over the mic, pretending to fiddle with her dress, and as she went in to kiss him on the cheek, her smile couldn't have been brighter.

'You didn't write that book,' he smiled, bending down to her.

'I'm afraid I did. I wrote it from some drafts I found in my uncle's possessions.' She paused. 'You knew him actually. Brendan Hillier?' Her breath felt hot on his cheek. 'He was notorious for chasing after beautiful young men like you. Is that how it all happened? Did he seduce you, Harry? Did he refuse to sign until he got what he really wanted from you? I bet he couldn't believe his luck when you turned up on his doorstep – a golden Adonis and a contract offer.'

'You're fucking mad,' he snarled under his breath, as she swapped cheeks.

'But then what happened? Did he forget his insulin? Did you keep him entertained in bed too long, drunk and insatiable? Did you let his pleas for help go unanswered?' She kissed the other cheek, a flicker of her tongue scorching him, her curves pushing into him ever so subtly. 'I'll bet that was an electric moment, wasn't it? The second you realized that if you just let him drift into unconsciousness, you could have it all. And you do have it all, Harry. Look at you. My uncle's made you an icon. You've even got an Oscar to your name. You're a global brand. A superstar. Nothing can touch you now. Right?'

He didn't respond. Couldn't. First James; now this.

She pulled back, beaming, and his eyes fell to the key around her neck. His key. He looked up at her as the pennies finally began to drop. The blackmail threat – it had all been a double bluff. She'd never given a damn about their earlier affair. He'd been so busy trying to destroy Cress, so sure James was behind it all, and all along she'd been hiding in plain sight. She'd needed a way in and he'd actually given her her very own key.

'I did tell you I wanted justice, Harry. But not for myself – for my uncle,' she said, fingering the key, showing him she'd been to the Kensington house, that she'd found the original manuscript, in his bedroom, in the Fortnum's bag. 'You were right, you know. That first night. Why would I stop at one measly million, when I was due all of it,' she whispered. 'But you know what's so sad about this, Harry? You made me fall in love with you again. I'd have shared it all with you. If we'd married, it would have been yours anyway. But then – when Kate and the baby . . .' She shrugged. 'Well, none of this would have had to happen.'

'None of what?' he said, growing cold.

'This,' she said, grabbing his hand.

Emily turned back to the audience and leant over the podium, Harry vaguely aware that he needed to stop her. But it felt hard to move, to react. The lights so hot. All those faces . . .

'I know I probably shouldn't say this, given that it's not scripted – although, neither was being snogged by my husband actually!' Emily laughed, and the world laughed with her.

'But even though I can't marry him, I just want to say what an amazing man I think Harry Hunter is.'

The crowd roared its approval and Harry flinched as he saw the camera swing back on to him. Emily gripped his hand tighter and raised it in the air, like a rally salute.

'The world needs more people like him!'

There was another cheer. It was like being at a rock concert.

'No, I mean it, America. He's unique. A true icon! Because, ladies and gentlemen, how many people do you know who'd give their *entire fortune* to charity? Please, Hollywood – give it up for Harry Hunter!'

Chapter Fifty-eight

The limo sped through the night, back to the hotel, its glamorous occupants dazed and exhausted.

Cress had never given so many interviews in her life, as journalists – in the wake of Harry's sudden and mysterious absence – clamoured around her for details of his switch from icon to benefactor.

She'd had a whale of a time with it all. 'I know Harry will want to talk about this *at length* with you all,' she beamed, knowing full well he couldn't imagine anything worse. 'But when the time is right! Right now he wants the money to do the talking, and the focus to be on the charities he's supporting. I will of course get my office to release a full and comprehensive list of those charities to you as soon as possible. In the meantime, I would also like to take this opportunity to formally welcome Emily Brookner to Sapphire Books, and you are invited to the press conference tomorrow morning for the details of the film deal for *The Wrong Prince*.'

Tor still had the hiccups, the last vestiges of the tears which had fallen steadily in the wake of James's departure, his gladstone between her pretty ankles, the Planed Spaces envelope twisted and wrung and battered and unread in her hands; Kate was glued to her mobile, trying to get through to London; Mark, after the shock of Greta's wanton indiscretion and the realization of how close he'd come to screwing things up with Cress, was succumbing to the jet-lag, his head resting on Cress's shoulder.

'I've been such a pillock,' he mumbled into her hair.

'I know,' Cress smiled, feeling the weight of a million lies lift off her like hoverflies.

'Although you've been a ruthless bitch too,' he added lovingly.

'I know,' Cress repeated, her smile growing wider.

'I think I had a mid-life crisis,' he drawled.

'You did.'

'But I'll make it up to you,' he mumbled.

'And I'll make it up to you too,' she smiled, rubbing his thigh. 'Believe me.'

When they pulled up outside the hotel, they trooped slowly out of the car, their shoes pinching, their make-up worn off, their dresses creased, their hair floppy. So different from eight hours ago, when they'd looked like supermodels stalking down the Versace catwalk.

Cress and Kate went up to the reception desk.

'I'd like a room for my friend here, please,' Cress instructed, full of her own importance. After tonight, everyone knew who she was.

'I'm sorry, ma'am, but we're fully booked.'

Cress raised her eyebrows at her.

'Actually, I think that if you look again, you'll realize you're not.'

'Uh . . .' The receptionist looked back down at the screen, perplexed. 'No, I'm sorry, ma'am, but we really are. This is the busiest night of the year for us.'

Cress leaned over the desk and lowered her voice.

'Is there a manager on duty I can speak to? Clearly I need

to deal with someone who has a little more authority.' The 'Robert, the fake butler' episode had proved to be useful leverage so far.

Kate leaned in, embarrassed by Cress's bullishness. She was clearly still on an adrenalin kick. 'Cress, it's fine. I can go elsewhere. Really.'

'Don't be ridiculous,' Cress hissed. 'You're staying here, with your friends.'

'I can pass you over to the manager, ma'am, but he'll only tell you what I've told you. The gentleman just over there took the last room,' the receptionist shrugged.

Cress looked round. A booted and suited businessman was walking towards the lifts, a copy of *The Times* sticking out of his briefcase.

Cress looked over disdainfully. And then screeched.

'Monty!'

Kate whipped round.

Monty turned and saw her, dishevelled and blooming and gorgeous, staring back at him.

'Kate?' he asked, incredulous. 'You're here?'

He ran towards her, not noticing he'd dropped his bags.

'Oh, Monty,' she cried, as he reached her, his hands automatically stroking her tummy. 'I've been ringing you solidly all night,' she said quietly, looking up at him. 'Where've you been? I thought you must be out with some new dollybird.'

He smiled. 'I was in Chicago. But then I saw you, on the telly and – I couldn't take my eyes off you. You looked so beautiful. And so bloody sad. I knew I had to come here and try to talk some sense into you.'

They looked at each other.

'Can you ever forgive me?' she whispered.

'What a daft question,' he twinkled, clasping her face in his hands and kissing her, the tears streaming down both their cheeks.

'Wait. There's something I have to tell you first, Monty, something you need to know,' she said, taking a deep breath. She felt unexpectedly nervous.

He kissed her eyelids and the tip of her nose. She tasted sweet, like rain.

'Billy's not your son. You're not a father, after all.'

She watched the emotions run across his face – confusion, disbelief, relief, disappointment – and, try as she might, she couldn't hold back the little smile twitching on her lips.

'But you're going to be.'

His eyes snapped up to hers. What?

She stepped back to make it easier for him to see what she was saying – letting him admire her ripe bump.

Slowly, he dropped his eyes downwards to where his hands were resting on her tummy.

'It's so hard,' he said, his voice thick with emotion, before jumping back suddenly. 'Was that a kick?'

She nodded, her eyes bright with tears. It was the moment she'd waited for her whole life.

'She's saying hello to her daddy,' she whispered.

Monty looked at her, a twinkle in his eye.

'I've told you before. She's a boy!'

Cress and Mark and Tor didn't intrude. The catch-ups could wait till breakfast. The Marfleets were well and truly in their own world.

They stepped into the lifts and pressed for their floors. The door was just closing when a porter carrying a muffin basket and a bunch of pink balloons jumped in. He pressed for the presidential floor and stood at the back of the lift, staring at the ceiling.

Cress stared at Tor meaningfully, but Tor pretended to busy herself with kicking off her shoes and stretching her feet. Not now, please. She was shattered. She'd had enough crying for one night.

The doors slid open at her floor a few seconds later.

'See you in the morning, guys,' she said wearily, sloping down the corridor, shoes in one hand, the tough leather bag banging on her shins.

She passed Hen's door – three rooms away from her own. The light was still on.

Feeling indignation flush her sleepy bones, she let herself into her room and unzipped the dress, letting it float to her feet like a puffy cloud. She pulled on her pyjamas and padded back down the hall, the dress back on its hanger.

She knocked on the door twice and stood back.

Hen answered, still fully dressed.

'Tor!' she exclaimed. 'I didn't expect to see you this evening. Was it a wonderful . . .'

'You're his *mother?*' Tor asked, rhetorically, completely disregarding Hen's line of conversation.

Hen fell silent. 'Ah. I see.' She stepped back and motioned behind her. 'You'd better come in.'

Tor walked in, placing the dress carefully on the bed and the gladstone on the floor.

'Thank you for lending me that,' she said primly, cross that she was beholden to her for her Cinderella moment. She wanted to be free, free from all of them.

Hen waved her hand lightly. 'I'm thrilled you wore it,' she said. 'It's been too long since it was last out of that bag.'

Tor stayed silent.

'Nightcap?' Hen offered, moving to the minibar. 'I've only got brandy, I'm afraid.'

Tor just shrugged. Whatever. She just needed something to make her eyes sting. Something to camouflage the fact she was on the verge of tears again. Because even though she was furious with Hen for hiding the fact she was James's mother – no, for being his mother – she was still her friend.

And right now, she needed a friend who wasn't having a life crisis of her own.

Hen handed her the drink and Tor took a big slug, shivering as it slid down and burned her.

Hen motioned for her to sit down, and Tor perched on the bed.

'How did you find out?' Hen asked quietly.

'The dress. He said his mother wore it the night she met his father.'

'Aaah,' Hen said, nodding. 'I did wonder whether that would trip him up. He's always loved that story, that dress. I thought seeing you in it might catch him off guard.'

Tor looked at her, shaking her head with disbelief.

'How can you sit there so calm about this, when all this time you've been betraying me?'

'Oh Tor, I've never betrayed you. Whatever you and I have talked about has stayed in my confidence. I didn't smuggle conversations back to James.'

'How could you not tell me? After all that time?'

Hen shrugged. 'Because he made me swear not to. He knew you'd run for the hills if you knew I was his mother.'

Tor stared at her, catching flies.

'You do realize what it is he's done, I take it? You're aware of his role in fucking up my life?'

Hen blanched at Tor's uncharacteristic invective.

'I know. He told me everything. He was beside himself after he saw you at the tennis. He'd just found out about Hugh. I've never seen him so agitated.'

'Did he order you to befriend me?'

Hen gave a small smile.

'How could he do that, Tor? Friendships come down to chemistry, not orders. But he asked me to keep an eye on you. Check you were OK, not locking yourself away, finding your feet in the village . . . But as soon as I met you, with your black teeth . . .' She smiled fondly at the memory. 'Well, I knew we'd be friends.'

She gave a big sigh. 'I'm glad that you know, actually. I wasn't comfortable with the fact that you didn't know James was my son. It made me feel as if I was lying to you, even though I tried very hard not to. It did mean I had to be economical with the truth on occasion. I kept telling James you should know, but by then you'd settled here, the children were making friends . . . What would have happened if I'd told you? Would you have left there too? Gone somewhere new? You deserved to be able to settle, Tor, to rebuild your life peacefully, among people who cared about you. You've been through enough.'

Tor pulled her knees up and pushed her teary face into them, the brandy long since past its limits as a disguise.

'It's such a mess, Hen. I don't even know where to begin with it all. He hates me now. Despises me.'

'Well, I know for a fact that's not true,' Hen said, coming to sit beside her and putting her arms around her. 'Quite the contrary. He's just frustrated that he can't resolve things with you.'

'Today's just been one long disaster,' Tor sniffed. 'I wish

we'd never come. We should have just stayed put in Burnham. From the moment I got on the plane, it's been one crisis after another. I just can't cope with any more. I'm a housewife. Not a sleuth.'

'I know, dear,' Hen said soothingly, shushing her. 'But it's all over now.'

Tor sat up and looked at her. 'Do you know? Has he told you? Has James told you what happened tonight?'

Hen nodded.

'So you know, then – about everything?'

'Mmmhmm. Cress does get herself into some pickles, doesn't she?'

Tor couldn't help but laugh.

'Yes, she does,' she sniffed. 'She drives me nuts with her melodramas. I don't know why she can't just be like other working mothers. Do the nine-to-five, drive the 4 x 4. Why does she have to start blackmailing the most famous man in the world?'

Hen laughed. 'When you put it like that . . .'

Tor gave a big sigh and looked down at her hands.

'I'm so sorry about Lily. It must have been an awful burden for you to live with.'

Hen started slightly. 'Well, it has been. Yes. But I'm just glad everything's out in the open now. Life is so much simpler when people just talk honestly.' She tipped her head to the side. 'Will you talk to James?'

Tor sniffed. 'There's no point. He doesn't want to talk to me any more. He doesn't even want to look at me.'

Hen raised her eyebrows, doubtfully.

'No, it's true, Hen. You didn't see him tonight. He's been pushed too far. I've accused him of things – dreadful things he could never have done. I don't know what I . . .' Her voice trailed off and she shook her head. 'Too much has been said. We can never be friends now.'

Hen said nothing, but nodded in understanding.

Tor stood up and pointed to his bag with her foot.

'Will you give this back to him? He left it behind earlier.'

'Of course.' She gave Tor another hug. 'Try to sleep. I'll see you in the morning.'

In spite of the day's high drama, Tor managed to sleep, and to sleep well. Whether it was the brandy or the ceaseless crying, jet-lag or just the pure stress of being sucked into Cress's maelstrom, she awoke eleven hours later to a note on the bedside table.

Don't panic! Am taking the children to Seaworld. Have a lie-in. We'll be back for supper.
Love Hen

Tor smiled. She had authorized a spare key for Hen to her room, which adjoined the children's, in case she had needed anything from them while she was at the awards yesterday.

She stretched sleepily and tried to drop back off, but her eyes caught sight of the digital clock. Twelve o'clock! She couldn't remember ever sleeping that long since ... since university.

She rolled on to her back and stared at the ceiling, as the previous day's events pushed forward. Emily. Harry. James. She felt the tears well, poised to jump, at the very thought of him. What had she done? Her accusations ...

The ceiling rose blurred out of focus, and by the time she could read the clock again, it was 12.38 p.m.

Tor tried to get a grip, swinging her legs lethargically out of bed. Crying wasn't going to bring him back. She rang Kate and Monty's room but they didn't pick up – she could well imagine what they were up to. And she knew Cress would be at her press conference by now.

She stood at the window and looked down upon LA. She was here. She might as well make the most of it. At the very least she needed a dress for the party tonight, though she couldn't think of anything worse than having to socialize again so soon.

She called up for room service – coffee and a croissant – while she showered, dried her hair, slipped into an antique pink silk jersey dress and pretended that she really was as fine as she looked.

Thirty minutes later, her sandals click-clacked over the marble floor, her hair swinging about her shoulders. She didn't notice Daniel Craig do a double-take as she crossed the lobby, looking freshly slept and perky.

Tor jumped into a cab waiting outside the hotel, and looked out at all the Californians walking their dogs, blading in their shorts, and taking for granted the leisurely lives they led under these sunny blue skies.

'Rodeo Drive,' she said to the driver. Not because she wanted to go there especially, but it was the only place she could think of off the top of her head.

She regretted it instantly once she was there, feeling intimidated by the big brands lining the clean, wide street. She couldn't imagine going in to any of them, much less trying anything on.

Slowly, she walked along the pavement, but shopping was poor therapy right now and she kept forgetting to look in the windows. She sighed heavily and looked up and down the street, wondering what to do and where to go.

Tiny, ferocious women were everywhere, marching like toy soldiers with shiny bags for drums.

The tears started falling again and she slapped them away hurriedly, mortified to be losing it so publicly. She turned to the nearest shop window to hide her face, catching sight of a dress as she did so.

It was beautiful. Tiny pink rosebuds were dotted on ivory satin, with pintuck gathering at the skirt and a cutaway neckline.

She pushed open the door, relieved to find the boutique busy inside. Music was – if not blasting, certainly pumping – out of the speakers and the assistants had a funky vibe going on, organizing shelves and manning the tills in skinny black jeans and diamanté-studded vests.

A pretty assistant came over, smiling. 'Hi there. Can I help you today?'

'I'd like to try that dress you've got in the window,' Tor faltered, aware her face was blotchy from crying.

'Sure. Here you go,' the assistant smiled, handing the dress to her. 'The fitting rooms are just over there.' She pointed to a row of large cubicles, alternately draped with floor-to-ceiling black and white velvet curtains.

Tor stepped out of her shoes and slipped on the dress. It slid easily over her body and she stared dispassionately in the mirror. It would do. It fitted like a dream, and a distant voice in her head said it looked incredible, even with her socks still on. She just . . . didn't care. She just knew she could go back to the hotel now. Coming out had been a mistake.

'Do you need any help with the dress, ma'am?' inquired the assistant, outside.

'No. I'm fine, thanks,' Tor said, as she heard the curtain pull back behind her anyway.

'No you're not,' said the deep voice that reverberated around her head all the time.

Tor spun round.

'What are you doing here?' she managed, as James leaned against the wall, arms and ankles crossed.

'I followed you from the hotel. Once I saw Daniel Craig giving you the eye, I realized I probably shouldn't let you out of my sight,' he said, grinning boyishly.

Tor stared at him. 'I would have thought you'd have been glad to see the back of me,' she said quietly.

He shrugged. 'I tried to give that a go, but . . .' He stared at her, intently. 'Anyway, I know you were trying to protect Cress.' He paused. 'Just like you tried to protect Kate that night.' He glanced down at his feet and then back at her. 'Do you still think I'm an arch-fiend?'

Tor swallowed, embarrassed. 'No.'

'And you know I'm not a new father, or a cheating bastard.'

Tor nodded, a smile beginning to break out.

'Amelia's one of my oldest friends, but we've never been lovers. She's hopelessly in love with a married man – a famous director. He'll never leave his family, even though she's had his baby. A little girl, by the way.' He stepped forward and gently brushed her hair off her shoulders. He stared down at her, so close.

'Oh. Name?' Tor asked, trying to concentrate.

'Maya.'

'Nice.'

'Yes.' He traced her collarbone with his thumb. 'I went to a few premieres with her when this other chap let her down. The papers put two and two together and made five. We agreed to let them. It meant she didn't have to answer their questions about the father's identity every time she popped out for milk,' he explained distractedly, his eyes running over her. She looked amazing in that dress.

He dragged his eyes back up to hers. 'I love you,' he said simply. 'Have done ever since I last met you in a changing room. I thought you were the sexiest, sweetest, funniest woman I'd ever met. And I'm sorry that I acted on it . . . what that led to.'

Tor nodded. She knew he was.

'Have I answered all your questions?' he asked, stroking her cheek, desperate to kiss her.

'Ummm,' she smiled, desperate for him to kiss her. 'Oh. No. I have got one more.'

'Fire,' he murmured, his eyes blazing. 'Make it quick.'

'Why do you have a letter from Planed Spaces in your bag?'

He stiffened a little – in the wrong way – and she added quickly: 'It fell out of your bag. Cress found it.'

'Uh-huh. Well – you can't be cross,' he said cautiously. 'You weren't supposed to know about it yet.'

She felt her heart dip. 'Know what?'

He stared at her for a moment. 'I bought your share in the partnership. For the children. I've put it in a trust for them. I was trying to make amends, do the right thing.' He looked at her, trying to read her mind. 'You said you wouldn't be cross.'

She shook her head. 'I'm not cross.'

'You're not? You look cross.'

'Uh-uh,' she whispered. 'This is my horny face,' she giggled, making him laugh.

She dropped her head back and he kissed her tenderly, exquisitely, slowly, as though they had the rest of their lives to spend in this changing room together.

She felt his hand move up her spine and a gentle tug as he pulled down the zip.

'I feel like I'm in a Bond film,' she smiled.

'Wrong James,' he whispered into her hair.

'Not for me.'

The dress slid silently to the floor, crumpling into an abject heap by way of apology for impeding the lovers.

'We're crushing the dress.'

'Housekeeping can deal with it later,' he murmured, pushing her up against the mirror, its cool surface making her gasp as it made contact with her skin.

'What are we doing?' she gasped, as his fingers wound through her hair.

He tipped her head back so that she found herself reflected in his rich, warm eyes.

'The inevitable,' he said.

Prima Donna

by

KAREN SWAN

ISBN: 978-1-4472-2374-0

**Breaking the rules was what she liked best.
That was her sport. Renegade, rebel, bad girl.
Getting away with it.**

Pia Soto is the sexy and glamorous prima ballerina, the Brazilian bombshell, who's shaking up the ballet world with her outrageous behaviour. She's wild and precocious, and she's a survivor. She's determined that no man will ever control her destiny. But ruthless financier Will Silk has Pia in his sights, and has other ideas . . .

Sophie O'Farrell is Pia's hapless, gawky assistant, the girl-next-door to Pia's prima donna, always either falling in love with the wrong man or just falling over. Sophie sets her own dreams aside to pick up the debris in Pia's wake, but she's no angel, and when a devastating accident threatens to cut short Pia's illustrious career, Sophie has to step out of the shadows and face up to the demons in her own life.

Christmas at Tiffany's

by

KAREN SWAN

ISBN: 978-0-330-53272-3

**Three cities, three seasons,
one chance to find the life that fits**

Cassie settled down too young, marrying her first serious boyfriend. Now, ten years later, she is betrayed and broken. With her marriage in tatters and no career or home of her own, she needs to work out where she belongs in the world and who she really is.

So begins a year-long trial as Cassie leaves her sheltered life in rural Scotland to stay with each of her best friends in the most glamorous cities in the world: New York, Paris and London. Exchanging the grouse moor and mousy hair for low-carb diets and high-end highlights, Cassie tries on each city for size as she attempts to track down the life she was supposed to have been leading, and with it, the man who was supposed to love her all along.

The Perfect Present

by

KAREN SWAN

ISBN: 978-0-330-53273-0

Memories are a gift . . .

Haunted by a past she can't escape, Laura Cunningham desires nothing more than to keep her world small and precise – her quiet relationship and growing jewellery business are all she needs to get by. Until the day when Rob Blake walks into her studio and commissions a necklace that will tell his enigmatic wife Cat's life in charms.

As Laura interviews Cat's family, friends and former lovers, she steps out of her world and into theirs – a charmed world where weekends are spent in Verbier and the air is lavender-scented, where friends are wild, extravagant and jealous, and a big love has to compete with grand passions.

Hearts are opened, secrets revealed and as the necklace begins to fill up with trinkets, Cat's intoxicating life envelops Laura's own. By the time she has to identify the final charm, Laura's metamorphosis is almost complete. But the last story left to tell has the power to change all of their lives forever, and Laura is forced to choose between who she really is and who it is she wants to be.

Christmas at Claridge's

by

KAREN SWAN

ISBN: 978-1-4472-1969-9

The best presents can't be wrapped

Portobello – home to the world-famous street market, Notting Hill Carnival . . . and Clem Alderton. She's the queen of the scene, the girl everyone wants to be or be with. But beneath the morning-after make-up, Clem is keeping a secret, and when she goes too far one reckless night she endangers everything – her home, her job and even her adored brother's love.

Portofino – a place of wild beauty and old-school glamour. Clem has been here once before and vowed never to return. But when a handsome stranger asks Clem to restore a neglected villa, it seems like the answer to her problems – if she can just face up to her past.

Claridge's – at Christmas, Clem is back in London working on a special commission for London's grandest hotel. But is this where her heart really lies?